ırk alleys and howls in the night."
*FOREWORD REVIEWS* (**starred review**)

"Gritty . . . Imaginative . . . Evocative."
*KIRKUS REVIEWS*

"A richly multilayered book . . . incorporates myth, fantasy and horror to form an increasingly tense and very moving story."
**Linda Hepworth, *NB MAGAZINE* (5 stars)**

"Kyle Richardson pumps blood into machinery in *Beast Heart*, bringing his characters to life in this clever, emotionally engaging novel. A writer to watch."
**Kaaron Warren, award-winning author of**
***Into Bones Like Oil* and *Tide of Stone***

"A wonderful and original mix of action, psychology and suspense. Blending steampunk and horror, it captures readers and leaves them wanting for more. Very highly recommended, for adults and teenagers alike."
**Seb Doubinsky, award-winning author of**
**the City-States Cycle series**

"Adventure, transformation, and two peculiar young characters searching for meaning in the hands they were dealt. An unexpected delight. Richardson brings us a deftly-written adventure that zigs when you expect it to zag, and begs for a sequel."
**Jacqui Castle, award-winning author of**
***The Seclusion***

"A rare treat that manages to seem familiar from the start yet surprise at every turn."
**G.D. Penman, author of**
***The Year of the Knife***

"*Beast Heart* beats with beautiful whimsy and honesty about the pains of adolescence, abuse, and bullying. It also nurtures hope that its heroes can hold on to their humanity."
**Rebecca Gomez Farrell, author of *Wings Unseen***

# BEAST
# HEART

## THE STEAMBOUND TRILOGY
## BOOK ONE

## KYLE RICHARDSON

Meerkat Press
Atlanta

Library of Congress Cataloging-in-Publication Data

Names: Richardson, Kyle, author.
Title: Beast heart / Kyle Richardson.
Description: Atlanta : Meerkat Press, LLC, [2020] | Series: The steambound trilogy ; book 1 | Summary: Gabby, who uses her clockwork glove to kill monsters like those that killed her mother, teams up with Kemple, who is trying to salvage the little humanity he has left, against a mysterious hunter.
Identifiers: LCCN 2019055243 (print) | LCCN 2019055244 (ebook) | ISBN 9781946154354 (paperback) | ISBN 9781946154361 (ebook)
Subjects: CYAC: Monsters--Fiction. | Shapeshifting--Fiction. | Adventure and adventurers--Fiction. | Science fiction.
Classification: LCC PZ7.1.R53324 Be 2020  (print) | LCC PZ7.1.R53324 (ebook) | DDC [Fic]--dc23
LC record available at https://lccn.loc.gov/2019055243
LC ebook record available at https://lccn.loc.gov/2019055244

Printed in the United States of America on acid-free paper.

Published in the United States of America by
Meerkat Press, LLC, Atlanta, Georgia
www.meerkatpress.com

Cover and book design by Tricia Reeks

*Dearest Michelle,*
*I wrote it sideways.*

# PART ONE

## A GIRL AND A BOY

# 1

"Can I take this stuff off?" Gabby asks, looking up into Mom's sky-blue eyes. "Please?"

Mom shifts on her seat and shakes her head, making her long yellow hair twirl and bounce. "We're next to the see the doctor," she says, for probably the tenth time this morning.

Gabby lets out an overloud sigh and slumps back in her chair. Somewhere between last night and this morning, the bandage around her hand turned dark and damp. Now it's so gray and sopping that she's afraid to even look at it. Plus, her fingers are really starting to ache under all that wet fabric. "I'll just take it off for a *minute*," she says.

Mom shakes her head again. "No. I told you, he'll see us soon."

Gabby groans. Today, *soon* feels more like *never*. She flits her goggle-eyed gaze around the room, just to find something worth looking at. Aside from the ugly green chairs and the dumb brown carpet and the weird little lanterns hanging from the ceiling, the doctor's office is pretty much empty. "He's probably just eating lunch in there," she says, pointing with her left hand—her good hand—at a closed door near the end of the hall.

Mom frowns at the door, then glances down at the flowers printed on her skirt. "I doubt it," she says, smoothing a wrinkle from one of the petals. "He's more likely reviewing your file." She forces a smile, her lips pulling a little too thin. Then she musses Gabby's hair. "Yours is a special case, after all."

Special. What a lousy word. Nothing about Gabby's hand *feels* special. It feels painful, if anything. And weird. And a little bit tingly. "I think something's wrong with me," she says, twisting her mouth. She kicks her legs along the edge of the seat, back and forth. The dress she's in—a starchy, bright yellow thing with miniature trees dotting the hem—bunches up around her knees, and she frowns at how thin her legs look inside all that fabric, like she hasn't eaten anything in weeks. "And I'm too skinny," she adds, kicking her legs harder.

Mom inhales slowly, the way she always does whenever she wants a moment to think, as if her thoughts are balloons that need careful inflating. "Nothing is wrong with you," she finally says. She reaches over and flattens the hem of Gabby's dress back down, covering up her knees. "And you're certainly not too skinny, either." She peers sideways at Gabby as if seeing her for the first time, then spreads her mouth into a big, toothy grin. "You're just right."

But of course she'd say that. She has to. It's like . . . standard Mom-speak, or something. "Oh, sure," Gabby shoots back, rolling her eyes behind her gray lenses. "I'm just perfect."

Mom raises a finger, almost threateningly, as if she plans to jab it, sword-like, right through Gabby's chest. But before she gets the chance, a balding man in a white smock steps into the room and clears his throat. "Gabrielle Lenton?" the man mumbles, dabbing a beige kerchief against his mouth.

Gabby gives Mom a victorious elbow jab to the ribs. "See?" she whispers. "He *was* eating!"

Mom ignores the comment, wraps her slender fingers around Gabby's arm, and tugs her to her feet. "Thank you, Doctor," she says, flashing an apologetic smile. "I know this is short notice and all, but—"

The man stuffs the kerchief into one of his pockets, then waves a hand like he's swatting away a bug. "No explanation necessary, Miss Lenton," he says, glancing at Gabby. He smiles in a way that makes his chubby face look even chubbier. Then he bends down, rests his palms on his knees, and speaks slowly and loudly, as if he thinks Gabby is deaf and dumb. "Hello again, Gabrielle," he calls out. "You're looking quite lovely today. Do you remember me?"

Gabby scrunches her face. How could she forget their new family doctor? They only have the one. "I do," she says flatly. Then, because Mom gives her arm a sharp squeeze, she adds, "And . . . thanks. For seeing me."

The doctor smiles, pats her head, and nods at Mom. "Oh, to be nine years old again, eh?" He says this in a voice that sounds half-joking, half-sad, and Mom gives him one of those pretty smiles she uses whenever she's at work—her eyes bunched, her teeth bare and gleaming.

Of all Mom's smiles, this one is her fakest.

"Well, then," the man says, clearly fooled by the smile, "let's have a look at that hand, shall we?"

Gabby's bandaged hand throbs, as if it knows it's being talked about, and she gulps as Mom nudges her along. They follow the doctor quietly, their shoes scuffing against the mud-colored carpet, Gabby holding her breath all the while. For some reason, it feels like they're going to a funeral.

# 2

When they enter the examination room, Gabby doesn't wait for the doctor to tell her what to do. She just climbs right up onto that crinkly mattress and slumps down onto her back. She knows the routine by now.

"Well," the doctor says with a chuckle, "somebody's done this enough times before."

Mom says something back, but Gabby doesn't hear it. She's too busy looking out the room's only window at the park across the street. From here, she can just make out the edge of a wooden swing. Two boys around her age are taking turns riding it. She stares at them, unblinking, through the dark lenses of her goggles, until the doctor clears his throat.

"I'm going to remove your bandages now, Gabrielle," he says, gently lifting her arm, "so I can get a better look at your hand. Is that okay with you?"

Gabby looks up at the doctor's smiling face, nods, then looks back at the park. The boys have wandered off somewhere, leaving the swing empty. She imagines herself in their place, sitting on the splintered wood, her dress rippling in the wind, her goggles shining in the sun. In her daydreams, she always has two normal hands. No wet bandages. No aches and pains. No reason to be examined by bald doctors. Aside from her lenses—which are, for some reason, always there, even in her fantasies—her daydream-self never has anything wrong with her at all.

"Hmm," the doctor says, unwrapping the damp gauze. "It's definitely . . ." He trails off, and Mom fills the silence by saying, "Yes, I know. Now it looks like . . . tinted glass?"

"That's one way to describe it," the doctor replies. He prods at Gabby's hand with his fingertips, pushing gently against her wrist until tiny jolts of pain streak through her knuckles. When she winces and tugs against his hold, he relaxes his grip. "Sorry, my dear," he says, lowering her arm.

It's the kind of sorry she's gotten used to hearing from the doctors before him. *Sorry, I don't know what to make of it*, or, *Sorry, I don't know what to do*, or her least favorite of all: *Sorry, I don't think it can be fixed.* She frowns and looks away from the window, settling her gaze on the eggshell-colored ceiling, instead. "So that's it, then?" she says. "I'm doomed?"

Mom sighs, and the doctor lets out a slow laugh. "Well, I wouldn't go that far," he says. "Though I would like to try something, if it's okay with your mother."

Gabby bunches her face. All the other doctors ended their examinations as soon as they apologized. None of them ever wanted to *try something.* She looks at Mom, who smiles softly and gives her a quick nod. "It's okay, sweetie," she says. "I'm here."

So Gabby exhales and peers back out the window as the doctor moves about the room, clattering objects and rummaging through drawers. At one point, it sounds like he's peeling open a roll of tape. Then it sounds like he's twisting open a peanut butter jar. Gabby forces herself not to look at any of it, not because she's afraid, but because doctor stuff always confuses her, and today she wants to stay clear and level, her mind as flat as a windless lake. Today, the doctor will tell her that everything is finally okay. Today, they *will* find a cure. Today—

"What I have here is a syringe," the doctor says, raising a large, metallic needle to the light. He holds it above Gabby like a trophy, like something he wants her to gape at and marvel over.

She scowls at it, instead. "No," she says. "No, thank you. I don't like needles." She widens her eyes behind her lenses and looks quickly at Mom, who squeezes her hand in response. "I haven't given you permission to inject my daughter with anything, Doctor," Mom says, looking hard into the man's brown eyes.

The doctor nods, as if he expected this response. "I completely understand your concern. Though I assure you, I won't be injecting anything into your daughter. My plan is to merely puncture the skin of her wrist." He looks down at Gabby and smiles again, as if he didn't just use the word *puncture.* As if he didn't just say that he wants to stab her with a needle. "The poke," he tells her, "will be very slight. Like a bug bite, nothing more. Then it'll be done, and I'll put the needle away, and you won't have to see it or be poked by it again. I give you my word."

Gabby chews on her lip. Doctors have been giving her *their word* for months now, and frankly, it hasn't done her any good. She looks back at Mom, whose face has become tight and wrinkled with concern.

"And what," Mom asks the man, "are you hoping to accomplish with this?"

"A release of hydrostatic pressure," the doctor says quickly. When his words only seem to confuse Mom more, he adds, in simpler terms: "To ease her discomfort."

Mom frowns, then slowly nods. "And the jar?" she asks.

The doctor shifts something under his arm, then gives Gabby a playful wink. "Call it a hunch."

Mom says nothing back, and Gabby clenches her teeth. What do hunches have to do with needles and jars? And what does *any* of this have to do with her sore hand? "After this," she says, "can I go?"

The doctor clears his throat. "Well, there'll still be some routine tests that I'd like to run, and—"

Gabby shakes her head and says more firmly, "I'd like to go after this. I don't feel like doing any more tests."

The doctor exhales and says, "I understand, Gabrielle, but—"

Mom finally speaks up. "I agree with my daughter on this. I'll grant you permission to prod her with that needle. But after that, I'm taking her home. Surely you can run any additional tests on her some other day."

The doctor sighs, and Gabby holds back a grin. She knows that sigh—it's the same one *she* uses whenever Mom gets into one of her difficult moods. When the only thing you can do is sigh back.

"Very well," says the doctor. "But I do insist that you bring Gabrielle back at your earliest convenience. If this procedure goes as I expect it will, there'll be many questions left unanswered. Time will be of the essence."

"I'm taking her home after that needle," Mom replies, her tone suddenly heavy and forceful, and the doctor says nothing back. He merely nods, lifts Gabby's arm, and slowly brings the syringe toward her wrist. "You'll feel a slight poke," he says. "It'll hurt for an instant, then the pain will be gone. Are you ready?"

Gabby isn't ready, no. She doesn't want to be ready. But Mom's hand tightens around hers so firmly that it feels like she has no choice. After all, Mom agreed to take her home, to make all of this go away if Gabby would just let the doctor poke her wrist. Just once. One jab from that needle, and it'll all be over. One quick prick of pain, and things'll be better. The doctor will hum, and Mom will sigh with relief, and Gabby will wince her eyelids apart to see that her hand has suddenly been cured—just like that!

Surely an outcome that perfect is worth a split-second of pain?

"I'm ready," she says, looking out the window once again. She finds the edge of that wooden swing and pins her eyes to it, locking her lens-covered stare in place.

The doctor clears his throat, lifts her wrist higher, then begins to count backward. "Three," he says.

Gabby swallows hard.

"Two," he says.

Mom sniffs loudly.

"One."

Mom's hand squeezes hers so hard it hurts, and Gabby pinches her eyes shut, smothering the world in darkness, tensing every muscle until her body feels hard as stone, ready for any impact.

The needle presses against her wrist and then the touch becomes painful, hot and searing, as if the metal tip has somehow caught fire. She whimpers, and just when she's about to cry out, the pain suddenly vanishes. Mom lets out a gasp. The doctor becomes a flurry of movement, shifting and grabbing, grunting and wrapping. The sound of unfurling tape returns. Something thuds dully against her forearm, then a different something presses against her elbow. Finally, there's a sound like water spraying. Mom's voice rises above it all, her words thin and off-key. "What is that? What's happening?"

When it's all over, the doctor drags his sleeve across his forehead and gives Gabby a pat on the arm. "You're a brave girl," he says. Then to Mom, he raises his eyebrows. "This is quite likely the first case of its kind."

Mom's face looks pale, like she's seen a ghost. "Is that supposed to be comforting?"

The doctor shrugs and gestures at Gabby. "Gabrielle, does your hand hurt anymore?"

Gabby relaxes her body and slowly wiggles her bad fingers. She waits for the dull throbs of pain that always come next, but nothing happens. There are no aches. Nothing tingles. There isn't *anything*, really. "It feels . . . good now," she says, letting the sound of her own strange words wash over her. *Good now.* How long has she waited to say such a thing?

"But . . ." Mom begins. She leaves the sentence dangling, unfinished, as if there's nothing else to be said, and the doctor rests a hand on her shoulder. "If you'd like me to proceed with some additional tests . . ." he says.

Mom shakes her head and shrugs off the man's touch. "No. I said I would take her home and that's what I'm going to do."

The doctor nods quickly. "Understood. Though I must insist, Miss Lenton, that you return as soon as possible. I have a few colleagues who would greatly appreciate seeing your daughter. They may provide some answers that I'm not yet able to."

Mom blinks dumbly at the doctor, then says, "Do you have something to . . . cover it up?"

Gabby scrunches her face all over again. Cover what up? Her hand? Isn't it fixed now? Why would she need to *cover* it? She lifts her head and tries to see her fixed fingers, but Mom gently pushes her shoulders back down onto the mattress. "Just a moment, sweetie," she says. The doctor pulls a thick green towel from somewhere beneath the mattress and hands it to Mom, who begins tying it around Gabby's forearm, knotting the fabric tightly, as if she's wrapping some horrible gift.

"That should discourage any curious eyes," the doctor says.

Again, Gabby frowns. Why would anyone be curious about her hand now? It feels fine. Why, she can even wiggle her fingers and . . . "It's okay. I can take the towel off," she says, reaching for the green fabric.

Mom shakes her head and grabs at Gabby's forearm, but Gabby is already pulling the knot loose, tugging the towel apart. "Honey, wait!" Mom shouts. "You don't understand!"

"Really, it's okay," Gabby says, yanking at the fabric. "I don't need a towel or bandages or—"

Mom grasps frantically at the towel, but Gabby twists out of her reach and tugs the last bit of fabric free. "See," she says proudly, lifting her hand up to the light. "It's ... it's ..."

But then she sees what Mom has been trying to hide, and all the warmth inside her suddenly darkens and crumples, as if a rock has formed behind her ribs, made of nothing but ash and burnt leaves. Her hand isn't fixed—not even close. It's sealed in a glass jar now, one that's been taped around her wrist, and the inside of the glass looks foggy and clouded, as if the doctor has filled it with smoke. No—as if her hand is *made* of smoke. "Wh-what?" she stammers.

Mom wraps the towel back around the jar and quickly ties it into place, but Gabby has already seen enough. "Is that ... is that my *hand*?"

The doctor rubs the back of his neck, and this time when he smiles, he looks proud. Excited, even. "Gabrielle," he says, bending close to her. He glances at Mom, whose face looks stiff and unreadable. "I believe," the doctor says, looking eagerly into Gabby's eyes, "that yours is the first ever instance of a body part turning entirely to steam."

Mom closes her eyes and lets out a choked sob, and Gabby knows she should be upset. She knows this is a bad thing. It couldn't possibly be *good*, anyway. She knows the cold, hard feeling behind her ribs is here to stay, and that she might as well get used to it. But all she does is lie down on the mattress and look back out the window, until her spectacled eyes find that wooden swing all over again.

This time, when she imagines herself perched on the seat, one of her hands is sealed in a glass jar, with her fingers pluming inside it, like mist.

# 3

The first thing Kemple says to the new girl is: "Stop." One word, hissed into the early morning quiet, as they both crouch in the dimly lit kitchen. Then, more urgently, he says: "Don't."

The girl swishes her dark bangs away from her eyes, shoots him a look that he can't quite read, then continues jiggling two hairpins inside the pantry lock. As if she doesn't know any better.

No—as if she doesn't even *care*.

Kemple crumples his face so hard, his mouth starts to hurt. Two months, he's been living in this rickety house. Eight weeks of learning Abner's heavy-handed rules. This girl, however, has only been here for a few *hours*, and already she's breaking one of the biggest rules of all—one that'll earn her the bruising, buckled end of a belt if Abner wakes up and catches her in the act. "The pantry is off limits," he tells the girl, his voice whispering over the cold tiles. "You're gonna get yourself hurt!"

But the girl just rolls her eyes at him and keeps fumbling with the lock. "I'm gonna get myself *starved to death* if I don't open this lock," she hisses back. "And between you and me, I'd rather be hurt than dead."

Kemple rubs the heels of his hands against his face. He's hungry, too. Heck, he's been hungry since he moved here. But an empty, trembling stomach is a small price to pay to avoid Abner's wrath. If *Kemple* could learn to live hungry, then the girl can do it, too. "He'll make us toast in the morning," he whispers. "That's what he does. And a cup of watery milk. It's not much, but you'll get used to it."

The girl squints at him in the low light, her green eyes shining behind her lashes. "Toast and watery milk," she says, rolling her eyes. "Wow. What a feast. Think I could keep all that in?"

Kemple shakes his head. He's just met this girl, and already he doesn't like her. She's reckless. Careless. And she clearly doesn't know how furious Abner can get.

"I'm telling you for your own good," he whispers, bunching his shirt in his hands, "Abner will hit you something fierce."

"So?" the girl says, lifting her chin high. "Won't be the first time I've been hit."

Kemple clamps his mouth shut. He's never heard someone say that they've been hit before. Isn't that supposed to be kept secret? Something dark and shameful? An admission that you've been *bad*? "Maybe you should learn your lesson, then," he says, creeping closer.

The girl scowls at his bare feet, and he drags his heels to a stop. "Or maybe you should learn to stand up for yourself," she says. Then something in the lock clicks. The girl's eyes widen and she gapes at him for a moment, as if she didn't expect her hairpin trick to actually work. Then she grabs the lock and wrenches it open.

The fear in Kemple turns thick and crunchy, like mud that's been left too long in the sun. It drags through his veins and crawls up his throat, and when he tries to speak, it makes his words come out gurgling, his tongue heavy and thick. "He's gonna wake up and find you here and . . . and you're gonna wish you'd listened to me!"

But the girl just lets the lock clatter to the floor. Then she swings open the pantry door and starts rummaging through the darkened shelves, crinkling packages with her fingers, shifting boxes with her elbows, tearing open bags with her teeth. "Oh, it's like a treasure chest in here," she mumbles, her mouth already full of something. "Come on! There's plenty here for you, too."

But Kemple already knows what's on those shelves. Dried meats. Baked chips. Cans of pork and beans. It's all the good food that Abner keeps for himself—the stuff that Kemple has been walloped over, just for daring to *ask* about it. No way is he even going near that pantry now that it's open. "Put it all back," he hisses. "Lock it away! I'm telling you now, before it's too late and—"

Somewhere in the shadow-draped house, Abner coughs, and the bed springs creak.

Kemple's heart collapses into his throat. If Abner so much as catches them out of bed at this hour, well . . . he doesn't even want to think about it. "He's waking up!" he whisper-shouts, giving the girl one last chance to escape.

She finally pokes her head out of the pantry and stares at him with wide, unblinking eyes. "Are you sure?" she asks, her voice thin and wobbly.

"Yes!" Kemple hisses. "Put it all back, now!"

The girl finally seems to realize the danger. She starts jamming things back onto the shelves, creasing their open edges shut. "Help me!" she whispers. A bag of onion skins flops to the floor. "I don't remember what order it's supposed to—"

Then it happens: a jar of sliced peaches slips off the uppermost shelf and tumbles into the open air. They both watch it twist and flip, as if it's falling in slow motion. The girl reaches out to catch it, but only manages to smack her knuckles against the lid. Then the jar hits the floor and shatters, throwing syrup and glass shards everywhere. The sound of the impact echoes through the house, and for a moment neither of them move.

Then Abner's raspy voice thunders down the hall. "What in the damn hell?!"

Kemple's breathing turns hard and jagged. There's no time to clean everything up. No time to put the food back on the shelves. There's no time for anything, really, except for the two of them to run. But what good would that do? Abner will find the mess. He'll know one of them did it. Then he'll stalk them through the house until he gets his hands on them both, and then . . . then . . . Kemple spots the girl's horrified face, and something in the way her bottom lip is quivering, like she's on the verge of tears, makes him realize a horrible truth: she's never been hit before. It was a lie, something she made up to sound tougher than she is. If she'd really been beaten by another Abner, she wouldn't look like such a rat in a trap right now. She'd be steeling herself, bracing her mind for what's about to come. Instead she sniffs, hugs her ribs in a helpless way, and whispers, "Please."

And he understands what she's asking. *Please, save me.*

*Please, don't let him get me.*

Then Abner appears, stomping down the hall without a shirt on, his red-gray hair sticking up in all directions around his scruffy face. His wild eyes take in the mess and his face contorts into the ugliest scowl Kemple has ever seen. Then his glare locks onto the girl's sniffling face. "Why, you little piece of—"

Kemple's voice shoots out of him before he even has a chance to think. "It was me!" he croaks, forcing his feet to move. He scuttles over to the girl and puts himself in front of her, blocking most of her from Abner's view. "She begged me not to," he lies, "but I was hungry, and I just wanted a few chips, is all."

Abner's crap-brown eyes tear into his. The man's stare feels like it's made out of razor blades. "You selfish little prick," Abner growls. He grabs Kemple by the elbow and yanks him so hard that something in his shoulder pops and turns hot. Then the man begins tugging off his belt. "You're gettin' ten hits for this," he snarls. "Then you're gonna clean every speck of this up!"

Kemple grinds his molars together and bunches his hands into fists. *Ten* hits. He's never gotten more than five. "I'm sorry," he says, more out of habit than anything.

"Yeah," Abner rasps, still tugging at his belt, "you're gonna be a hell of a lot *more* sorry in a minute." Then, spotting the girl, the man jerks his head toward the hall. "You get on back to bed, Josephyn," he snaps. "You stay good, and you'll never have to get no belt hits like Kemple, here."

The girl's eyes find Kemple's, and she stares at him blankly, her gaze wet and unblinking. Then Abner yells, "Get!" and the girl bursts into movement, her skinny body lunging down the hall.

Abner sighs loudly, then wraps the tip of the belt around his hand, leaving the buckled end dangling in front of Kemple, the rusted brass glinting in the half-light. "Ten hits," the man reminds him, "for every one of your greedy little bastard fingers."

Kemple turns his back to Abner and braces his hands against the pantry door. He knows the routine by now. Knows to relax his shoulders—tensing them only makes it hurt worse. Glass shards and cold syrup slop against his toes, and the air suddenly feels hot and stifling, as if the house has become an oven filled with too much smoke and steam. He knows the girl must be crouching somewhere, trying not to listen to his punishment—punishment that should've been hers. When Abner inhales and shuffles his feet against the tiles, Kemple repeats the girl's name in his head—the name of the girl he saved. *Josephyn*. Something small and warm inflates in his chest. A tiny bubble of pride. Even in this horrible place, he's managed to do something good.

Then the belt buckle whistles through the air, and Kemple squeezes his eyes shut, bracing for the pain to come.

# 4

Gabby spends the next few days scowling at the jar taped to her wrist, until the fog inside the glass no longer resembles her hand at all. Now, no matter what angle she turns the jar, her hand just looks like a milky, rain-filled cloud. Numb. Featureless. Strange.

By the third day, she can't take it anymore. "I can't spend my life like this," she tells Mom, raising her jarred hand to the light. "I don't even know what this *is*."

Mom smooths her own hair behind her ears and sighs tiredly. She looks haggard this morning, which is unusual for her. The skin under her eyes is tinted purple, and the lines around her mouth have become so deep, they almost look like cracks. She leans against the kitchen sink, twists open the faucet, and stares blankly at the gray, silty water sputtering out of the pipe. "I've been trying to find someone, Gabs," she says, twisting the faucet closed again. "It's not as easy as you think."

Easy? Something in Gabby bends, almost to the point of breaking. She's never thought of any of this as *easy*. "My hand is in a jar, Mom! And it doesn't even look like a *hand* anymore." She flicks her good thumbnail against the glass, making the mist inside twist and swell. "Why can't we just go back to the bald doctor? He didn't seem worried at all."

"That's exactly what bothered me about him," Mom says, shaking her head. "He didn't want to help, Gabs. He wanted to turn you into a circus act."

Gabby flexes her eyebrows and imagines herself sitting inside one of those red fabric tents, the ones with wood chips and peanut shells strewn across the ground, her flowered dress stained from grease off a dirty stool. She imagines all the suited men and parasol-toting women coming to see her, their eyes wide as they peer at the cloudy jar on the end of her arm, their mouths open so far that she can see the pinks of their tongues. She'd even have a fancy name painted on a sign above her, like *The Girl With The Jarred Cloud Hand*, or something. And though Mom clearly means this as something to avoid, Gabby honestly can't see what would be so bad about any of it. With all that kind of attention, she'd eventually attract doctors and healers from around the world, until one of them thought up a cure.

Then she'd just be a normal, two-handed girl, with a pair of thick goggles for eyes. And wouldn't that be nice?

"I don't think a circus act would be so terrible," she says.

Mom scoffs and tugs at the strings around the middle of her dress, cinching the corseted fabric in place. "There's one person we could try," she says, stepping in front of the hallway mirror. She twists her body this way and that, frowns at her reflection, then scoops her leather purse off the counter. Coins clink inside.

Gabby frowns at that. There was a time when Mom's purse didn't make a sound. Back then, she carried paper bills instead of metal. Life was easier—being an airship stewardess paid well. But nowadays, flying has become such an ordinary, everyday thing that folks like Mom aren't really *needed* anymore.

Who needs a stewardess to offer you lemonade and tea when you can buy your own airship, with cupholders built right into the pilot's seat?

"You look pretty today," Gabby says, only partway lying. Mom always looks nice, but today she looks the *least* pretty she's been in weeks.

Mom relaxes her face into a tired grin. "Thank you, honey," she says softly. When Gabby frowns at the jar on her hand again, Mom says, "Okay, then. Get your boots on. We'll see what the engineer has to say."

Something lifts inside Gabby, like an airship taking flight. An *engineer* sounds like an important job. And important people always know how to make things right. She scrambles to the doorway and tugs on her boots with her good hand, not even bothering to knot the heavy laces. She must look rather sad in her frilled pants, her starchy gray shirt, and an oversized jar on her wrist. Especially next to Mom, who still looks like an airship stewardess, even though it's been months since she strolled in the sky.

But maybe looking sad is a good thing. It might make the engineer feel sorry for her, which might make him want to help her even more. She twists the lenses of her goggles a few clicks to the left, magnifying her eyes just a bit. Then she practices her most pitiful pout.

Mom plucks their apartment key off the rusted nail in the wall, nudges Gabby out the door beside her, and quietly clicks the lock into place. The look she gives Gabby is more worried than hopeful, but Gabby just shakes her head. "This is going to turn out well," she says, patting Mom's thigh with the jar. "I can feel our good luck growing."

This is . . . mostly a lie. The only thing she *really* feels is a wispy, slick sort of pressure around her smoky hand, as if her ghostly fingertips have finally discovered the edges of the jar.

As if her steam hand has decided it wants *out*.

# 5

The carriage they take is rickety, painted the color of spoiled meat, and smells like the inside of a barn. Every time the scruffy driver hits a new patch of cobbles, the whole coach jitters and shakes, and Gabby learns to hug the jar to her chest, just to stop it from slipping right off her wrist and shattering against the floorboards.

It brings a new question to mind, one she hasn't wondered about before: what would happen if the jar really did break? Would her steamy hand just hover there, clinging to her wrist like a ghost? Or would her fogged knuckles keep spreading apart until her whole hand drifts away, forever lost in the open air?

And would it hurt, either way?

She makes a point of remembering these questions so she can ask them aloud later. The engineer might have an answer or two.

"When my hand is back to normal," she tells Mom, raising her voice over the noise of the carriage, "I'm going to learn to play the piano."

Mom squints out the coach's grimy window, then looks over at Gabby blankly, as if she's been thinking about something else this whole time. "What's that again, dear?" she says, rubbing Gabby's hair.

"Piano," Gabby says. She lifts her jarred hand, holds it beside her good hand, and does her best imitation of fingering an invisible row of ivory keys. "I want to learn."

Mom frowns, and it's the saddest looking frown Gabby has seen on her in a long time. "Why would you want such a thing?"

Gabby crumples her face. Why does Mom always need a reason for everything? Can't she just *want* something for the sake of wanting it? "I don't know," she admits. "Maybe so that everyone can watch me play and say things like, *Oh, what a lovely, two-handed girl*, or, *And to think, she used to have a ghost hand in a jar!*"

She smiles as she says this, but when she looks up, Mom's mouth is tight and quivering, and her eyes look swollen with tears. Mom turns away and presses her nose against the carriage window. "I'd like that for you very much, Gabs," she says quietly. Then, with a brighter tone to her voice, one that sounds almost forced, she adds, "Or, if things *don't* work out with the engineer, you could always learn to play the drums." She glances sideways at Gabby and musters a smile, but her eyes look red and damp.

Gabby stays quiet the rest of the ride, with Mom's voice echoing in her head, like a charred heart pumping out burnt, tarry blood.

*. . . if things* don't *work out with the engineer . . .*

It's the first time Mom has suggested that things might *not* go as planned, and the thought alone makes Gabby's heart wobble. She frowns and stuffs her jarred hand into the shadows below the seat cushion, just so she won't have to look at it anymore.

# 6

The engineer doesn't seem at all surprised by the jar on Gabby's hand. He squints at it closely, flexing his sunburnt face, as if he's trying to see not just into the glass, but right *through* the mist of her hand itself. Then he grunts and gives Mom a quick tilt of his head. "Yeah," he says, "I can do something about that." His eyes narrow and he adds, "All depends on how much I'm getting paid, though."

Mom must be ready for this, because her hand is already inside her purse. She pulls out a brown fabric pouch and gives it a shake, making the coins inside clink together. "Will this be enough?" she asks, handing over the pouch.

The engineer unties the little bag, looks inside, and frowns. "Not enough for anything fancy," he says. "Some brass, some leather. Some iron and glass. It'll be functional, but . . ." He looks Mom up and down, his gray-eyed gaze roaming across her ribboned yellow hair, her corseted dress, her polished white shoes—this outfit that makes her look like she should be strolling down a carpeted aisle in the sky, offering drinks and reassuring scared passengers, not standing here in the gravel and dirt, talking about money with a grungy engineer. The man shakes his head and says, "It definitely won't be pretty to look at."

Mom sighs and says, "That's fine. Functional is better than a jar."

Gabby looks around and frowns. On the way over here, she imagined the engineer as a wizard—big robe, floppy hat and all. A man who doesn't have time to trim his beard because he's too busy being wise and traveling to exotic lands. The kind of guy who writes spells and slays dragons. But the engineer doesn't even have a hat, or a beard, or a robe—all he's got on is a pair of grease-stained blue coveralls, his dark boots splattered with white paint. And instead of some mystical, cavernous lair, his place looks more like a scrapyard—the rocky ground around them littered with the twisted frames of old airships, rusted metal plates, and the splintered spokes of huge carriage wheels. Come to think of it, the engineer looks like the *least* magical person Gabby has ever seen. How can he possibly turn her hand back to normal? "I want to find a different engineer," she says, not meeting Mom's eyes.

It's the engineer who responds. "Your mother already paid me, girl," he says with a chuckle.

He doesn't say this cruelly, but his words grate on Gabby all the same. Him and his raspy, non-wizardly voice. His ordinary, *nobody* voice. Her cheeks flush and she clenches her misty hand inside the jar, turning the cloud into a milky knot behind the glass. "Then un-pay her," she says, aiming her dark lenses right at his boring gray eyes, like she's pointing the barrel of a gun.

The engineer flattens his lips into a line, then turns his back to her. "It'll take me about an hour," he says, looking at Mom. He jerks his chin toward a nearby hill covered with dry grass and torn strips of leather. "There's an airfield on the other side of that slope. Your kid might like watching it, or whatever. I'll give you a holler when it's done."

Gabby wants to tell the engineer that she's already seen *plenty* of airfields, thank you very much, but before she has the chance, Mom grabs her by the elbow, flashes her fake work smile at the man, and tells him, "Thank you. That sounds perfect."

# 7

The airfield is small and ancient, its roads sun-bleached and crumbling at the edges. From the looks of it, there used to be white lines painted onto the cement, to give the dirigibles something to aim for when they drifted in to land. But even those have become so worn and faded that they're practically invisible now. Gabby frowns and leans her chest against the rusted fence, letting her arms dangle over the other side, her jar clinking dully against the chain links. "What's so perfect about this airfield?" she says to Mom. "It's all beat-up, and it's terribly plain." She points her goggles at Mom's squinting eyes and says, "It's a lot like the engineer, actually."

Mom takes a deep breath and lets it out quietly. The wind whips her yellow bangs against her forehead, and she brings a hand to her face, shielding her eyes from the sun. "He's not going to fix your hand, Gabs," she says. She stares intently at a small white airship that's sitting lopsided on the grass, just beside the pavement. "He's going to make it useful, though. You'll be able to function just like everyone else."

Gabby narrows her eyes behind her lenses. Function? What kind of word is that? It makes it sound like she's part machine—like a human appliance. "I don't want to function," she says, leaning harder against the fence. She slaps the jar against the metal, making the glass clang. "I want to be *normal*, like everyone else."

This actually makes Mom laugh. "Oh, honey," she says, brushing a stray lock of hair behind her ear, "normal is so overrated." She looks down at Gabby's spectacles. It's bright out today—the sky a sharp, piercing blue—so she probably can't see Gabby's eyes through her lenses. But their gazes lock anyway, and Mom smiles warmly. "One day," she says softly, "you'll understand how special it is to be . . . well, *special*."

Gabby's mouth goes dry, and she tries to force some spit over her tongue, just so she can swallow comfortably. Part of her wants to argue, to point out that Mom couldn't possibly know what it's like to be her; to have such huge, clunky goggles and a hand that looks like warm breath on a cold day; to have jet-black hair and blurry green eyes and stupid freckles all over her nose and cheeks; and most of all, Mom wouldn't know how it feels to be skinny and straight in all the places where so many other girls already have curves, to be all but *invisible* to anyone her own age. But she doesn't say anything at all. She just stays there, slumped over the top of the metal fence, while a pair of rickety, lime-green airships wobble across the sky above them, practicing their take-offs and landings.

The hour passes quickly, and before long, the engineer's voice catches in the wind, his gravelly accent flattening his words into a steady, unchanging tone. "I've finished the glove. Bring the girl to try it on."

Mom looks down at Gabby and offers an encouraging smile. "Well, then. Let's see how it turned out."

But Gabby is suddenly too numb to respond, her mind teetering off-balance. The engineer hasn't done anything to fix her hand—he simply built her a stinking *glove* to cover it up.

Mom wraps her slender fingers around Gabby's bad wrist, gripping the gray tape that holds the jar around her hand, and they take their time trudging down the dry hillside. Mom seems eager—hopeful, even—but Gabby's insides are all warbling heat and chalky cinder. It doesn't matter what color the glove will be, or how it'll feel, or what the stupid thing will look like. No, she's already decided: she's going to *hate* everything about it.

And not even Mom will change her mind.

# 8

It takes days for the sting of Abner's belt to finally stop wrenching tears from Kemple's eyes. He spends the time lying facedown on his scratchy cot in nothing but a pair of tattered shorts, his arms dangling over the edges, his fingertips grazing the floorboards.

Abner, at least, leaves him a box of saltine crackers and a jug of dirty water—just enough to keep him from starving to death.

Right before it happened, Kemple was actually foolish enough to think he'd done a good thing—helping Josephyn escape her first ever lashing. But since then, the girl has been like a ghost. He hasn't seen her or heard from her in days. It's like she somehow up and left, leaving him to suffer from his injuries alone. And now that he's had a few days to think it over, well . . . if he had the power to go back in time, he'd tell Abner the truth, right then and there. He'd let the girl feel what he's feeling now. Let *her* know what it's like to lie here, slumped over hour after hour, with these scorching hot bruises stinging *her* back, like so many merciless licks from a dragon's tongue.

Let Josephyn know what it's like to cry alone for so long. To have nobody to tell her that it'll all be okay in the end. Let *her*—

"Hi," says a small, wavering voice, and Kemple twists his head around to find the girl standing in his doorway. She looks the same way she did that first night: skinny, wide-eyed, with a sharp, angular face, as if she's spent a lot of time looking into a mirror, honing that permanent scowl of hers. But her lips are flexed into a smile.

He grumbles and turns his head away. Smiling or not, he'd rather she leave him alone, just so he can finish hating her in peace. "Why don't you go break into something else?" he mutters. "Then Abner can wallop *you* this time."

The girl says nothing. Instead, she steps quietly into his room. Her bare feet scuff against the floorboards, like a cat's tail swishing gently back and forth.

"I said *go away*," he mutters into the fabric of his cot.

"No," the girl replies, her voice annoyingly casual, "you told me to *break into something else*. So that's what I'm doing. I'm breaking into your room."

Kemple frowns. His room is hardly a room at all—a sad fact that Abner makes sure of. There's a cot, a dusty closet, a battered little dresser with some shabby clothes inside, and a grimy window with a lock on it to keep it from opening. Really, if he had to describe it, he'd call it more of a prison cell than anything else. "Be my guest," he says, closing his eyes. "There's nothing here worth taking."

Josephyn makes a thoughtful noise in the back of her throat, then her cat-tail feet swish around the room. Kemple tries not to listen—tries not to *care*—but he finds himself straining to hear anyway, just so he can follow her movement. She moves toward the closet, then toward the dresser. Then she makes her way to the window and lingers there for a while, as if she's looking out at the dry, grassy fields beyond the house, her gaze fixed on that lonely dirt road that he's spent so many afternoons staring at—that never-ending path that quietly promises so many things. Adventure. Escape. Freedom. Then the girl sniffs, shuffles over to his cot, and stands so close that he can hear her slow, steady breathing. Suddenly he's aware of how pitiful he must look, lying here shirtless, with all those long, red welts peppered across his spine and shoulder blades. He tries to roll over, but the pain on his back flares up again, like a fresh splash of acid on his skin, and a whimper escapes his lips.

"I'm sorry, Kemple." She pushes the words out slowly, as if it's hard for her to apologize. As if she's not used to doing it. "I'm sorry you got this because of me."

The apology sounds genuine, but something inside him isn't ready to let go. That anger keeps twisting and blazing in his gut, like he's swallowed a miniature sun, and just the thought of letting it fizzle away makes his teeth clench and grit. It wouldn't be *fair* for him to get such a beating, and for her to expect it to all be okay, just because she says a few lousy words. "You *should* be sorry," he says, letting the sun inside him scorch his ribs. "Letting me take the blame for you? That makes you a terrible person, you know."

The girl replies quickly, her voice lashing out, her tone suddenly hard and thick. "I didn't ask you to do anything for me."

For a split second, Kemple actually cringes, half-expecting her words to come with the smacking sting of a buckle. But when nothing happens, he rolls over to face her, wincing as the cot scrapes his skin. "You did ask me," he says, scowling at her bird-like face. "You said *please*." And she really, truly did. He's replayed that exact moment in his mind so many times. No *way* is he letting her pretend it never happened.

Josephyn looks back at him, matching his scowl, like she's the smaller, girl-version of himself. Then her expression softens, and she gives him a nod.

"Yeah, okay," she says. "Maybe I did." She brushes her dark bangs away from her eyes and says quickly, "But I'm still here, saying sorry for it. That has to count for something."

The sun moves inside him, sliding its heat up his stomach, lodging its flames in his throat, and it takes him a moment to realize that it's trying to escape, to be free, to burst out into the open air so it can wither away completely, like a flame trying to leap off its wick. But he swallows the rage back down, holding it in place. He's not ready to forgive her yet. Not while the skin of his back still feels like it's made of smoldering coals. "Apologies count for nothing," he tells her, turning his face away. Then, as if Abner is speaking through him, he says, "Now *get*."

But the girl doesn't move. She just stands there, breathing steadily, probably staring daggers at him. Then she says quietly, "I don't believe you. I think you're already forgiving me, you're just too stubborn to admit it. But that's okay. Stubborn is good. It's what'll keep bastards like Abner from getting under your skin."

Kemple says nothing back. The girl talks like she knows everything, but she's only just met Abner. She's only seen the *beginning* of life in this man's miserable house. Let her live here for a few months like he has, then she'll know better. She'll learn what he's learned the hard way: bastards like Abner will *always* find a way under your skin. "Just let me alone," he mutters. "It hurts, and I can't cry with your stupid face watching me."

Josephyn sighs and places something bulky on his cot, nestling it under the crook of his elbow. Then her cat-tail feet swish across the floor. He listens as she pauses at the doorway—maybe to look back at him, or maybe to say something else. Whatever it is, she must decide against it, because her footsteps then move briskly into the hall, until they've faded away completely.

He frowns at the dingy closet and waits for a moment, letting the dull silence of the house drape over him like an invisible sheet. Then he looks down at the thing she left under his arm.

It's a wrinkled paper bag—one of those empty grocery packages that Abner likes to hoard in the cabinet under the kitchen sink. Inside is an old can opener and small tin can, the label faded and half-peeled. He reads the can quietly, barely moving his lips. "Pork and beans," he whispers. Abner's favorite. The man must not've noticed this one missing from his stash.

The can feels weighty in Kemple's grip, and not just in a physical way. No, it's as if he's holding an actual bar of *gold*. And despite his best effort to cling to that ball of anger in his gut, the fire quickly goes out, all that heat withering into a plume of cool, damp smoke.

He stuffs the can back into the bag, reaches over the edge of the cot, and slips the package quietly into the top drawer of his dresser. His own secret treasure. Then he slumps back onto the cot and rests his knuckles against his eyes, doing his best not to smirk.

"Okay, Josephyn," he mutters under his breath. "Apology accepted."

# 9

If Gabby could have one superpower right now, she'd want the ability to make herself heavier—so heavy that not even an airship would be able to lift her. Or at least so heavy that an adult couldn't possibly pick her up. "I'm not going," she says, for at least the tenth time this morning. She lets her body go limp in Mom's arms, willing all the weight in the universe into her legs and back.

But Mom is frustratingly determined this morning. She hugs Gabby tighter to her chest, almost in a bear hug, and drags her down the hall. "I have a job interview today, Gabs," she says through her teeth. "You won't ruin this for me. And you will *not* miss your first day of school."

But Mom doesn't understand. How could she, with her two perfect hands? She doesn't know the looks Gabby will get from the other kids. The whispers. The snickers. The things they'll throw at her back whenever she isn't looking. It was bad enough last year when she showed up wearing her goggles. Now that there's a permanent chunk of metal and leather where her hand should be? Heck, she can already picture the horrified looks on their faces. "I'm a *freak*," she says, lifting her clockwork glove and wiggling her steamy fingers inside it.

The gears along her knuckles twist and click, and the valve above her wrist lets out a tiny spurt of steam. She points at it, as if even the glove agrees with her. "See?" she says, looking hard at Mom's exasperated face. "They'll eat me alive in there."

Mom just rolls her eyes and wrestles Gabby onto their tattered living room couch. The orange fabric wheezes out a tiny cloud of dust, and Gabby swats at it with her mechanical hand, as if smacking at some dirty air could possibly erase her frustration.

"Your prosthetic is completely fine, Gabs," Mom says, jamming a pair of long green socks onto Gabby's feet. "Do you think you're the only girl in the world with something different about you?" Mom tugs at Gabby's pant legs, flattening the creased hems back down around her ankles.

Gabby waits until she's done, then reaches down and bunches the hems back up around her calves.

Mom sighs loudly and runs a hand through her coiffed hair. "Honestly? Sometimes I think you exist just to make my life more difficult."

The comment stings, and Mom seems to realize it, because she quickly shakes her head. "I didn't mean that," she says with another sigh. "I'm just . . . we're running low on money, sweetie. I need today to go well, so we won't have to move again. Do you understand?"

Gabby knots her arms over her chest and pouts. Why is it always *her* that needs to understand? Why can't Mom ever be the one to listen? "I understand that you're okay with sending me off to the most miserable day of my life so far," she grumbles.

Mom's shoulders sag, like she's melting. Then she glances at the wooden clock on the wall and her mouth pulls into a line. "Negotiations are over," she says. "You're going to school, and I'm going to my interview, and today will turn out to be *wonderful* for us both." She flashes one of her dazzling smiles—all shiny teeth and twinkling eyes and so much fakeness that it makes Gabby angry, her nose and cheeks flushing with heat. Then Mom actually has the nerve to ruffle her hair. "You'll see, Gabs," she whispers. "We'll both see."

But she doesn't look at Gabby's lenses when she says this, as if even *she* doesn't believe it.

The rest of the morning unravels in a dizzying blur. They both scarf down stale slices of bread with strawberry jam that tastes more bitter than sweet, and the milk is so thin today that they might as well be drinking cloudy water. Neither of them say a word while they eat. Then Mom stuffs a banana into Gabby's satchel, loops the bag over Gabby's shoulder, and places her clockwork hand on top of it all, patting Gabby's head like she's a well-behaved pet. "There," she says, looking Gabby up and down. When she notices Gabby's scowl, she tilts her head and says softly, "I wish you could see yourself the way I see you. Then you'd know how lovely you really are."

The comment is so ridiculous that Gabby doesn't even bother arguing with it. She just shakes her head and steps out the door, clenching her clockwork fingers around her satchel so hard that the leather nearly rips. She stays like that, with her mechanical fingers digging into the side of her bag, while Mom leads her into the hallway and locks the door behind them. She stays like that while they trudge down the ugly yellow stairs, and while they wait on the curb beneath a bleary gray sky, and while Mom hails a carriage that jostles them over the wooden bridge that cuts through Iron Bay like a huge, splintering belt. She even stays like that when the carriage drops her off outside the school, while Mom waves and smiles her fake smile, her voice as cheerful as it is empty. "It'll all turn out great. You'll see!"

Then the carriage steers away and Gabby turns to see the other kids lingering on the steps by the front doors, with their normal hands and their non-goggled eyes and their sneers and whispers and horrible pointed fingers, and suddenly Gabby's boots are stomping along the cobbles, not toward the school but *away* from it. She swings her clockwork hand, glares through her tinted lenses, and runs until the sounds of the school wither away, until the only noises left are the squawks of gulls overhead, and the rumble of machinery far in the distance.

Only then does she allow herself to cry.

# 10

Kemple is standing at his bedroom window, looking blankly through the dirty glass at that lonely road to nowhere, when Abner knocks on the wall and clears his throat. There's no door to Kemple's room—it was taken off the hinges long before he moved in—so it's the wood frame that Abner raps against, knocking out an impatient rhythm. "Got your shirt on, I see," says the man in that gravelly, bitter voice of his.

It's hard to tell what kind of response Abner expects, so Kemple just shrugs and turns away from the window, not quite meeting the man's eyes. "Still hurts," he says, tugging at his shirt collar, "but not so bad that I can't get dressed anymore." This is . . . not exactly true. His back still hurts like all heck. But he's tired of lying around like a mushroom on a log, waiting for his body to heal. So today he forced himself onto his feet, and he tugged the loosest shirt he owns over his head, grimacing and wincing all the while. The cotton is rough and thin—a sign that it was cheaply made and has gone through a few too many washings—and it grits like sandpaper against his skin. But at least he feels like a boy again, and not just an injured victim. Like he's finally returned to the human race. "And," he says simply, "I felt ready to get up."

Abner clucks his tongue. "Well, it's about time. You act like I branded you with a cattle prod. Now, if you had *my* pops, maybe you would've. So consider yourself lucky you got me instead, boy."

Kemple scrunches his face and nods, not because he agrees, but because it's what the man expects of him. Honestly though, he can't imagine a universe where *anyone* would call themselves lucky to have Abner. "Yeah," he mutters. "I guess."

"You *guess*," Abner says, dragging out the word as if something about it disgusts him. He steps into the room, his shoes tracking dirt and grime onto the floorboards, and Kemple glances sideways at the muddy shoe prints, wincing inwardly. He'll have to clean *that* slop up, now. And Abner doesn't own a mop—or if he does, he never lets Kemple use it. These kinds of jobs have always been given to him with nothing but a tattered rag and a rusted, soap-filled bucket. "Suppose you want me to clean the floor now," Kemple says.

Abner looks down at his tracks, shakes his head, then drags a dirty hand through his hair. "I ain't worried about it," he says. "You and what's-her-name can scrub it off later."

"Josephyn," Kemple says automatically. Immediately, he bites his lip. He shouldn't have spoken so quickly. Shouldn't have mentioned her name. Should've acted like he didn't even know the girl at all—or at least pretended that he didn't care. "I mean," he says, trying to look casual, "I think that's her name, anyway." He flicks his gaze up to Abner's scruffy face.

The man scowls back with his crap-brown eyes, slithering his sour glare all over Kemple's face, as if Kemple's thoughts have been carved right onto his skin. As if the bastard is reading his mind. "So you two got an alliance going now, hmm? Is that it?"

Kemple shakes his head, but Abner's eyes grow even narrower. The man is a royal jerk, but he isn't stupid. "Was gonna give you the day off," Abner says. He rubs his calloused hands along the seams of his gray coveralls, as if he's searching for a pocket. "But seeing as you and the girl got a bond now, I figure: why should she have to pick up *your* slack, when you two can just work together, like good little bastards? What do you say to that?"

Kemple bunches his lips. Honestly, that sounds more like a kindness than a punishment. But he sure as heck won't say that to Abner's face—the man *hates* kindness. Sees it as a weakness. "I think," Kemple says, weighing his words carefully, "that you know best."

This seems to make Abner relax just a tad, his shoulders lowering, his fingers going slack. His eyes widen and he nods, as if he approves. "Damn right I know best," he says, jabbing a finger toward Kemple. "And don't you ever forget it, boy." Then the man turns and leaves the room, his heavy footsteps clomping down the hall. "There's two buckets of smelt on the counter," he calls out. "You and the girl are both gonna clean it all up. And it better be done by the time I get back, or I'll put you back down on that cot with a whole slew of fresh welts, you hear?"

Before Kemple has a chance to reply, the screen door creaks and slams shut. It clatters as Abner twists the lock, and the house fills with that familiar throb of silence—that calm after the storm. Then Josephyn's cat-tail feet swish up the hall. She pokes her skinny face around the doorframe and raises an eyebrow at Kemple, her sparkling green eyes fixed on his blue-gray shirt. When she looks back at his face, her expression is tight, her brow knitted with confusion. "What the heck is *smelt*?"

Kemple sighs and steps past her, dragging his heels along the dusty floorboards. She follows him to the kitchen, stalking quietly behind him, as if she's afraid

Abner might leap out from the shadows. "Smelt is . . ." he begins to say, but the only word he can think of is *disgusting*. "It's fish," he says. "Slimy, awful-smelling fish." He glances back at her grimacing face and says, "And I'm gonna chop their heads off. Then you're gonna scoop out their guts. Otherwise, we'll both be in for it when he gets back." He emphasizes the word *both*, just so she understands that this time he *won't* be taking the belt for her. This time, if things go wrong, it'll be her own skin on the line.

She seems to get the message, nodding slowly. Then she brushes her bangs away from her eyes—a useless motion, as her hair just falls right back into place. She stares at him for a moment, her eyes pinched and unreadable, before finally saying, "Why do I have to do the guts?"

# 11

Abner's scissors are rusted and dull, so it takes Kemple a few tries to cut off the fish's head. "You have to cut it at an angle," he says, "just behind the gills. Like this." When he finally squeezes the blades through the rubbery flesh, the head falls into the sink, hitting the metal basin with a soft, wet thud. The head's eyes and mouth stay wide open, as if the fish is somehow surprised, and Josephyn lets out a groan. "This is awful," she says, shaking her head. "How can you even stand it?"

The question sounds layered, as if she's asking about more than just beheaded fish, and Kemple can only shrug. "You get used to Abner's ways, after a while," he says. "He's really not that bad, once you get to know him."

Josephyn gives him a hard look. "*Not that bad?*" Her hand finds its way to his back, her palm pressing gently between his shoulder blades, and her touch is like fire against his skin. Like the fabric of his shirt is turning to flames.

He cringes, flinches away, and almost drops the scissors to the floor.

"Yeah," Josephyn says, crossing her arms. "Not that bad, huh?"

Something inside Kemple clenches, and he finds himself grinding his teeth. "It was your stupid fault anyway," he says, jamming the scissors into the fish's headless body. He cuts a jagged line down its belly, then shoves the slimy thing toward her. "And if you don't want it to be your turn next, then you should probably get started on the guts."

Josephyn glares at the tiny corpse glistening on his palm. Then she snatches the thing from him and does exactly like he told her to: she stuffs her finger into the cut, drags the sticky innards out, and slops them down into the sink with a whimper. "Oh, foul," she says.

And it *is* foul. Easily one of the foulest things Abner has ever made Kemple do. But foul is better than painful, so he doesn't hesitate when he reaches for the next fish, plucking it quickly from the putrid bucket. "We do this well," he says, scissoring off the next head, "and maybe he'll give us some."

"Oh," Josephyn says, rolling her eyes. "Nasty, headless fish bodies? I can hardly wait."

Kemple says nothing back. What's the use of arguing, anyway? She clearly doesn't get it. So what if the fish is foul? So what if she doesn't want to eat any? The whole point is to stay on Abner's good side. To not give him a reason to lash out. To do what he asks, and to do it well—that's the secret to avoiding fresh bruises. "Make sure you push your finger all the way in," he says, cutting open another belly. "If you leave any gunk behind, he'll throw a fit."

Josephyn scowls at the next fish he hands her, but she does as she's told, jamming her finger so roughly into the thing that it makes a squelching sound. This time, she almost gags.

They stay like this for a while, side by side at the kitchen sink, with him cutting, her scooping, and the sun streaking through the window in dusty, grime-pinched beams, until the tension in Kemple's chest finally begins to ease, and the roar in his head quiets down. Maybe she's finally getting it. Maybe she actually understands. As long as they behave like good little servants, Abner won't have a reason to show his teeth.

But then Josephyn clears her throat, and Kemple's chest goes tight once more. "From what I can tell," she says, slapping another scoop of fish guts into the sink, "Abner leaves us alone enough, now and then, to lose track of what we're doing."

Kemple lops off another head and sighs. The scissors are starting to get slippery in his fingers, the metal slick with awful juices, and he squeezes the handle until his hand starts to throb. "He goes out, yeah," he says, slicing another belly. "But he always knows what we've been doing."

Josephyn snatches the fish body from him and drags out the guts without even looking. She stares at his face the whole time, her mouth flexed into a stiff line. "He knows *afterward*," she says. Another clump of innards hits the sink basin with a wet slap, and she raises her eyebrows at him, as if she's trying to tell him something without actually using the words.

But the stink of the fish has his head feeling cloudy, his thoughts blurring together. Whatever Josephyn is trying to tell him, he's almost certain that it's *not* going to make Abner happy. "I don't know what you're getting at," he says, "but I've been here way longer than you. I know him way better than you. And I know that if you want to avoid pain and tears, you do what he tells you to do, and you hope that he approves when you're done."

Josephyn's face softens, her eyebrows bending upward, until she looks like she might cry. "That's a horrible way to live," she says, studying his face. "Don't tell me you're okay with that."

But honestly, he doesn't know *what* he's okay with anymore. Things were fine until she showed up. Okay, well . . . maybe not *fine*, but at least he had a system.

The days were hard and the nights were short, but the little things kept him going. Like gazing at that lonely road that could lead to anywhere. Or the weekly porch sweepings while Abner sat on his chair, swigging liquor from a bottle until he passed out, leaving Kemple to stand there with a splintered broomstick in his grip, the hot wind caressing his face like a reassuring hand. Or—

"Oh, my God," Josephyn mutters. "You actually *are* okay with it."

Kemple's face turns hot and he reaches down into the bucket, but he's already holding a fish. "I'm not okay with it," he finally says, pressing the scissor blades into the fish's silvery gills, "I've just . . . learned to deal."

Josephyn shakes her head, and he watches her drag the back of her wrist against her forehead, smearing a few beads of sweat into her eyebrows. "This is the fourth foster home I've been in," she says, glaring up at the dirty window. "And you know what *I* learned?"

Kemple shakes his head, not because he doesn't know, but because he doesn't *want* to know. "We still got another bucket to do before he gets back, and he specifically told me—"

"I learned how to get away," she says, her words hitting the air like a mallet. She looks at him with her face as blank as can be, all the emotion drained out of her features. "And I'm getting away from this one, too," she says. "The only question left is: will the boy who took a beating for me be brave enough to come along? Or would he rather stay behind, scooping guts from stinky fish until he's all sour and grown up, with nobody but Abner to keep him company?"

Kemple bites his lip and tries not to imagine that exact scenario, but it fills his mind anyway. Him growing tall and lean. Abner growing fat and even more bitter. Bucket after bucket of foul smelt to be cleaned, and dusty porches to be swept, and an endless road that's always achingly out of reach, its edges forever leading to nowhere.

And something close to a sob escapes his lips. "I don't want that," he mumbles.

Josephyn's mouth quirks, the edges of her lips curling up. "Then let's make a plan," she whispers.

Kemple squeezes the scissors shut, chopping off one more head at the gills. This time when it tumbles into the sink, it doesn't look surprised—it looks like it's *listening.* "Okay," he whispers back. The word feels jagged coming out of him, like something dangerous and forbidden, and he finds himself holding back a grin.

# 12

Gabby doesn't get much time to cry at the docks. A few minutes, maybe. A quarter of an hour, at most. Eventually a man in a bowler cap notices her, and soon after that a blue carriage with a domed roof arrives, the coach's wheels creeping right up to the edge of the pier. As soon as the driver steps out, his wide body wrapped in a shiny gray uniform, that murky feeling in Gabby's chest thickens even more, and she tilts her goggles away from her cheeks until her trapped tears fall to the wood.

She's never been in trouble with the *law* before.

The officer looks at her sternly, and she watches his gaze settle on her clockwork hand. His eyes narrow with suspicion. Then he jerks his chin toward the coach and mutters a single, commanding word: "In."

Gabby knows she should listen, knows she should *obey*, but for the briefest of moments, she imagines a boy with messy hair the color of dark soil swooping down in an airship, his arm outstretched, his glittering eyes locked onto her goggles. "Take my hand!" he calls out, and she reaches up with her clockwork glove to twine her brass-plated fingers between his. And he doesn't grimace or wince or pull away at all, he just smiles and grips onto her even tighter; then she's lifted up, her boots dangling above the pier, the wind whipping her hair against her ears and fluttering her clothes against her skin, and the officer shouts and even fires a pistol, but the airship's engine roars and the gondola rises and the boy pulls her into his arms and takes her away—to safety and freedom, to a land where goggled eyes can be fixed with a single medicine drop, and where steamy hands can be cured with a pill.

But when none of that happens, the officer gets impatient, grabs her by her elbow, and shoves her—a little too roughly—into the backseat of the coach. Then he stuffs himself into the driver's seat and says flatly, "Where do you live?"

Gabby whispers her address like she's losing a secret.

The officer grunts and steers the carriage away from the docks, revving the engine the whole way, rattling the wheels over the cobbles. The ride is terribly uncomfortable—the coach bucks at every turn like an angry horse, and the seat-back presses against Gabby's spine like a pair of calloused hands—but she keeps her forehead jammed against the window, her lenses clinking against the glass, her eyes fixed on that imaginary airship as it shrinks into the clouds above the sea.

# 13

Kemple won't say it aloud, but Josephyn's plan is really quite clever. He's beginning to see this as her defining trait: cleverness. Her mind never seems to stop working. Which probably explains why she's been able to break out of three foster homes so far—if her word is true.

Still, even a clever plan feels risky when it involves Abner. Especially when it's about trying to *escape* from him. Kemple frowns and sweeps more dust off the porch, dragging the broom slowly along the sun-bleached wood. "I don't know," he whispers, keeping his voice as soft as he can. "It still seems dangerous."

Josephyn kneels by the window beside him and dips her hands into a bucket of gray, soapy water. "That's why it'll work," she whispers, swishing her hands inside the murky liquid. "It's the last thing he'd expect us to do."

Kemple frowns but continues sweeping, just to keep the bristles rustling against the wood. Abner fell asleep a good ten minutes ago. Now he's slumped in the padded chair at the end of the porch, with an empty liquor bottle propped against his thigh. But Kemple isn't ready to set the broom down yet. Not until the bastard starts snoring. "Maybe it's the *first* thing he'd expect," Kemple whispers.

Josephyn pulls a grimy sponge from the bucket and smears it against the window, soaking the glass between the iron bars. "He thinks he owns us," she says, using her normal speaking voice. "And he thinks we're okay with that." She shoots Kemple a hard look, as if she expects him to argue with her. When he says nothing back, she relaxes her face and says, "And when he wakes up, we'll be long gone from this hellhole." She glances at Abner and gives him a sloppy salute, leaving dirty soap bubbles on her bangs.

Kemple looks out at the dry fields, his gaze lingering on that lonely dirt road beneath the cloudless sky. It's around noon, which usually means chores and more chores, but today the midday feels like a huge box that's been opened, its insides dark and mysterious. Like a gift just waiting to be torn into.

Or like a bomb that's ready to go off.

"If he catches us," he hisses, "we're done for. Who knows what he'll do?"

Josephyn sighs and throws the sponge into the bucket, making the foamy water splash against her trousers. "And if we stay? Then we're done for, too." She points a glistening finger in Abner's direction and says, "Besides, who knows if we'll get another chance like this?"

Kemple doesn't want to admit it, but she's right. She would know—this was *her* doing, after all. She was the one to suggest to Abner that they clean the porch. And she was the one to offer the man a drink. The rest practically took care of itself—once the jerk starts chugging, he usually doesn't stop—but it was still *Josephyn* who put the wheels into motion.

And even *she* wouldn't be daring enough to try the same trick on Abner twice.

"Okay," he whispers, "but we don't even know where we're going."

Josephyn cracks a smile, as if this is all part of the plan. "That's the best part of all," she says. "Imagine the possibilities."

Kemple chews his bottom lip and tries to imagine their lives without Abner, but his mind doesn't want to cooperate. When he pictures them riding in a carriage through an open field, there's Abner, sitting in the front seat, glaring back at them through the driver's mirror. When he pictures them clambering onto an airship, there's Abner, dressed in a pilot's uniform, scowling down at the unpunched tickets in their hands. In every scenario he can think of, the man is somehow there, clinging to them like a hungry leech. "I can't see us getting away," Kemple mutters.

Josephyn frowns, shoves the bucket away from her, and points angrily at his face. "See? You can't even *fantasize* about getting away from him. That's exactly why we need to go."

"But . . ." Kemple starts to say. But there isn't anything else *to* say. He glances at Abner, who's already snoring, his mouth so slack that a thin line of drool is trickling down his chin. Right now the guy looks harmless, his body sagging awkwardly in his chair, and Kemple almost feels sorry for the bastard. When he finally wakes up, he'll be all alone, with nothing around him but an abandoned broom and a rusted bucket full of dirty water. But then Kemple's gaze lands on the man's calloused hands, and any pity he has for the jerk suddenly turns hard and cold, like the bruising end of a belt. "Go screw yourself, old man," he mutters under his breath. Then, louder, he says, "I hope you choke on your own spit!"

Josephyn's eyes grow wide, and she whirls around to look at Abner, her body already poised to run. But the man just snorts, shifts on his chair, and pulls the empty bottle tighter against his hip.

"That's our cue to leave," Josephyn says, and this time Kemple doesn't argue, doesn't shake his head, doesn't even think, *What if . . . ?* He simply sets the broom down on the weathered porch and squints out at that endless dirt road.

Josephyn leaves her bucket and steps beside him, and for a moment they just stand there, gazing out at that path to nowhere. No . . . that path to *anywhere*. Then, without even saying a word, they both hop off the porch and begin to run, their bare feet slapping against the parched earth, their tattered clothes rippling in the wind.

Neither of them dare to look back.

# 14

The officer explains everything to Mom with a bored look on his face, as if it's the most common thing in the world for him to find a metal-handed girl crying alone at the docks. "Guy in a cleaning crew spotted her," he says, his eyes flicking toward Gabby's lenses. "First-time offenders like her get off with a warning." He looks back at Mom and grins in a way that makes Gabby feel soiled. "But her name is in the records now. So if she's caught leaving school again . . ." He lets the sentence trail away, and Gabby finds herself leaning forward, just so she can hear the man better.

What's the punishment for a second-time offender? Will they toss her in jail? Stone her? Bind her wrists and ankles, then toss her into the sea?

But the officer says nothing else. He just nods at Mom, as if the conversation has finished. As if Gabby's future punishment is as obvious as rust on wet metal. His beady-eyed gaze settles on her glove once more, then he steps into the hall and pulls the door shut behind him.

Mom stands still for a moment, her shoulders rising and falling from the weight of her breathing, and she stays that way until the sound of the officer's footsteps fade into silence. Then she becomes all noise and movement, her hair streaming behind her like flames. "What were you thinking, Gabs? Do you realize what could've happened to you? Do you understand how much *worse* this all could've been?"

Gabby twists the hem of her blouse between the tips of her metal fingers. There's probably a correct answer to these kinds of questions, but whatever it is, she sure can't think of it. So she goes with the truth, instead. "I don't like the way they look at me." Of course, by *they* she doesn't just mean the kids at school, but *everybody*. The whole darn, stupid *world*.

Mom takes a deep breath and lets it out slowly, as if she's trying to deflate until she's nothing but empty skin. Then she sighs and swipes her bangs away from her forehead. "Honey, if I had a coin for every time someone looked at me sourly," she mutters, "we'd be as rich as royalty."

Gabby just scoffs. She doesn't want to be rich or famous or talented or any of that—she just wants to be normal. Boringly, forgettably, plain as stale bread *normal*, with two working hands and two functioning eyes and nobody looking at her as if they're trying to figure out just where she went wrong. "Maybe I should just chop my hand off," she grumbles. A stray lock of hair sticks to her goggles and she tries to brush it away, but she uses the wrong hand, and her metal fingers clack uselessly against her lenses. "And gouge my eyes out, while I'm at it."

Mom's face becomes the stiffest Gabby has ever seen, her eyes as sharp as blades. "Don't you ever let me catch you saying something like that again, Gabrielle." When Gabby says nothing back, Mom's expression softens, and she lets out a tired sigh. "Today was supposed to be a good day," she says. Her voice falls in a way that makes Gabby think of leaves tumbling off a tree. "You were supposed to make new friends," she continues, looking blankly at the far wall, "and I was supposed to come home with good news." She waves her hand aimlessly, like she's trying to scoop something meaningful from the air. Then she looks sadly at her empty palm and says, "Instead, *this* is what we got."

Gabby tenses her face and rubs her good hand against her glove's leather straps, trailing her fingertips along the frayed edges. Some strange, older part of her thinks that she should rest that hand against Mom—to massage her shoulder or pat her back, to tell her that it'll all be okay—but isn't that kind of stuff *Mom's* job? Isn't Mom supposed to be the one comforting *her*? "You didn't get the job?" she asks quietly.

Mom shakes her head and looks down at her orange dress. Right now she looks like a fruit—her clothes all bright and dimpled, her hair curled up into a citrusy bloom—and when she unzips Gabby's satchel, pulls out that overripe banana, and begins peeling off those black-speckled strips of skin, Gabby can't help but laugh.

Mom takes a miserable bite out of the thing and takes her time chewing before mumbling, "What's so funny about any of this?"

Gabby doesn't have a good response. Honestly, nothing about today *feels* funny. It feels wrong and ugly and jagged, as if someone came along and opened the book of their lives and angrily tore out a page. "I don't know," she says, eyeing her glove's pressure valve. She waits for it to spurt out another silvery plume, but the nozzle stays still and quiet. When she finally looks back at Mom, Mom's eyes are fixed on her goggles, her candy-blue irises glittering.

"Tell you what," Mom says, forcing a smile. "How about we make each other a promise?"

Gabby tries not to frown, but it comes out anyway. She doesn't like promises—they're too fragile. All they seem to do is break. "Promise what?"

"I promise to do better." Mom raises her hand like she's in school all over again. Then she looks at Gabby and adds, "If you promise to do better, too."

Gabby avoids the obvious question—do better at *what?*—and suggests something simpler, instead. "I promise," she says, lifting her mechanical hand as high as she can, "to try."

Mom blinks up at Gabby's clockwork glove, then flattens her lips in a way that's not quite a frown, but not quite a smile, either. "I suppose that'll have to do." She steps close to Gabby, wraps her fingers around Gabby's geared wrist, and gently pulls her arm back down to her side.

Gabby doesn't resist, even though a part of her wants to flail, to thrash, to remind Mom that she's not just some *doll* to be moved around.

"Now then," Mom says, mussing Gabby's hair, "I'm going to take a nice, hot shower. I'd like to . . . wash this whole day off and start clean." She winks at Gabby's lenses. "When I'm done, we can get some ice cream. Smooth things over. Talk it out, girl-to-girl. How's that sound?"

To be honest, it sounds like a giant broom sweeping Gabby's worries under another rug. As if a lousy fudge sundae will somehow make her forget all about her terrible glove. As if a dusting of sprinkles will somehow make the wisps of her fingers turn whole again. But Mom's face looks delicate and hopeful, like a child's, and Gabby finds herself nodding, just to avoid disappointing her twice in the same day. "Yeah," she mumbles. "Sounds nice."

The lie slips out easily, like breathing.

# 15

That little voice in Kemple's head keeps bouncing around, like an echo that just won't quit.

*... We should keep moving. Don't stop. Don't let Abner catch up. We should...*

The voice is probably right, but the only thing Kemple wants to do right now is stand here with his mouth open and stare. Josephyn, at least, seems eager to do the same, though it's hard for either of them to decide where to look.

Above them, whale-sized dirigibles rumble through the smog, their propellers thrumming the air so forcefully that Kemple can feel the reverberations thundering through his ribs. Around them, driverless carriages rattle over the cobbles, their giant brass wheels maneuvering down the busy streets as if steered by magic alone. Important-looking men march along the sidewalks in satin-lined hats and vested suits that look more expensive than Abner's entire home, and the women appear even more extravagant, their coiffed hair wrapped in shiny silk bonnets, their perfumed bodies clasped in hourglass-shaped skirts that sweep just inches above the pavement. Clothed horses carry their riders as if on display, and street vendors lift up their shiny contraptions, letting their gears glint and their flues gush, and the noise of it all is like a never-ending thrum of blood in Kemple's ears.

Everyone looks like they're shifting or floating, like they're all part of the same monstrous machine, every cog with their own special purpose.

Everyone except him and Josephyn.

He frowns and tugs on his ratty clothes, and Josephyn grimaces and paws at her messy hair, and they both look exactly like what they are: a pair of filthy runaways. Two nobodies who don't belong. "Maybe this was a bad idea," he says, raising his voice over the noise.

Josephyn looks at him quickly, her eyes bright and wide. "What do you mean? This is even *better* than we could've hoped for!" She spreads her arms wide—gesturing at the rain-slicked streets, at the hulking buildings, at the thundering, smoke-filled skies—and she leans forward, like she's eager to hug it all at once. Then she looks at him expectantly, *impatiently*, as if whatever it is she's trying to tell him is the most obvious thing in the universe.

But it *isn't* obvious. Not to him. All he sees are important people and expensive machines and things that don't line up with his world. He doesn't fit in a place like this—this city that feels like a gaping maw with towering concrete teeth. One wrong step, and Iron Bay will chew them up and spit out their bones. "It's like a nightmare," he mutters, hunching his shoulders against the oily wind.

"It's like a *dream*," Josephyn counters. She leans her head back and lets the chemical-drenched air wash over her. "Don't you see? With all this madness rumbling about, how could Abner ever hope to find us?"

Kemple cocks his head and eyes the city again. It still looks the same—daunting, chaotic, frightening—but no matter how closely he peers and how hard he strains, his mind can't seem to conjure up an image of Abner anywhere. "He'd... *hate* this place," he admits. "He'd want nothing to do with any of it."

Josephyn turns to him and lets the dirty air sweep her bangs away from her eyes. "And that," she says, nudging him in the ribs, "is exactly why we're here to stay."

# 16

Gabby stabs limply at the paper bowl in front of her, jabbing a wooden spoon into her melted scoop of ice cream. She uses her good hand to do this, keeping her glove tucked under the table, carefully hidden from view. Having that officer scowl at her hand was already embarrassing enough—she'd rather not deal with any more stares or whispers today.

Still, the glove ticks relentlessly on her lap, like an iron heart wrapped around her fingers, and she tries her best to ignore it.

"Isn't this great?" Mom asks, a little too cheerfully. She finished her own bowl a while ago—chocolate with strawberry swirls, the same combination she always gets. Since then, she's been watching the carriages drive along the road beside them. Or, more accurately, she's been *pretending* to watch the carriages drive by—mostly she's just been sneaking quick, subtle glances in Gabby's direction. As if she thinks Gabby won't notice.

As if the fact that Gabby wears thick, tinted goggles somehow makes her blind to Mom's nosiness.

"Yep. Just us girls," Mom says, "out on the town. Enjoying a little treat." She smooths her blonde locks behind her ears and sneaks another obvious glance at Gabby.

Gabby lifts her spoon, tilts it over, and lets the ice cream glop back down, like a drizzle of creamy snot. Her stomach twists a little, as if it's trying to hide. "You can stop staring at me," she says, jamming the spoon back into the bowl. "It's kind of creepy."

Mom lets out a low sigh. This time when she looks at Gabby, she doesn't bother to hide it. "We should probably talk, Gabs."

Gabby pushes the bowl away and relaxes a bit. Honestly, *talking* sounds a heck of a lot better than what they've been doing for the past ten minutes. "Okay," she says, plopping her gloved hand onto the table. Her iron palm thuds loudly against the wood, and the nozzle beside her thumb lets out a whistling spurt of steam. "Let's talk about *this*."

Mom blinks at the glove with wide eyes, her face a mixture of curiosity and regret. Then she flips a switch in her head—at least, that's how Gabby imagines she does it, like a mechanical being twisting a dial inside her copper-wired brain—and her signature *air-stewardess* poise returns. She sits up so straight that her spine might as well be a metal rod. Her smile spreads until even her eyes are flexing. And her teeth glint so brightly that, even with Gabby's lenses on, she finds herself needing to squint.

"It's a wondrous device, if I do say so myself," Mom says, her voice all honey and practiced charm. "Quality construction. Multi-functional. I'm even thinking of getting one myself."

Gabby just rolls her eyes. She's been watching this same routine of Mom's for as long as she can remember. Empty compliments. Fake enthusiasm. Nothing but glitter and noise. "This thing is a jail cell," she counters. "Not just for my hand, but for my entire stupid *life*." She quivers the wisps of her fingers inside the glove, and the burnished gears and silver levers respond, twisting and clacking those ugly brass-plated fingertips against the tabletop. The leather straps around her wrist strain and creak. "There's nothing wondrous about any of it," she mutters, her voice nearly a whisper.

Mom must flip the switch in her mind again, because she sags in her chair, her toothy smile collapsing into a frown. "So what do you want me to do about it, Gabs?" she asks tiredly. "Wave my magic wand and make everything all okay?" She turns away and watches an orange coach rattle past before saying, "Because if I could do such a thing for you, I'd do it in a heartbeat." She sneaks another sideways glance at Gabby. This time, she doesn't look nosy or fake—she just looks . . . sad. "You know that, right? That I'd do anything for you?"

But Gabby doesn't feel like talking anymore. Lately, everything is just . . . awful. The ice cream is awful. The weather is awful. The noise from the traffic is awful and the kids at school are awful and the officer who took her home was awful and her goggles are awful and, of course, her machine hand is the most awful thing of all, and she reaches forward with her good hand, plucks the spoon from her bowl, and jams a dripping smear of vanilla ice cream into her mouth, just so Mom won't notice the tremble in her lips, or the clenching in her cheeks, or the hot tears spilling out under her lenses.

But Mom is staring at her now with those unblinking *Mom* eyes, eyes that don't seem to miss a thing, and before Gabby even has a chance to hide the hitch in her breathing, Mom climbs out of her seat, swoops around the table, and scoops Gabby into her arms.

Around them, the carriages rattle and the pedestrians clomp and the airships rumble and groan, and there must be a hundred pairs of eyes watching them, a hundred mouths frowning, a hundred voices whispering, *judging* this air stewardess who isn't up in the sky where she belongs, and this goggle-eyed girl with a horrible machine hand, sobbing in her arms. But Gabby doesn't care. She definitely *will*, after the moment has passed—her cheeks will burn and her heart will clench, and *God*, what if kids her age saw her? How pathetic will she have looked?—but right now, Mom is real and here and *with her*, not just smiling *at* her or talking *at* her or telling her what to do.

For the moment, however brief it may be, Gabby isn't alone in this world.

# 17

Kemple is still gawking at the airships overhead when Josephyn says, "We should probably get some better clothes, if we want to fit in."

"Fit in?" Kemple mumbles. The words put a sinking feeling in his chest, like there's a half-chewed piece of fish lodged in his throat, and he finds himself swallowing hard, as if he can somehow gulp the sensation away. His life so far has been a collection of dusty foster homes—each one temporary, every one worse than the last. *Fitting in* has never exactly been the goal. No, it's always been about shrinking down and fading away—making himself as small and unnoticeable as possible. To do what he's told, and to do it well enough to be excused, but not so well that he's remembered. Just enough to be forgotten until the next chore comes around. But what Josephyn is suggesting now, it's . . . well, it's a whole different way of thinking. Of *living*. He drags his eyes away from a blue-sailed dirigible and frowns at her.

She frowns back at him even more.

"How are we supposed to buy clothing, then?" he asks. "We don't even have money."

Josephyn chuckles and shakes her head, as if he's the dumbest boy she's ever met. "Who said anything about money?" She gives him a wink that makes his inside curl in a dark, worrisome way, and he opens his mouth to argue, to complain, to warn her that shop owners in the city probably do a heck of a lot worse to thieves than Abner ever did to *him*. But she lunges ahead before he can utter a word, and he watches her run toward the smoke-strewn streets with her teeth clenched, her dark bangs whipping against her forehead like a pirate's flag.

He hesitates, just long enough to glance back the way they came. His eyes roam over those parched fields full of so much dirt and weeds, fields where the homes have barred windows and locked doors, where foster parents hoard food and swing belts until an aching stomach and an injured back become a way of life—until the only thing a kid can do is peer longingly through a dirty pane of glass at some winding, endless road. He stares until something sour clenches in his gut, then he turns back to see Josephyn duck behind an oversized carriage, vanishing from sight.

"Fit in," he mumbles again. Surely he can pull at least *that* much off.

He sighs, shrugs against the wind, and sprints into the smog and the noise, his bare feet slapping against the gritty cobbles.

# 18

Gabby is lying on her bed, trying *not* to glare at her clockwork hand for the hundredth time today, when Mom marches into the room and slaps a beige envelope onto the blanket beside her. "*Ta-da!*" Mom sings. "I found us a compromise."

Gabby blinks at the envelope for a moment, eyeing the beige thing through the dark tint of her lenses. Then she rolls away. Whatever gave Mom the idea that she wanted to *compromise*? "Unless there's a cure for my hand in there," she says, tugging at a loose blanket thread, "I don't want it."

"Maybe there *is* a cure in there," Mom says, cryptically. "Maybe all your hopes and dreams will be one step closer to coming true, once you see what's under that flap."

If only. "Or maybe my mom is just trying a little too hard," Gabby mutters back.

Mom sighs and sits beside her, making the mattress shift and creak. "Look, I'm making an effort here," she says, smoothing Gabby's hair behind her ear. "Meet me in the middle and try, too? If I remember correctly, you promised to at least do that much for me."

Gabby frowns, rolls back over, and plucks the stupid envelope off the blanket with a sweep of her gear-wrapped hand. "Happy?" she grumbles.

Mom shakes her head and gives her a *you know that's not what I meant* look. "I'll be happy when you *open* it, Miss Gloom."

Gabby tries to hold onto her scowl, but a smile tug at her lips. *Miss Gloom* has a rather nice ring to it. Like the name of a superpowered villainess. *Miss Gloom and Her Vaporous Hand of Doom*. At least in the world of fantasy, the bad guys are allowed to be . . . different. "I open this, and you'll go away?" she says, crinkling the envelope with her brass-plated fingers. "No more pep talks or ice cream trips?"

"You open it, read it, and tell me what you think about it," Mom corrects. She slides her voice over her words, as if Gabby is nothing more than an airship passenger who's asked something dumb—like how to work a seatbelt. "You do all that for me," Mom says, "and *then* I'll leave you alone."

So Gabby does exactly that, grumbling all the while. She tears open the envelope. She unfolds the creased parchment inside. And when the paper is finally unfurled and stretched flat, she gapes at the big block letters printed on it, while Mom smirks quietly beside her. "Is this real?" she whispers, jiggling the flyer.

Mom nods, making the blonde waves of her hair bounce and sway. "As real as your two front teeth."

Something in Gabby's chest expands, like a dirigible preparing to take flight. "*The First Annual Inventors of the Future Convention*," she reads aloud, sliding her goggled eyes over each glossy word. "*Witness the Creations of Tomorrow!*"

Below the words is a hand-inked sketch of a girl in a fluttering dress, her face tilted up at a cloudy sky, her eyes wide and glittering. Clutched in her hands is a device with thick gears, liquid-filled tubes, and what looks like a rippling flag.

Whatever the drawing is supposed to mean, Gabby has no clue. But it fills her veins with a dizzying sort of heat, and she has a hard time pulling her gaze away.

"Sounds marvelous, doesn't it?" Mom says, giving the edge of the flyer a flick with her thumbnail. "I saw this on the way home and thought: now here's something my Gabrielle would love. And what better way to take our minds off everything than a busy convention, full of fancy gadgets and whirring devices?"

Gabby grins. Of course, Mom is wrong about one thing: not even an event like this would take her mind off everything. Certainly not when it comes to her horrendous clockwork glove. But a convention full of *inventors*? A gathering of scientists who build contraptions to change the world?

What better place for a girl with a steamy hand to find someone who can craft her a cure?

Mom tilts her head and studies Gabby, her sky-blue eyes gleaming with pride. "Now there's the smile I've been waiting for," she says, mussing Gabby's hair.

But Gabby is too distracted to respond, her mind a whirlwind of possibilities. She glances down at her mechanical glove and watches the nozzle by her thumb spurt out a dismal puff of mist, as if it knows its time is running out. As if it understands that, soon, it might very well be gone. And this time when she smiles and her eyes well with tears, she doesn't bother to wipe them away. Instead she leaves her goggles on, trapping the moisture on her lashes, holding the feeling in place until her room looks like it's been flooded by a trembling sea. Until the girl on the flyer looks like she's peering up from an ocean floor, her gaze fixed on the cotton-smeared waves.

# 19

Over the next few days, Josephyn steals the city, one tiny piece at a time. Kemple watches it all with his head lowered and his body rigid, as if the buckled end of a belt might come whipping toward them at any moment. But Abner never shows up to drag them back home. And the store owners never seem to notice the dark-haired girl with emerald eyes slinking between the shelves.

Right now they're in a bookstore, of all places. Why, though—Kemple has no clue. But Josephyn weaves through the aisles like a shark, her head bobbing up and down, so she must have *some* sort of a plan. He stumbles after her like an injured dog, pulling at his too-snug pants and shrugging inside his too-narrow shirt. They didn't have much time to find good-fitting clothes the other day. Josephyn threw a coin at the window, and when the shopkeeper turned toward the noise, they both lunged for the first clothes within reach. Now the only outfit he owns feels like it's trying to strangle him. He'd never admit it out loud, but a part of him rather misses the dingy clothes he wore before— the earth-colored shirts and those tattered trousers that Abner always seemed to pluck out of donation bins. They weren't much to look at, but at least they were *comfortable*. "What are we doing here?" he hisses, keeping his voice down. "Shouldn't we be looking for food?"

"We'll do that soon," Josephyn replies, without looking back. "But first, we each need a story."

Kemple wrinkles his face. Josephyn has been acting like this ever since she ran into the city—like she's suddenly an expert on living in Iron Bay. As if she didn't spend her childhood growing up in battered foster homes, just like him. "Why would we need a *story*?" he whispers back. Her answer will probably be something ridiculous—he's known her for only a few days now, but already it's clear that ridiculous answers are her favorite kind. Still, at least she gives him answers. With Abner, his questions were always met with toothy glares and narrow-eyed scowls. Or worse.

"Stories are excuses," Josephyn says, stopping beside a display of thick, dog-eared books. She plucks one off its wooden shelf—a fat, orange thing with the hand-drawn image of a gray whale swimming across its cover—and she takes a moment to skim its pages. She flips through the book in a hurry, as if there's something important hiding between the words, something that might disappear if she takes too long to find it. Then she glances at the last page, frowns, and jams the book sloppily back onto the shelf. "That one's no good," she says, marching ahead. "There weren't any pirates in it." Before he can even ask, she says over her shoulder, "A story without pirates isn't even a story at all."

Kemple frowns at that, but his mind is still snagged on her answer from earlier. He staggers after her, stopping just long enough to straighten the whale-covered book. "What do you mean, *stories are excuses*?" he whispers, following her around a corner. "What do we need excuses for?"

Josephyn huffs, as if she's never heard such a stupid question. "So if anyone catches us doing something we're not supposed to," she says, rolling her eyes at him, "then we just hold up our books and say that we were busy reading, so how could we possibly do anything bad?" She stops and jams a finger against Kemple's chest, wrinkling the fabric of his new, uncomfortable shirt. "That means we have to actually read the books, too," she whispers. "That way, if anyone asks us about them, we don't have to lie or guess. We just tell them what happened. All the best parts. Like who killed who. Who fell in love. Who cried and which ship had the biggest sail, and how the captain lost his compass in a sword fight, so later on, he accidentally steered his whole crew off the edge of the world." She raises an eyebrow and says, "Then whoever is questioning us, they'll just shrug and leave us alone, because our story is our excuse. It's what'll keep us *safe*. Get it?"

Kemple nods, even though he doesn't *really* get it. Why would talking about sword fights and lost ship captains convince *anyone* of their innocence? It sure as heck wouldn't work on Abner. "But what if—"

Josephyn shoves a book into his hands before he can finish the question. "There," she says, giving the dusty cover a smack with her palm. "That one has dragons in it. And knives. And a princess that needs to be saved, or something. You know, boy stuff."

He blinks at the cover, his eyes tracing the shimmering outline of a huge, smoking dragon. The creature looms over a man holding a blade, like it's one breath away from stretching out its neck and snapping the man in half with its jaws. But something about the way the man is standing—his legs wide apart, his chin held high, his knife pointed up and at the ready—makes Kemple's insides twist and bloom. The book looks . . . dangerous. Forbidden, even. Like something not meant to be seen. "I don't know," he says, handing the book back to her. "*You* read it."

But Josephyn just pushes the thing back toward him and turns away. "Too bad," she says, stalking farther down the aisle, her eyes scanning the shelves. "It's yours, Belt Boy. I'm going to get my own."

Then she's gone—her slender body vanishing around another corner—and Kemple finds himself grinding his teeth. "*Belt Boy*?" he mutters. He looks down at the book and stares at the snake-eyed dragon and the knife-wielding man below it, and it takes him a moment to piece it all together, to finally grasp why Josephyn chose *this* book for him, out of all the books here: *he* is the man with the blade. And the smoke-wrapped dragon is Abner. Or maybe . . . maybe he *and* Josephyn are the man, and the dragon is . . . everyone else in the world.

Somewhere in the store, the clerk must be watching them, prowling behind them like a cat on the hunt, so Kemple makes his next move slowly, keeping his back to the front counter, his chest pressed against a shelf. In one smooth motion he lifts the bottom of his shirt, tucks the book against his stomach, and yanks the shirt back down.

Josephyn appears soon after, with her own shirt bulging above her hip. "Got your excuse?" she says, giving him a wink.

For a split second, Kemple's mind fills with flames and wings and slashing teeth—like the last thing a man might see before getting devoured by a monstrous dragon—but then the image shifts in his head until he and Josephyn are standing on the deck of a huge, creaking ship, watching its bow crash into towering, white-foamed waves. Neither of them holds a compass, and they're probably sailing blindly toward the edge of the world, but still, it all feels . . . nice. It feels *right*. So he grins at Josephyn, and she grins back. Then they sprint out of the shop together, carrying their excuses away from the storekeeper's angry shouts, their new clothes rippling in the wind.

Josephyn runs like she's steering a whole fleet into battle, with a lit cannon sizzling beside her. He clambers after her a bit more clumsily, a bit more *urgently*, as if a set of smoke-wrapped jaws really *is* following close behind. As if the only thing he has to fend off a ravenous beast is a blade that fits in the palm of his hand.

# 20

Gabby has been struggling to tape the flyer to her bedroom wall for the past . . . well, it feels like an *hour* now. The problem is the bumpy, ripply plaster—the tape doesn't stick to it well enough. It keeps bunching and creasing and curling away, like it'd rather be doing something else. Gabby sighs, folds the dusty tape over the edge of the parchment, and is in the middle of peeling off a fresh piece with her metal fingers when Mom steps into the room and clears her throat. "So, I've got an offer for you." The doorframe creaks, likely from Mom leaning against it—which means that she's trying to look casual. As if whatever's on her mind is no big deal. Which probably means that it is.

"Sorry," Gabby says, shaking her head and jamming another piece of tape onto the flyer. "I'm chock full of offers already."

Mom chuffs out a laugh. "Very funny. But really, Gabs, if we're going to attend this . . . *thing*, then there's something you'll have to do for me."

Gabby presses the parchment to the wall, then sighs when it slips off again. "It's called a *convention*," she says, trying another spot beside her window. She tilts the flyer to the left, then to the right. When neither position seems to work, she frowns and angles the page to the left again. "It's okay to say it, Mom," she says, pressing an extra strip of tape along the flyer's gritty edge. "It's not a scary thing." All the folds of unusable tape have begun to form a thick border around the flyer, but Gabby doesn't mind. Actually, she rather kind of likes it. It gives the flyer a sort of visual *weight*, like it's a picture inside its own frame. Somehow the tape takes hold, and she steps back to inspect her work. She twists her lenses until the wall looks far away, like a memory from some time long ago.

The flyer looks . . . centered. For the most part. And it seems to be secure. Gabby smiles at it for a moment, eyeing the hand-drawn girl on the bottom of the page. If Gabby tilts her head just right, it almost looks like the girl is staring out the window, waiting for the future to arrive. Gabby turns to look at Mom and says, "Okay. What do you want me to do?"

Mom folds her arms and leans against the doorframe even more, as if whatever she's about to say is so plain and boring that it's not even worth saying out loud.

Gabby braces for the opposite.

"School," Mom finally says.

Instinctively, Gabby's nose scrunches. These days, even *hearing* that word leaves a sourness in her stomach. "What about it?" she mumbles.

"I want you to go," Mom says, looking firmly at Gabby's lenses.

Gabby's breath leaves her without her even trying, like it's eager to escape her body. Like it wants to avoid this whole conversation before it gets any further. In its place, something hot and bitter fills her chest—something that almost feels like *jealousy*. Wouldn't it be nice if she could drift out of a room so easily? To just turn to air and float away, whenever she doesn't feel like hanging around? "Well, I *don't* want to go," Gabby mutters. "So . . . there's that."

Mom is dressed like a man today, her legs lost in a pair of dark, billowy pants. The rest of her is wrapped in a hard-shouldered green jacket, like she's ready to stomp off into battle. Like she knew this argument was going to happen and dressed for the occasion. The only thing she's missing is a thick, shiny helmet. "Gabs . . ."

"And did you already forget our little ice cream trip?" Gabby adds. "Do I need to cry again just so you believe me?"

Mom unfolds her arms and paws at her blonde hair, messing up the loose knot she's tied into it. "I know *exactly* how much the idea of school upsets you," she says, glancing at the flyer. She cocks her head, as if she's only now noticing the hand-drawn girl at the bottom of the page. Then she looks back at Gabby and offers a weak smile. "That's why I'm only asking for one week. Five school days. Attend your classes. Keep your nose in your books. Shrug off the looks and the stares and the whispers, or whatever else it is the other kids might throw your way. Then, after you've done all that, we can go to the convention together."

It's a typical *Mom* move, one that Gabby should've seen coming the moment Mom tossed the flyer onto her bed. Her machine hand clenches until the leather straps squeak from the strain. "And if I say no?"

Mom eyes her glove, then shakes her head slowly. "No school, no convention. That's my offer. Take it or leave it, honey."

Gabby frowns and looks back at the flyer. The girl on the parchment looks worried now, as if she's gaping up at a flurry of gathering storm clouds. A week of suffering, for one day of hope—that's what Mom is offering. Five days of getting teased and mocked, of being harassed and avoided at the same time, just to have the *chance* of finding someone who can turn her steamy hand back to flesh and bone. She sighs. Then she moves the tingling wisps of her fingers inside the gears, sliding and stretching and twisting those smoky tendrils until her iron fingers curl toward her burnished palm, and her brass-plated thumb points to the ceiling.

Mom eyes the gesture cautiously, like she's afraid the glove might explode into a thousand rusty shards if she even so much as *looks* at it wrong. "Is that a *thumbs up?*"

Gabby nods and twists her goggles, narrowing her vision until she's peering at nothing but a dark, dust-speckled gap between two floorboards. The gap looks like the entrance to a bottomless cave, one that plunges all the way down to the fiery center of the earth, and Gabby imagines herself stretching her arms up and reluctantly diving in. "Fine," she mutters. "Five days of hell, then I get my reward."

Mom crosses the distance between them and pulls Gabby into an awkward, stiff-jacketed hug. "No," Mom says, patting her back, "five days of learning that the kids at your school aren't as bad as you think. Then a day of gawking at gadgets with your poor, clueless Mom." Mom winks playfully, but Gabby just looks back at the flyer, her lens-tinted gaze catching on the girl's hand-sketched jaw. There's a tension there that Gabby didn't notice before, a tightness in the girl's angular face, like she knows something that everyone else doesn't. As if there's something else coming their way, something that only she can see—something even *worse* than an ink-lined storm swelling on the horizon.

# 21

Nighttime in Iron Bay is nothing like the dull, cricket-filled quiet that used to surround Abner's house—the weighty silence that always drenched Kemple's room like a spilled cup of watery milk. No, *here* the streets thrum with clattering vehicles, and the skies never seem to stop rumbling, and the voices endlessly murmur and shout, all hours of the night. But even worse than all of that are the *cats*. Tonight, a group of them won't stop yowling, and the heat in Kemple's limbs is starting to blaze. "I hate them," he says, twisting in his limp sleeping bag.

In the murky darkness beside him, Josephyn twists inside her own sleeping bag. The sound of her movement makes Kemple think of autumn—of leaves the color of burnt metal rustling down a rocky hillside. He shakes his head and frowns. They've been living in Iron Bay for almost a week, and already he's forgotten what season it is. In this city, it's always the same. Same temperature. Same bitter, sour air. Same relentless wave of noise. When she doesn't say anything, he reaches across the gritty rooftop until his fingers find the cotton edge of her sleeping bag. Beneath the fabric is a hard lump—her elbow, or maybe a shoulder. He gives it a quick shake. "Josie?"

Josephyn groans in the dark, and the lump moves away from his touch. "I told you not to call me that," she mumbles, her voice slurring. "Nicknames are for pets." She yawns and smacks her lips together. "What time is it?"

"Still night," he says, rolling onto his back. Above them, the sky is a smear of splotchy ink, the stars hidden behind a layer of dirty clouds. A part of him wonders if there's a place in the world where the sky *always* looks this way. "I can't sleep," he says. "The stupid cats won't shut up."

Josephyn says nothing, and he imagines her eyes narrowing against the wind as she listens to the city, her ears taking in every clattering wheel, every thrumming propeller, every shout and screeching mew. The whole concept of sleeping on a roof is still new and awkward to him, but it doesn't seem to bother her at all.

Maybe she's always slept this way—out in the open, beneath the bare sky—even back when she lived in foster homes.

Maybe this is why she was so quick to run to the city: because of all the empty rooftops to choose from.

When she finally speaks up, her voice makes him flinch. "So make them stop," she says flatly, "if they're bothering you so much." Her sleeping bag rustles again, and Kemple can tell, without even touching the lumpy fabric, that she's rolled away from him, ending the conversation. Soon she'll be lightly snoring, her lips pulled into a thin smile, her mind filling with adventures of pirates on the sea.

Kemple crumples his face, pinches his eyes shut, and tries to pull himself toward his own sleep, as if it were a physical thing that he could just plunge into, like a lake full of fish that haven't yet been scissored apart. But down in the alley below, the cats yowl even louder, and before he even realizes what he's doing, he wriggles out of his sleeping bag, crawls to the edge of the roof, and begins climbing the metal ladder down the side of the building.

The rungs feel icy against the soles of his feet, and his knuckles keep scraping against the bricks behind the ladder, but he keeps his mind off the climb by mumbling to himself. "Make them stop," he says. "Scare them off, that's all." It *should* be easy enough. But his heart begins to thud against his ribs, and the closer he gets to the alley's mews and hisses, the more he finds his muscles tensing, his body slowing down. By the time he reaches the end of the ladder, the cats are almost deafening. He steps off the last rung and hangs for a long while, dangling in the dark like a mouse on a string.

He could leave the cats alone, climb back up, and squirm into his sleeping bag with his fingers plugged in his ears. Eventually he'd fall asleep, and Josephyn would never have to know that he'd actually gotten *scared* of a few stupid strays.

But what's there to fear about a bunch of cats, anyway? He's dealt with so much worse. Heck, he's dealt with *Abner* and his horrible belt. A handful of scraggly animals should be nothing to worry about.

. . . and yet . . .

He frowns, shakes his head, and looks up at the sky as if an answer might be there, floating in the cloud-smeared darkness, waiting for him to notice it. Of course, there isn't anything to see but the brown edge of the building and the black, starless void behind it.

No help from the universe, there.

So he makes up his mind on his own: he'll call it quits, climb back to the roof, and hide his fear from Josephyn like it's just another book stuffed under his shirt. Tomorrow, if the cats come back, perhaps he'll give it another try. Maybe he'll be braver then.

He swings his legs and pulls, but his arms are suddenly too weak to do anything more. He imagines himself hanging over a dark, rippling lake, full of huge, gray-skinned monsters with mouths the size of tents, but even the fear of being eaten alive—of being pulled down into the cold, dark depths by some cruel, soulless beast—even *that* doesn't give his arms strength. Before he can think of a worse scenario, his fingers slip free from the rung. He gasps, falls the last few feet to the grimy pavement, and lands in an awkward crouch.

Only then does he allow himself to breathe.

The cats are . . . everywhere. Beside the gutters, around the dumpsters, pressed against the cracks in the walls—their movement is so continuous that the buildings seem to be shivering. The glow from the street has turned the alley a dirty yellow, making every cat look like it's wrapped in a brassy sheen. Any other night, he'd probably find it pretty. Or, at least *interesting*. Tonight, though, every slitted eye just looks menacing, every tiny body coiled like a dangerous spring.

He shouldn't have climbed down the ladder. Heck, he shouldn't have even left his sleeping bag at all.

But he's here now. And the cats, for the moment, have stopped howling, their knife-slit eyes fixed on his.

In the book he's been reading, the hero, Quint, always seems to stumble into situations like this. In the beginning, the guy fought his way out of a tunnel full of man-eating worms. Later, some bad guys shackled him and dumped him into a half-frozen sea. He escaped that, too. In the part that Kemple hasn't finished yet, an evil sorceress splashes pig's blood all over Quint and throws him into a giant spider's web. The spider is the size of an elephant. Kemple doesn't have to guess what'll happen next—Quint will obviously get away in the nick of time.

But Kemple isn't Quint. He doesn't have bulging muscles, an immunity to poison, or an enchanted switchblade that can slice through dragon skin. The only thing he has are four skinny limbs, a scratchy voice, and a heart that feels like it's trying to thump itself right out of his chest.

He tries his voice, first, hissing like an animal. "Get out of here, you stupid cats!"

A few of the strays cock their heads and swivel their ears toward him, but none of them turn to leave.

So he tries again, louder this time. "I said, *get!*"

The closest cat yowls, baring its fangs, and the ones behind it do the same.

Kemple plucks a crumpled can from the damp street and throws it at the largest cat—an orange-striped monster that almost looks like a long-tailed *bear*. The can bounces off the animal's side and clatters against the pavement. The creature lets out an angry hiss, but it doesn't run away. None of them do. The *opposite* happens, actually: they each lower their ears and begin stalking toward him, like a pride of lions closing in on an injured buffalo.

Kemple's head fills with a disturbing image: the headlines that'll be stamped onto the news pamphlets tomorrow, the ink bright-red and dripping. *STRAY CATS EAT BOY ALIVE. BLACK-HAIRED GIRL SAYS SHE HEARD NOTHING—WAS TOO BUSY READING A BOOK.* This brings a question to mind, one that he hasn't worried about before: if animals ever *did* eat him alive, would Josephyn even care?

Would she cry over the boy who saved her from Abner's belt? Or would she shrug and move onto the next big city, eager to find more pantries to rummage through, and more bookstores to plunder?

Honestly, he's not sure either way.

But the cats don't give him more time to wonder—the closest ones lunge at him with their paws outstretched, and Kemple somehow finds the strength to jump up and grab onto the ladder. He yanks and grunts and thrashes until he's gets a leg up over the bottom rung. Then he climbs like he's running up a wall.

The cats don't follow, and for that he breathes a sigh of relief. He wouldn't know what to do if they could clamber up the sides of buildings, too.

By the time he reaches the roof and wriggles back into his sleeping bag, he's panting and his too-tight clothes are damp with sweat.

In the alley below, a few of the cats mew, and a can rattles against the pavement. After that the night stays relatively quiet, with only the low hum of the city warbling in the air. Kemple grins and looks over at the dark lump of Josephyn's sleeping bag. His arm twitches, as if it's eager to reach out and shake her, to pull her out of those pirate-infested seas so he can tell her all about the *real* adventure he just had. But he keeps his hands inside the fabric and forces his eyes shut. Let her conquer a few more ships. Let her find that buried treasure. He'll tell her in the morning, when they're both bleary-eyed and wild-haired and on the hunt for food.

Something stings near his foot, and the pain makes him smile even wider. One of the cats must've scratched him on his way up. He reaches down and probes the wound with his fingers, tracing the burning line from his heel to his ankle.

Now Josephyn will *have* to believe him—he's got undeniable proof.

He rolls his back to the city, curls his body inside the fabric, and breathes in the peppery stench of the roof until it's the only thing he can smell. When his sleep finally comes, it does so slowly and hauntingly, settling over him like a cloud that's fallen from the sky. He lets the feeling move through his skin and sink into his bones, until his mind is nothing but an ink-black drain, crumpling his thoughts and pulling them down into a bottomless void. The last thought to be swept away is a good one—one that pulls his lips into a grin: *Hopefully, the scratch leaves a scar.*

# 22

The school week drags itself along in much the way Gabby expected it would: with taunts and whispers and crumpled wads of paper thrown at the back of her hair. Most of the bullying comes from a boy named Zachariah Wells—a gruff-voiced kid with short red hair, dark blue eyes, and a sour-looking face that Gabby constantly fantasizes about punching with the most jagged edge of her glove, just so she can watch him bleed. But she made a promise to Mom—to *try*, at least; to stick it out, for the convention's sake—so she doesn't shout back at the boys when they call her things like *Toaster Hand*, *Tin Girl*, and *Ugly Automa-Tonia*. She doesn't throw her books at the scowling girls who mutter and scoff whenever she walks by. Most of all, she doesn't shove Zachariah Wells against the wall and hammer his already-scrunched nose, until the bones in his face crunch under the weight of her brass-plated knuckles.

All she does is fix her goggled eyes on the teachers, and take notes with her good hand, and clench the wisps of her bad hand inside the gears, until her metal glove is nothing more than a ball of taut leather and glittering lead.

She survives in this way until Friday, to the last class of the day, to the point where the bell clatters through the halls and the students whoop and clamber out of their chairs, stuffing their books and pencils into their bags in a frenzy. Gabby takes her time, packing her things slowly, just to make sure she's the last one out. Life is easier when she stays *behind* everyone—she's more of a target when they can see her back.

On his way past her desk, Zachariah leans over and whispers in her ear, "Just so you know, we're all hoping you fall into a sewer drain and never come back. You'd probably like it down there, anyway. You'd fit right in."

When she turns to glare at him, the boy actually *spits* in her face. She gasps and nearly falls out of her chair, and before she can do anything else, the jerk runs away, laughing his ugly laugh, until it's only her in the classroom, smearing her sleeve against her goggles. His saliva leaves sticky white streaks on her lenses, and for a brief, fiery instant, her heart twists and her throat clenches and her eyes threaten to flood with stinging-hot tears. But she buries the feeling, smothering it under the weight of a single, jaw-clenching promise: she *will* find a cure for her hand, one way or another. It *will* be flesh and bone, once more.

And when that finally happens, she'll smash that hand into the face of Zachariah Wells, again and again and again, until somebody makes her stop—or until there's nothing left for her to hit.

# 23

Josephyn watches Kemple with her brow furrowed, like he's a wheel missing a spoke. They're perched on the edge of their roof, ankles dangling over the rusted gutter. Beside them, their sleeping bags lie in a wrinkled heap. Josephyn takes a thick bite out of the blueberry muffin they're sharing, then hands it back to him. The muffin has a red crown stamped onto the bottom of it. Two blocks away, that same logo is painted onto the side of a breakfast cart. Kemple tries not to think about it, but he can't help wondering: how long until the woman in the cart finally notices one of her muffins is missing? And when she finally does, will he and Josephyn hear the woman's angry shouts from all the way up here? He squeezes the muffin gently, as if it might have an answer for him.

A blueberry rolls off the pastry and plummets to the alley below.

"There's something different about you today," Josephyn mumbles. Her lips are caked with crumbs, and her fingertips are stained blue, but she doesn't bother to wipe off any of the mess. Instead, she narrows her eyes and looks him up and down.

"I told you," he says, peeling off a chunk and popping it into his mouth, "I fought off a herd of cats." He says this casually, like it's no big deal. Like he's the kind of boy who does this stuff all the time.

Like he's the real-life version of Quint.

"Pride," Josephyn says, shaking her head. "A whole bunch of cats is called a *pride*." She yanks the muffin from his hands and takes another bite. "And I don't believe you fought them off," she says, her voice muffled and thin. "I would've heard something."

Kemple shrugs. It's actually a bit surprising that she *didn't* hear something last night. If his yelling didn't wake her, then the noise of his ladder escape must've surely made her *stir*. "Maybe you did hear something," he says, grabbing at the muffin again. The thing is half eaten now, its edges glistening from her spit. He dabs his shirt against the wettest part, then takes another bite.

Josephyn watches him for a moment longer, then leans forward and peers down at the alley below. It's lifeless now, full of nothing but damp cobbles and ragged bits of trash blown in from the morning commuters. Somewhere in the distant, cloud-filled sky, an airship blasts its horn. "Well, whatever," she finally says, leaning back on her elbows. She licks at her fingers and adds, without looking at him, "If you really did fight off a whole pride, then good for you."

It's hard to tell if she means this or not—the more he gets to know her, the more he's come to learn that her lies sound pretty much the same as her truths. All he can do is guess. Right now, he'd like to think that she's being honest. "Thanks," he says. When she doesn't reach for the muffin again, he jams the rest of it into his mouth and gulps it down quickly. Then he leans back, just like her, and says, "I even got a mark to prove it."

This makes her sit up a little straighter. "Show me."

So he does, slowly, lifting his foot to the light and turning it so she can see the scrape. The line is redder than he expected it to be, and the skin around the wound is puffy and tinted purple. He frowns a little. It looks more like a bruise than a battle scar. He was hoping for something a little more . . . epic.

Josephyn frowns, too, but in a way that makes her look worried. "That doesn't look . . . healthy," she says, prodding at his ankle with her thumb knuckle. His skin lightens when she touches it, then darkens again when she pulls away. She blinks a few times, then asks, "Does it hurt?"

He shakes his head. Actually, he hardly feels it at all. To prove it, he reaches down and flicks his nail against the scrape. He feels the impact of the flick, but that's about it. "It's mostly numb," he says, letting his foot dangle over the gutter again. He smirks at Josephyn, the way he imagines Quint would, and says, "Guess I'm just tough like that."

Josephyn stares at his ankle a bit longer with her face crumpled, like she's figuring something out. Then she shrugs, gets her feet under her, and stands up on the edge of the roof, curling her toes over the ledge. "Well, just keep an eye on it. In my excuse," she says, nodding at the book-shaped lump in her sleeping bag, "there's a pirate who gets stabbed in the leg by a rusty sword. After a while, his leg starts to get real sick." She reaches up to the sky and stretches, arching her back like a cat. "They have a nurse on the ship," she continues, "and she keeps frowning at the pirate every night while she sharpens her saw." Josephyn smooths her dark bangs away from her forehead and looks him square in the eyes. "It's like she knows that she's going to have to cut off his leg, eventually."

Kemple looks down at the puffy, violet scrape on his ankle, and suddenly he doesn't feel like Quint anymore. No—now he just feels like a dumb pirate with a doomed limb. "Wha-what happens next?" he stammers, looking back at Josephyn.

But she isn't there anymore—she's already on the ladder, climbing down to the alley below. "I haven't read past that part yet," she calls out, her voice bouncing off the bricks. "Your guess is as good as mine."

But he doesn't have to guess. He frowns and scuttles after her, clambering down the rungs, stamping against the ladder with every step, but his stupid foot stays numb and cool, like it's waiting for something *more* to wake it up.

Or like it's already said goodbye.

# 24

Today, it feels like Gabby is made out of a thousand glittering wicks, every one of them lit and smoking. *"The First Annual Inventors of the Future Convention,"* she calls out, skimming her lens-tinted eyes over the flyer's bold text, as if she hasn't already read—and *reread*—these same words at least a thousand times by now. *"Witness the Creations of Tomorrow!"* She's standing in front of her window, letting the orange daylight wash over her. Usually she avoids standing so close to the glass—anyone from the street below could glance up and see her goggled face and her metal-wrapped hand—but right now she feels . . . bold. Invincible, even. Like nothing can get in her way, ever again.

When Mom doesn't respond, Gabby yells out, "Did you catch that last part?"

"I did," Mom calls back, her voice wafting from the kitchen. "It'll all be wonderful, dear. I'm sure of it." She sounds cheerful, but distracted, as if there are other, more *important* things on her mind.

Not Gabby, though. Ever since she woke up this morning, every thought in her head has circled around this same blazing point, like a fleet of airships all tethered to a single, glittering dock.

The convention is *today.* Which means that, by this time tomorrow, she'll have already met the inventor who's going to build her a cure.

She grins until her cheeks start to hurt.

"Are you sure you didn't skip any classes?" Mom asks, her voice curled by a smile. The kitchen echoes with the sounds of her packing—dishes clinking, zippers opening, water splashing into a jug. "Maybe we should stop by your school to check," she teases. "You wouldn't mind if we showed up to the convention a little late, would you?"

*"Ha, ha,"* Gabby replies flatly. "Not funny at all."

Mom lets out a chuckle. "I thought it was a *little* funny."

Gabby doesn't respond. She's too busy looking in the mirror now, studying her reflection. It took days to finally pick an outfit that didn't make her groan. Today she wears it proudly, with her chin high and her chest pushed out. Pinstriped beret, leather jacket over an egg-colored shirt, snug pants with a few too many pockets, and the thickest, cream-colored boots she owns. Of all the mismatched items in her closet, this was the best combination she could come up with. In it, her thick goggles and her gear-wrapped hand almost look like they fit. Like they *belong*.

Like she's practically an inventor, herself.

She fusses with the cap a few times, pushing the dark mess of her hair down over the top of her goggles. Then she gives her reflection a sophisticated nod. "Lenton," she mumbles. "Gabby Lenton."

For the first time in a long while, she doesn't hate the way she looks.

Mom's heels clack against the kitchen floor, and she calls out playfully, "Do I have time to take a shower? How about a nap? Maybe we should just call it off and attend next year, what do you think?"

But Gabby is past the point of being bothered. Not even Mom's terrible sense of humor can fluster her today. "Let's go, let's go," she says, stomping down the hall. Her boots thunder against the wooden floor. Her clockwork hand ticks and whirs. "If you make one more joke about calling this off, I'm just going to leave without you."

Mom looks up from behind the kitchen counter and flashes a toothy smile. Her hair is pulled back into a loose bun, her blonde locks flaring behind her head like a starburst. "I'd like to see that," she says, looping a large fabric bag over her shoulder. Her green dress wrinkles under the weight of the satchel. "My one and only daughter, navigating the city all by herself." A hint of her fake stewardess poise shows through—that familiar tension in the lines around her mouth, the smooth glassiness of her eyes—but for the most part, she seems just as excited as Gabby.

"I wouldn't get lost," Gabby says proudly. "I'd just follow anyone who's dressed like me." She twirls around like a fashion model, just so Mom can get a better look at her outfit.

"Well," Mom says with a nod, "you certainly look like you belong."

Gabby starts to laugh, but something prickles in her chest—a sharp, sudden ache in the space around her heart, and her smile collapses into a frown. For a brief, fleeting instant, she actually *misses* Mom, as if this is nothing more than a memory—a moment that she'll look back on some day with tear-filled eyes.

It's almost like . . . like she's already lost Mom without even realizing it.

She grimaces and shakes her head until the ugly feeling fades away. It leaves her body slowly, like sludge draining out of her veins. By the time it's gone, she's already forgotten what made her sad in the first place. "I think I look like an inventor," she says, picking up the conversation where they left off.

But Mom's smile looks awkward now, like someone glued it onto her face, and her eyes are distant, unfocused. "You'd make an outstanding inventor," she mumbles.

Gabby tugs on the lapels of her jacket and wiggles her toes inside her boots. "I *would* make a great inventor." She says this loudly, as if her voice alone can somehow break the spell that's got Mom so distracted.

It almost seems to work. Mom blinks and looks at her with wide, sparkling eyes, and Gabby waits for a glimpse of the Mom she *used to* have, before life became so complicated—the Mom who got excited about everything, no matter how silly; the Mom whose smile was never fake at all. But just when that version of Mom is about to surface, someone knocks hard on the front door, and Mom's face clouds all over again, the glint in her eyes turning soft and dull. "Now who could that be?" she mutters.

"You know we can't have visitors today," Gabby says sourly, as if this is somehow Mom's fault. "Today is—"

"I'm completely aware of what today means to you, Gabs," Mom says. She tilts her head toward the hall. "Why don't you go wash up, and I'll kindly tell whoever it is to *get lost*." She winks, then sticks her nose up in the air, like she's trying to look tough, and Gabby can't help snickering.

Sometimes, Mom is alright.

"Then we're off to the convention?" Gabby asks.

"Then we're off," Mom says with a nod.

Gabby smiles, jogs to the bathroom, and shuts the door before the universe can throw any more interruptions her way. Mom's melodic voice warbles through the wood, followed by a man's gruff accent, and Gabby cranks the rusted handle on the wall until the grimy bulb on the ceiling flickers and glows, bathing the tiny room in a dim yellow haze. She shakes her head at her reflection, making her messy bangs bounce against her goggles, and she twists her beret this way and that, until she finds the most *inventor-like* tilt of the cap: angled down, forward, and to the left.

The man's voice gets louder. Mom's voice rises, too, and Gabby almost feels sorry for the stranger—out of everyone she knows, Mom is by far the best at telling people off. Eventually the door slams and the apartment fills with a thick sort of silence—a calm, victorious sound that makes Gabby's smile stretch even wider. Then Mom's muffled voice trembles through the wood.

". . . Gabby?"

"Almost done," Gabby sings back.

The silence returns, and Gabby fills the quiet with her own sounds: water trickling in the sink, a chalky bar of soap squeaking against her leather straps, the bristles of her wire brush scrubbing gently against her brass-plated knuckles. She *loathes* her machine hand, but it's still a visible part of her. And though she doesn't know much about inventors, it's probably safe to guess that they won't want to help her if her clockwork glove looks *filthy*. So she lathers the glove's straps, rinses them off, then oils them until they shine. She treats the rest of her glove just as carefully, running a damp wire brush along every cog and lever. Afterward, she gives everything a quick wipe with a tight-knitted cloth, then rubs the tiniest dab of grease along the joints—just enough to keep the metal slick and smooth.

When she's all done, the pressure valve lets out a thick burst of steam, as if the glove itself approves. Gabby wiggles her ghostly hand inside the gears, and the glove responds with quick, clattering movements, every piece of it glimmering in the dull light. If she squints just right, it almost looks like her hand is wrapped in *gold*.

She swings open the bathroom door with a dramatic sweep of her arm, but Mom isn't there to see it. A pair of heeled shoes lie scattered on the kitchen floor, and the pantry door is slightly open. Glass jars clink inside the storage space, and the floor echoes with the sound of Mom's stockinged feet as she stumbles around.

Gabby frowns, slumps onto one of their rickety kitchen stools, and drums her brass-plated fingertips against the tabletop until the clockwork in her glove goes through another revolution, the valve above her thumb sputtering out a puff of steam. Her frown hardens. At this rate, they'll *never* get to the convention in time. "Mom," she whines. "Come *on*."

Mom mumbles something soft and quiet, something that almost sounds like a whisper, and Gabby's insides start to boil. Mom had *all week* to pack for today! What the heck could she need from the pantry that's so darn important? Cans of beets? Stale bread? A dumb box of baking soda? "Mom!" she yells.

When Mom *still* doesn't respond, Gabby leaps off the stool, stomps to the pantry door, and flings the stupid thing open so hard that it nearly yanks right off its hinges. "What on earth are you—"

The question crumbles apart on her lips before she can finish asking it. Inside the pantry, two pairs of eyes stare back at her: her mother's—wide and veiny—and the fiery eyes of . . . something else. Something *not* human.

The creature has its furred mouth clamped around Mom's throat, and her blood is . . . everywhere. Mom lets out a wet, sputtering gasp, and Gabby takes a half step backward, as if she can somehow step back in time, back to where everything was fine, where Mom wasn't hurt and bleeding, where strangers knocking on doors were nothing but inconveniences and monsters just plain *didn't exist*.

But it doesn't work. The creature is still there, looming like a brown-furred lion in the dark, its oversized jaws biting into Mom, its slitted yellow eyes fixed unflinchingly on Gabby's lenses.

Gabby looks wildly at Mom—at the one person in the world who's supposed to make all of this right again—but Mom's eyes are closed now, her face slackened, her body lying limp in the monster's grip, as if she's simply fallen asleep.

No—as if . . . as if she . . .

A word shoves its way to the front of Gabby's mind—an awful word, the *worst* word—but she holds it down, pushes it back, squeezes it tight with everything she has, just so it won't escape. Just so it can't become real.

The creature shifts its weight, jostling Mom in a terrible way, and the word in Gabby's head finally bursts, the pieces of it scattering inside her heart and tearing through her veins like a million shards of rust. Like a planet-sized mound of sludge that can never be washed off.

Mom is . . . she's . . .

All those word crumbs sound at once, echoing under her skin, pounding in her head like a brass-knuckled fist. *Dead dead DEAD!*

And Gabby starts to scream.

# 25

The chill moves through Kemple's veins like a worm, slithering from one body part to the next. In the morning it's in his leg, lingering just above his scratched ankle. At lunch, it moves to his side, wrapping around his hip. By the time the sun slips down the cloudy wall of the sky, the coolness has oozed into his chest and settled around his sternum like a spidery chunk of ice, its tendrils grazing his throat. He curls in his sleeping bag and hugs the dingy cotton to his neck, as if the thin fabric can somehow warm him from the inside out.

It doesn't.

"M-maybe you could light a f-fire?" he stammers.

Josephyn shakes her head. "We're criminals. If we put flames on this roof, every officer in the city will look and up and think, 'That's where the bad guys must be.' And then, you know what they'll do to us?"

Kemple shivers and shakes his head.

"They'll separate us and lock us away in different parts of the world, so we can never find each other again." She nods at the open book on her lap and says, "That's what the general did to the twins, two chapters ago. Is that what you want to happen to us?"

Kemple wants to shout that he and Josephyn *aren't twins*, and that *there is no general*, and that maybe, sometimes, a book is *just a stupid book*—but to say all this would take too much breath and way too much effort, so he merely groans and rolls away until the side of his face presses against the gritty rooftop. Then he squeezes his eyes shut. He imagines sizzling wicks and blazing trees, volcanoes spewing frothing hot lava. But the cold spot inside him only stretches and grows.

"What you should've done," Josephyn says, turning a page in her book, "is stay away from the cats. So what if they were noisy? You got yourself scraped and now you're so sick that you can't do anything but lie down." She takes a deep breath, like she's about to give him a speech. "In my excuse, a few pages ago, a guy jumped off a bridge because he wanted to impress the maid's sister. He landed wrong and twisted his knee, and now he needs a cane to walk. Everyone can hear him clomping around before he's even entered a room. Sure, the maid's sister still smiles at him and laughs at his awkward jokes, but her insides don't twist into knots for him—not as much as they used to. In her head, she used to call him *dreamy*. Now she calls him *foolhardy*." Josephyn grows quiet and stays that way for a long while. Then she says softly, "That's what you are, Kemple. Foolhardy."

Kemple sighs and wraps himself tighter in his sleeping bag. Josephyn's excuse sounds incredibly boring to read. Twisted knees? Cane-clomping? Maids whose insides twist into knots? It's the kind of story that would definitely have him snoring by the end of the first page. Luckily, he got the book with a dragon on the cover. *Quint* never worries about stupid stuff like being *foolhardy*. If he ever jumped off a bridge and twisted his ankle, he'd just grit his teeth, march through the pain, and slash his magical blade at any hungry monsters that leapt his way. "T-tell me about something r-real, then," he mutters.

Josephyn claps her book shut, then moves around on her sleeping bag. "What do you mean, *real*?"

Kemple grits his teeth and wills his heart to pump harder, to bathe his insides with hot, steaming blood. But the icy knot just grows even more. Now it's a hand wrapping around his neck, its cold fingers gripping his throat. "S-stuff that's actually h-happened," he says. "Dis-distract me."

Josephyn doesn't say anything for a long time, and Kemple's body sags. Falling asleep for her should be no problem. She doesn't have a numb scratch on her ankle to worry about, or a cold spot growing in her chest. She doesn't have to be afraid of those cats coming back for her in the night, or wonder what part of her body the chill will move to next. All she has to do is nestle in her sleeping bag, close her eyes, and think about dumb maids whose insides clench, and foolhardy men who limp around with noisy canes, until her boredom is so thick and heavy that it just pulls her down into a bottomless sleep where—

"Grand," she finally says, and her voice is so small and distant that it almost sounds like it's coming from somewhere else. "That's my real name. Grand Aliston. Can you believe it?"

Kemple sits up slowly, keeping the sleeping bag still tucked around him, and turns to look at her in the darkness. "Your first n-name is *Grand*?"

A thick cloud sweeps above them, blotting out the stars, and Josephyn turns from a sad-looking girl to a featureless silhouette, the shape of her outlined against the gray-violet sky. Kemple watches her silhouette as she shakes her head. "That's what I was born with. And it's what the people called me at all those different places, until I was old enough to realize that if my parents never bothered to stick around for *me*, then why should *I* bother to keep their stupid name?"

By the time she's done speaking, her voice is so high and wobbly that Kemple finds himself bracing for the sound of her crying—that first, bitter sob that always seems to come, no matter how hard you try to stop it. But Josephyn stays quiet, and for a while they just listen to the vehicles churning on the streets below, until finally the cold spot in his neck reaches up and grazes his jaw. "S-so," he says, just to keep his mind off the chill, "what made you ch-choose *Josephyn*?"

"I don't know," she says quickly. Then, more slowly, she adds, "I guess I . . . just liked the sound of it. Like I wanted to grow into it."

Kemple watches her silhouette lean back until it vanishes into the darkness of the roof. Then he listens to her move around in her sleeping bag. Soon she'll be snoring gently, and he'll still be awake, replaying their conversation in his head until the drone of the city finally lulls him into his own restless sleep. And when he wakes in the morning, that cold ache will have moved somewhere frighteningly new. Maybe into his *brain* or his *eyes* or—

"This is the part," Josephyn blurts out, "where you're supposed to tell me that I made a good choice."

Kemple eyes the dark space where her sleeping bag should be. "W-what?"

"My name. Your job is to make me feel better about it. That's how it works." Her sleeping bag rustles, and he imagines her rolling onto her side, propping her head up on her hand, and studying him with the same narrow-eyed gaze that she always seems to use on him these days. "If I share something personal," she continues, "you're supposed to make me feel good about it. Otherwise, what's the point?"

This sounds like the kind of logic that she found in a book—like something the maid's sister would say to the limping man. But Kemple is starting to get tired in a thick, garbled way, and the ice block in his jaw is finally starting to thaw—so he doesn't bother to argue. "I think you m-made the perfect choice," he says. He relaxes a little in his sleeping bag, loosening the fabric around his neck, letting in some of the cool night air. "When I think of you," he adds, closing his eyes, "it's hard not to think of you as *Josephyn*."

Josephyn stays quiet for a long while before finally whispering, "Thanks." Her voice quivers a little as she says, "What about your name?"

But Kemple is suddenly too tired to answer. The sounds of the night all muddle together until the hum is like a lead weight pushing down on his brain. He tries to mumble something about the ice in his face, something to make her understand, but the roof is like a giant mouth opening beneath him, and the next thing he knows, the mouth is swallowing him whole, pulling him down into a sleep so dark and dreamless, he might as well be dead.

# 26

The officers that show up to examine Mom's body are nothing like the one who found Gabby crying at the docks. At least with him, she saw a *hint* of humanity. An *almost*-touch of concern. But the officers streaming into the apartment now are practically machines—their faces stiff and expressionless, their eyes narrow and unblinking. They move around her with their notepads open and their instruments dangling from their hips, as if she isn't there. As if the fact that she's sobbing on the floor with her goggles pressed against her knees doesn't even matter at all.

And maybe, in the grand scheme of things, it doesn't. Maybe this is their way of telling her that no amount of tears will bring Mom back. Maybe the world really *is* this cruel and—

"Gabrielle?" says a gruff voice.

Gabby flinches at the sound of her name, not because it startles her, but because it's coming from a *stranger*—a stranger who's only here because Mom *isn't* here, because Mom is . . . she's . . . Gabby's heart wrenches so hard that it feels like it might shatter, and she hugs her legs tighter to her chest, burying her face deeper into the gap between her knees, as if she can somehow fold herself into a ball of lead and roll away forever.

Still, the voice persists. Gently. Stubbornly. "Gabrielle, can I chat with you for a bit?"

The voice has a noticeable accent. Something southern and heavy, as if the man's words are made of hot wax, making them bend and droop at the edges. Any other day, Gabby might've found it comforting. Today, it just makes her want to thrust out her clockwork hand, pinch the man's lips between her brass-plated fingers, and rip his mouth right off his face. "Go away," she whines into the fabric of her pants. "Just . . . all of it go away."

"Would make it so, if I could," the voice responds. The kitchen echoes with a blur of noises—shoes thumping against the tiles, quills scratching against parchment, a heavy cloth bag sliding across the floor—but the man's words seem to move in front of it all, as if he's trying to use his voice to shield her from everything. As if he knows just how closely she's listening. "Lost my own mama when I was around your age," the stranger says. He clears his throat and moves closer to her, and she catches a whiff of his peppery scent: like old liquor and wood smoke and flowery chemicals. "Thought the world had ended," he continues. "Thought to myself: what's the point of even going on? But then, you know what happened?"

Gabby shakes her head against her knees, not to answer his question, but because she doesn't *want* to know what happened. The only thing she wants is for Mom to be alright, for her eyes to blink and her mouth to twitch and all that sticky blood to suck back into her body, to inflate her veins and warm her skin and, oh, what Gabby would give just to see Mom's fake smile again, or to watch her climb into one of those fancy dresses that always fit so perfectly, like they'd been made just for her, or even to hear more of her stupid advice about boys or—

"It started to hurt less," the man says quietly. He's moved closer now—so close that it almost sounds like he's talking inside her head. "Little by little the pain began to numb, and my tears dried up. And every day that passed, I got that much stronger."

The man sounds so much like Mom right now that Gabby lets out a groan. "I don't want a lousy pep talk," she mumbles.

The stranger clears his throat. "Fair enough. What *do* you want, then?"

Here, Gabby finally looks up at the man. Her hair is stuck to her lenses, and her eyes are wobbly with tears, so it's hard to make out anything more than just the barest of details. The man looks old—around Mom's age, maybe even older—and he's wearing a beige hat. His face is tanned and scruffy, and his white shirt is wrinkled, and his yellow tie has sea animals on it—whales or dolphins, she's not sure which.

In all the ways that Mom seemed put together, this man appears to be crumbling apart. How on earth could he possibly help her? He looks like he can't even help himself. She jams her face back into the gap between her knees and mumbles, "Nothing. I don't want anything. Now can you *go*?"

Instead of leaving, the man grunts and sits down beside her. He lets out a sigh, as if it's a huge relief to finally rest on the floor. "I can go," he says, "but these other guys, they'll want to stay and ask you questions. They'll want to look at your clothes, and your hair, and even your skin, and by the time they're done, you'll be so far beyond miserable that you'll wish old Shaw had stuck around, just to save you from it all."

When she lifts her face to look at him again, he's got his hand out, ready to shake. "That's me," he says with a lopsided smirk, "in case you didn't catch the hint." With his other hand, he tugs on the brim of his hat. "Detective Shaw, at your service."

Gabby scowls at the man's outstretched hand. "Am I supposed to like you now?" she says bitterly. "The girl who just . . ." Her voice tightens, and her next few words come out in a whisper. ". . . who just *lost her Mom.*" She waits while a stream of fresh tears floods the inside of her lenses. Then she tilts her goggles open and lets the warm droplets run down her face. They land on her pants, on the floor, on her glove. Everywhere. "You think I want to make *friends* with some stupid detective?"

Shaw removes his hat and presses it gently over his knee, covering up a worn patch on his trousers. "I do think that, actually," he says. "I think if anyone in the world needs a friend right now, Gabrielle, it's you."

She glances at him again, and he smiles easily, like someone who's never needed to fake a smile in his life. Like someone who's never even *considered* it. And though some raw, wild part of her wants to lash out at him—to batter him the same way that monster ravaged Mom—another, more delicate part of her wants nothing more than to see him smile again, to be reassured that there's still a *reason* to smile. To be reminded that there's still some good in this world. She sniffs, drags her sleeve against her wet nose, and mutters the first thing that comes to mind: "Why do you even care?"

Shaw jams his lips together and scrunches his face, as if she's just asked him the most difficult question there is. "Why, indeed," he mumbles. He scratches at his gray-brown hair for a moment, then leans close to her and whispers, "Because you, Gabrielle, are the only person who can help me. And because I'm the only person who's willing to help you." He leans back, jams his hat onto his head, and stands slowly, wincing just a little. Then he reaches out a hand for her to grab. "And," he says firmly, "I'm the one who's offering you a chance to get even. You help me find the thing that hurt your Mom, and I promise you this: I'll do whatever I can to kill it."

Gabby blinks dumbly at the detective, at this man who isn't offering comfort or safety, at this *stranger* who's only offering *revenge.* She peers at the officers around them, who're busy rummaging through the apartment, sweeping and prodding at the dust in the corners, shifting and poking at the objects in the drawers. She looks at the pantry doorway and the blood-splattered shelves inside, until the ache in her heart digs so far down that it might as well be in her bones. Then she glances at Shaw's outstretched hand—at his grubby fingers with their too-short nails, at his skin that looks so dusty and beat-up that no amount of soap could ever wash it clean—and before she even realizes what she's doing, she reaches up with her clockwork hand, wraps her geared fingers around his wrist, and pulls herself up onto her boots.

Shaw eyes her metal hand for a moment, then gives her an approving nod, and she stands there awkwardly, blinking hard behind her fogged lenses and tugging at the seams of her outfit. Her clothes feel so ridiculous now that she can hardly bear to look at them. "What now?" she mutters.

Shaw frees his hand from her grip and gently pats her shoulder. "Now," he says, nodding at the front door, "we get out of here, and you tell me everything you know."

Gabby frowns at the open hallway, at that dim plaster tunnel that she's walked through with Mom so many times before. Something sharp and jagged scrapes at the space behind her ribs, and she quickly looks away from the hall to rest her teary gaze on her boots. "Then what?"

"Then," Shaw says, his voice squeezing to a whisper, "I'll teach you how to catch a beast."

# 27

By the time the chill reaches Kemple's head, it's become a blazing fever. The heat scorches every part of him, from his face all the way down to his toes, until even his nails and hair feel burnt. He tries to distract himself by skimming the next chapter in his book, but his fingers are so numb that he can barely feel the pages, and his mind has trouble holding onto the words. He groans, slaps the book shut, and tosses it to the edge of the roof.

Josephyn straightens beside him and sets her own novel onto the edge of her sleeping bag. "Hey," she says, scrambling toward the gutter, "don't be throwing this away." She scoops his book off the roof and sweeps her hand against the cover, brushing gravel and dirt off the dragon's wings. "I told you, we *need* our excuses."

Kemple just scoffs. They've been living in this city so long that the days and nights have begun to blur together, and not *once* have they needed their excuses. When she tries to hand the thing back to him, he shakes his head and rolls away. "I feel like I've been sick inside this sleeping bag for years," he says, dragging his wrist across his damp forehead. Even his sweat feels like it's boiling.

"It hasn't been that long," Josephyn replies. She crouches down, sets his book next to hers, then pokes her thumb against his swollen ankle. Her touch leaves a pale mark in the center of his bruise, and they both watch as it slowly fades away. "You've been drifting in and out of sleep, for the most part," she says. "I thought about cutting your leg off, just like the nurse did when . . ." She trails off with a frown and nods at her book. "Well, you probably don't want to hear the rest of it."

She's right. The last thing he wants to hear right now is some dumb story about a lovestruck maid's sister. What he wants—what he *really* wants—is someone to look at his ankle and tell him that it'll be alright. Someone who's seen this kind of injury before. Someone with medical training. Someone like—

"A doctor," Josephyn says, squinting hard at his face. "That's what you're thinking about right now, isn't it? That you want a doctor?"

Kemple gapes at her for a moment, then slowly nods. His neck muscles feel like they're ready to burst into flames. "I'm not doing so good," he says. "And I'm pretty sure it's getting worse."

Josephyn nods sadly, like she's been waiting for this exact conversation. No—as if she's been *fearing* it. She looks at him for a moment, her green eyes roaming all over his flushed face. Then she leans over the gutter and peers down at the streets below. "You hear that?" she says, closing her eyes.

Kemple scrunches his face and listens, but there isn't anything to hear except the monotonous roar of the city—the same clanking warble that he's learned to ignore. "I don't hear anything different," he grumbles.

Josephyn keeps her eyes closed and smiles. "That's right," she says, opening her eyes. Her gaze flicks toward his, and her irises suddenly look sharp—like a pair of razor-edged discs. "Nothing's different. We're still here, and they're still there, and everything is how it should be."

He looks away before her stare can cut him. "Everything's *not* how it should be," he mutters. "If it was, I wouldn't have a numb, discolored leg." He kicks his bad heel against the roof, and the impact sends a shiver of tingles up his shin. "And," he says, tugging the sleeping bag back over his leg, "I wouldn't be burning up right now."

Josephyn rolls her eyes. "What I mean is, everything is how it should be with *you and me*." When he just blinks at her, she sighs, turns her back to him, and stands up on the gutter. The metal groans under her weight, but she just spreads her arms wide, like she's a bird preparing to take flight. "And if you hunt down a doctor," she says, tiptoeing along the gutter, "you'll just screw everything up." Halfway to the corner of the roof, she stops, kicks her leg out, and twirls on her grime-stained toes. For a brief, teetering moment, she looks graceful—*beautiful* even, with the clouds stretching endlessly behind her—like a ballerina spinning on a gray-curtained stage. But then she wobbles, stumbles back onto the roof, and hisses as a jagged piece of the gutter snags on her heel—and just like that, the illusion is gone. "See that?" she says, pointing at her foot.

Kemple squints at the dark droplet of blood oozing from her heel. "Yeah?"

"That's proof, right there," she says, kicking the blood away. "You've already upset the balance. Now everything's falling apart."

Kemple shakes his head so hard that his sweat-drenched bangs slap against his forehead. "You mean like how I was doing fine at Abner's until *you* came along?"

Josephyn gasps so loud that it's almost funny. "So now you're going to attack *me*, is that it? Blame me for your injury?" Her face twists until he barely recognizes her. "Act like it's *my* fault that you got scratched?"

"I'm not blaming you for that," he says, looking away. He stares at the foot-shaped lump under his sleeping bag, until the heat in his ears makes him dizzy. "I just . . . want to see a doctor. To make sure I'll be okay."

"And what about us, then?" Josephyn says. "In case you forgot, we're not supposed to be in Iron Bay." When he doesn't answer, she lowers her voice, her tone suddenly hard and serious. "The moment a doctor looks at you, our whole ruse is up. They'll figure out who we are. They'll realize we don't belong."

She's right, of course. If he's learned anything about Josephyn in the time he's known her, it's that when it comes to these kinds of things—surviving, escaping, *belonging*—she's never wrong. But he's also clearly *ill*, and with the way this fever has gripped him, it'd be darn near *suicide* to ignore it. "So what do you suggest I do?" he mutters, shoving the words through his clenched teeth. "Wait it out? Hope it'll fix itself?" He drags his arm across his flushed face and shakes the sticky sweat off. "Because that's obviously not working."

Josephyn lifts her eyebrows and jabs a finger toward her book. "There's a part where the nurse has to get medicines, before the amputation. And they're all named in there. I memorized them, in case we'd need them. Laudanum and chloroform and morphine and . . . well, what I mean is: I could do it. I could fix you."

But Kemple has heard enough. The anger rises so quickly in him that it almost feels like he's going to throw up. Instead of puke, though, it's *words* that fly out of him, every one of them scalding hot. "It's just a story, Josephyn!" he shouts. He flings the sleeping bag off his leg and kicks at the dirty air. "A stupid, good-for-nothing *story*! Somebody made it all up, and you're sitting here, acting like it's *real*!"

Josephyn covers her lips with her hands and staggers backward, as if he just slapped her in the mouth. When she finally speaks, her voice is thin and muffled by her fingers. "What're you saying?"

The heat pools in Kemple's eyes, making everything look like it's glowing red. The rooftops. The rocky clouds. Josephyn and her messy hair and her dagger-like gaze. "I'm saying it's all fake," he snarls. "All *useless*." He's standing now, his body swaying in the sticky breeze. His too-snug clothes blaze against his skin. "And I never thought that you, of all people, would be dumb enough to believe any of it."

Josephyn shakes her head slowly and keeps her fingers clamped over her lips. "You don't even get it," she says. "Of course it's all pretend. Of course I *know* that." She drops her arms to her side and stares at him until her eyes start to glisten, tears swelling under her lashes. "What *you* don't understand is that everyone has a *thing*. An inside joke. A place. A moment." She points at the two books on her sleeping bag and glares at him so hard that her eyes almost look like they're going to fly out of her head. "This was *our* thing, Kemple," she mumbles. "And you just . . . you *killed* it."

The redness in his vision softens until everything on the roof turns pink, then orange. The heat in his head drains into his neck, too, leaving his skull cold and numb. He tries to wrap his thoughts around what Josephyn just said, but his mind feels foggy and distant. Dreamlike. His gaze flicks toward the books on her sleeping bag, and his features sag on their own: his eyes drooping, his mouth collapsing into a frown. Was this actually their *thing*? How could he not have known?

Did he really just screw everything up?

"Maybe," he says, taking a wobbly step toward her, "maybe we can—"

But Josephyn takes a step backward, keeping the distance between them. "You know what?" she says, looking out at the other rooftops, "maybe you *should* see a doctor after all." She glances at his swollen ankle and says, "Maybe then you'll see what a mistake you've made. Maybe then you'll realize that you should've stayed here all along."

Kemple frowns at the violet-tinged bruise creeping up his shin. Right now, the wound doesn't even look real. It looks like something strange and fake that's been plastered onto his skin—like oil and mud and thick, curdled paint. Like something that'll wash right off. Like something *make-believe*. "And if I do go?" he says, looking back at her face.

She meets his gaze and says flatly, "Then . . . I guess that'll be the end of us." She trudges over to her sleeping bag, slides the books off, then slowly rolls the fabric into a dirty ball. "And I'm not going to stick around and wait for some badges to scoop me up. Not even for you." She tucks the wad under her arm, marches to the fire escape ladder, and begins climbing down the rungs. When only her head is visible, she stops and looks up at him. The wind picks up, whipping her bangs against her forehead. The skin under her eyes is red and glistening.

And here, Kemple feels it: the gravity. The weight. The heaviness of this moment, where the next thing he says and does could change everything, forever. But the fever has come back, too, and the heat of it is suddenly flooding his veins, squeezing his lungs, searing his skin from the inside out. The more he tries to ignore it, the hotter everything gets, until it feels like he might explode. Josephyn stares at him patiently, as if she's waiting for him to find the right words, the perfect combination of sounds to make everything between them better again. But the only thing he can think to say is: "What if you're wrong? What if I find help, and everything turns out okay?"

Her face droops and she looks away, and Kemple doesn't even have to guess: she was clearly expecting something more from him. When she finally meets his eyes again, her expression is so flat and bare that it almost looks like she's wearing a mask. "I hope I am," she mutters. "Then I hope you find me to say *I told you so.*" She smiles so wide that it almost looks genuine. Then she whispers, "Don't lose your excuse, Belt Boy."

Before Kemple can say anything back, the girl formerly known as *Grand Aliston* dips out of sight without even so much as a goodbye. By the time he staggers to the gutter and squints down the rusted ladder, she's already gone, leaving nothing behind but a long, lonely stretch of weather-worn buildings and burnt-coal streets.

He tries to yell out her name, but the heat puddling in his brain is so thick and heavy that all he can do is slump forward. The world around him turns soft and creamy, like a cup of spoiled milk, and when he finally begins to move down the ladder, he can't tell if he's actually climbing, or if he's simply *falling* to the alley below.

# 28

Gabby walks from her apartment to the street below as if she's made of steam: every inch of her numb and disconnected. From Detective Shaw's perspective, she must be stumbling, because he keeps reaching out to grab her hand.

She keeps shoving him away.

"I can walk just fine," she mutters, without looking up at the man's unfamiliar face. "I'm nine years old."

The detective drops his arm with a shrug and says, "It's not your age I'm worried about." He strides ahead, leading her across the empty road, as if he's already taken the role of her new parent. As if replacing Mom could ever be so simple.

She makes sure to keep a large distance between them.

A few carriages rumble at the end of the block, and somewhere in the clouds above them, an airship blasts its horn. Shaw stops on the sidewalk and waits for the noise to fade before turning to her. "You've been through quite an ordeal," he says. "It's normal to lose control of a lot of things—your emotions, your body. Your spirit."

Gabby steps onto the curb beside him, crosses her arms over her chest, and scoffs so hard that she actually spits into the wind. "My *spirit*? Don't tell me you believe in ghosts." She says this with a grimace, as if the words taste sour coming out of her mouth.

Shaw frowns at her and says, "Don't tell me you *don't*. It'd be pretty sad if this life is the only one we get, don't you think?"

Gabby scowls at the sidewalk and twists her lenses until everything looks small and distant, like she's peering at the earth from an impossible height. She's never actually thought about spirits or the afterlife—it's the kind of talk that Mom would've simply laughed away. But now that Mom is . . . well, now that she's *not here* anymore, maybe the detective has a point. The idea of Mom drifting like a yellow-haired ghost is a heck of a lot better than the thought of her body lying in a casket underground and . . . and . . .

Her throat clenches and she turns her back to Shaw. She will *not* let him see her cry again.

"Look," the detective says, "I've got a place for you to stay. You'll have your own room, your own bathroom, and I almost always eat out, so the kitchen and anything in it will be for you, too. Plus, I've been told that the bed is really quite comfortable."

Gabby's mind flutters back into her own bedroom. Even in her thoughts, the poster with the hand-drawn girl on it is still there, taped lopsidedly to the wall next to her window. Already, the thing feels like a cruel leftover from a previous life. Like a joke that the universe put there to taunt her—a future that'll never come to pass. "I'm never sleeping again," she mutters. She burns her stare into the cracked sidewalk. "Or eating, for that matter. So you can keep your place to yourself."

Shaw sighs, and the sound is completely foreign—nothing like the thick, airy sigh that Mom used to have whenever she was lost in thought. No, this one is quick and choppy, like a dirty burst of steam from an old exhaust pipe. "Tell you what," the detective says, tapping her on the shoulder. "If you promise to just *look* at it, I promise to leave you alone for the rest of the day. How's that sound?"

It sounds like a lie, if Gabby is being completely honest. Like one of those half-truths that adults use just to trick kids into agreeing. But it's the best offer he's given her so far, so she untwists her lenses, presses her lips into a hard line, and gives the man a reluctant nod.

"Okay then," he says, clapping his hands together. "To my place, it is."

Shaw whistles sharply at a nearby carriage, and Gabby looks away as the vehicle turns and lurches toward them. She doesn't look at the thick-armed driver, or at the detective standing rigidly beside her. She doesn't look at the sun-bleached building that she grew up in, either, or at the wide lobby door that's already being roped off by officers. The only thing she looks at is the dreary gray sky, because if she looks anywhere else, the tears filling her eyes will spill out into her goggles. And if she starts bawling now, she's not sure she'll ever find a way to stop again.

# 29

Kemple has been dreaming for a while now. He knows it's a dream because the sky is red, and somehow he's been chained to a clocktower, his arms and legs shackled to huge brass knobs on the rusted clock face. Every time the giant minute hand shifts, it inches just a little bit closer. If he doesn't find a way to wriggle free soon, the thing will crush him into a bloody mess. This probably isn't as bad as it seems—if he gets killed in a nightmare, won't he just . . . *wake up*?—but something about the whole scenario feels terrifyingly *real*, and the closer the minute hand gets, the more he begins to wonder: what if this isn't a dream, after all?

What if this really *is* happening?

He yanks against the chains, but whoever bound him clearly knew what they were doing. The metal links are knotted so tightly around his wrists and ankles that it hurts to even move them. And the harder he struggles, the more the blood-red sky seems to darken, as if the clouds are somehow bleeding.

Then there are the *birds*. They keep circling him—thick, ebony-feathered beasts with glistening orange beaks and talons the color of wet ink. It started with only a few, but now there are over a dozen fluttering through the sky with their beady, unblinking eyes fixed hungrily on him. Their claws scrape at the smoke-filled air, as if they're practicing the movements they'll need to tear the meat from his bones.

"Only a dream," he croaks, pushing his words through his cracked lips. Then, louder, because he's still not convinced, he calls out, "Just a nightmare!"

But the ache in his leg is startlingly cold and piercing, and when he looks down at his ankle, his gash from the alley cat is still there, all swollen and purple and *real*—as real as the crimson sky and the predatory birds and the chains around his limbs that refuse to budge—and somewhere down in the city below, so far down that it's lost in the eerie shadows, a creature lets out a monstrous, guttural roar. The sound echoes off the buildings and slashes across the rooftops, and somehow Kemple knows, without logic or reason, that the bellow is meant for him. Suddenly he isn't scared of the looming minute hand, or the ravenous birds.

No, now his only fear is the beast.

What'll happen if he doesn't get free in time? Will the creature slash its way out of the darkness? Will it climb into the light? Will it close in on him while he's still strapped to this terrible clocktower? And which of these threats will be the one to finally end him: the clock, the birds, or the monster lurking in the dark?

He spots Josephyn on a nearby rooftop, her eyes downcast, her lips pulled taut, and her disappointment in him is so obvious that she doesn't need to utter a word. *This wouldn't have happened*, her body language says, *if you'd just listened to me. Now look where it's gotten you.*

Part of him wants to argue, to *shout* at the girl who breaks open pantry locks, who upheaves *lives*, but what's the use of arguing with the friend who's no longer here? What's the point in talking back to the *stranger* who abandoned him on a rooftop?

Heck, what's the use of doing anything at all?

He sags against the chains, and the minute hand lurches closer, and the birds multiply and swarm until it looks like there are hundreds of them, all waiting for their turn to rip at his skin. And beneath it all, the monster's growl changes into a voice—a gravelly, relentless rasp of a single, ominous word: *Soon.*

The word thunders through the air, shuddering against his clothes and vibrating the bones in his chest, until it feels like his own horrible heartbeat. He pinches his eyes shut as the voice hammers on. *Soon. Soon. Soon . . .*

When he opens his eyes again, he's no longer chained to a clocktower beneath a bloody sky—now he's tethered to a stiff mattress under a white-hot lantern, and there's a gray-haired woman peering down at his scrunched face. "Well, look who's finally awake," the woman says. Her thick-lipped smile makes him shiver, and she watches him with a tense frown until the tremor leaves his limbs.

"Hospital," he whispers. Somehow, he made it here.

"Indeed," the woman says. "It's a good thing someone found you when they did, too. You lost a considerable amount of blood." She presses a finger to his wrist and holds it there for a moment before saying, "The cold flashes are normal, by the way. They're from the painkillers. My name is Agatha. I've been looking after you since—"

Kemple clears his throat and forces out a raspy question. "Where's Josephyn?"

Agatha gives him pitying look. "I have no idea, my dear. Is she a family member of yours? A friend, perhaps?"

Kemple looks away and says in a sad whisper, "She used to be both."

"Well," Agatha says with annoying cheer, "perhaps she'll come to see you, after all. Serious injuries have a curious way of bringing things back together again."

Her words catch in his chest like thorns. *Serious injuries?* His thoughts spiral down into his arms and legs, but everything from his neck down feels . . . numb. Absent. He tries to lift his head, but a fresh gush of pain floods his neck, and he lets out a withering groan.

"Easy there," Agatha says. She tugs on a pair of fabric gloves, then gently prods at his throat with her fingers. "It's not every day that someone survives a fall like you did." Her touch moves down his body in a stiff, clinical manner, her gloved fingertips poking at all his aching parts. "You should be thankful. With time and therapy, you might very well make it back to your previous self, with little more than a limp to show for it." Her face reappears beneath the glaring lamp, and he suddenly notices how old she looks—as if she's spent a few too many decades tending to other injured kids like him. The wrinkles around her eyes deepen, and her lips pull back into a gummy smile. "Wouldn't that be grand?"

"Grand," he repeats dully. Grand Aliston. The thief with night-black hair and emerald eyes. The girl who entered his life just long enough to derail it forever. Something cold and hard hitches in his chest, and he squeezes his words around the lump. "What about my books?"

Agatha blinks at him. "Books, dear?"

"I had books," he says weakly. He tries to lift an arm to point, but his hands feel like they've turned to lead. He gives up with a sigh and says, "Up on the roof. They were . . . important."

Agatha twists her face and offers him a consoling shrug. "Perhaps they're still where you left them, then."

Kemple winces his eyes shut. He pictures the violent Iron Bay air battering his sleeping bag and mercilessly tearing pages out of each novel. He imagines people on the streets lifting the brims of their hats so they can look up at the papers fluttering from the sky. He thinks of Josephyn, too, perched on some other rooftop with her sleeping bag still twisted into a ball under her arm, her eyes fixed on the ragged pieces of their *excuses* as the wind scatters them across the city. Suddenly his arms and legs fill with heat and pressure, as if his veins have been stuffed with hot coals. "I need to find them," he says, straining to sit up.

"*Excuse* me," Agatha says, pressing her hands to his chest. "You need nothing of the sort. What you *need* is rest and fluids, and perhaps another dose of—"

"You don't *understand*," Kemple growls, his voice thickening in a menacing way. "I can't let anything bad happen to them. They're all I have left!"

Agatha's face turns hard and she lets out a sharp *tsk*. "I need some help in here," she calls out, and it takes Kemple a moment to realize that she's not talking to *him* anymore. "Another sedative would be terrific, thanks." Her words come out scratchy and stern—nothing like the smooth, sugary voice she used on him just a moment ago—and something about the change makes his insides tighten and his teeth clench.

Agatha isn't here to help him—she's here to hold him against his will. And he doesn't even need to guess what'll happen next: Josephyn already warned him about all of it. "You can't keep me here," he says, squirming under the woman's hands. The numbness in his limbs has started to drain away. In its place is a new, tingly sensation: like coiled springs and scorching hot air and animal muscles bulging inside too-thin skin.

Agatha's face twists with surprise, and she presses her hands more firmly against his chest, using her weight to hold him down on the mattress. "Stop this, right now!" she snarls. "You're only going to hurt yourself. If you'd just lie still for a moment longer, you'll—"

But Kemple's mind has become a drum, with Josephyn's voice smacking it like a mallet. *They'll separate us and lock us away . . . so we can never find each other again.*

*Don't lose your excuse, Belt Boy.*

*Don't lose . . .*

*Don't . . .*

The springs inside him suddenly uncoil. The hot coals erupt into steam. And Agatha, determined as she is, is no match for the flames rising in him. The straps around his wrists and ankles snap free. Agatha staggers back and falls to the floor. And before Kemple even realizes what he's doing, he stumbles past her and sprints down a slick-tiled hallway with his teeth bared, his eyes wildly searching for the nearest exit.

As he runs, the image of Agatha's horrified face blazes in his mind. The woman wasn't just scared of him—she was gaping at him as if he'd turned into a *monster.*

# 30

Gabby's thoughts are so scattered that she doesn't remember leaving the carriage with Shaw. She doesn't remember entering his apartment building, either, or stepping through his front door, or even hearing him speak to her at all. The only thing she remembers is Mom. Mom, and her sun-colored hair and her cheerfully bad advice and all those promises they made to each other, promises that'll stay forever broken from here on out. Her throat tightens and her eyes start to burn, the tears already welling up inside her. Before the feeling can get any worse, she turns to the detective and twists her lenses, magnifying the room and zooming in on his face until his tired, crinkly eyes are the only things she can see.

His irises are brown and pale, as if they're made of sun-parched dirt. The dullness seems to fit him—plain, simple. Nothing fancy or complicated at all. If he had night-blue eyes or irises the color of exotic ferns, she probably wouldn't trust him at all.

After a moment, Shaw seems to notice her staring. He looks away, clears his throat, and steps quickly into his tiny kitchen. He begins moving things around— pots, dishes, silverware. He does this in an aimless way, as if he doesn't know what else to do with his hands. Without looking at her, he mutters, "Trying to figure out if you should trust me, is that it?"

Gabby looks away and shakes her head. "I don't know what I'm trying to figure out," she admits.

"Well," Shaw says, sliding a drawer open, "this is obviously the kitchen. Where you're standing is the living room. Down the hall to the left is the bathroom. To the right is my room. And back a little further—well, that'll be . . . your room." He lingers on these last two words, stretching them out carefully, as if they're old and fragile and ready to break apart at the slightest jostle or shake.

Gabby tries not to think about it, but her mind wrestles with the clues, anyway. Maybe Shaw used to have someone—just like she used to have Mom.

Maybe the detective is just as broken as she is.

"Do you have any magazines?" she asks.

Shaw frowns in a way that almost looks angry. "Reading material," he mutters. "So obvious. Now why didn't I think of that?"

Gabby shrugs and looks down at the fabric couch beside her. To be honest, she isn't hoping for anything to read. She just wants pictures to look at. Advertisements to scan. Images to lose herself in. Her eyes roam over the sofa's coffee-stained pattern: green leaves and yellow rose petals scattered beneath thick, gray clouds. The zoom of her lenses makes the clouds look checkered—every gray puff showing its stitches and seams. "It's fine," she mutters. She glances back at the kitchen, and her gaze catches on Shaw's stubbly jaw before landing on the splintered countertop. There, her eyes find something that makes her stomach quiver. "Is that—?"

Shaw follows her gaze to the thick manila folder resting on the counter, and his lips sag into a frown. "That would be all my research on cases . . . similar to your mother's." His eyes find her lenses, and he stares at them for a moment, as if he can see right through the tinted glass. As if he can read every emotion filling her eyes—all the horror, all the dread, all that burning curiosity.

A tense few seconds pass between them. Then they both speak at the same time, their voices blurring together into a jumble of noise.

"—I want to see it."

"—Absolutely not."

Gabby twists her lenses until the room shrinks back to a normal size. "You want to keep me occupied?" She lifts her clockwork hand and points her metal index finger at the folder. "Well, there's my reading material."

Shaw slams a drawer closed, scoops the folder off the counter, and tucks it under his arm. "I said *no*. You're not even a decade old, Gabrielle. This information here? This is about *homicides*. Do you even know what that word means?"

Gabby drops her arm to her side and scowls until her face hurts. "That's a file about stuff related to *my mom*, who was a part of my life this morning, and *now she's not*." Her eyes dampen and she clenches her misty hand inside those gears, curling her mechanical fingers into a shuddering, glittering fist. "If there's anything in the world I should be reading right now, it's *that*," she says, raising her voice. "If there's anyone in the world who has the right to see it, it's *me!*"

The detective shakes his head, yanks open a cabinet above him, and stuffs the folder inside. "This is the last thing you need to see," he says, shutting the door. "Especially today." When she opens her mouth to shout, to *scream*, he cuts her off with a sharp wave of his hand. "I'm not trying to be cruel. I have every intention of showing you this file. Really. Just . . ." He lowers his hand and looks at her pleadingly. "Just not right now. Not today. Give yourself time to grieve.

To heal. Then, when you're ready, I promise you, Gabrielle Lenton: we'll brave this folder together."

Gabby glares at him in trembling silence—not because she can't think of anything to say, but because there's so *much* to say that her mind can't hold it all together. Her muscles shudder. Her stomach burns. The gears on her clockwork hand tick and whir. If her rage were a fire right now, she'd burn this whole stupid apartment down to its foundation.

Shaw holds his ground behind the counter with his dull eyes fixed, unflinchingly, on her goggles. He doesn't move. He doesn't blink. He doesn't even *breathe*.

Gabby finally breaks the silence, her body whirling into motion. She twists around, lifts her metal glove, and slams it down on the couch's armrest. Her brass knuckles tear through the ugly rose petals. Her iron gears chew through the fabric clouds. She punches and screams and rips at the sofa until the air around her is nothing but a whirl of dust and cotton, until the couch's wooden skeleton is exposed and splintered, until her cries wobble and fade and her body crumples, and suddenly she's on the floor and sobbing.

The detective rushes over and wraps her in a violent hug, his thick arms squeezing her tight. "It's okay," he rasps. "It's alright. You let it out, girl. You let it all out until there's nothing left to let out anymore."

Gabby jams her goggled face against his coat, burying herself under all that scratchy fabric. The detective grips her shoulders and rubs her spine, and though his touch is gentle and reassuring—fatherly, even—it's also horribly unfamiliar, a painful reminder that the only person she has left in the world is a haggard man who's nothing but a *stranger*.

She curls against him, balling herself as small as she can, and she wails Mom's name until her voice gives out.

# 31

Kemple scrambles through the hospital with his heart hammering against his ribs, his mind a wet cloud of noise. Everything feels wrong and out of place, as if he somehow fell into another world and lost everything *normal* along the way. His head feels clogged. His blood feels syrupy. Even the too-snug outfit that he stole with Josephyn is gone—in its place is a faded green robe that keeps slipping off his shoulders and billowing around his waist. To make matters worse, the only clear thought he's been able to dredge up is a single, pitiful word: *roof.* He needs to find a roof. Any roof will do. Somewhere high where the air is pure and the sky is open all around him, where he isn't trapped inside a building with hallways like giant shelves, as if he's nothing more than a can of beans that's been stuffed into a pantry.

He imagines Abner's monstrous hand sweeping through the halls, those grubby fingers eager to snatch him up, and the thought alone makes his blood run cool. He quickly scans the corridors, but they all look exactly the same.

Where the heck is the way *out*?

Somewhere in the glossy maze behind him, Agatha shouts, her words screechy and jumbled by the distance. Other voices respond—deeper, gruffer voices that fill Kemple's head with images of scissored fish bellies and swinging belt buckles, voices that make the skin on his back sting and the space around his heart tremble—and his legs move on their own, pulling him aimlessly down the nearest corridor. He turns a corner and tumbles over a metal cart filled with towels. He skitters down a ramp and crashes against a table cluttered with vials and tubes. When he finally finds a thick red door that seems to lead outside, he skids to a stop and scowls at the thing, as if he's looking at some kind of a trick.

As if, on the other side of the door, Abner is waiting with an arm raised and a thick belt wrapped around his merciless fist.

But suddenly Kemple isn't afraid. He isn't worried. Heck, he isn't . . . *anything*, really. Somewhere between the rooftop and here, something about him changed.

He isn't sure how it happened, or what the change even *means*, but the twisting, disorienting gravity of it is undeniable. It fills his bones. It radiates off his skin. And somehow he knows, without even having to think about it, that Abner is now a part of his *previous* life—a life that's been erased forever. Now there's a *new* monster to worry about, something without a face or a name or even a body—something that exists only in the center of his mind like a horrible knot of pressure. Like a creature slumbering between his thoughts with its clawed limbs tucked menacingly against its sides.

Like a demon ready to wake.

"Hey, you!" shouts a woman behind him, her voice sharp with anger.

Kemple's heart clatters in his chest and he lunges for the door without looking back. His fingers fumble with the handle. His teeth scrape against his tongue.

"If you're the kid they're calling about," the woman yells, her voice uncomfortably close now, "then you're in a hell of a lot of trouble, boy!"

The monster twitches in his head, and he finally manages to twist the handle open. He jams his palm against the door and pauses, just long to glance over his shoulder. He scowls at the woman's stiff-looking dress and mumbles, "I'm already in more trouble than you know." Then he shoves the door open, lunges into the sour city air, and slams the door shut behind him before the woman has a chance to reply.

Outside, the sky is a dizzying swirl of color and light. He squeezes his eyes shut, but the brightness still floods through his eyelids. He staggers back with a snarl, jamming his forearm over his face.

Ever since he and Josephyn found Iron Bay, the air over the city has always looked dull and dismal. Since when did looking at the daylight *hurt*?

The door behind him thuds and the handle jiggles, and the sound is like an electric jolt to his heart. He inhales quickly, then staggers away from the building, out into the blinding city. With his eyes still hidden behind his arm, his other senses fill in the gaps: hot cobbles under his bare feet, bitter spit on his tongue, the stench of old smoke burning his sinuses and the roar of vehicles swirling around him. It's overwhelming and maddening and a little bit frightening, and the only place he can think to go is *up*—up to the rooftops where his sleeping bag still lies, scattered in a dingy heap beside his and Josephyn's excuses.

Up, to the only place in the world that feels sane and familiar anymore.

He bumps into someone's hip, and a heavy pair of hands shoves him roughly. "Watch where you're going, idiot!" He mumbles an apology and staggers to the side, only to clip his leg against something hard. A carriage horn blasts in his ear, and a woman's shrill voice knifes through the air. "Get off th' road, ya fool!"

His path through the city continues this way for what feels like forever—every sidewalk littered with violent arms and legs, every cobbled street cluttered with horn-blaring vehicles and neighing horses. By the time he stumbles into the quiet of an abandoned alley, his muscles feel bruised, his ears are ringing, and he's pretty sure he's bleeding in a few places. But then his fingertips graze the metal curve of a ladder, and he lets out a sigh of relief.

Now all he has to do is reach out and step up, one rusted rung at a time, until—

"There he is!" someone shouts, and Kemple gnashes his teeth at the sound of the woman's familiar tone—all that sourness where there used to be sweetness, all that anger where there used to be sympathy.

He barely knows Agatha, but already he hates her.

"Stay away!" he snarls. With his eyes still closed, and the sky still glaring against his eyelids, he clenches his fingers around the first rung and leaps, pulling himself up. His arms shudder from the strain and his lungs burn from the effort, but soon the struggle eases, and his muscles soften, and his mouth greedily sucks in the cool, damp air. He lifts himself farther, yanking his body upward, throwing himself toward the roof until he's moving so quickly that he's climbing the ladder three rungs at a time. Until it feels like he's *flying*. Before long he reaches the top, yanks himself over the gutter, and lands in an effortless crouch, his toes digging comfortably into the gravelly rooftop. The motion jostles something in his head, and the creature between his thoughts seems to move, slinking that much closer to the surface.

Somewhere in the alley far below, Agatha's shout rings out, all that harshness in her voice replaced by a thin, confused warble. "What on this hellish green earth *are you*?"

Kemple says nothing—because not even he knows the answer anymore.

# 32

Gabby spends the next few days wandering aimlessly around Shaw's apartment, like a spider without a web. Everything about the man's place grates on her—the way he hangs the head of his toothbrush over the edge of the bathroom sink, the way he dries his plates and bowls by setting them upside down on the countertop. Even the way he sits annoys her: with his back to the center of the room, his chair angled toward the far wall, his half-lidded eyes staring blankly at the dull plaster, as if he's searching the cracked paint for clues.

It's like he's *trying* to upset her with every little thing he does. As if he doesn't *want* her to feel at home. Every night, she lies on her borrowed bed with her eyes wide open in the dark, her eyelashes quivering behind her dirty lenses.

On the third morning, while she's limply pushing her spoon into a gray smear of oatmeal, Shaw glances up from his own bowl and says quickly, "You feel like going out for a carriage ride?"

She doesn't. Not really. Lately she doesn't feel like doing anything except breathing—and even then, she'd be fine if she stopped doing that, too. But a carriage ride sounds infinitely better than hanging around inside the detective's frustrating apartment, so she nods, adjusts her goggles, and lets out a dismal sigh.

"That's the spirit," Shaw says, with just the tiniest hint of sarcasm.

Gabby ignores the jab, clattering her brass knuckles against the man's wooden table. She pushes the gray mush around her bowl until the detective finishes eating. Then they head out, moving through a routine that's so much like the one she used to have with Mom: locking the front door, clomping down a dimly lit stairwell, stepping out into the smoke-stained air of the city with her boots scraping against the dirty sidewalk.

Shaw hails a coach with a quick, sharp whistle, and Gabby doesn't pay attention when he mumbles directions to the driver—she just climbs onto the padded seat in the back and fixes her goggled eyes on the side window, her mechanical hand stuffed carefully under her thigh. Then she glances down at her outfit and frowns. Dingy leather jacket. A long-sleeved shirt the color of rotten eggs. Snug pants with too many darn pockets, and monstrous boots the color of spit. Somewhere along the way she lost her beret—now her hair just sits limply on her head like a mound of oily grass. She tenses and checks her coat sleeves for blood—*Mom's* blood. Blood that, in that horrible moment, looked too *red* to be real. Too *horrible* to be true. But aside from a few smears of dirt and dust, her jacket is mostly clean. She lets out a quivering sigh, slumps back into the seat, and notices Shaw watching her from the opposite bench. The man gives her a sad smile, then says quietly, "You didn't get any on you."

Gabby scowls and folds her arms over her chest, hiding most of her sleeves. He's clearly trying to be nice, but today *nice* just feels . . . annoying. "It's none of your business what I get on me."

Shaw chuckles and shifts on his seat. "I suppose you're right. I've been told I have a habit of sticking my nose where it don't belong."

Gabby twists her face and searches her mind for something Mom used to say about *her*, but her thoughts just keep circling around that terrible pantry door and the nightmarish creature lurking within. Eventually she gives up and looks out the window, resting the frame of her goggles against the faded glass. Crumpled buildings and scraggly trees slide by in a jittery blur, until it all looks so frustratingly similar. So pointless. The carriage's wheels clatter against the road. The engine hums and groans. Her clockwork hand clacks and lets out a sputter of steam, and the drone of it all makes her teeth grit. Finally, she breaks the silence with a whisper: "Where are we going?"

"You'll see," Shaw replies, and he says it with such a sense of finality that she doesn't bother asking anything more.

When the coach finally grinds to a stop, they're in a part of Iron Bay that she doesn't recognize. The trees are thick. The ground is sloped. Tiny statues litter the grass. Off in the distance, in an opening beneath the dreary sky, a dozen or so people are standing around, hugging and shaking hands. They're dressed nicely—the men in pressed suits, the women in flowing dresses with thick, floppy-brimmed hats—but something about the way they're standing tugs on Gabby's insides. She frowns and looks away from the glass, pinning her gaze on the detective's stiff face. "What is this?" she asks.

The driver clears his throat, opens his door, and glances back at her and Shaw. For the first time today, Gabby sees the man's face: wrinkled forehead, violet eyes, a short beard the color of hay. The man looks sad in a way that makes her angry. His gaze meets hers for an instant, then he looks at Shaw. "I'll wait outside 'til you're done," he says.

Shaw nods and the man leaves the vehicle, closing the door with a heavy click.

Gabby stares at the detective in silence for a moment, until the moment turns sour and awkward. She straightens on her seat and asks again, "What *is* this?"

Shaw blinks slowly, then looks out the window, fixing his gaze on the group of people in the distance. "I figured, keeping a way's off would be better. Thought you'd prefer it this way." He reaches inside his vest, pulls out a tiny pair of metallic binoculars, and begins carefully wiping the lenses with the hem of his shirt.

Gabby squints at the man. Something about him looks different today. His clothes are less wrinkled. His hair is less greasy. Even the scruff on his face looks shorter, neater.

For some reason, he cleaned up.

The mystery yanks at her brain, like it's eager to unravel her thoughts. She hardens her face, instead, and says firmly, "What. Is. This?"

Shaw sighs, sets the binoculars on the seat cushion beside him, and taps his thumbnail against his lip. This, she's learned, is his *thinking* pose, and her ghostly hand twitches inside her clockwork glove, her misty fingers vibrating with a sudden urge to reach out and smack his thumb away from his mouth, to knock his stupid hand away from his face, not just *now*, but *every single time* the man stops to think, because what has thinking ever done for *her*?

What did thinking ever do for *Mom*?

"We're at a cemetery, Gabrielle," Shaw blurts out, and Gabby's eyes flick up to meet his. He stares back at her lenses, his expression soft and unreadable, until something blooms and expands inside her. A flame. A fire.

An inferno.

Suddenly, it all makes sense. The carriage ride. The sad-faced driver. The well-dressed strangers hugging on the grass. "You . . . you took me to my Mom's *funeral*?" she says, her voice quivering with rage.

"Not *to* it," Shaw says, lifting the binoculars to his face. He points the tiny lenses at the group of people and watches them for a moment. Then he lowers the binoculars and nods at her. "I took you *near* it. What you do from here is a matter of choice."

Gabby quickly turns the other way and fixes her scowl on the cloud-stuffed sky. "If this was your carriage," she growls, "I'd punch my clockwork fingers into its stupid engine and tear everything out."

"You're angry," he says flatly. "I get that. And I hate to break it to you, kiddo, but that anger won't go away anytime soon. Not if you just let it simmer." He goes quiet for a moment, as if he's waiting for her to say something. When she doesn't, he sighs and says, "That's why we're here. To move past it. Or at least to try."

A rabbit-shaped cloud drifts into view, and Gabby flexes the skin around her eyes. She imagines the rabbit's head tearing off, blood-red clouds sputtering from its jagged cloud-neck. For some reason, this comforts her. "We're here because you tricked me," she mutters.

"All you have to do is look," Shaw replies. "I've seen you work those goggles of yours. I know you don't need binoculars like I do. I know that all you need to do is twist those lenses to see the faces of those folks standing over there."

The rabbit-shaped cloud bends and loses its shape. Now it looks more like a whale without fins. Gabby frowns and looks down at the coach's worn upholstery, her eyes lingering on places where the leather has cracked and split. The fabric looks a lot like how she feels: fractured, tattered. Broken. "What the heck is that supposed to accomplish?" she snaps. "I don't even *know* them."

Shaw makes a thoughtful noise, and Gabby knows, without even looking, that he's tapping his stupid thumbnail against his lip again. "You may not know them," he says, "but they knew your mom. They lost her, too."

She turns her head toward the window, then catches herself and squeezes her eyes shut. So what if they lost Mom? Nobody lost Mom like *she* did.

Nobody *loved* Mom like she did.

She pinches her eyes shut even harder and says, "I don't care about them. I don't care about *anyone*."

Something warm and firm wraps around her knee, and she flinches for instant, her mind filling with an image of dark, gaping jaws and huge, bloodstained teeth. Then she realizes that it's just Shaw's grubby hand on her leg. He gives her kneecap a gentle squeeze and says, "I think you do care. I think what happened to you is the worst thing to ever happen to a little girl, but I also think that you're made of stronger stuff than you put on."

Gabby winces her eyes apart and glares at Shaw. Her vision is soft and watery. "So the hell what?" she snarls.

"So prove it to me," he says, pulling his hand away. He jerks his chin toward the window. "Show me you're not just some bitter kid who'll grow up filled with hate. Show me that you still got some goodness left in you." He reaches across the space between them and taps his fingers against the edge of her goggles. "Look at those people over there and tell me what you see."

So Gabby turns and looks, twisting her lenses until she can see the strangers' faces up close—not because he's asking her to, but to prove him *wrong*. She *is* just some bitter kid who'll grow up filled with hate. And she *doesn't* have any goodness left in her. She knows this because, ever since she found Mom in that pantry, there's been a coldness inside her where there should be warmth. A void where something important was torn away. So whatever it is that Shaw sees in her, he's clearly mistaken. She's nothing but damaged goods now. Shattered past the point of repair. A freakish little girl with ugly goggles and a hideous mechanical hand, someone who'd be better off left for . . .

For . . .

She hesitates, then twists her lenses a little more, zooming in on the tanned face of a woman with long black hair.

The woman is crying in a private sort of way, as if she doesn't want anyone else to notice. Gabby turns her head and her gaze catches on the face of a man standing beside the woman. His jaw is clenched. His eyes downcast. His neck looks stiff with strain.

For the next minute or so, Gabby watches the group, scanning every face, watching every emotion. Finally, she sags back in her seat and twists her goggles until the world returns to its normal size.

"Well?" Shaw asks. "What did you see?"

She takes her time thinking the question over, until she finds an answer that she's comfortable with. "I saw that . . . I'm not the only person hurting over Mom."

"That's what I saw, too," Shaw says, tucking his binoculars back under his vest. "And how'd it make you feel?"

This time she answers quickly, blurting out every emotion that's coursing through her veins. "Sad. Scared. Confused." She glances at Shaw's thin-lipped face and says, "But mostly *angry*."

Shaw chews on his lip for a moment, then reaches up and knocks hard on the carriage's roof. "Then your anger is what we'll use."

Something moves in the corner of Gabby's vision, and she turns to see the driver limping back toward the coach, his weathered hand rubbing against his sand-colored beard. The man doesn't look sad anymore—now he just looks tired. And the anger she felt toward him earlier has faded. Now she just feels sorry for the guy. She turns back to Shaw and says quietly, "Use for what?"

Shaw gives her a wink, as if he's hiding some monstrous secret. As if the answer to her question isn't something he can say out loud. And when the driver opens the door and climbs in with a sigh, the detective leans over and whispers in her ear, "I think you're ready to see that folder now."

# 33

Sometime during Kemple's stay at the hospital, Iron Bay must've changed. Now everything about the city feels too bright, too loud, too . . . *rancid*. The glow from every street lamp burns his eyes. The clatter of each passing carriage scrapes against his eardrums. Even the scent of the people walking along the sidewalks has become unbearable—now everyone smells like filth and rotting meat. Like food that's been left out so long it's started to grow fur.

Not that he has time to stand around sniffing the air. For the past few days, he's been on the run—from Agatha and the hospital staff, from the fever that keeps leaving and coming back, from the strange tilt of this new world that seems to never go away, as if he hasn't woken up completely. As if a part of him is still caught in that dream where he's strapped to a clocktower with that giant minute hand lurching closer. The one where those voracious birds keep circling around him, while some terrible creature drags itself up from the city's shadowy depths.

The one where he's waiting to find out which horrible thing will kill him first.

This morning he's sprawled out on a tarry rooftop, the edges of it plastered with peeling white paint. His eyes are crusted with dried tears. His jaw is tight and sore. His mouth tastes bitter and foul. On top of it all, he hasn't slept a wink since he escaped up that rusted ladder. How could he? His mind won't stop hammering him with questions.

*What if he—?*

*How did they—?*

*Why does it ever—?*

The worst part is that the questions never *finish*. They just bloat inside him in shattered fragments, dangling like strange puzzle pieces, until finally they droop and slough apart, like flowers shriveling to death. Like plants with poisoned roots.

At first, he tried finishing the questions himself, just to stuff some quiet into his head. But the effort made his mind lurch and the world spin until he felt like throwing up. Now he doesn't bother. He'd rather be confused than nauseous.

For now, he keeps everything small and simple. Sit up. Rub his face. Wince up at the dreary sky.

Lately it's the short, slow movements that seem to agree with his body the most.

He squints down at the fabric over his ribs and grimaces. His hospital robe isn't green and loose anymore—now it's a grungy brown-gray mess that's begun to unravel at the seams. Really, it hardly resembles a robe at all. He closes his eyes and tries to picture the snug outfit he stole with Josephyn, but even that tiny memory feels too heavy to dredge up. He sighs and imagines simple things, instead: Dark clouds. Gray smoke. Shaggy black fur and thick, jagged claws and—

Something clinks nearby and his ears flinch, his eyelids snapping open. He turns his head toward the sound—slowly, carefully—until his bleary eyes catch a glimpse of the source: a bearded, haggard old man, crouching on another rooftop.

The man is too far away to see clearly, but even from here it's obvious that the stranger is like Kemple: Dirty. Broken. Not really *living*, but . . . surviving.

*Existing*, one pointless breath at a time.

At first Kemple simply looks away, dragging his gaze back onto the roof. If he waits long enough, the stranger will finish whatever he's doing and wander away. Then the city will be Kemple's again: Filthy and foreign. Noisy and putrid. Stuffed with so many people and things but at the same time so utterly *empty*.

But is that really what he *wants* right now? To be alone? To be left up on some strange rooftop, like a discarded piece of trash?

How would a life like this be any better than the one he suffered through with Abner?

He glances at the other building and watches the old man shuffle across the rooftop. His body is hunched. His head is lowered. But his arms move quickly and with purpose: sifting and prodding, lifting and squeezing.

It takes Kemple a moment to remember the word for what the man is doing. "Scavenging," he rasps. His throat is scratchy and raw, and he flinches at the alien sound of his own voice, as if it came from someone else. Is this the first time he's spoken since his escape from Agatha? And what was it he yelled to her? Something about leaving, or taking, or—

The old man looks up from his own rooftop and their eyes meet, their gazes locking together. Even from a distance, Kemple notices the man's wildness—the way he *cowers* instead of stands, the way he *moves* instead of walks. Is this how Kemple looks, too? Has he become a sort of animal in human skin? Is this stranger his unavoidable future?

Kemple watches the man in silence. The man watches him back. For a long while, neither of them move. Then the stranger jerks his head and twists away, and suddenly the man is stumbling across the roof with surprising speed. He drops a few things from his rumpled clothing—small, shiny objects like empty cans and rusted bolts—and Kemple's mind drags another word from the dark pool of his thoughts and shoves it through his gaping mouth: "Fleeing."

The man is running away . . . from *him*.

The realization feels silly, at first. Like something he should laugh at. Why would anyone run from *him*? But just as he starts to chuckle, something inside him shifts and darkens, like a curtain being yanked over a window to block the light. The laugh dies in his throat. His mouth tightens. His lips pulls back over his teeth. And that silly feeling inside him curls inward and hardens until it's as jagged and sharp as a claw.

The man is running from him like a rat scrambling from an alley cat. The man is running from him like *prey*.

Before Kemple even realizes what he's doing, he's up and running, too—not away from the man but *toward* him, closing the gap between them one wild step at a time. His robe chafes against his skin. His brain sloshes in his skull. The world staggers and twirls and he braces for another violent wave of nausea . . . but it never comes. Instead, everything sharpens and clears. The dizziness falls out of him like a coin slipping through a slot. The confusion whisks out of his head, too, like fog sweeping away from a strong gust of wind. In its place, one thought remains—a command that pulses through him like its own heartbeat: *Chase him. Catch him. Hunt him down.*

So he does, panting and snarling and grinning—actually *grinning*. The chase moves from one rooftop to the next, over and through the noise of the city, like a scissor blade slicing through the belly of a fish. The man stumbles and hurls himself over the gaps between the buildings, his stride slowing with every roof. Kemple follows him steadily, loping and leaping with the foul-smelling wind dragging in his hair and the yellow-gray sky pummeling him with its sticky heat.

On each building, the stranger makes a misstep: tripping over a pipe here, bumping into a vent there, crashing against a protruding gutter. Each time, Kemple gains on the man a little more. By the time they reach the sixth rooftop, the air has begun to reek with the man's sour stench, like old milk and stale bread and fear—so much *fear*. Kemple throws himself onto the edge of the roof and skids his heels against the tarry shingles, and the man twists around and shouts out a garble of noise before throwing the contents of his pockets at Kemple: bits of wood and scraps of metal, bread crusts and dirty shards of glass.

Kemple flinches from the attack, lifting his arms to his face and ducking from instinct. The debris rains down on him in scattered bursts, peppering his hair and skin, but it doesn't hurt at all. It doesn't even sting. Soon the air clears and Kemple looks up to see the man plunging his bandage-wrapped hands into his pockets, as if he's searching for something else to throw. As if he's looking for something with a little more weight to it.

Kemple doesn't give him the chance. He lowers his head and barrels forward, and suddenly the rooftop is tilting, and the man's bearded face is under him, his wrinkled eyes wide with terror. Kemple's arms move on their own, swinging and thrashing, his fingers stiff and bent like claws. Spit flies through the air. Bloody fabric mixes with it. The stranger screams and flails and tries to shove Kemple off, but Kemple pulls himself closer and tears at the man harder. The pulse in his ears becomes a pounding drum and the man's scruffy face gets redder and wetter, and the stranger's wails become so high-pitched and grating that Kemple has an urge to bite down on the bastard's dirty throat, to sink his teeth into the man's windpipe, to *rip* and *tear* until that horrible yelling finally stops and—

The man's veiny eyes meet Kemple's, and Kemple sees it clearly: the man's horror, his despair, his look of *pleading*—not just for a stop to the violence, but to be *spared*. To not have his life end in this awful way above the city, up on some abandoned rooftop.

Suddenly the world loses its balance. The drums in Kemple's ears fade away. The crispness in his head sloughs apart. That familiar nausea rolls in, like a tidal surge rising from his gut, and he staggers off the man and falls back onto the roof's gritty shingles.

The man gasps, rolls onto his hands and knees, and starts crawling away slowly. Weakly. Eventually he reaches the edge of the roof and groans his way down the ladder, and Kemple waits until the stranger is gone completely before staggering to his feet. He spots the man's trail off the building, like a huge snail streak on the shingles: Torn strips of fabric. Broken bits of trash. Long, glistening smears of red. The sight makes something wrench in his stomach. Bitterness swells in his throat. He looks down at his hands and stares numbly at the man's blood glistening under his fingernails, until his own voice starts to drone in his skull, blaring out a single word: *Wrong. Wrong. WRONG!*

"What," he whispers, "is *happening* to me?"

The city doesn't answer him. It just keeps churning and humming all around him, as if nothing has changed at all.

# 34

Shaw leads Gabby into his room slowly, as if he's unsure of how she'll react. "My desk is over there," he says, almost apologetically. He nods at a wooden table that's been wedged into a corner and gives her elbow a nudge. "Go on," he says. "Investigate. I know you want to."

He's right. As much as she hates to admit it, she *is* curious. Of all the places in Shaw's tiny apartment, his room seems to hold the most unanswered questions. The drawers all have keyholes on them. The walls are littered with rectangular stains, as if they once had pictures hanging from the plaster. And the bed always seems to be neatly made in the same way, as if the detective never actually sleeps on it. Instead of walking farther into the room, though, Gabby just twists her lenses, expanding her vision until the desk in the corner is all she can see. The tabletop looks gritty and is mostly bare, except for a brass picture frame leaning against the wall. Gabby scans the frame, then frowns when she notices there isn't anything in it. The glass is bare, and the edges of the frame are coated with a thick layer of dust. She twists her lenses until the room pulls back into view, then points at the empty frame with her clockwork hand. "Where'd the picture go?"

Shaw frowns at the frame, then looks softly at her goggles. "Tucked away," he says. "So I don't always have to see it." He pauses, then looks away. "Sometimes it's nice to be reminded of things. Other times, it's nicer to forget."

Before she can ask anything more, Shaw clears his throat and nods at the rickety stool beside his desk. "I only got the one seat. And with me being the old man here, I plan on using it. So before we get started, I suggest you grab a chair from the kitchen. Otherwise, you'll have to stand."

Gabby shrugs in a way that she hopes looks casual, even though her insides are suddenly buzzing. "I don't mind standing."

Shaw raises an eyebrow, then nods at her. "Alright then." He gives the folder under his arm a pat, then trudges to the desk. "What," he says, easing himself down onto the stool, "is the first thing you want to know?" He sets the folder on the desk and carefully nudges it with his thumbs, until the thing is perfectly centered on the dingy tabletop. "Keep in mind," he adds, glancing back at her, "it's still *my* folder. *My* research. So I reserve the right to withhold any information that I deem fit." He narrows his eyes and says, "And yes, I know this relates to your mom. And yes, I know how much this means to you. That's why I'm letting you peek behind the curtain. But that's all today is, Gabrielle. A peek. And if things go well, then later on, you can peek a little more. Deal?"

Gabby nods easily, even though the buzzing inside her has turned into a trumpet blast. Her steamy hand quivers inside her glove.

Shaw gestures for her to come closer, but the room suddenly feels too large to walk across—too *dangerous*—so she shakes her head and crosses her arms over her chest. "I'm fine here," she mutters.

"Suit yourself." The detective opens the folder, revealing a sheet of parchment that's cluttered with handwritten notes. Then he glances back at her and says, "Your first question?"

Gabby eyes the exposed page, and her good hand instinctively moves toward her goggles, her fingers automatically wrapping around the frame. But she stops herself from twisting the lenses. What if she reads something she's not supposed to?

What if she sees something . . . awful?

"These are just questions of my own," Shaw says, tapping his thumb knuckle against the first page. As usual, the man seems to have a knack at guessing what she's thinking. "Wonderings of mine. Ideas I've been kicking around. Nothing to be concerned about."

Gabby brings her hand back down to her side and tightens her grip around her ribs. "Nothing to be concerned about?" she mutters.

Shaw's expression softens. "Probably not the best figure of speech," he says. "What I mean is, now's your chance to ask away. Don't hold your questions in. They'll just fester and burn. Trust me—I know from experience."

Gabby's gaze flicks back to that empty picture frame, and she frowns at it until the thrumming inside her narrows to a white-hot point, like the tip of a knife that's been held to a fire. "What's it called?" she blurts out.

Shaw twists around on his stool to face her. "What's *what* called?"

"The thing," she says, looking away from his eyes. "The . . . monster that attacked my mom."

Shaw nods as if he expected this question. Or as if he approves. "We call them the *Ailouroi*." When she doesn't say anything back, he adds, "It's the old Greek word for *cat*. Granted, the thing you saw was obviously nothing like a household feline."

Gabby's misty fingers clench inside the gears, digging her brass fingertips into her side. Her ribs start to ache, but she doesn't move the glove away. Right now, she *needs* the pain. It's the only thing keeping her from screaming. "And how," she says, her voice trembling slightly, "do I kill them?"

Shaw's eyebrows rise up, wrinkling his forehead. Then he shakes his head. Clearly, he wasn't expecting this question.

Clearly, he doesn't approve.

"Don't you want to know where they come from? Or how they're made? Or what they wan—"

Gabby's glove wrenches even tighter, and there's a sound of tearing fabric as her metal fingertips rip a hole in the seam of her jacket. "*How*," she says more firmly, "*do I kill them?*"

Shaw sighs, turns back around to face his desk, and gently closes the folder. "I thought you were ready to learn," he mumbles. His words come out softly, as if he's talking more to himself than her. Or as if he's talking to someone else altogether. "Obviously, I was wrong."

But nothing about this *feels* wrong. If anything, Gabby feels more *right* than she has in days, as if this conversation was meant to happen all along. As if the question she's asking is the only one worth mentioning at all. Suddenly she's yelling at the top of her lungs, her voice strained and hoarse. "Damn you, Shaw! *Tell me how to kill them!*"

Shaw whirls around, his face taut and flushed. "Now you calm down right now!" he yells back, chopping his hand through the air. "This isn't the way at all, Gabrielle. There ain't no shortcuts here. Not when the stakes are so high. You can't just—"

Gabby scoffs so hard that it actually startles the detective. She's so *fed up* with being told what to do. So *sick* of being told to wait. Wait for *what*, anyway? For another one of those things to find someone else's mom? For Shaw's folder to get even thicker? "You tell me how to kill them right now," she blurts out, "or so help me God, I'll run away from you and figure it out myself!"

Shaw blinks at her and shakes his head. "You wouldn't."

Clearly, he doesn't know her as well as he thinks. "I've been caught running away before," she replies flatly. "You're a detective—check my file to see if I'm lying."

Shaw clamps his mouth shut and glares at her, the muscles tense around his jaw.

Gabby narrows her eyes behind her lenses and glares right back.

Finally, the detective throws his hands in the air and scoops the folder off the desk. "Fine," he growls. "You want to know how to kill the beast? You want to see what it takes?" He yanks open the folder and roughly shoves the pages aside until he finds one with an image on it—a hand-inked illustration. Something dark and red. Something that he doesn't even bother to glance at before angrily thrusting it toward her. "There," he says, staring grimly at her goggles. "See for yourself, Gabrielle."

Gabby reaches out with her clockwork hand, snatches the page from him, and turns it over impatiently. Her lens-tinted eyes roam all over the picture, and at first she can't even tell what she's looking at. Then the details begin to pull together, and everything starts to make sense. The image is of a yellow-furred creature, much like the one she saw perched over Mom. This one, though, is sprawled out on a dirty street with its fanged jaws gaping, its long tongue hanging out, its slitted eyes wide and glossy. The drawing is muddled and discolored in the middle, where the monster's chest should be, and it takes Gabby a moment to realize that she's looking at an artist's depiction of blood. No, of *gore*. Of torn skin and shattered bones, of syrupy fluids and ruptured organs and . . . and . . . and suddenly Gabby's insides are twisting and rising, as if her own organs are struggling to climb out of her body. She gags, drops the picture, and scrambles to the bathroom.

She makes it to the toilet just in time to spit up the measly amount of oatmeal she ate this morning. Then her stomach wrenches again and she throws up even more, over and over, until her insides feel like they've torn apart. Until the only thing left for her to do is cough, and gasp, and sob against the cold porcelain.

Eventually Shaw steps into the bathroom and leans quietly against the doorway. The folder is no longer tucked under his arm, and he doesn't look mad anymore. Now he just looks sad. He studies the mess she made in the toilet, then says softly, "The best way to kill an Aílouros?" His gaze slides down her face and settles on her twitching glove. "You have to tear out the thing's spoiled heart."

For a long while, Gabby doesn't say anything at all. She doesn't *feel* anything, either—except for a dull, distant throb in the space where her heart should be. Eventually she drags her sleeve against her chin, smearing away a glob of spit, and pushes her goggles up onto her forehead so she can look Shaw in the eyes. She lifts her clockwork hand and flexes her ghostly fingers inside. The gears twist and click. The valve by her thumb lets out a spurting gush of steam.

Shaw squints at her metal fist as if she's holding a weapon. Then he meets her eyes again. He stares at her steadily, as if he knows what she's about to say. As if he's been waiting for her to say it all along.

"Promise you'll teach me how?" she whispers.

Shaw flattens his lips into a grim line and nods slowly, easily, as if the motion is rehearsed.

As if he's made this exact promise to someone else before.

# 35

Kemple stays on the rooftop the whole day, until the sky ripens from a pale gray to a bronzed, dirty yellow. He spends the time gathering the stranger's leftovers into a dirty pile: lantern shards, rusted bolts, strips of bloody fabric. He arranges them by size and color and texture: the largest, darkest, and roughest at one end; the smallest, smoothest, and brightest at the other. He's not sure why he even bothers—it's just a meaningless heap of trash. But something about the slow, deliberate act of collecting these things has made his shoulders relax and the noise in his head shrink away. Now, instead of a deafening roar in his skull, there's only a distant, muffled groan.

He's hungry, though. And sore all over. And though the air is thick and warm this evening, his skin is surprisingly cold, as if his body is somehow missing a layer of fur. He shivers, squeezes his robed arms around his scraped knees, and glares at the tiny pile of litter, as if it's the *trash*'s fault that he ended up here, alone and on the run.

As if it's anyone's fault but his own.

But it *is* his fault, isn't it? Josephyn even warned him about it. If he'd simply listened to her instead of argued, if he'd just trusted her instead of thinking he knew better, maybe now he'd be *with* her instead of wondering where she is. Instead of *missing* her. Maybe now they'd both be reading more of their excuses. Perhaps she'd even tell him if the nurse finally sawed off the pirate's leg or not.

Of all the questions circling around in his head, this one seems to bother him the most. Did the pirate's leg get worse? Or did it get better on its own?

He lifts the dirt-crusted edge of his robe and glances down at his swollen ankle. The scrape is a jagged line now, the color of burnt coal. The skin around it is yellowish brown. All in all, it looks more like a burn than a bruise. He frowns and lowers the robe. He'd rather not look at it anymore. Heck, he'd rather not even *think* about it. Besides, he's dealt with worse. The bloody welts Abner used to leave on his back probably looked just as—

A man shouts from a nearby alley, and Kemple's whole body jerks from the sound. "I *specifically* requested three feet of nickel-plated wiring!" the man yells.

"I remember what you asked for," another man shouts back. "And I don't got it. So get lost!"

"This is unacceptable! I have a deadline that must be met, and I *refuse* to be delayed by your incompetence!"

The shouting continues, both voices swelling with anger, and though the argument sounds private, like something Kemple isn't meant to hear, he finds himself creeping toward the sound anyway. His foot aches in a numb sort of way, so his movement is more of a hobble than a stride, but he eventually reaches the edge of the roof and slumps quietly against it. He lets his head hang over the moldy gutter, its hard edge digging into his throat.

Below him—so far down that if he fell, he'd probably have enough time to scream *twice* before hitting the pavement—two men are standing across from one another in the center of a narrow alley. Their arms slash at the air, as if they're trying to scare each other off. One is tall and thin, his gray coat billowing around him like a cape. The other is short and broad, with a dirty yellow jacket that looks a lot like the inside of an unflushed toilet. Kemple watches the pair argue while an airship roars overhead, the hum of its engine distorting the men's voices, flattening their words into growls and hisses. By the time the dirigible passes, the two men have fallen silent. They nod at each other as if they've reached an agreement, and the man in the urine-colored jacket reaches for a narrow bag on his hip. The other man watches with his chin held high and his arms crossed over his chest—a stance that Kemple knows all too well. Abner used it on him all the time. In fact, the man's face probably looks *exactly* like Abner's right now—the skin around his mouth tense and wrinkled, his eyes narrowed in an impatient scowl.

The mental image makes Kemple's teeth grit. Maybe the yellow-coated man is a former foster child, like him. Maybe that arm-crossed glower is something that *all* foster kids get thrown at them, even after they're all grown up.

Kemple is halfway toward hating the tall man when the yellow-coated man suddenly hands over something small and shiny. Then the two men briskly part ways without saying a word, walking in opposite directions.

Kemple frowns and rubs the underside of his chin against the gutter's crumpled edge. He was hoping for something a little more . . . exciting. A fistfight, maybe, to distract him from the ache in his leg. Or perhaps a foot-chase, just to take his mind off the slow drumming in his veins.

But the yellow-coated man simply disappears around a corner, slipping quietly into the night. Kemple turns to watch the tall man do the same at the other end of the alley, but instead of stepping out onto the street, the man stops and stands there for a moment, his body rigid and still, as if he's forgotten something terribly important. "You can stop hiding now," the man calls out.

Something streaks through Kemple's chest, like a scissor blade dragging across his heart, and he flattens his body against the edge of the roof, making himself as small as possible. The gutter bites the skin of his throat so hard that he's certain it's drawn blood, but he doesn't move. He doesn't even breathe.

Can the man see him? Has he known Kemple was watching all along?

Most importantly of all: is he *dangerous*?

"I don't know why you insist on cowering in the dark," the man says. His long gray coat flutters around him, its thick fabric swishing in the dark. "You have every right to walk the streets. No one will harass you."

Kemple crumples his face. He can think of a few people who'd be *eager* to harass him, actually. Agatha. Abner. Heck, even *Josephyn* would want a word or two with him. Clearly, the tall man doesn't know him as well as he seems to think.

The man sighs loudly, then turns his head and glances back over his shoulder. Kemple tries to see his face, but the distance between them is too large, and the man's features are lost in shadow. Eventually the man shakes his head and says, "Do I have to drag you out myself?"

Kemple's fists clench on their own, his eyes narrowing to slits. *You try it, old man*, he wants to say. *You just see what happens.* But he bites his lip and stays quiet, instead, while a surge of heat rushes through him, like boiling water gushing from a cracked pipe. He has a sudden, violent urge to leap over the roof's edge completely—to surrender himself to gravity, to make the space between himself and the tall man vanish an instant, just so he can do to him the same thing that he did to the stranger this morning: to slash, and tear, and *ruin*. But before he can do anything at all, a new voice catches in the air, its words bent under an accent that's strangely thin and melodic. Feminine.

"Must you always strive to embarrass me?"

Kemple blinks dumbly as a girl steps from the shadows, her slender figure draped in a long overcoat. She walks to the tall man with quick, rigid steps, like an insect closing in on its prey. When she's close enough to touch him—to *attack* him—the man reaches out, wraps an arm around her shoulders, and musses her dark, stringy hair. "I never strive to do any such thing," he says.

Kemple wrinkles his brow until a word fills his head, crowding out his thoughts: *daughter*. The girl is the man's child. Not a foster kid but a real one—bound not just by name, but by *blood*. The realization feels like a splinter in his mind. Like a punch to the gut from the universe. *Here*, it seems to say, *is the very thing that you are not. The very thing that you'll never be.*

Kemple scowls and turns away. The alley isn't interesting anymore. Now it's just more of the awful same: another reminder of how alone he really is. He twists his body and pushes off the gutter, his gaze locking back onto the stranger's pile of rubbish. Maybe he'll arrange it by smell this time, just to do something different. Just to keep himself distracted. But the gutter shudders under him, the metal squealing beneath his weight, and suddenly the whole thing snaps and rips away from the rooftop, yanking him with it, out into the open air.

For a split second, Kemple actually laughs. This couldn't possibly be real. But then the gutter buckles and cracks apart, and suddenly he's falling—*truly* falling. His laugh turns into a yell, all vowels and no words, and he flails his arms and legs, searching for something solid to touch, searching for *anything* to hold onto. The night rushes past him as if the whole city is leaping up toward the clouds, and his thoughts turn from a garbled hum to an ear-splitting screech, his skull all noise and fury. Somewhere beneath the rushing air, the tall man shouts a name: "Viola!" Then Kemple's body flips over and he glimpses the glittering cobblestones rushing up to meet him. He squeezes his eyes shut and braces for the smack of a thousand belt buckles at once—his final, life-ending lashing—and there, seared into the ink of his eyelids, is an image of Josephyn with her eyes downcast, her face tilted away, as if she doesn't want to see what happens next.

Then his body hits the ground, and he waits for the pain of a hundred shattered bones and a dozen ruptured organs, for the agony of his skin tearing and his brain bursting within his own crushed skull . . . but all he feels is coarse fabric and cold metal under his limbs, and the stiff, awkward hug of skinny arms squeezing him against a motionless chest.

He opens his eyes to find himself inches from a girl's slender face—if it could be called a *face* at all. Her cheeks are curved metal plates. Her lips look like twisted ropes. Only her eyes seem vaguely normal—glossy and creamy like a pair of glass marbles, with irises the color of scorched sand. Beside them, tiny gears shudder and twist. Around the girl's features is a crusty halo of black hair, and beneath that: the lowered hood of a grease-stained overcoat. The girl's neck is visible where the fabric is parted, and Kemple eyes the metallic plunge of her throat, so much like the curve of a giant spoon, until the confusing mess in his head twists into something harder and more defined.

He's . . . being held by a *monster*.

The strange, mechanized girl turns her head away and calls out into the darkened alley, "I caught him. He seems unharmed. Though, he saw my face. Shall I kill him for it?"

"No," responds the tall man. "Not yet." A moment later, the man appears behind the girl, his light brown eyes peering down at Kemple from over her shoulder. The man looks nothing like Abner—his face is kind, his expression soft—and for that Kemple supposes he should feel grateful. But he doesn't feel *anything* right now, other than a bone-rattling clench of . . . fear. Of *horror*.

He tries to speak, but only manages a gasp.

"I suspect," the tall man says, his eyes locking onto Kemple's, his lips pulling down into a frown, "that something else is already killing him for us."

Kemple opens his mouth to argue, to *shout*, but the tall man shakes his head, presses a calloused finger to Kemple's lips, and says, "Shh. Now, a question for you: if I had the power to do so, would you allow me to save your life?"

Kemple sputters out a laugh. What kind of ridiculous question is that? "Of course," he rasps—or he tries to, anyway. To the girl and the tall man, his words probably sound like little more than wet air.

"Very well," the tall man says. He offers Kemple a flicker of a smile, then he looks at the girl and nods. "Wipe that frown off your face, Viola. We have ourselves a new project to work on."

Viola scoffs in a metallic way, her arms stiffening beneath the thick fabric of her coat. The ridges of her muscles dig into the soft parts of Kemple's back and hips, and for a brief moment, he wonders if the rest of her is just as cold and angular. Is *any* part of her soft and warm? The question feels unusually large, as if he's trying to stuff a planet into his head, and soon everything about him feels impossibly heavy. His head. His heart. His *soul*—if there even is such a thing. He lets his eyes droop shut, and he listens to the rhythm from two pairs of footsteps: one soft and whisking, the other heavy and clomping. Then even that disappears. His last thought before falling asleep is a single, flailing question: *What would Josephyn do?*

*How would* she *escape?*

But of course, no answer comes. His emerald-eyed friend is gone. Now the only girl in his life is carrying him off to who knows where . . . and she doesn't even seem to be *human*.

# PART TWO

## A HUNTRESS AND A BEAST

# 36

Brielle has been trying to sleep for the past hour or so—*trying* being the key word. Mostly, her mind has been stuck in that foggy realm between asleep and awake, that space where pain and pleasure blend, where sounds seem to warble from an unimaginable distance and the tears welling in her eyes feel like they've been set on fire, as if at any moment one might slip loose and scorch a trail down the side of her face, igniting her starchy sheets and her lumpy mattress and her cramped little apartment, and even the garbage-strewn streets themselves, until the whole city is nothing but a towering inferno and—

The door thuds hard, once, twice, the sound echoing through her dusty apartment, and Brielle bolts upright with her hair matted over her face, her clockwork glove tangled in her sheets. She was dreaming about . . . something. Something involving . . . fire? She rubs at her face with her good hand and tries to pull the dream back into place, but it just slips away even more. Eventually it's gone completely, leaving nothing but a faint quiver in her gut and a vague sense of regret.

"Gone," she whispers with a frown. It's the story of her life—she's become such an expert at losing things.

The door thuds again. This time, the knock comes with a voice. "Gabrielle," says a man. His tone is dry, impatient, and all-too familiar. "Get up. We got problems."

Brielle sighs, uses her wrist to rub the dampness from her eyes, and yanks her glove free from the sheet. It's too early for *problems*. Too early for anything, really. "Shaw," she groans, "I'm trying to sleep." She squints at the violet sky through her grimy living room window and says, "Come back later. You know, when the sun is up? When normal people interact?"

Shaw grunts through the door. "You don't sleep. Said so yourself. And since when do you think of either of us as *normal*?"

Brielle grits her teeth and brushes her hair behind her ears. As always, the man has a point. "Just give me a minute, will you?"

The door stays quiet for a brief, merciful moment, and Brielle lets the silence wash over her until the tightness in her chest eases, the ripples in her mind going flat. Soon, she's back in that clear and level place. Calm as a windless lake.

"Still alive in there?" Shaw barks. "I'm dying of old age, standing here."

Brielle rolls her eyes behind her smudged lenses and swings her legs off the mattress. Her bare feet scuff against the dusty wood floor. "I'm not dressed," she calls out, looking down at her pale nightshirt. She stands and tugs at her gray cotton pants. They're fitting loose today. All these years of climbing up rusted ladders and sprinting across crumbling rooftops, and she still has sticks for legs.

"So *get* dressed," Shaw says through the door. "But make it quick. Like I said: we got problems."

She listens for that telltale *hitch* in Shaw's voice—that tiny warble between his words whenever something has truly upset him. Today, it isn't there. His voice is steady. His words are flat. Whatever the problem is, it's clearly something minor. "Why're you rushing me?" she calls out.

Shaw says nothing back, so she trudges over to her doorless wardrobe and peers at the stretched-out shirts hanging from the rod. The selection is dreary: all blacks and browns and muted grays, the necklines tattered and thin. She plucks the nearest one off its hanger, yanks it down over her nightshirt, and pulls the torn sleeve over her bulky glove. Then she steps to the side and blinks at her reflection in the cracked wall mirror. Her goggled-eyed gaze roams all over her dirt-colored top, as if she's searching for . . . well, she doesn't know *what* she's looking for, honestly. An answer, perhaps? A question? Something out of the norm? Whatever it is, she doesn't find it, so she gives herself a nod. Her shirt is a decent choice. Today feels like a *brown* day, if there ever was such a thing.

"Okay," Shaw calls out, "now I'm definitely dead. Message the coroner. Tell him some poor old man passed away while waiting for a girl to choose an outfit."

Brielle sighs, marches to the door, and wrenches the deadbolt loose. "You're the one who woke *me* up," she says, dragging the door open. "I'm perfectly entitled to make you wait."

Shaw stands in the narrow hallway, looking even more haggard than usual. His hair juts up on one side of his head and lies ridiculously flat on the other. He hasn't shaved in days. And his outfit looks like it was slapped together in the dark—a wrinkled green coat atop a coffee-stained pair of blue trousers. He's even tried to knot himself a necktie. It looks more like a narrow, lopsided scarf. To top it all off, the man is holding one arm mysteriously—no, *suspiciously*—behind his back.

Brielle narrows her eyes to slits. "What's going on? You look like . . ." She tilts her head and looks him up and down a little closer. It's hard to tell *what* he looks like right now. Certainly not like his usual self. ". . . like a carnival spat you out, I suppose."

Shaw smirks at his jacket and smooths a wrinkle from one of the lapels. "That's the look I was going for," he says. He glances back at her and winks. "*Carnival spit.*" Before she even has a chance to roll her eyes, he lifts his hidden arm, revealing a wrinkled paper bag. He gives it a dramatic shake. "Didn't have anything nice to wrap with," he grumbles, "so you'll just have to tear through this."

Brielle blinks dumbly at the bag for a moment. Then she understands. Her face droops and she turns her back to Shaw, as if she can somehow avoid what's coming next by simply walking away. "Let's not do this, okay?"

Shaw clears his throat and shakes the bag harder. "If you don't open it," he says, "I will. Paid good money for this. I'm not letting it go to waste."

She's tempted to say, *Open it, then. See if I care.* But that wouldn't be fair at all. Shaw has been nothing but kind to her. And if he really did pay *good money* for whatever's inside that bag, then she practically *has* to open it. She lived with him long enough to know just how little the city pays him. Long enough to see just how much of a struggle it's been for him to make ends meet. So she groans her way to her lumpy sofa, flops down onto it, and grudgingly says, "Okay. I'll open it. But that's all. No cake. No wishes. And absolutely *no singing.*"

Shaw steps into her apartment and gently pulls the door shut behind him. Then he takes a moment to glance around with that *detective* stare of his. His eyes touch everything: the windows that she never bothers to wipe, the grimy floorboards that've moved so far past dusty that they practically feel carpeted, the furniture that's so battered it's a wonder any of it is still standing at all. And of course, *her.* Finally he reaches for the lantern on the wall and twists it on. A dull yellow glow floods the room. "There," he says, blinking in the light, "that's . . . slightly better."

Brielle clamps her jaw and braces for another one of his grating lectures on *cleanliness.* Instead he merely says, "I've never met anyone who hates celebrating their birthday as much as you."

*Birthday.* The word puts a sour taste in her mouth and an even worse feeling in her gut. Birthdays are for people who *like* remembering how far they've come. For those who *don't* want to forget. "It's just a dumb tradition," she says, waving her clockwork hand in the air. Dust particles swirl around her brass knuckles and stick to the leather straps around her wrist. "Why would anyone be happy about getting *older*? It just means you're one year closer to dying."

And one year farther away from Mom.

Shaw barks out a laugh and turns to look at the window. His profile flickers from the lights down in the harbor. "You're sixteen, Gabrielle," he says teasingly.

"Not ninety." He rests his forehead against the glass and studies the view like he's examining a crime scene. "Take a break. Lighten up. Enjoy the scenery."

Brielle lets her glove plop down on the cushion beside her. More dust plumes into the air. She's been living here for years now, her sixth-floor apartment towering over the dark waters of the bay, yet she can't remember the last time she glanced out the window like that. Just to . . . *look*. Perhaps this is proof that something truly *is* wrong with her.

Maybe staring blankly through dingy panes of glass is the kind of thing that only normal people do.

"Have you ever known me to lighten up?" she asks.

Shaw turns away from the window and shakes his head. "No," he admits. "Can't say that I have."

She cracks a challenging smile. "So why should I start now?"

The detective raises his arms defensively, as if she's got him at gunpoint. "I can list over a dozen reasons," he says, "but then you'll just kick me out."

Her grin widens. "You know me best."

"I do," he says, rubbing at his messy hair. He tosses the paper bag in the air, and they both watch as it lands with a dull thump on the cushion beside her glove. "Which is why I also know that you'll appreciate what's inside."

Brielle's smile fades. *Appreciation* takes energy. Effort. It means being thankful for something that she never even asked for in the first place. She squints at the bag and says, "Can I unwrap it later?"

Shaw sits on the armrest across from her and shakes his head. "Nice try. You already said you'd open it." He taps a calloused knuckle against his temple. "My memory is a steel trap. Sorry, doll—there's no escaping this one."

Brielle is tempted to point out that there's *always* an escape, if you look hard enough. Heck, it's one of the first lessons *he* taught her. But Shaw's face looks fragile right now, his skin too tight and too wrinkled, as if something has been drying him out from the inside for a long time now. As if he's one firm touch away from crumbling apart completely. So she sighs, scoops the bag off the couch, and plunges her good hand inside.

Her fingertips brush against hard edges and sharp corners, and though she doesn't want to guess—doesn't want to ruin the surprise, for his sake—her mind puts words to everything she's touching, anyway. *Wood. Glass. Metal. Fabric.* Already she has an idea of what it might be, but she stops herself from thinking its name. Instead she just frowns and says, "You shouldn't have."

"Nonsense," Shaw mutters. He eyes the bag impatiently and says, "Don't just grope the darn thing. Pull it out already and see."

So she does, grudgingly. And what she sees is exactly what she guessed: a thick, antique-looking picture frame.

Shaw rubs at the stubble on his jaw. "You were always looking at it on my desk. Most of the time, I don't even think you knew that I noticed. And I figured, why keep it empty in my dismal room when it can be put to better use somewhere else? So, *voilà*. Happy Birthday, Gabrielle."

Brielle turns the frame over in her hand and smiles at it, even though the thing just makes her want to frown. This is supposed to be *his*. It *belongs* to him. She can practically feel the memories—his memories—radiating off its coffee-stained edges. "Thanks," she says, stuffing it back into the wrinkled paper bag. "But I don't have anything to put inside it."

Shaw raises an eyebrow. "You think I didn't think of that?" He nods at the bag and says, "There's a card in there, too. Give it a read."

But she just shakes her head. A gift *and* a card? This is becoming too much. "I said I'd open it. *It*. Singular. You already know how much I hate this."

Shaw sighs heavily. "The card is part of the *it*."

"And I'll read the card," she says. "But not now. The frame is more than enough. Right now I'm hungry," she lies, "and if I'm going to make something to eat, I'll need to clean up the mess in my kitchen first."

The detective frowns at her, his stare piercing right through the dark tint of her lenses. He doesn't bother to glance at her kitchen. If he did, he'd see that the countertop and the sink are as bare as can be. But he already seems to know that. "You've always been a terrible liar," he says. "But don't worry—it's a good trait. The *convincing* liars, they're the ones you gotta worry about." The detective stands with a groan. Then he reaches over and musses her tangled hair. "I'll leave you to your moping," he says, "because I know that's what you want right now."

Brielle opens her mouth to argue, just for the sake of it, but Shaw just shakes his head. "It's fine. I got some files to look over, anyway. Just promise me you'll read the card when I'm gone."

Brielle nods and says, "I will." And she means it. Maybe not today. Maybe not tomorrow. But she will, eventually.

"Alright then," Shaw mutters. He pinches the air above his head, like he's tipping the brim of an invisible hat. Then the man who raised her since she was nine quietly leaves her apartment, shutting the door gently behind him.

Brielle watches the closed door while, somewhere inside her, another version of herself feels like it's trying to get out. A younger her. Or at least a less jaded one. The feeling lasts for only a moment. Then it fades away completely, leaving just a hint of sadness in its wake. She sighs and tilts the paper bag until the frame tumbles free, pulling the card out with it.

It's more of a creased page than a card, actually. Brielle recognizes the parchment's dull tint—Shaw had reams of the stuff tucked away inside his drawers.

She unfolds the sheet carefully, using her metal fingertips, and reads the man's slanted handwriting aloud.

> *"I found this inside your file. Been holding onto it for a special occasion. Sweet sixteen seems special enough, don't you think? Now you got somewhere to put it. I'm proud of you, kiddo, no matter what you call yourself. —Shaw."*

Below the words is a photograph—one of those brown-hued, long-exposure shots, where the edges look like swirled mud. Inside the mud is a smiling girl who looks about her age. The girl is clad in a blue-collared shirt. Her hair is thick and golden. Her lips are tinted pink. Instead of looking straight ahead, the girl's eyes are tilted up, her gaze locked on something beyond the picture's edge.

Brielle studies the girl for a long while before it finally hits her: this is *Mom*. Mom when she was *her* age.

Mom when she was still . . . alive.

That old, gritty tide of emotion threatens to surge to the surface again. All that fiery pain and trembling anger. That horrible knot of questions with no possible answers. Before the feeling has a chance to claw past her chest, Brielle stuffs the photograph back into the bag, wraps her geared fingers around the package, and squeezes her misty hand inside her glove until her metal fingers creak from the pressure, until the bag is nothing more than a crumpled wad of trash. Then she squeezes even tighter, locking her glove in place, just to make sure the picture has no chance of ever being smoothed flat again.

# 37

Kemple hammers his fist against the warehouse door, again and again, until the heel of his hand starts to ache. Then he glances over his shoulder and eyes the crumpled bicycle beside him. The thing is chained to a slat on the side of the building, its rusted spokes curled inward, its handlebars bolted to a pair of exhaust flues. He tries to picture Gideon on the seat, the man's narrow coat billowing behind him like a gray sail in the wind, but the image is so ridiculous that he chokes on a laugh. No way would that man ever be caught riding around on a cycle—steam-powered or not.

Which means that the bike must belong to Viola.

Viola, and her face like a rusted carriage grill. Viola, and her stride like a hungry praying mantis. Viola, the copper-veined girl with a hot-blooded temper who's never said a word to him that wasn't laced with anger or disdain.

Of course, when the corrugated door finally slides open, it's *her* sand-colored eyes that blink out at him from the building's shadowy interior. The gears lining her cheeks twist and contract, crumpling her surprised face into a scowl. "*You,*" she says bitterly. "What business do you have here?" Before he says a word, she adds sharply, "Haven't you caused enough trouble already, *monster*?"

Monster. He tries to laugh off the insult, but the word still stings. He *is* a monster. That's why he's here, after all. "I need to see Gideon," he says, avoiding her mechanical stare.

"Of course you do," Viola snaps, wielding that unsettling ability of hers to sound like she's yelling without even raising her voice. "You always need *something*. You're like a parasite—you just keep leeching and leeching." She opens the door a bit more, revealing that familiar raincoat of hers. The fabric so grayed and tattered these days that it looks more like a cape and cowl. Like she's some kind of mechanized supervillain. All she needs to complete the outfit is a mask to cover those inhuman eyes. She tilts her head condescendingly and says, "What happens when Father is gone? What will you do then, *mutt*? How will you function without someone to hold your pitiful hand?"

The question isn't new to Kemple—he's asked himself the same thing countless times. And the only answer he's been able to come up with is a resounding *I don't know*. But no way would he ever admit such a thing to her. Viola doesn't have a compassionate bone in her body—heck, she doesn't have *bones* at all. "I could ask you the same question," he says, meeting her dagger-like glare.

"And what," she hisses, "is that supposed to mean?"

If she wasn't such a psychopath, he'd step through the doorway, spin her around, and slap the iron handle on her back—the one he's seen Gideon wind again and again. The one that keeps that black-metal heart of hers from grinding to a halt once and for all. But Viola is made of iron and serrated wire, of high-tension cables and so much burnished brass. One wrong step, and she wouldn't hesitate to remind him just how fragile the human body can be. So he uses his words, instead. "What will *you* do when Gideon isn't around to wind your heart anymore?" He holds her stare and says, "What happens to a puppet when her strings are finally cut?"

Viola's eyes narrow into two gleaming slits.

He mirrors the look right back at her.

They stay like this for a long, awkward moment, trapped in a blinkless stalemate—neither of them daring to move. Finally, a voice from somewhere behind Viola breaks the tension. "Would you fools cut it out already? I swear, sibling rivalry is a parent's worst burden."

Viola's scowl softens to a frown. "He's only here to complicate our lives further," she calls out.

Gideon responds slowly, his voice dull and haggard. "I . . . welcome complications," he says. "The challenge is refreshing."

Viola lowers her shoulders and sighs in a not-quite human way. Then she opens the door fully and steps to the side, avoiding Kemple's gaze. "If he wasn't here right now . . ." she says, her voice low and threatening.

But Kemple is tired of jousting with Gideon's clockwork daughter. He has bigger concerns on his mind. Worse threats to deal with. He stalks past Viola without saying a word, keeping one hand clutched to his chest, his fingers absently probing the gritty fabric of his shirt. Beneath it, his own metal handle shudders and whirs. And beneath *that*, down in the space where only his heart should be, something cold and dark begins to move.

# 38

Brielle takes a swig of water from the kitchen faucet, slurping straight from the tap. The water is lukewarm and chalky—a taste that she's grown used to over the years—and she gulps until she feels swollen with the stuff, as if this might somehow wash away the quivering guilt that Shaw's so-called "gift" left in her gut.

As if a few mouthfuls of silty water can somehow erase the memory of that awful photograph.

Mom looked happy then. Truly happy. As if she had everything in the world to look forward to. As if she didn't have a single regret. As if she never planned to have a daughter at all.

Brielle coughs on the water and lurches away from the sink, wrenching the faucet shut.

Well, it doesn't *matter* what Mom looked like then. Right now, she looks like a corpse.

Brielle frowns, smears her sleeve against her wet chin, and trudges over to the sofa. Beneath it lie her ragged boots—the last pair of decent footwear she owns. She stuffs her bare feet inside, makes quick work of the buckles, then scoops her leather satchel off the armrest. She checks the bag's contents in a rush, just to make sure everything is still there. Hatchet, poisoned vials, dart pistol, chains. The only tools a girl in Iron Bay really needs.

Satisfied, she heads out the door without a second glance, stopping only once to wrench the key in the lock.

The deadbolt thuds reassuringly into place.

Today, Shaw threw her for a loop. But loops can be broken. *Anything* can be broken with the right amount of pressure.

She may be sixteen now, but Shaw was wrong about one thing: there's nothing *sweet* about her at all. No—today she's out for blood.

# 39

Viola follows Kemple into the gloomy warehouse, her metallic footfalls mimicking his own. Any other day, he'd mock her for it. The jagged clockwork girl, always trying so hard to be human. Always denying what she really is on the off chance that maybe, just maybe, she'll finally get it right.

But today he just . . . doesn't have it in him. Taunting Viola *should* come easily—she's a walking engine part, for heck's sake. What chance does she have of ever becoming a *real* girl? But when he tries to force out the words, his mind just throws up a wall. After all: isn't he here seeking the same thing? A chance to be normal? A way to finally shrug off the curse?

Didn't he come here in hopes of a cure?

"Still in your head, I see," Viola says to his back. "Always muttering to yourself. For such a stupid boy, you sure do think a lot."

Kemple stiffens from a sudden, violent urge to spin around and shake her clattering arms. She's been calling him a *boy* since the day they met. But he's nearly seventeen now. Practically a man. She, meanwhile, is still trapped in that rusting body of a sour-faced ten-year-old girl.

"Struck a nerve, didn't I?" she rasps. "The poor, stupid boy got his feelings hurt."

Kemple finally stops walking. His hands ball into fists.

Viola skids to a halt, too. "Oh, got your knuckles out already?" She clicks her metal tongue in a way that's probably meant to sound disappointed. "Stupid boy, always trying to solve your problems with brute force. Well, come on then. Turn and face me. Throw a punch. See how far it'll get you."

Kemple is about to do exactly that when Gideon's voice swims out of the shadows. "Enough! I tire of this, Viola. You know your duties today. I expect them to be completed by the hour's end."

Viola stammers in protest, but Gideon cuts her short with a booming, *"Now!"*

Kemple winces from the shout. Gideon shouldn't be yelling, not in his condition.

Even *if* Viola deserves it. But then the mechanical girl scuttles away, grumbling to herself, and he can't help but grin. "Don't fall into a vise," he whispers after her. "Would hate to see that ugly face of yours made even uglier."

She spits back a flurry of curses, and he smiles even more.

"My warning applies to you, too, Kemple," Gideon says, his gravelly voice filling the dark hallway.

Kemple holds back a chuckle. A warning from Gideon has always been toothless. The man is everything that Abner wasn't: kind, generous, thoughtful. Come to think of it, he can't remember a time when Gideon ever raised a hand in anger. Not toward *him*, anyway. And certainly not toward Viola. "She's always giving me grief," he tells the man. "She deserves to have some thrown back at her." He flashes a mischievous grin and turns to look Gideon in the eye, but what he sees wipes the smile right off his face.

Gideon leans instead of stands, his weight supported by a pair of wooden crutches. His signature gray coat isn't gray anymore—now the fabric hangs off him like a chalky white veil. His eyes are dark and sunken. His nose looks creased and splotchy. And his skin has become so thin and tight that Kemple can practically see the man's bones.

Gideon doesn't just look sick now—the man looks completely *broken*. Like he's one step away from tumbling headlong into the grave. "Gideon . . ."

The man forces a pained smile, lifts a hand off one of his crutches, and swats weakly at the air. "Spare me the pity," he rasps. "I'm fully aware of how I look."

Kemple fidgets with his hands, then looks away. If the man *really* knew how badly he looked, he'd be in a medic's care right now.

"Enough concern," Gideon says, as if reading his mind. He shuffles his crutches around, making the wooden legs creak. Then he turns and hobbles back toward the shadows, jerking his head for Kemple to follow. "Tell me why you're here, son. I'd say you look well, but we both know that isn't the truth."

Kemple sighs. The last time he saw Gideon in person, the man was leaning over the hood of a carriage, eagerly twisting a wrench. Now the poor guy looks like he can barely stand without falling over. "Where is it now?" he asks the man, as gently as he can.

Gideon stops struggling with his crutches and lets out a ragged breath. "In my blood now. Liver. Kidneys. I . . . suspect my lungs, too."

Kemple doesn't say anything back. It's hard to fathom so much sickness in one frail body. So much darkness in a man who was once a beacon of light. He prods the iron crank under his shirt and tries *not* to remember the day Gideon installed it, but the memories come rushing back, anyway. The blinding lights glaring down on him. Viola's impatient scowl partially hidden under a medical mask. The hardness of the table beneath him, its metal ridges digging sharply into the tender scars on his back. And of course, he remembers the jagged saw that Gideon used to cut him open, its spinning teeth so much like those of a hungry shark.

Kemple hadn't felt any of the pain, at least. In that moment, Viola's love for chemicals stopped being something for him to make fun of. From that day on, he became grateful for it. But he did *feel* the procedure, even though her elixir turned him cold and numb. He felt the tugging, and the shifting, and that horrible, relentless *pressure* as Gideon tethered all those gears and tubes to his heart.

"Perhaps not a permanent fix," the man said, "but this should keep the beast at bay."

Kemple tried to respond then—to thank Gideon, to thank even *Viola*—but his tongue felt like a soggy wad of cotton, and his words came out in a wet, meaningless garble.

It was Viola who responded to him, not Gideon. And her words were characteristically blunt. "You are in Father's debt now, boy," she said, her gear-wrapped eyes clenching, her pupils shrinking to dark needlepoints. "And, for that matter: *mine.*"

The memory falls apart after that. Even the years that followed—all that time spent trying to *fit in* with this new, bizarre family of his—it all seems like a muddled blur now, as if, ever since Gideon implanted that device in his chest, Kemple's mind stopped working properly.

As if the act of stuffing the monster back into his veins somehow ruined his memory, too.

But now . . . now . . .

"I can tell something's not right," he says, trying to put the feeling into words.

Gideon sags on his crutches, then slowly collapses into a leather chair. "You and me both," the man wheezes. He smiles faintly in the dark, the lines of his face going smooth for a moment. Somewhere high above them, deep in the shadowy rafters, a ceiling fan creaks and turns. "I'd offer you a seat, dear boy," the man says, his face tightening again, "but this is the only one I have left."

Kemple shakes his head. "It's fine," he says. "The problem isn't in my legs."

Gideon seems to catch on. His eyebrows jut up. His teeth clamp over his lip. His eyes slide down Kemple's face and catch on the metallic lump under his shirt. "Your crank has begun to fail," the man declares.

*Fail.* The word feels like a towering cliff. Like the peak of some huge, rocky mountain—one that Kemple is about to be thrown off. "The dreams have been coming back," he says. "And I can feel it moving sometimes. Like a shadow inside me . . . trying to get out."

Gideon nods slowly, as if he expected this all along. "Viola's potions are acts of brilliance. She takes alchemy to the level of near-magic. But it's all just science, in the end. And . . ." He winces and gasps, and Kemple watches the pain flicker across the man's face, like a bolt of electricity streaking over his skull, constricting his features one at a time. When it passes, Gideon lets out a trembling sigh and picks up where he left off. ". . . even science has its limits."

Kemple crumples his face. He expected something more. Something . . . *different*, at least. "It sounds like you're telling me—"

"I can't help you," Gideon says quickly. "Not the way you want me to." He looks down at his bony hands and slowly wriggles his fingers. "Had you come to me sooner, I might've been willing to try. But now . . ."

Kemple doesn't need to hear any more. "What about Viola, then?" he tries, but the words sound even *worse* aloud. Viola would never help him—not in a thousand years. Not without Gideon's command. "You could tell her to mix a new batch," he says quickly. Childishly, even. "You could teach her how to use the saw. You could—"

"Kemple," Gideon says softly. The weakness of his voice sounds like a hammer-fall. "I'm dying, my boy. From ashes to the ether. Viola's task, as we speak, is to secure my funeral arrangements."

As if on cue, the warehouse echoes with the sound of Viola's terrible clockwork footfalls, her insectile stride moving closer and closer. When she finally appears beside Kemple, she doesn't even glance his way. Her metallic gaze sticks to Gideon like glue. "It has all been arranged," she says softly.

Gideon nods at her weakly. "Excellent work, daughter. One less . . . complication to worry about."

Kemple opens his mouth to say something, *anything*, but nothing comes to mind. For the first time since they found him, tumbling out of a dirty night sky, he's reminded of just how alone he really is in this world. The three of them aren't a family—not anymore. Now there's only Gideon and his dutiful clockwork child. A pair. A duo. And then there's *him*: the disconnected wheel. The boy who's slowly becoming a monster.

"I need to rest," Gideon whispers, to nobody in particular. "Another . . . fit is coming."

Kemple moves toward the man, but Viola steps in his way—her short, slender body forcefully blocking his path. "That," she hisses, "is your cue to leave, *monster*."

Kemple looks past her, toward the man who raised him since he was nine, but Gideon's face is pinched now, his eyes closed, his features wracked with pain. "I'll come back," he whispers to the man, "if only to say goodbye."

Gideon doesn't respond. Instead, it's Viola who speaks. "That *was* your goodbye, stupid boy." She turns her back to Kemple, strides quickly toward Gideon, and carefully lifts him in her spindly arms. The man sags pitifully against her, and she carries him off into the darkness without another word, her tattered coat billowing behind her.

Kemple stands for a long while, staring blankly into the shadows while the sound of her footsteps fade away. Then he leaves the warehouse slowly, carefully sliding the door shut behind him. The metal clangs, shudders, and goes painfully quiet. Only then does he allow himself to cry.

# 40

Brielle cuts through the city like a blade through spoiled meat. Across sidewalks. Through alleyways. Onto the barren rooftops. She doesn't have any destination in mind—she just wants out. Out of her dismal apartment. Out of her head. Out of . . . everything.

Too bad Shaw's so-called "gift" won't leave her alone. No—now that image of Mom feels branded into her brain. Every time she closes her eyes, there's Mom, looking so young. So hopeful. So . . . horribly naive.

Brielle grits her teeth and shakes her head roughly, as if she can somehow jostle the memory loose. As if the roiling heat in her veins could ever be cooled by a simple jerk of the neck.

If only things could be so easy.

Today, Iron Bay feels extra chaotic. Carriages careen over the cobbled streets. Horses buck and thrash against their restraints. Pedestrians jostle against one another, as if the sidewalks have somehow become valuable property. Even the airships seem to have lost their gentle, whalelike sway—now the sky looks like a wild sea, with every dirigible behaving like a predator on the hunt.

And isn't *that* what she needs right now? A hunt? A furious, primal, blood-to-bone *chase*, girl against monster, human against beast? And not just for the climbing, the leaping, or the lunging—but for that final, thrusting act of plunging her clockwork fist into the chest of a creature that the universe never intended to be. A creature that God would *want* her to slay.

She needs that right now—all of it. It's been too long since her last kill. She made a promise to protect the city, to not rest as long as those demons are out there, to keep searching until every last one has been found, and cornered, and torn open by her gear-wrapped hand. And though the promise was something she merely whispered to the sky—something that not even Shaw knows about—it's still a promise that means something. If nothing else, it matters to *her*.

So she stalks the city like an Aílouros herself, slinking through the trash in the darkest of alleys. Crouching on the most cluttered of rooftops. Twisting her lenses until the world is swollen and bloated, until she can see the frown on every stranger's twisted face, every wrinkle around their red-rimmed eyes.

And then, sometime in the afternoon, when her hunger pains have come and gone and the sun is slowly gliding down the gray wall of the sky, this is when she spots him: a thin young man in a patchy wool coat, with straw-colored hair, mud-brown eyes, and a pair of too-cracked lips. It's the lips that catch her attention: he's the only person for blocks who happens to be smiling.

No—more than smiling. He's *grinning*, like there's something terrible on his mind.

Like he's a monster in disguise. A creature on the hunt.

Brielle's ghostly hand twitches inside her glove, as if her body is eager to get started, and she twists her lenses back to a normal view. The streets expand. The buildings loom. And the young man shrinks down until he's the size of a rodent—like an animal she could end with just a flick of her iron fingers. "Okay, guy," she whispers, leaning close to the edge of the roof. "Let's dance."

The young man moves quickly through the crowded sidewalk, threading a path that looks . . . well, if she's being completely honest, it looks *random*. Pointless, even. Her frown deepens and she wraps her clockwork hand around the roof's gutter, her geared fingers denting the metal. What the heck is he up to?

She studies him as he steps around a woman in a floppy hat. He twirls and walks the other way. Then he stops, nods, and dodges a man in a white coat, spinning around again to face the other direction. Two young girls scamper beside him, laughing and tossing a stuffed rabbit back and forth, and Brielle watches as he eyes the pair with that suspicious grin of his. Then he turns away and strolls off once more.

A few minutes pass this way before Brielle finally gets it: he's not crazy, he's just searching for the perfect victim. A wolf in disguise, looking for the right lamb to sink his teeth into.

For a moment, her concentration falters. Her vision clouds. Her hearing dulls. Her mind fills with a single, unfurling question, like a flower bud peeling apart: if she had the power to go back in time, to somehow glimpse the monster who took Mom's life, to watch the thing in its human form before that horrible act, is *this* what she would've seen? A shifty young man, prowling through a crowd of strangers, his terrible gaze eventually locking onto Mom?

And was she *with* Mom at the time? Did the beast see *her*, too? Did it glimpse her chunky goggles and her prosthetic hand? Did it study the frown on her face? And if so, at what point did the monster make a conscious choice to end her mother's life? Was it a playful flip of Mom's bright yellow hair? A flash of her toothy smile?

Or was it something *Brielle* did, herself? Was *she* the tipping point? Did she grumble something that finally made the monster's head snap forward, its attention zeroing in on them? And if so, what words did she mumble? What did she *say* that led to Mom's demise?

*. . . What the heck did she SAY?*

There's a sound of metal wrenching apart, and Brielle blinks behind her lenses, her attention snapping back into place. She looks down at her clockwork glove and frowns. Between her metal fingers, the gutter has been pinched into shards.

It's not the first building she's damaged because of her guilty conscience. Once, she tore apart an entire roof, stripping it all the way down to the tar. But that was in the early days, when the pain was fresh, the wound still raw. Back before her emotions hardened into the scars they are today.

Back when Shaw knew better than to give her a *Mom*-related gift.

She shakes her head and glances back at the young man on the sidewalk.

But the creep isn't there anymore.

Her body stiffens and she eyes the sidewalk frantically, her gaze flicking from body to body, face to face. None of the pedestrians seem to notice the young man's absence. They frown and glare, their expressions a mixture of boredom and fatigue, like cattle meandering through a grassy field, unaware that a lion was just among them.

The fools.

Brielle is tempted to lean over the edge of the roof and shout to the crowd, to scold them, to *terrify* them, but just as she's about to, something moves quickly in the corner of her vision. She turns and catches a glimpse of the young man's woolen coat as he lunges down an alley at the end of the block.

She'd know that move anywhere—it's the same one *she* uses whenever she closes in on one of those beasts. It's a three-step process, really. Steer the target away from prying eyes. Limit its space to maneuver. Then, move in for the kill.

Which means that the young man has finally chosen a victim.

Which also means that she doesn't have much time—not if she wants to save them. If nothing else, the Aílouroi are certainly . . . efficient at what they do.

She wraps her clockwork hand around the copper downspout and leaps over the roof's crumpled edge. Her steamy fingers contract inside her glove, squeezing all those intricate gears, collapsing all those shifting panels. Metal grinds against metal. Sparks fly between her iron fingers. The muscles in her arm and around her ribs strain against her weight, and she looks at the cobbles as they rush up to meet her. The downspout creaks and shudders all the way down. By the time her boots hit the ground, she's already mid-stride, sprinting toward the alley at the end of the block.

She tucks her satchel against her hip and takes the quickest possible path: a diagonal line, right through the center of everything. Drivers blare their horns. Men curse on the sidewalk. Women gasp and stumble out of the way. A carthorse even tries to kick her when she skids beneath it, but the kick, just like everything else in her life, is too little, too late.

By the time she reaches the mouth of the alley, she's panting and slick with sweat, and the street behind her is in an uproar.

Not like it matters, anyway. She's never been one to fit in; a square peg in a city full of round holes. A freak in a land of normalcy. An . . . exception to the rule. It's the only thing she really has in common with the Aílouroi—in this world, neither of them belong. But at least she's still a *person*. Still a part of the human race. Still willing to *protect* others instead of preying on them.

So when she lunges into the narrow side street, she's not expecting a young man—she's expecting a creature with its fangs already out, its body no longer human at all.

Instead, what she sees is the same young man, with nothing different about him other than a flimsy knife clutched in his fist, the blade cracked and dull. He's cornered a young brunette with large, frightened eyes. Her hair is pulled back, her dress bright and sleek. The girl keeps looking at the dirty bricks around her and shaking her head, as if she refuses to believe that any of this is happening.

"Your purse," the young man growls. "Wallet. Coins. Jewelry. Anything valuable of yours—it's mine now. Scream even once, and I'll slice you ear to ear." He slashes clumsily at the air in a downward stroke, then adds a quick jab, like he's visually punctuating the sentence. *Exclamation point.*

Brielle stops herself from reaching into her satchel and just . . . watches the pair, instead. Mostly because none of this makes sense. Aílouroi never want anything *valuable*. And they certainly don't make demands. All they crave is flesh to tear into. Blood to slurp. Bones to chew and crunch. This creep, however, only seems to want trinkets and jewels. Which must mean that . . . Brielle has stumbled upon a mugging.

A common, plain-as-dirt, daylight *robbery*.

And here she is, poised at the front of the alley with all these monster-killing weapons in her satchel, her blood pumping hard, her body aching for a *war*.

She blurts out a ridiculous laugh, and the two spin around to look at her, their faces stretched with surprise. Then the girl's expression shifts from shock to relief. "Help me!" she says, gaping at Brielle's metal hand. "He . . . he's trying to—"

The young man whirls on the girl, shaking the knife above his head. "I warned you, one peep and you're *cut open!*" He glances over his shoulder at Brielle, looks her up and down, then grimaces in a way that reminds her of snot-nosed kids and crumpled wads of paper, of cramped wooden desks and hallway bells that seemed to take forever to ring, of an endless wave of chest-clenching anger and a horrible boy named Zachariah Wells. "Get out of here, freak," the young man growls. He shakes his head and says, "Or I'll cut *you* open, too."

Normally, she'd laugh at a fool like this. But the brunette reminds her of herself in a way, like the Gabby she might've been if her life had turned out differently. A Gabby from a universe where moms don't die in crowded pantries, and monsters don't exist. And just like that, something inside her falls away. A shroud. A chain. A wall. Whatever it is that separates her from that cloud of rage in her veins, it vanishes in an instant. Her face turns hard. Her limbs blaze with heat. And before the young man has a chance to react, Brielle is upon him, knocking him down, kicking his useless blade away.

The girl shrieks, scrambles away from them both, and disappears around the corner where the alley meets the street, her panicked footsteps vanishing into the din of the crowd. The sound fills Brielle with an odd sense of relief, as if she really *did* just rescue another version of herself. As if now the world has one less problem to be solved. One less wrong to be righted. One less—

"You bitch!" the young man spits, and Brielle blinks just in time to see the creep's calloused knuckles rush toward her face. She jerks away, swinging her shoulders back, but the punch connects anyway, jolting her head back and knocking her goggles loose. The world tilts and reels for an instant, and for that split second, she feels like a little girl again—a tiny, helpless thing in a world that's too big to manage, too menacing to face. Then the feeling is gone, replaced by a rage so hot and scalding, it's a miracle she doesn't burst into flames.

She rams her shoulder into the young man's chest. He coughs and falls back. She pins his biceps under her knees. He shouts and bucks his hips. Her ghostly hand collapses into a point, condensing her iron glove into a leather-bound fist, and she hits him again and again, until his screams turn to gasps and his gasps turn to whimpers, until his face is a ruined mess of spit and bruised flesh and her clockwork hand is dripping with sticky blood, until all the struggle goes out of him completely and he finally just *lies there*, groaning and twitching, looking the way she always wanted Zachariah Wells to look.

Only then does she stop to look around. Only then does she realize what she's done.

Somewhere in the street, the girl's voice rings out, her words thin and rushed. "They're this way!" she shouts. "He had a knife and she . . . she had a *gun* where her hand should've been!" Her words are followed by a flurry of footsteps and shouting voices, and Brielle instinctively leaps to her boots. She grabs onto the nearest fire escape ladder, scrambles up the rungs, and hurls herself onto the building's jagged roof just as the girl's voice reaches the mouth of the alley.

"What the hell?" someone yells.

"Is that the mugger?" shouts another.

"Someone check for a pulse," says a third.

"Oh my God," the girl replies, her voice faint and distant. "Oh my God."

Brielle slouches lower against the copper gutter, hiding herself from view, and she tries not to hear the shock in the girl's reply, the tremble in her voice. The horror in her words. But it's there, just the same. All of it. Undeniably. Impossible to ignore.

For the first time ever, she finally gets it: she's no different from the Aílouroi. Not really. Her and them? They're just two different kinds of monster.

# 41

Kemple trudges to the harbor in a daze. He takes the back routes, meandering behind the abandoned factories, just to avoid being seen. His eyes burn and his cracked loafers scuff out a lonely rhythm against the salt-crusted docks, and though he tries not to think about Gideon's miserable last words to him, they wriggle through his thoughts anyway, like poisonous snakes moving through a field of tall grass.

*I'm dying, my boy. From ashes to the ether.*

It shouldn't come as a surprise—he and Viola both knew this was coming, sooner or later. He just . . . thought it would be *later*. Thought he would have more time.

Thought he wouldn't need to *grieve*.

Is *that* what he's doing right now? Grieving? Mourning for the man who replaced Abner's cruelty with his own unique brand of discipline? Of kindness? Of . . . fatherly love?

Kemple scrunches his face. No—*love* isn't the right word. Whatever he had with Gideon, it wasn't love. *That* the old man saved for his mechanical daughter alone. But Gideon *did* call Kemple his "second-finest creation" once, on a night when Viola was out running errands, and the stars above their warehouse looked like a thousand glimmering insect eyes. The old man drank a bit too much liquor that day—an ugly habit that reminded Kemple of Abner, in the worst of ways. But Gideon wasn't Abner. Booze didn't turn him cruel and violent. Instead it just seemed to . . . flatten him out, like a giant rolling pin, smoothing all his edges. And for a long while, as they waited for Viola to return with supplies from the evening marketplace, Kemple sat beside the old man on the warehouse roof, with their faces turned up to the sky. The man mumbled for a bit, talking about a girl whose name Kemple didn't quite hear—a girl who Gideon wished Kemple had gotten a chance to meet. "Sometimes," the man said, "if I squint enough to erase the seams on her face, if I look away just enough to blur the gears around her eyes, I'd swear Viola was *her*." Gideon fell quiet for a moment. Then he said softly,

"Those are the days, Kemple, when it hurts the most. Like an actual, physical *ache* around my heart."

Gideon stopped talking then, his body shifting noisily inside his starchy clothes, and Kemple only nodded in the starlight, not because he didn't know what to say, but because speaking felt . . . unnecessary. Oh, he had questions, sure. He wanted to know the girl's name. He wondered how Gideon had known her. And, like always, he wished to ask the man why Viola despised him so much. But he stayed silent through it all until finally Gideon spoke again, his voice filled with a thoughtful kind of weight. "Viola is a miracle, Kemple. Life, from an assortment of lifeless things. She is . . . my masterwork. My greatest enduring achievement."

Kemple tried not roll his eyes too hard. If there was one thing he hated about Gideon, it was the way the man always spoke so highly of Viola, as if he couldn't see how spiteful and hate-filled she truly was. As if he didn't realize that he'd created a monster. "I suppose she's . . . an impressive piece of work," he managed to say.

"As are you," Gideon replied. When Kemple said nothing back, the man asked, "Where is the beast right now?"

Kemple didn't have to ponder the question for long. The monster was always there, lurking just beneath the surface of his awareness. Sometimes it was a pressure between his ribs. Other times it was an inky blot of heat behind his eyes. Tonight it felt like a slippery mass behind his lungs. Like a predatory eel searching for food, or a legless fish looking for a way out. "In my chest," he finally muttered. "Under each breath."

Gideon made a thoughtful noise in his throat. "And your crank?"

Kemple thumbed the iron handle through the fabric of his shirt. It still amazed him that this tiny metal object had the power to restrain that animal inside him. "Still working," he whispered. "Miraculously."

"It's no miracle," Gideon replied gently. "Merely science." Then, after a pause that seemed like it would never end, the old man said, "I know I speak highly of Viola, and I know I do it often. But you, Kemple, are my second-finest creation. And a close second, at that."

Kemple smiled then—a big, goofy grin that he hoped Gideon couldn't see. "Thanks," he muttered.

"Hmm," was all Gideon said back.

Viola returned soon after, her steam-cycle sputtering noisily up the road, and the two of them left the roof carefully, without saying another word. The moment was gone. Gideon's buzz had worn off. Now their lives would return to its usual form, with Viola and Gideon behaving like daughter and father, and Kemple being the odd one out. But he was grateful, all the same. Gideon had given him something that Abner never could've: a brief sense of belonging. A touch of concern.

A glimpse of how things might've been if his life had turned out differently—if he'd grown up with a *dad*.

Now, though, none of that will ever happen again. Gideon is dying. And Viola clearly feels like it's her responsibility to shut out Kemple completely. And with the way the pressure in his chest has been swelling lately—like a wall of water shoving against a flimsily locked door—it feels like it's only a matter of time before the crank on his chest stops working altogether. If that happens, the monster in his veins will finally be . . . loose. Unrestrained. *Free*. And he doesn't even want to *imagine* what kinds of horrors that would lead to.

He stops at the edge of the pier and frowns at the choppy waters of the bay. Nearby, a dozen sun-bleached yachts slosh against their mooring lines. In the distance, a buoy clangs somberly. He glances at his own weather-battered boat, his gaze roaming over her grimy windows, her paint-peeling hull, her dark and tattered mainsail. But he doesn't leave the pier. Instead he just stares blankly at his pitiful floating home while a plan unfurls in his head.

So what if Gideon is too sick to help? So what if Viola hates his guts? He knows the warehouse as well as either of them—heck, he lived there for years. He knows where Gideon keeps his tools and his notes. He knows where Viola stores her potions. And he knows that, if he doesn't try something soon, none of this will matter at all. If he doesn't act fast, eventually he'll be . . . *lost*.

"Tonight," he mutters, his eyes tracing the gray curve of the sky. Once the sun is gone, he'll break into Gideon's workshop and find what he needs in the man's chicken-scratch notes. He'll borrow Viola's elixirs, too—the ones she uses for pain. And then, well . . . then comes the hard part. His mind fills with an image of a spinning saw blade, of metal teeth that grind and rip, of tubes that curl and slosh—but he pushes the thought aside. He focuses, instead, on that monstrous quiver inside his heart—that dark, wriggling thing, like a parasitic slug just waiting to be torn away. Then he touches the crank on his chest, pinching the rusted metal through the threads of his shirt.

Tonight, he'll kill the beast inside him, once and for all.

Tonight, he slays the dragon.

# 42

Brielle puts some distance between herself and the alley, leaping quietly from roof to roof. She keeps her mind still, her attention narrowed to a point. One step after another. One ledge after the next. The city warbles and thrums around her, its evening pulse growing stronger with every passing minute, but she tunes it all out until she reaches her apartment rooftop.

Only then does she allow herself to think. To remember. To *feel*.

She didn't mean to leave that young man lying on the cobbles, gasping and bleeding, his face looking like a squashed tomato. She didn't mean to turn a petty mugging into an assault, either. And she *certainly* didn't mean to leave the alley feeling more like a beast than the girl who hunts them.

But . . . that's exactly what happened.

To top it all off, when the brunette came back and saw what Brielle had done, the girl didn't call for a medic. She didn't shout for Brielle to be found, either. She didn't do any of the dozen or so things that Brielle would've expected. Instead, the girl stammered about *God*. As if God had let this happen.

As if God has anything to do with Brielle's unique brand of madness.

And that's what this is, isn't it? *Madness?* A complete and utter mental disconnect from the norm? How many years has it been now? She's been living on the edge of society for so long, hunting creatures that shouldn't even exist. How could anyone do all that and *not* go a little . . . insane?

The thought alone makes her shudder, and she climbs down the side of her apartment building with her misty fingers quivering inside her glove. She's never thought of herself as crazy before. An outcast, sure. A freak, even. But . . . *crazy?* By the time she yanks open her living room window and climbs inside, the word has become a deafening roar in her skull. *Crazy. Crazy. CRAZY.*

She scoops her satchel over her head and lets it fall to the floor with a thud. Then she kicks off her boots, one by one. Finally she unfastens her goggles and sets them on the kitchen counter, angling the lenses toward the front door like a second pair of eyes. Her apartment turns blurry and soft—all those sharp angles bending into curves, all those colors turning splotchy and faint—and she makes her way to the bathroom with her bare gaze fixed on . . . nothing at all.

If she really *is* crazy, wouldn't Shaw have said so by now? Wouldn't he have warned her? Wouldn't he have done *something* to bring her back?

She plugs the drain in the bathroom sink, twists the faucet on, and lets the silty water flood the basin to the lip. Then she wrenches the faucet off, squeezes her eyes shut, and plunges her face into the water, submerging herself all the way up to her ears. The water gushes over the edge of the sink, soaking her shirt and her pants and sloshing against her toes, but instead of coming back up for air, she just grips the basin with her good hand and holds herself under until the water in her ears sounds like an avalanche bearing down, until the pressure in her lungs turns steaming hot, until the darkness behind her eyelids turns white and sparkling and the knot in her head finally unravels into a clear, unbroken line of reasoning. If she really *has* gone crazy, it's not because of Shaw. It's not even because of Mom. No, if she's truly lost her mind, it's because of her awful *hand*—the part of her that she's always avoided facing head on. The piece of her that she's forever wished to be gone. The horrible ghost of a limb that—

Her body lurches for air, that aching need to *breathe* overriding everything, and she tears herself from the water with a violent gasp. She curls around the sink and coughs and gags until the roar in her ears sinks away and that glitter fades from her vision. By the time she recovers, her mind has sharpened, her thoughts condensing to a needlelike point: if she really has gone crazy, there's only one person who can fix it. The only man in her life who ever promised *answers*. The only person in the world who peered at her misty fingers with a genuine smile on his face, as if he *welcomed* her condition. As if he knew just what to do.

She unplugs the drain and waits for the water to slurp away. Then she trudges down the hallway with her wet feet slapping against the floorboards. She scoops her goggles off the counter, latches them in place, and marches to the far corner of the living room where her dust-covered telegraph sits. On most days, the thing reminds her of a broken lamp—something she should've thrown away a long time ago. Right now, though, it looks like a huge, twisted *key*. Like the final piece of a puzzle.

A beautiful, gear-wrapped solution to the misty problem attached to her wrist.

She kneels beside the device, smears some of the dust and grime off its knobs, and cranks the handle until it clicks.

The tubes shudder. The gears whine and whir. Then the contraption settles down, like it's waiting for her to tell it what to do.

According to Shaw, the thing can hold up to four lines of text. For this message, she only needs one.

She taps the lettered keys carefully, gives the handle another twist, then yanks the lever across the wooden base. The machine clatters away, shoving her words through the wires attached to it, and she watches it all through her water-streaked lenses, squinting until she can almost see her message moving in the cables like a tiny ball of light, snaking its way across town. She pictures Shaw's face, too, when he receives her message—his thumb on his lip, his eyebrows crumpled with confusion.

*Can you track down someone for me?*

The telegraph falls silent for a minute. The minute turns to several. Then the machine finally trembles and spits out a thin strip of parchment, with a row of freshly printed words glistening along its edge.

*I'm a detective—what do you think? Just send me the details.*

Brielle frowns and pictures the bald doctor from her youth—the one who taped her hand in a jar; the one *Mom* took her to see—and her stomach lurches until it feels like she's riding a wooden swing. "Now what the heck," she mumbles, narrowing her eyes to slits, "was his *name?*"

# 43

The night comes slowly to Iron Bay. The stars crawl through the clouds. The moon drags itself out from behind the horizon. The sky grudgingly bleeds its color away. It all unfolds in such a sluggish way that Kemple can't help wondering: does the universe know what he's planning to do?

Is it giving him time to reconsider?

He ponders this for a moment, then shakes his head and shoves the thought aside. The universe doesn't care about him. Never has, never will. Which is more than fine by him. Who needs it, anyway?

When has it *ever* done anything good for him?

Really, if the universe has taught him anything, it's that he can only rely on *himself*. Not the stars. Not fate. Not even lock-picking girls who pretend to be your friend, only to leave you in the end.

No, there's just . . . him, and him alone.

He frowns inside his boat's tiny cabin and stares at the empty shelves lining the walls. There was a time, once, when he had the urge to fill those shelves with meaningful things. Cans of beans. Rusted scissors. Books to use as excuses. But eventually the urge faded, and now . . . well, now here he is, staring at a row of shelves that've done nothing but collect dust over the years.

He should probably feel bad about this, but he doesn't. Right now he doesn't feel anything other than a pressing need to get dressed. So he stuffs his battered shoes onto his feet, drags his pants up around his legs, and shrugs on a shirt that's so worn and faded, its gray fabric looks more like bleached chalk. For an instant his mind slips into the past, back to a carpeted store filled with racks of expensive clothes. Back to a time when he wasn't truly alone. He and Josephyn each stole an outfit that day. The one he chose turned out to be a bit too small and too stiff, but he was proud of it all the same. It was . . . *his*. Like he was shedding one more piece of his old life. A snake growing a new husk of skin.

The clothes he's wearing now don't have any of that magic—they're just machine-cut layers of fabric. Impersonal and meaningless. He sighs, tugs on the seams a bit, then leaves the cabin quietly, his shoes thumping dully against the deck. The *Nameless* rocks beneath him, her rickety hull creaking against the sway of the tide, and his eyes catch on the glittering water. Maybe he could just . . . journey out into the waves. Just him, his boat, and the salt-crusted water. He could wrench the sail taut and wrestle with the wheel, let the wind and the sun have its way with him. Let the beast inside him finally do what it's always wanted: to crawl out of his skin. To be *free*.

Perhaps he'd be better that way. Isolated from the world. Alone and adrift. Surrounded by nothing but deep, dark water, on a boat that's one hard jolt away from sinking to the bottom forever.

What would it be like to die on the sea?

He shakes his head again—more violently this time—and finally clambers onto the dock. He checks his pocket, too, just to make sure he hasn't forgotten the one tool he has for the job. The only tool he needs.

The key is just where he left it, tucked neatly inside the fabric of his pants, the weight of it digging against his thigh. The day Gideon made it, the thing looked like a priceless jewel—like some mystical artifact that should only be touched with gloved hands. "This," the old man said, wagging it in the air, "is for you, and you alone. You're part of the family now. And you're certainly old enough to wander on your own." He pressed the key into Kemple's palm, then looked him sternly in the eyes. "Don't lose it. I'll only make the one."

And Kemple *didn't* lose it. Not through all the years he lived in that gloomy warehouse, growing from a boy to a young man. Not through all the ferocious quarrels he had with Viola, either. Not even through all the days he spent crouching on rooftops, scowling down at the city like a gargoyle. He never once came close to losing the key, because the key meant *home*. It meant that, somewhere in this cold, gray world, he actually *belonged*.

Which is probably why the key feels so much like a *knife* right now. Like a tiny, hooked dagger, ready to be plunged into Gideon's back. A betrayal just waiting to happen.

He frowns, adjusts his pocket until the weight of the key isn't so noticeable, then heads off toward Gideon's with his jaw clenched tight, the crank on his chest shuddering with every step. By the time he reaches the warehouse, the night has settled over everything like a salt-flecked sheet, smothering the city in darkness. The pressure in his chest has swelled, too. Now it feels like an impossible weight—like a huge furred body weighing him down from the inside.

Like too much animal muscle trapped inside not enough skin.

For a long while, he simply peers at the dirty walls of the building where he spent so much of his youth, his eyes scanning every grimy window, every twisted hinge, every rust-stained rivet and bolt. Tonight, none of it looks familiar. It's a small mercy that he doesn't question.

He'd rather feel like he's breaking into a stranger's house than the home of someone who once cared for him—even if the feeling is just an illusion.

He pauses at the metal door just long enough to listen to the silence behind it. Then he pulls the key from his pocket, slips it into the lock, and twists his wrist until the tumbler clicks. The sound echoes in the damp night air, ricocheting off the nearby buildings, and he winces at the heaviness of it all—that thick, indelible *weight*, not just of the noise, but of the whole moment itself.

Once he opens this door, there's no turning back. He'll be in it, come hell or high water.

He takes a deep breath, slides the door open, and quietly slinks inside. He moves quickly in the dark, prowling across that familiar concrete floor, sneaking between those rusted shelves, weaving a path through the same cluttered space that he's strolled through so many times before. Tonight, everything feels a little tilted. A little . . . off. Like he's wearing someone else's spectacles, or looking through a different pair of eyes. He supposes it makes sense. He's a *stranger* now, eyeing things that don't belong to him. An outsider, wandering through a place where he doesn't belong.

Is this how Viola sees the world? Is this why she's always so full of . . . rage?

He shakes his head and keeps moving, ducking past a broken table, stepping over a heap of stray tools. Viola's state of mind is the last thing he needs to be worrying about right now.

He sneaks deeper into the warehouse, passing beneath the darkened rafters, stopping whenever a stray gust of wind whistles through the cracked windowpanes. By the time he reaches Gideon's workbench and finds the man's ragged notebook, his nerves feel like a web of frayed wires. He tucks the booklet into the waist of his pants, nestling it against the small of his back. Then, because his heartbeat refuses to ease, he mutters, "Calm down." As if *that* ever worked for anybody.

He scoops whatever tools are in reach off the warped table—locking clamps, rusted scissors, that horrible saw with teeth like a hungry shark—and bundles them all into the bottom of his shirt. Then he makes his way to Viola's storage room as quickly as he can. Unless she's changed the way she does things, her numbing potions should be sealed in dark amber jars.

For what he's about to do, he'll probably need several.

The door to the room is open, as expected, its interior draped in shadow. He steps lightly through the doorway, then stops abruptly, nearly dropping the tools.

Viola is standing in the center of the room with her arms crossed, her face taut with anger, her eyes fixed menacingly on his. Behind her, the elixir-filled jars glint teasingly inside a glass cabinet. So close, yet so out of reach. "It's about time," Viola rasps. The gears around her eyes constrict with an audible click. "Honestly, I was starting to worry that you'd be too much of a coward to show up."

Kemple hesitates in the doorway. He could escape right now. Could throw the tools at her if she tries to stop him. He could barrel out through the front door and never come back. But what good would that do? He'd still have that horrible beast inside him, straining to get out. And if he ever decides to break in again, Gideon will have surely changed the locks.

No—there's only one way out of this: he'll have to go *through* Viola. She may be made of iron and brass, but she's still just a girl in a child's body.

Just a bratty clockwork *kid*.

He steps through the doorway and tosses the scissors, the saw, and Gideon's notebook onto the cement floor. Not the locking clamps, though. Those he keeps clutched in his hand, like a mallet ready to swing. "How'd you know I'd come?"

"You're a stupid boy," Viola says flatly, as if this explains everything. Her eyes flick down, and her gaze locks onto the clamps in his grip. Her scowl hardens. "Stupidity is predictable."

Kemple matches her glare. A dozen comebacks spring to mind—most of them insults—but what finally slips through his clenched teeth is a question: "Why do you hate me so much?"

Viola pauses, her grimace faltering, and for an instant she almost looks like a normal girl—her eyes wide and unblinking, her bangs hanging limply over her forehead, her lips clamped into a thin, determined line. If he didn't know better, he'd think she was just a small, delicate thing. The kind of clockwork child that Gideon probably had in mind when he decided to build her. A mechanical sweetheart, full of nothing but gears and unquestioning love.

The illusion doesn't last long. Soon her face contracts, pinching all the innocence right out of her features. She tugs on the hem of her hooded coat and takes a menacing step toward him, her iron foot clacking against the cement. "You inserted yourself into Father's life without permission," she says. She takes another heavy step forward. "You absorbed his generosity without offering anything in return." She puffs out her chest and stalks even closer. "You took and you took, and whenever my back was turned, you deceived and manipulated Father, wriggling closer to his heart like some horrible bloodworm." She pauses, then takes one last step, finally closing the distance between them, the edge of her coat brushing against his shirt. If she could breathe right now, he'd be able to feel every angry pant of hers. Instead, the air in front of her remains still. The only sound in the tiny room comes from under the iron framework of her chest—the steady whir and click of her geared heart.

The noise is like a whisper. Like a threat.

"Why do I hate you?" she growls. She stares at him unflinchingly, her pupils contracted into pinpoints. "Because all you've ever done is try to take Father from me."

This . . . is not the answer he expected at all. He expected *jealousy*, sure—he's human, she's not. Of course she'd despise him for being a living, breathing thing, when she was merely assembled in a lab. And why *wouldn't* she hate him for it? He's done nothing but rub it in her face since the day they met—since the moment she asked Gideon if she could kill him. But to hate him *because* of Gideon? Because of some twisted belief of hers that he somehow wants the man for *himself*? "That's the most ridiculous thing I ever heard," he says, spitting the words right at her gear-wrapped face. He takes a step back, just to put some space between them, and adds, "I don't want Gideon any more than you want me."

Viola prowls forward, closing the gap between them again. "Then you're an even stupider boy than I thought," she snarls. "You *should* want Gideon, after everything he's done for you—none of which you deserved."

That cold, dark spot around his heart starts to tremble, and he squeezes the clamps against his palm. He's running out of time—he can feel it slipping away, one blood cell at a time, like sand grains spilling down an hourglass. "I'm done arguing with you, Viola."

He tries to shove past her, but she holds her ground. Stubbornly. Solidly. Like a girl-shaped lead weight, she grinds her feet against the cement and lifts her face challengingly. "And *I'm* done letting you use Father," she says. "Or me. Or anything that belongs to us." When he tries to sidestep her, she matches the motion, blocking his path once more. "That means no more of our tools," she grumbles. "No more of my potions. No more *anything* for you, stupid boy."

Kemple bites his tongue, but his words spill out anyway. "I'm slipping away, Viola! One lousy heartbeat at a time. I can feel it moving closer to the surface every day, straining to get out. Straining to . . . to . . . I don't know. To do something horrible."

Viola's expression doesn't change, not even by a millimeter. "Why should I care what happens to you?"

He falls silent, not because he can't think of a reason, but because none of the reasons seem to *matter*. Why *should* she care what happens to him? When has she *ever* cared about him? The only person in the world that she cares about at all is . . . is . . . "Gideon," he says softly.

This finally gets a response from her—her eyes flaring, her unnatural lips pulling back to reveal those too-perfect teeth. "What about him?" she growls.

"If the monster in me ever gets out," he says, "who do you think it'll go after first? Some random stranger? Or the man who built the device that kept it locked away all these years?" It's a bluff if he's ever said one. All theory and no proof. Who knows what the beast in his blood truly wants? Who knows if it's even *aware*?

Really, all it's been to him is a knot of pressure and a wave of cravings—a dark, relentless urge to hurt and maim. To *kill*.

But Viola doesn't know any of that. And with the way her face changes—her brow lowering, her lips curling back, the spark in her eyes turning bright and fiery—it's clear that the bluff hits home. "How *dare* you threaten Father," she says, her voice as dark as ever, "after all he's done for you?"

It's a valid question. If Gideon were here, Kemple wouldn't have a reasonable answer. But Gideon *isn't* here. And when it comes to egging Viola on, reasonable answers are a lot less effective than good old-fashioned spite. "I'm not threatening your old man," he says. This time, it's his turn to invade *her* personal space. He leans forward, crowding her until she grimaces and moves back. Then he says flatly, "I'm threatening *you*."

"With what?" she says, sneering at his hand. "A rusted tool?" Her eyes meet his and her mouth quirks into a bitter grin. "Help you or you'll clamp me to death?"

He's tempted to point out that, technically, she needs to be *alive* in order to die—but they've danced around that confusing topic before. So he goes for the direct route, instead. "I'm threatening you with *guilt*. With responsibility. With the fact that I'm asking you to help me while you still can. Otherwise, who knows what might happen? Who knows what you can *prevent*?"

Viola studies him with those creepy eyes of hers, and for a moment it seems like she's actually considering his words. He imagines the tiny gears in her head churning and grinding—her thoughts streaking like lightning bolts through the tangled wires in her skull. But then her expression clouds, and he can already guess what's coming next. "I can prevent you from ever being a problem in our lives again," she says. This time when she steps toward him, it's clear she doesn't plan on stopping.

"So, that's it then?" he says, gripping the clamps tighter. He moves back into the doorway, just to give himself more space to maneuver. "Negotiations are over?"

"You've always wanted your shot at me," she says, curling her sleeves up over her forearms. "Now's your chance to take it." She flexes her hands, contracting the brass coils around her wrists. Then, with a voice that almost sounds like a human whisper, she rasps, "But you better not miss, stupid boy. Father won't show up to save you this time."

She's right about one thing: he *has* always wanted to take a shot at her. Not to put her down, of course—but to simply wipe that smug scowl off her metal face, if only for a little while. That was then, though. Before the crank in his chest began to fail. Before the elixirs in his blood turned thin and watery.

Before the creature inside wanted *out*.

"A few of your painkillers," he says, showing her his bare palm. "That's all I want.

I've got everything else I need." When she doesn't respond, he adds, "Consider them a parting gift. I'll take them and be gone. Your way to get rid of me forever."

Her frown turns into a dark, mischievous smirk—one that puts a shiver in his spine. "I know a better way to get rid of you forever," she says. She pauses, just long enough for her words to sink in.

Then he watches as Gideon's clockwork daughter, the almost-girl who caught him in that alley all those years ago, lunges for his throat.

The irony is almost beautiful: the mechanical being that saved his life is now leaping toward him to *end* it. It'd be enough to make him laugh—if it wasn't so disturbing. Instead, he instinctively swings the clamps at her.

Metal clangs against metal, the impact jolting the bones in his wrist, and Viola's head snaps back. Her outstretched fingers scrape at his jaw as she stumbles past him, off-balance. She twists her torso back toward him, pivoting her body in an inhuman way, but her ankles cross and she clatters to the floor, her shoulder crunching through the doorframe. Wood splinters and chunks of plaster rain down on her wiry hair, and she shakes them off with a mechanical jerk of her head. "You're a rat in human skin," she snarls. "Gideon can't see it, but I can." She climbs back to her feet and squares her shoulders, blocking the doorway with her tiny iron body. "And when I'm done with you here, he'll finally see it, too."

She's probably right. He can't think of an excuse that would fool Gideon at this point, not after everything that's happened. He broke into the man's warehouse in the middle of the night, with a key that should've been returned long ago. He stole the man's notebook, too, and swiped a few of his tools. Now he just smacked the man's clockwork daughter in the face with a set of metal clamps. Heck, she could call him worse than *a rat* right now, and she'd be completely justified in doing so.

But it takes two to tango. If she had just *helped* him instead of arguing with him, if she'd just given him the elixirs like he asked . . .

The pressure in his chest twists and drags, like a sticky ball rolling around his heart, and his thoughts shrivel up like burnt leaves. It doesn't matter what Viola *should've* done. What matters is that her potions are still there, tucked behind that glass, just waiting to be taken.

He whirls around and lunges for the cabinet before she has a chance to react.

Viola lets out a surprised yelp, then clambers after him—her coat rustling, her feet clomping, the gears in her legs whirring and whining. Everything about her movement sounds *panicked*, reckless, and he has a fleeting urge to turn around and taunt her for it.

So much for the girl who always acts like she's in control.

But now isn't the time to heckle. He grabs the burnished knob on the cabinet door and flings the thing open so hard the glass fractures against its wood frame. Then he grasps at the nearest jar: a short, squat thing the color of burnt syrup, with a glob of silvery liquid inside. His fingertips brush the dark glass. His thumb grazes the lid. Then his shirt tightens around his neck and he's yanked backward so forcefully, his shoes lift off the floor.

This isn't the first time he's scuffled with Viola—but it *is* the first time she's pulled him off the ground. The first time she's used her actual strength.

Suddenly a pair of locking clamps doesn't feel like nearly enough. But it's all he has, so he swings the things behind him until he connects with something solid—her arm, maybe, or that scrawny neck of hers. Whatever it is, it's enough to make her curse and let go of his shirt, and he falls hard to the floor. The impact knocks the breath out of him, but only for an instant. Then he's up and moving, scrambling for the cabinet once again. If he can just get *one* jar, maybe that'll be enough to dull the pain so he's not flat-out screaming when he finally cuts through his skin and—

The air around him shifts, like it's being shoved by something huge and monstrous, then Viola is upon him once again, her narrow body pressed like a blade against his back. Her arm wraps around his throat, the gears in her elbow contract with a violent click, and his neck stops being a neck—now it's nothing but a knot of pain. Suddenly the jars don't matter anymore. Neither does the device around his heart.

No, all that matters right now is that a mechanical arm is choking the life out of him.

"Viola," he gasps, "don't!" He tries to pry her arm away, but Gideon built her like a tank—he'd have better luck trying to pull a steam engine apart with his bare hands. "This," he says, pushing his words out in a hiss, "isn't the way!"

But her grip only tightens, squeezing his windpipe and filling his vision with sparks. When she speaks this time, her voice comes out in a whisper, her mouth mere inches from his ear. "This is the *only* way." Her next words are barely audible, like silk rustling in the wind. "Goodbye, stupid boy."

Kemple closes his eyes and waits for the moment everyone talks about whenever death is mentioned: that brief, fleeting instant where a person's life flashes before their eyes. He braces for a glimpse of Abner's ugly face. He prepares for a slow-motion replay of the first time he looked into Josephyn's eyes. He even waits to be reminded of the things he's long since forgotten, like the sound of his mother's voice when he was finally pushed out of the womb. Was she screaming then? Crying?

Did she *regret* bringing him into the world?

None of that happens, though. Instead an angry, rasping voice echoes throughout the room. *"What on Earth is the meaning of this?"*

The question makes his eyes snap open, his body going stiff. Gideon. He tries to twist around to look at the man—to apologize, to *explain*—but Viola's grip is like a vice, pinning him in place. The only thing he manages to do is let out a pitiful wheeze.

"Father," Viola says, "I caught him. He broke in with the intention of stealing our properties. Even admitted it himself."

The silence that follows is more painful than Viola's arm. Kemple doesn't even need to see Gideon to know the hurt and disappointment creasing his face. "Is this true, son?" the old man whispers. "Have you returned just to betray me?"

When Kemple doesn't answer—*can't* answer—Viola adjusts her grip, giving his throat just enough room to breathe. He instinctively gasps for air.

Gideon waits until he's done panting, then repeats the question more forcefully. "Is it *true?*"

Kemple wants to deny it, to find the right combination of words that bends the truth *just enough* to put the blame somewhere else. But he knows that the moment Viola spins him around, the *instant* his eyes meet Gideon's, the man's withering gaze will burn right through him. And any lie he's told up to that point—well, it'll just crumble apart.

So he simply says . . . nothing at all.

Viola gives him a painful shake and growls, "Father asked you a question, stupid boy."

But he stays quiet. Because silence is the only weapon he has left.

Gideon lets out a tired sigh and says, "Let me see his face."

Viola grumbles something—a mutter that sounds like the grinding of gears—and then she does what Kemple would never expect a mechanical girl to do: she makes a mistake.

For a split second, she lets him go.

The moment doesn't last long. And the space between her arm and his throat is so slight, he can still feel the rough fabric of her coat brushing his skin.

But it's enough.

He leaps up, jams his shoes against the edge of the cabinet, and shoves himself backward with a strength that isn't his alone—a strength that comes from some dark, deep place between his veins. A strength that feels more animal than human.

Viola's body goes rigid against him—all those cogs and pistons snapping into place, every cord and sinew resisting his weight—but the power in him swells, shoving against his skin, and she finally loses her balance, stumbling back and away.

He falls to the floor, free and unrestrained.

Then Gideon makes a sound that Kemple never thought he'd hear from the man: he screams. Shrilly. Agonizingly.

Kemple rolls to his side and looks at the doorway just in time for Viola to block his view. Her movements are quick and jerky, like a puppet on electrified strings, but then she puts her back to him and crouches at the doorframe, and he immediately understands.

Gideon. He knocked her into *Gideon*.

"No," she hisses. "No, no, *no!*" She lowers her head to look closer at the old man, and here Kemple sees everything. The blood on the floor. Gideon's trembling hands. The splintered chunk of the doorframe sticking out of the man's chest. Gideon coughs and gags, and when he tries to speak, his words come out in a sickening gurgle.

Kemple squeezes his eyes shut and looks away, but that only makes the sound of the man's suffering that much worse. He hears every hack and sputter. Every scuff of the man's polished shoes. Every whimper and sob coming out of Viola's iron-wrapped throat.

Then the room falls eerily silent. When Kemple looks up again, he finds Viola staring back at him, her face slick and taut, her marbled eyes quivering with dark, oily tears. Gideon is limp in her arms, his eyes closed, his chest glistening with blood, and the whole scene looks so final and permanent that Kemple can hardly believe *he* was the cause of it all. That he made this happen.

That *he* took Gideon away from this world.

"Monster," Viola says, and Kemple doesn't even try to argue. Of all the insults she could throw at him, this one seems the most accurate. She pulls Gideon's body close to her little-girl chest, as if her touch might somehow comfort him, and for an instant it looks like their roles have reversed: the child becoming the parent. The old man reverting to an infant.

All the while, Viola's unblinking eyes never look away from Kemple's. "Beast," she growls. "*Demon.*"

Her words stab into him, slicing his insides in a way that a knife never could. The beast strains against his heart, too, thrashing to be free, but he presses the feeling down until it's nothing but a cold, flat line under his ribs. Then he staggers to his feet and stumbles through the doorway, stepping over Gideon's sprawled legs. He makes sure not to look at the man—he can't handle seeing what he's done. Even a *glance* at Gideon's wrinkled face would be enough to break him right now.

Viola scowls up at him with a look that could melt the sun, and all he can think to whisper is, "Sorry." Of all the useless things to say, *this* is what he comes up with. *Sorry.*

Viola doesn't say a thing. She just keeps staring at him, drilling her hateful glare into his skull until he turns away and trudges back the way he came, maneuvering through the cluttered warehouse like a rat that's just escaped a trap. Only when he reaches the front door, and gently slides it open, does she finally speak, her voice thundering throughout the warehouse. "I'll find you, stupid boy," she calls out.

Her words are gravelly and trembling with emotion. "And when I do, I'll ram my arm through your worthless chest and rip out your blackened heart."

Kemple ducks through the doorway and slips into the night without uttering a word back—not because there isn't anything to left to say . . . but because he fully believes her.

# 44

Brielle spends a good ten minutes racking her brain before she's finally forced to admit it: she can't remember the name of the doctor from her childhood. So she types *other* details into the telegraph: the part of town where the man's office used to be. The shape of his bald head. The way the carpets in his office looked like sun-dried mud.

The telegraph goes quiet for a while afterward, and the longer the silence lasts, the more her brow creases. What if Shaw wandered away on his end?

What if she's typing to *nobody*?

But then the machine shudders and spits out a short response, and she nearly leaps to her feet. She quickly scans the message through her water-streaked lenses.

*6294 Ivory Lane.*

She's never heard of the place. But no matter. *Someone* in this city must know where it is. She tears the paper off, stuffs her damp feet into her boots, shrugs her satchel on, and hurries out of the apartment.

How could she have gone so long without doing this? Even with only the vaguest of details, Shaw managed to find the doctor's address in a matter of *minutes*. And to think, she could've met with the man years ago. Could've asked him to treat her. Heck, he might've even found her a *cure* by now.

It's enough to make her want to scream.

But right now she needs to focus. She still has to *get* to the address, first. Then she can pity herself all she wants—she already spent her childhood mastering the art of it.

The night air feels especially heavy, even for Iron Bay. Like it's full of potential. She takes a steadying breath, steps into the glow of the nearest streetlamp, and waves her clockwork glove until a dull green carriage pulls up, its engine coughing out pink steam and gray smoke. The driver leans out the window and narrows his eyes at her, the rest of his face hidden under a red kerchief. "Where to?" he says flatly.

Brielle hands him the paper without letting go of its ragged edge. "Do you know this address?"

The man eyes her the same way everyone else does: like he doesn't know what the heck he's supposed to be looking at. Then he squints at the paper in her hand. "Halfway across town," he says sourly. "You got the money for it?"

She doesn't, no—but she nods anyway, and a minute later they're clattering down the darkened road. She catches the driver scowling at her through the mirror, his sour gaze roaming all over her clockwork hand, and she stuffs the glove under her satchel, just so he won't have anything to look at. The rest of the ride she spends slumped in the coach's back seat with her goggled eyes fixed on the telegraph paper, as if the address printed on it is some sort of code, hiding a wondrous secret.

"*6294 Ivory Lane*," she mutters. She doesn't know the street, but it sounds promising. Like something out of a fairytale. She imagines castles with darkened moats, towers made of glass, and cottages wrapped in magical spells, until the coach finally squeals to a stop. "We're here," the driver grunts.

She glances out the window and frowns. Ivory Lane looks like any other street in Iron Bay: worn down and dirty, the pavement riddled with cracks. Even the house at the end of the curb looks dismal—its gray siding sloughing off, its walls sagging at the edges. Above the white front door, someone has painted the numbers *6294* in thick, red ink. It makes the address look like a warning.

*Beware.*

Her frown tightens and she looks away from the glass, meeting the driver's squinty gaze in the mirror. "Are you sure this is the right house?"

The man scoffs under his kerchief and glances bitterly at the road. "Big, ugly goggles like that. Surely you can *read*, can't you?"

She has a brief, fleeting urge to raise her clockwork hand and drive it down into the cushion beside her—to do the same thing to the man's carriage that she did to Shaw's couch all those years ago. But she clamps the feeling down and exits the carriage slowly, wrenching the door open with her clockwork fingers, hard enough to make the handle twist and bend.

Let the jerk find the damage later.

"Hey!" the man calls out, just as she's slamming the door shut. "You forget something? You don't get a free ride just for being a freak."

The urge to do something violent comes back, and this time she doesn't fight it. She lunges around the carriage and pushes her goggled face right into the man's open window. "Say it again," she snarls, shoving the words through her clenched teeth. "Call me a freak." She raises her gloved hand for the man to see, balling it into an iron fist. "I *dare* you."

The man shrinks away from her, his eyes wide and veiny, and he yanks the carriage into gear so suddenly that the engine makes a grinding sound. Smoke billows out from the grill. The whole vehicle sputters and shakes. "Find your own way back!" the driver yells. Then the coach lurches away from the curb and clatters down the darkened street.

She watches it go with her shoulders hunched, her glove still clenched into a fist. She should've done more to damage the cab—the guy deserved worse. But at least she didn't have to pay. As for what he said—so what if she's stuck here? Surely the doctor has a vehicle of his own. He could give her a ride back home—*after* looking at her steamy hand, of course.

*After* whipping up a cure.

For the first time in a long while, she finds herself smiling. Actually *smiling*. But then she turns around to get a better look at the house, and her smile falters. The paint isn't just cracked and peeling—it's all but torn away. The windows are in even worse condition: every pane is cracked and smeared, or just plain missing altogether, revealing an interior as dark as ink. And the lawn is so overgrown with weeds that she can't tell where the walkway used to be, or if there ever was one at all.

The place doesn't just look shabby—it looks downright *abandoned*.

She glances at the slip of paper in her hand and lets out a ragged sigh. Of *course* the doctor doesn't live here anymore. Of *course* it's just another dead end. Why did she expect anything different?

When in her life have things *ever* been easy?

She kicks at the curb with her boot, and the concrete is so old and cracked that it actually crumbles apart. So she kicks at the shards, too, scattering them over the street, but the heat in her chest keeps simmering, like water boiling in a pot. Like wood chips and coal being torched in an oven. Finally, she can't take it anymore. She grabs one of the rocks with her good hand, whirls around to glare at the empty house, and hurls the debris at the nearest window. The glass shatters inward, the sound echoing down the street, and she waits for the pressure in her veins to ease, for the heat to dwindle away.

It doesn't. It grows instead, spreading through her like a wildfire, igniting her bones and muscles and scorching her skin until she has to *move*, until she can't *not* move, and suddenly she's storming over the curb, stomping through the weeds, and leaping onto the house's battered porch. Up close, the building doesn't just look pitiful—it looks like it's *taunting* her. This ugly, useless home with its blood-red numbers and its dirty, crooked walls. This worthless waste of space. She gnashes her teeth and grabs at the house with her clockwork hand, squeezing her misty fingers throughout the glove's gears until the porch beams crunch between her brass fingertips and the doorframe shatters under her iron palm. Paint chips and wood splinters rain down around her, and somewhere on the desolate road behind her, a carriage screeches to a stop. But *she* doesn't stop. She keeps wrenching and tearing, hitting and clawing, bashing and snarling until a man's voice bellows into the night, his tone rough and sharp. "Hey! *Knock it off!*"

She stops and scowls at the damage she's done—damage that she hasn't *finished* doing—and two words burn through her mind: *the driver.* Of course he'd come back to demand payment. As if her night isn't already ruined enough. She whirls around, fully expecting to see the kerchiefed man standing in the street with a menacing friend by his side. Or perhaps with a weapon clutched in his hands.

But the man she locks eyes with isn't the driver at all—it's Shaw.

Shaw, climbing out of a police carriage. Shaw, grimacing at her in the way that only a disappointed father could.

Her face grows hot, and even though he can't see her eyes through her lenses, she finds herself avoiding his gaze.

"Soon as I sent you this address," he says, slamming the driver's door and step-ping onto the curb, "I learned that this house has been empty for years." He glances at the broken porch around her and lets out a tired sigh. "Should've known you'd rush over here without waiting to hear more." He pins his eyes to her lenses, and his frown darkens. "Empty or not, you don't have a right to damage this property."

The anger is still smoldering inside her, bubbling like froth in the spaces between her muscles, so when she speaks, her words come out like claws. "Is this what you came here for? To lecture me? Because I can do without it, thanks." She glances down at her glove and spots a small clump of plaster stuck between the gears around her knuckles. She curls her fingers until the cogs whine and twist, crunching the debris into powder. "I'm sixteen now," she says, watching the dust fall to the porch. "I live on my own. You don't have to look after me anymore."

"Oh," Shaw says casually, "is that what this is? You flexing your independence?" He strides slowly through the tall grass, like he's in no hurry at all. Like he didn't just catch her in the act of attacking an empty home. "Let me tell you, Gabby— you've got one twisted idea of what it means to behave like an adult."

Gabby. The name alone makes her teeth grit. Gabby was weak. Gabby was a *coward.* Gabby let Mom slip away. "I don't go by that name anymore," she snaps. "It's *Brielle* now." She flexes her clockwork fingers and studies her knuckles, just to make sure the gears are clean. Then she looks up at him and adds, "I'm no longer a dumb little girl."

Shaw chuckles and points at the fractured porch around her. "Really? Could've fooled me."

The man has a history of annoying her, but he's never once gone far enough to actually *piss her off* . . . until now. Her hand flares inside her glove, like it's eager to crunch through something harder than old wood and plaster. Like it's hoping to break some *bones.* "Just get out of here, will you?" she says, stalking off the porch. "You leave me alone, and I'll leave the stupid house alone. Deal? Then everyone's happy."

Shaw shakes his head in a slow, sad way. "What were you thinking would happen here? That you'd find the doctor? That he'd restore your hand?" His gaze slides down to her dust-covered glove. Then he says quietly, "There's nothing about you that needs fixing, Brielle."

She scowls and storms past him, avoiding not just his eyes, but his entire body. What would he know? What would *anyone* know about what it's like to be her? "Thanks for the pep talk," she says, with as much sarcasm as she can muster. "It's exactly what I wanted to hear."

He reaches out and grabs her elbow, stopping her just before she reaches the curb. When she spins around to glare at him, he says gently, "Just wait. There's another reason I came here."

"What?" she says, yanking her arm free. "Something else about me that you want to criticize?"

"If I ever criticize you for anything," he says grimly, "it's because I know you're capable of doing better."

She tries to think of a reply, but nothing good comes to mind. In the end, all she manages is a grunt. "So why come here, then? Just to check on me? To make sure I'm looking both ways before crossing the street? To ask if I'm taking my vitamins?"

Shaw grins in a tired way. "Those *are* things worth worrying about, actually," he says. "But no. I came here because there was a disturbance in the warehouse district tonight. An investigating officer found a property with its door wide open and . . . a body inside, still warm." His voice drops to a whisper and he leans in close. "There was a journal, too, full of sketches and notes. And it's got Aílouros written all over it. How much do you want to bet one was involved?"

The bitterness in Brielle fades—all that heat morphing into something thicker. Something deeper and more firmly set. Something closer to rage. To *pain*. Without waiting to be asked, she stomps to the police carriage, yanks open the passenger door, and climbs onto the leather seat. When Shaw just blinks at her from the tall grass, she calls out through the window, "Well? Come on. If there's any trail to follow, it's getting colder by the second."

The man raises an eyebrow, clearly recognizing the words—it's what *he* taught her, after all. He sweeps an arm around, gesturing vaguely at the battered house. "And you expect me to just ignore all this?"

Brielle looks down at her grime-coated pants and says quietly, "We can grumble our apologies on the way." She has no intention of saying she's sorry, of course. And he probably knows it, too. But it's enough to pull a nod out of him. Enough to get him back into the coach. He twists the ignition crank, wrenches the vehicle into gear, and says grimly, "I know you're no stranger to blood, but there's a lot of it. And the scene is still fresh." He glances sideways at her, his lips pulling taut, and steers the carriage into the road. "So try not to smudge it all up. We're just going to study the clues. No setting off on your own. No *avenging* the victim. I don't want any more blood spilled tonight. Deal?"

Brielle swipes restlessly at the dirt on her pants and mutters under her breath, "*No promises.*"

# 45

Kemple staggers back to the docks in a daze. He moves slowly, stumbling down the shadowy roads with one hand clutching the crank on his chest, the other pressed tightly over his mouth. Tears keep blurring his vision, making the star-flecked sky quiver and stretch, and the back of his throat keeps squeezing shut, making him cough and gag.

Gideon is gone now. Forever. And it's all because of *him*.

To top it all off, the man's death has only made those monstrous urges inside him swell even more. Now it's worse than just a ball of pressure—now it feels like his heart is trying to rip itself from his chest.

He grips the handle through the fabric of his shirt and squeezes it just enough to feel the gears under his sternum resist, to feel the springs beneath his ribs tighten, to feel the pain around his heart flare like a torch. Then he curses and lets his hands fall to his side.

When did *this* become his life? Alone, on the run, with a demon in his blood, an old man's death on his hands, and a clockwork girl's rage trailing after him. How did he ever fall into such a bottomless hole?

How can he ever hope to get out?

He gulps back a sob and stumbles down a maze of trash-strewn alleys and hoof-worn streets, keeping his legs moving, his shoes dragging, until the air turns salty and warm and his ears fill with the familiar sound of water sloshing against sun-bleached wood. The docks. At least he made it this far. He sighs and staggers around a corner, then stops when he sees the sagging pier and the dark, glittering water around it, its surface littered with slow-rocking boats. The *Nameless* is still there, tethered where he left her, her battered hull sloshing against the waves. The sight of her is like gravity, pulling his shoulders forward, dragging his legs ahead. A few more strides and he'll be safe inside that musty cabin. Tucked away like a key in a lock. Like an insect in a shell.

Like a beast in a cave.

But he drags his heels to a stop as soon as his shoes clomp onto the pier.

What good would it do to cower in his boat? How would that solve anything? And what'll he do when the darkness inside him finally comes spilling out, with no device to hold it back? His mind flashes back to a gray rooftop, to that horrible moment when he threw himself onto a bearded stranger—to the first time in his life when the animal in him actually bared its fangs.

Is that what he has to look forward to—a complete and utter loss of control? A frenzied bloodlust? An insatiable craving to *kill*?

He frowns at the *Nameless* and eyes her fractured mast until a word forms in his mind: *help*. The word expands outward, blooming and spreading throughout his skull until it's a full-fledged idea. A *plan*.

He needs to get help. Not just any help, but the *right* kind. Help that he should've sought out years ago. He glances one last time at the *Nameless*, his gaze sliding across her paint-stripped deck, then he turns and trudges back toward the city.

It's time he introduced himself to the authorities. Properly. They deserve to know what he's done. They need to know what he's *capable* of doing, too—even if he doesn't fully know, himself. At the very least, they can lock him away. Shackle him in a cell. Bury him behind bars until the monster comes out, so they can see the evil in him with their own eyes.

Maybe, after all the fish bellies have been sliced and the belt buckles have done their bruising, after the stolen books have been read and so many rooftops have been slept on, after the gears and tubes have been hooked to his heart and the elixirs in his blood have finally thinned to water—after all that, maybe a prison cell is where he truly belongs.

# 46

Shaw parks the carriage beside a large, dark warehouse and twists the ignition crank, stilling the engine. In the quiet that follows, he sighs and looks down at the wheel.

It's a pose that Brielle knows all too well. He's thinking about something dark and important—something involving her. "What?" she says. "It's not like I destroyed the whole house or something. And nobody even lives there, anyway."

The detective shakes his head, then turns on his seat to look her up and down. After a moment that stretches too long, he frowns and says, "You look like a girl who just committed a crime."

Brielle sighs and glares out the window, fixing her lens-tinted gaze on an old, weather-battered lift truck. "That's because I'm a freak," she grumbles, aiming her words at the rusted vehicle. The thing looks like it's been sitting there for centuries. "Freaks always seem suspicious."

Shaw exhales and glances at himself in the mirror. "I'm not even going to respond to that," he says. "I've told you so many times: there's nothing wrong with you." He frowns at his reflection and rubs his palms against his brown-gray stubble. "What I mean is: you're covered with grime, your hair is a mess, and you've got an *angry juvenile* posture right now, one that I'm sure no amount of words can cure."

Honestly, none of that sounds bad at all. "So what?" she says, emphasizing her *angry juvenile posture.* "Last I checked, I'm not competing in a beauty pageant anytime soon."

Shaw carefully paws at his frizzy hair, like he's hoping it'll somehow lie flat instead of jutting up everywhere. When that doesn't work, he mumbles a curse and looks away from the mirror. "Some important people will probably show up at the scene tonight. I know reputation doesn't mean much to you, but it should. *Yours* included."

Brielle grimaces and sticks out her tongue. Shaw always worries about the dumbest things. "You just said nothing is wrong with me, not even thirty seconds ago. Now you're acting like *everything* is wrong with me. So which is it? You can't have it both ways."

Shaw fixes his gaze on her lenses and forces an uneven smile. "To me, you're completely fine," he says. "But to someone else, you look like you just . . ." He waves a hand uselessly in the air. "I don't know."

"Like I spent the last hour tearing apart an abandoned house?" she guesses.

Shaw nods. "Something like that. And again, it don't matter one way or another to me. But if you want to help me investigate here, you need to look the part. Otherwise, one of the higher-ups will just toss you out the door. And I won't be able to do nothing about it." He glances at her hopefully—with his eyebrows raised and his lips bunched—and the expression looks so ridiculous on him that she groans out a weak, "Fine."

*Fine*, she'll clean up, even though it all seems so pointless. Or maybe, more accurately: *fine*, she'll play the good surrogate daughter in front of his peers, but only because it matters to him. "But I'm keeping what I figure out to myself," she says, jabbing a clockwork finger in his direction. "They can do their own detective work."

Shaw cracks a smile and nods. "Deal. Now go dust yourself off. The clock is ticking."

So she does as she's told, clambering out of the carriage and slapping at her clothes and swishing her hair, letting the dust and dirt fall off her in a cloud. The air is thick with the stench of burnt oil and the sound of a thousand crickets, but she pays attention to none of it—her mind is too busy preparing itself for the scene they're about to walk into. She needs this. The distraction. The challenge. It's been so long since she's had a good puzzle to ponder—something to take her focus off that horrible, five-fingered ghost inside her glove.

Something to help her forget about Mom.

When the debris finally stops falling off her, she smooths her bangs away from her lenses and looks grimly at Shaw through the passenger window. "There," she says, striking a mannequin's pose. "Do I look *presentable* now, Your Majesty?"

Shaw rolls his eyes and climbs out of the coach. "Good enough, I suppose." He slams the door and gives the carriage roof a hard smack with his palm. "Come on. Let's put those goggles of yours to good use."

She nods, tucks her satchel against her side, and follows him around the warehouse. The detective moves slowly and carefully, his head on a swivel, his gaze constantly darting around. He looks at the road, at the building, at the sky. Twice, he appears to be looking at nothing at all. By the time they reach the front of the warehouse, he seems to have figured something out. "I counted six side windows and doors," he says, muttering over his shoulder. "Yet, none of them appear to have been used to get in." He waits a few seconds, then asks quietly, "Why do you think that is?"

Brielle lets the question simmer in her head for a moment. Then she blurts out the most obvious response: "The violence was domestic."

Shaw nods. "And if it wasn't?"

"Then . . . whoever wanted in already had a key?"

Shaw lets out a satisfied grunt. "Couldn't have said it better myself."

Brielle tries not to smile, but it sneaks out anyway. She's missed this—not just the detective work, but her and Shaw *doing* things. Together. Like a family. "So what now?"

"Now," he says, gesturing at the front of the building, "we fight off the wolves."

Brielle glances over his shoulder to see a group of officers crowding around the open front door. They look the way Shaw probably once looked: young, rigid, mean. The buckles on their dark uniforms glint in the dim light. Their faces are hard and angular. For an instant her mind throws her back in time, back to that horrible moment when she first met Shaw—the only comforting presence in a room full of officers who couldn't have cared less about her. The memory vanishes quickly, leaving nothing behind but a lingering wave of anger, hot and smothering. "Just seeing them makes me want to bash their faces in," she hisses.

Shaw chuckles and shakes his head. "Best if I do the talking, then," he jokes. But then he glances over his shoulder and eyes her seriously. "Stay here," he says. "Wait for my signal."

So she does—not because she's scared, but because she knows this is important to him. If she had things *her* way, she'd stomp up to the officers right now, shove herself into their personal space, and *dare* them to piss her off. She's heard more than enough, from Shaw himself, of the things they say about her. The nicknames, the gossip. The cruel *orphan* jokes . . .

She bites her tongue so hard it starts to bleed.

Shaw approaches the men slowly, like he's sneaking up on a flock of birds. He strides through the dark weeds with his arms loose and his shoulders swaying in a phony, casual way—and it all looks so . . . utterly ridiculous. She'd laugh if she wasn't so mad. But she *is* mad, so all she does is scowl even more.

The men turn when they see him, and then they take turns glancing over his shoulder, their bitter gazes landing on her. They share words, their voices low and muffled, and one of them even laughs. Then Shaw places himself between them, stealing their attention back.

The detective mutters a question. A few of the men shake their heads. Shaw makes an angry gesture, swiping his arm down like he's slashing a sword. The tallest man shrugs, like he's unimpressed. Finally, Shaw raises his voice enough for Brielle to hear his words. "—every right to be here! I've been training her since—" The wind picks up, drowning out the rest of his complaint, but she's heard enough to understand the problem: they don't want her here.

Like every other lousy person in this world, they don't think that she *belongs*.

And of course they'd feel that way. What do they contribute, anyway? All they do is stand around in their ugly outfits and their stupid badges, running their mouths and being useless. They're spectators, nothing more. Glorified bumps on logs. They don't hunt down the monsters like she does. They don't *risk their necks for a cause.*

And they certainly don't have a right to stop her from doing what she came here for: to look for the clues that they'll invariably miss. To study the patterns that they'll never see.

To *solve* the kind of crime that they could never understand. The kind of crime that *made her* who she is today.

She clenches her glove into a leathery ball of metal and stalks forward, crunching the dry weeds under her boots. Shaw may be too polite to shove past them—but not her. Heck, she'll do it with a smile.

The closer she gets, the more details she notices. The tool-lined shelves standing just beyond the open doorway. The modified bicycle leaning against the building like an afterthought. The bloody footprints trailing away from the warehouse in an almost mechanical fashion, every stain evenly spaced apart.

Shaw would've spotted all of this too, no doubt. And he's probably formed a few theories already, tying all the clues together. She's tempted to pull him aside, just so she can ask him what's on his mind. What's the thread knotting all of this together? What's the answer to the question that she hasn't yet thought to ask?

But then she reaches the place where the weeds turn to gravel, where the distance between herself and the officers is finally small enough to hear their voices clearly, and one of them mutters something that makes her drag her heels to a stop. "Must be something crazy in the air tonight," the man says. "Just heard some punk is trying to turn himself in at the Bay station. Claims there's a *demon in his veins.*" The officer's voice rises at the end, curling his words into a mocking tone, and the other men share a chuckle, like it's all a big joke. Then Shaw turns around and spots her standing here, so much closer to the building than where he left her, so fully *within earshot*, and his eyes go wide with understanding. With *worry*. He raises his hands and says, "Gabby, *wait*," but it's too little, too late.

She whirls around and sprints for the carriage, her clockwork hand pumping in the wind. Shaw yells out something, and a second later she hears the rustle and thud of him chasing after her, his body crashing through the overgrowth. But she's younger than him. Faster, too. And by the time he reaches the place where she just was, she's already clambering inside the coach. Already winding the ignition. Already wrenching the engine on.

The motor groans and shudders. Smoke and steam gush from the grill. Shaw stumbles around the edge of the warehouse, his body flattened into a silhouette, and when he sees her backing the carriage away, he yells out in a garbled voice: "Not without planning it first! You don't know anything about this! Going in blind is how you get killed!" When she merely revs the engine harder, he shouts, "Your mom wouldn't want it this way!"

His words make her pause, but only for a second. Then she narrows her eyes and stomps on the pedal. The engine growls, the wheels spin on the pavement, and she steers the coach around in a flurry of gravel and smoke. Her satchel shifts against her hip. Her lenses fog, then clear. Then she's off, speeding down the dark streets while Shaw's flailing body shrinks to a dot in the mirror.

For all the things the detective has been right about in her life, he's wrong about the most important thing of all: Mom *would've* wanted it this way. Because this way means that someone else might live. Slay the beast, save a soul.

. . . If only someone had done the same for Mom.

Brielle squeezes her clockwork glove around the steering wheel, crunching finger-shaped indentations into the rubber, and she yanks the carriage into a higher gear. Somewhere near the bay, there's a young man saying he has a demon in his blood. And she's got just the right tool to punch it clean out of him.

# 47

Kemple leans his forehead against the thick-paned window and groans—not from the ache around his heart or the endless thrumming in his head, but because he just plain doesn't know what else to say. "I'm not crazy," he says, slapping his palm against the countertop. "I know it sounds that way, but I'm really not. If you'll just lock me up for the night, you'll see that I'm telling the truth."

The officer on the other side of the glass scowls and shakes his head. "Now, you hear that right there?" the man says, tilting his head. He drags his fingers through his blonde hair and cups a calloused hand around his ear, like he's listening to something far in the distance. "That's the sound of me not giving a damn." He looks over Kemple's head and makes a big deal of studying the smudges in the night sky, as if to say, *Even those dumb, dirty clouds are more interesting than you.* Then he glances back at Kemple and grimaces. "The only way you're getting locked up is if you commit a crime. And with the way you're so suspiciously *eager* to be locked away, I'd even go as far as making sure you *don't* go behind bars. Hell only knows what kind of twisted reason you've got for wanting such a thing."

Kemple lets out another frustrated groan and kicks at the brick-lined building. When he finally spotted this police station, it looked like a shimmering lantern in the dark. Like a glint of hope in a sea of putrid ink. But now, well . . . now it's feeling like another lousy dead end. How many ways can he say that he thinks he's . . . *infected*? How many times must he repeat himself before this badge-wearing idiot finally catches on? "There's. Something. Wrong. With. Me," he says, growling every word.

"Well," the officer says, glancing around at nobody, "would you look at that? The kid is finally right about something." The man chuckles dryly at his own joke. Then his face grows tight and serious. "For the last time, I'm telling you: get lost." He glances at the telegraph beside him, and for a moment it looks like he might use the thing a second time—not just to report Kemple's odd request again, but maybe to ask for backup. Or to ask for something, anyway. *Anything.*

But when the man shakes his head and turns away from the machine, Kemple's shoulders sag even more. "I've already filed a description of your . . . *problem*," the officer says bitterly. "And frankly, I've given you a hell of a lot more patience than you deserve." The man jabs a finger against the smudged window and grumbles, "So if you don't get out of my sight in next ten seconds, I'm going to contact the asylum. I'm sure they'd love to toss your scrawny hide into a padded room." He squints at Kemple through the cloudy glass and mutters, "How's that sound, *Mr. Something's Wrong?*"

To be honest, it doesn't sound anywhere *near* strong enough. Not to hold the awful pressure inside him, anyway. Not to keep the beast in his blood sealed away. No, what Kemple needs is shackles and bars. Chemicals, too. He needs concrete and metal, tethers and straps. He needs Viola's potions and Gideon's devices and Josephyn's worldly insights, and even *then*, he's not sure if all that would be enough. The heat in his chest expands, stretching from an orb into a spike, and he curls around the jagged spot with a groan. "I'm telling you," he gasps, "there's a monster in me that wants out!"

The officer sighs angrily, steps away from the window, and starts jabbing at the keys on the telegraph beside him. "That's it," he says. "I'm done trying to be nice." He twists a lever on the side of the machine and the whole contraption jostles and whirs. "Stick around, kid," the man says, scrunching his face. "I'm sure they've got a straitjacket in just your size."

Kemple imagines his arms ripping through a pair of fabric restraints. He pictures his hands tearing apart a room with cushioned walls. He thinks of the asylum workers, too, with their terrified eyes and their distorted screams when the thing inside him finally breaks loose. When it finally makes him do what it's always wanted: to rip, to tear. To *kill*. Worst of all, he thinks of all that fresh, glistening *blood*. So much blood. All of it spilled because of *him*. "You're making the worst mistake," he mutters.

When the officer merely scowls, Kemple grabs at the crank on his chest. Maybe Gideon's device has one last twist in it. Maybe there's enough of Viola's concoction still trickling through his blood. All he needs is a little more time. Just enough to stave off the beast.

But the instant his fingers graze the handle under his shirt, a lance of pain stabs at his heart. He gasps and staggers away from the window, away from the useless officer, away from the telegraph that's luring more *fresh meat* toward the demon in his skin. The officer yells after him but he just stumbles farther away, staggering over the slippery cobbles, aiming his body toward the darkest parts of the city—toward the shadows where, hopefully, there'll be somewhere decent to hide, somewhere sheltered and secure, somewhere strong enough to hold him when that horrible pressure in his blood finally curls him inside out.

Viola's inhuman face flashes in his mind—her oil-slicked eyes narrowed to slits, the gears on her cheeks glinting like knives, her mouth twisted into a menacing snarl—but he shoves the thought away. He can't worry about her right now. For crap's sake, he can barely *walk*.

Josephyn streaks through his head, too, like a green-eyed comet scraping the inside of his skull. What would she say to him if she were here now? What would *she* suggest he do? The question feels like an endless bucket of smelt. Like a book where every word has been smeared into a blur. There must be an answer, somewhere. There's *always* an answer if you look hard enough, isn't there? But the more he tries to find it, the more his thoughts keep crumbling away, until there's nothing in his head but a monstrous ache and a single, thrumming word: *gone*.

It's all *gone*. Everything and everyone that's ever mattered to him: *gone*. Gideon and his fatherly guidance. Josephyn and her sisterly concern. Even Abner—that belt-whipping bastard of a man—even *his* absence feels like a loss now; like just another failure in a list of mistakes that runs all the way back to the beginning of Kemple's life.

And it makes sense, doesn't it? All he does is *lose* things. All he's good for is letting everything fall apart.

So when the night air fills with the roar of an approaching carriage, when the cobbles glint from the orange glow of the vehicle's headlamps, when the driver wrenches the coach to a stop and leaps out to yell at him—her slender face half hidden under a pair of tinted goggles, her right arm lost in the bulk of a prosthetic hand—this is why he finally *lets go*. Of everything. His sorrow for Gideon. His regret over Josephyn. His hatred of Abner. Even that deep-rooted anguish over the mother he can't remember—the woman who *created him*, who brought him into this world only to abandon him without ever leaving a reason why—even *that*, he lets drift quietly away. And when all that awfulness is gone, and the only thing left is a trembling thread in his spine, a frayed cord dangling in the center of his being—that final line between himself and the monster within—he lets go of *that*, too. Lets it fall away. Lets it plummet into that dark, empty void. Because why not?

What else can he possibly lose?

For one delicate moment, everything feels right in the world. He looks up at the starless murk of the sky, fills his lungs with the sulfur-tinged air, and for the first time in God-only-knows how long, he relaxes his mouth into a big, careless smile.

Then the pressure in his heart finally gushes outward, like a dam breaking deep in the center of his chest. Everything after that is *pain*.

# 48

The moment Brielle leaps out of the carriage, the *instant* she sees the boy's pained eyes, Shaw's voice blares in her head like a siren.

*Not without planning it, first! You don't know anything about this!*

Maybe, just maybe, he was right. She's never hunted an Aílouros that still looked *human*.

Is it murder if you kill a monster while it still has a face?

On the drive here, she didn't consider this at all. What's there to think about when it comes to slaying a beast? You track it down. Immobilize it. Then you rip out the thing's ugly heart. It's a simple, three-step process that she's been following for years now. But never once has she needed to deal with a creature that hadn't yet . . . changed.

Should she attack while it still looks like a person? Should she wait until it's done?

If she plunges her clockwork glove into the thing's chest now, will the heart inside still look *human*?

The questions fill her mind, twining around her thoughts, until her head feels stuffed with wool. So she doesn't bother to think—she merely shouts the same words that she's heard Shaw use so many times before: "Get on the ground!"

The boy winces, his face blanching in the glow of the carriage's headlamps, and her gaze flicks over him, taking in every awful detail. Thick, tousled hair the color of dark soil—hair that looks like it hasn't been washed for days; hard, narrow eyes with night-blue irises, his pupils as sharp as needlepoints; and an angular chin set firmly beneath a mouth that looks both tender and cruel. In another time, under different circumstances, she might even consider him *handsome*. Right now, though, everything about him bothers her. No, it's worse than that—everything about him *enrages* her, from his stupid chalk-white shirt to his grime-covered pants, all the way down to his dumb, tattered shoes.

So what if it looks like life has dragged him through the mud? Is she supposed to feel sorry for him? He hasn't had it worse than *her*, she can guarantee that much. And she isn't the one with a monster in her blood.

She unlatches her satchel, scoops out her dart pistol, and aims it at him like she's jabbing a sword. The cartridge glints through the slot in the barrel, the vial inside full of brown, syrupy poison, and he seems to understand the threat. His eyebrows lift. His body tenses. For a split second it looks like he's about to speak. But then his face clouds and his expression changes—his eyes squeezing shut, his brow wrinkling, his features pulling tight. He doubles over and lets out an agonized howl, and Brielle tightens her grip around the gun, her fingertip brushing the trigger.

If there was ever a perfect moment to shoot, this would be it.

. . . But her finger refuses to move. It just *stays there*, frozen in place, as if her good hand has become a glove of its own, with its geared joints rusted shut. She grits her teeth and tries again, but this time her *mind* gets in the way, her thoughts pluming like smoke.

Why does it seem like the boy doesn't want this? Why does it look like he's struggling for *control*?

She keeps her eyes on him, her gaze steady and unblinking behind her dark lenses, while her mind swirls with doubt. Every Aílouros she's encountered has been simple and primitive—their actions as predictable as rain from a cloudy sky. They hunt, they feed, and when cornered, they lash out in the most direct of ways: claws out, jaws open, those catlike ears pulled back against their skulls. They're *reactive* animals at best, spurred on by the most basic of instincts. And they sure as heck don't have a self-aware bone in their fur-covered bodies.

So why does the boy look like he's *fighting* the change?

Shaw has reminded her, time and again, how the disease changes a person. How inhuman they become. How it rewires their brains until they *want* all that monstrous strength. Until that insatiable bloodlust becomes their defining trait.

But looking at the boy now, well . . . could Shaw have been wrong?

The boy drops to his knees and smacks his knuckles against the cobbles. His back tightens. His shoulder blades jut against his shirt. He angles his head and lets out a sound that's halfway between a growl and a scream.

Brielle inhales sharply and tries to squeeze the trigger again.

But again, her finger won't comply.

"Damn it," she grumbles. What's stopping her? It's not like the poison will finish the boy off. She's darted enough of these demons to know that all the serum does is stun them—stiffening those muscles, paralyzing the joints. Holding the creature in place just long enough for her to . . . finish the job.

But the more she eyes the boy, the more she sees it: his pain. His *agony*. A kind of suffering that looks so much more than physical. He looks the way *she* must've looked to Shaw the first time they met: broken, pitiful. Dangling at the frayed end of that existential rope.

It's all the more reason to shoot him, isn't it? To put him out of his misery? To end his suffering while he's still at least *somewhat* human? She waits a moment longer, with the pistol aimed squarely at the boy's heaving chest, as if the universe might give her a sign.

Instead the boy yells out again, his voice deep and guttural, and she watches with wide eyes as his fingernails stretch into long, yellowed points.

"Okay," she mutters, "that's enough of that." This time when she squeezes the trigger, her finger bends without a hint of resistance.

The pistol fires with a metallic *pop*, knocking the handle back against her iron palm. A small cloud of steam and smoke swirl around the gun, and the dart whistles through the air like a poison-tipped bullet, straight for the boy's throat.

One second, that's all the dart needs to find its target. A thousand milliseconds from the gun's barrel to the boy's delicate skin. The tiniest fraction of a minute, just long enough for Brielle to tense and hold her breath.

Just as the dart is about to make contact, though, the boy yelps and lurches from a sudden twinge of pain—a lurch that moves his throat a few inches to the left—and those measly inches are enough to make all the difference.

The dart whizzes harmlessly past him and clatters pitifully to the darkened cobbles.

Brielle mutters a colorful curse. Compression guns are excellent for single shots, but they're a terrible pain to reset. Which means there's no time to reload. She jams the gun back into her satchel and thrashes her hand around inside the leather folds until her knuckles smack against a thick loop of copper chains. They feel extra sturdy tonight. Sturdy is good. Sturdy is reassuring. She yanks the links out and sweeps her clockwork glove against the outer coil until the grappling hook at the end of the chain snags on her wrist. Then she lunges forward, not because she *wants* things to be close and personal, but because there's no other choice. The longer she waits, the less of a boy he'll be—and the more of a monster he'll become.

His eyes flick up to meet her goggles, and she can already see the changes in him: his pupils elongated, his jaw distended, the skin on his cheeks turning dark and splotchy. He parts his lips with a rasp and suddenly his teeth aren't teeth anymore—now he's got a mouth full of *fangs*.

Fangs, just like the ones that sank into Mom's neck.

Brielle's insides twitch in a cold, dark way, and she runs harder, closing the distance between herself and the boy as if she's closing in on that pantry door all over again.

As if, this time, she can finally save Mom.

The boy roars with a voice that's no longer human. His face scrunches and tufts with thick, dark hair. He reaches out with an arm that's begun to tear through his sleeve and rakes the air with a claw-like hand. But his movements are flailing and unfocused. Panicked. Confused.

Brielle doesn't waste a second. She leaps in close and rams her knee against his chin, snapping his inhuman head back and knocking him off-balance. The boy who's not quite a boy anymore howls and slashes at her chest, but she dodges the blow with a twirl, pivoting away from his claws and yanking the hook off her wrist in one smooth motion. There's a sound of stretching and tearing from the boy—not just from his clothes, but from thicker, wetter, *internal* things. Like tendons and cartilage, ligaments and skin. When the boy bellows again, she almost feels sorry for him.

Almost.

But then her mind shudders with the memory of that half-open pantry, its interior draped in shadow, its shelves coated with gore, and any hint of pity she has for the boy evaporates in an instant. She swings the hook down in a hard, curving slice, and the metal prongs stab into the creature's meaty shoulder.

The monster roars and thrashes, and she leaps back just enough to get out of its terrible reach. Then she gives the chain a hard yank with her clockwork glove, pulling the thing to its knees.

For a moment the creature just stays there, kneeling and heaving, its breath steaming around its monstrous face, its body still swelling through those tattered clothes, its fur still growing out of its skin.

It's a strange sight, this half-changed being, and Brielle can't decide if it looks more like a monstrous cat, or like an ape with some dog genes thrown in. Maybe a little bit of everything. Its posture is definitely feline, though, from the snarling lips to the menacing hunch, all the way down to that serpentine tail.

Like a carnival version of some ravenous man-tiger, with shredded clothing instead of stripes.

Again her insides tighten, her nerves tingling, her muscles taut like wires. The tension is familiar—that readiness before the kill, the build-up before the release—and she curls her wispy fingers inside her glove, balling those iron fingers into a brass-knuckled battering ram.

The perfect instrument for smashing through inhuman chests.

She parts her lips to say *goodbye* to the thing that was once a boy, but the monster's eyes flick upward before she can get the word out, and their gazes connect in a startling way, the darkness of his crescent-shaped pupils slicing right through the tint of her lenses.

For a moment she just stands there with her clockwork fist raised, her body pinned in place by the beast's unflinching stare. It's not the eye contact that stills her, but the murk of emotions roiling beneath it: Anger and despair. Panic and fury. And with it: a slow, gentle tilt of the creature's head that almost looks like a *plea*.

*Kill me*, it seems to say.

But her arm is frozen in place. Since when do demons want to die?

*End it*, the creature seems to beg.

Her body shudders with the strain. What kind of monster asks for mercy?

The beast furrows its brow, narrows its yellowed eyes, and twists its maw with confusion. *What're you waiting for?*

It's a question with no answer. A puzzle with no solution. What on earth is *wrong* with her? She screams out a garble of vowels and drives her metal fist in the only direction it'll move: down and away, toward the cobbles beneath her boots, smashing a knuckle-shaped crater into the street.

The creature rasps and thrashes against the hook in its shoulder, yanking the chain taut, and when Brielle looks up at the thing's eyes again, all that awareness is suddenly gone. In its place is the same look she's seen a hundred times over: that empty, cavernous yearning for *blood*.

Now the thing truly *is* a monster.

Now the boy is truly gone.

Brielle rears back, pivots her weight forward, and this time when she drives her clockwork fist toward the monster's chest, her mind stays mercifully quiet, her head undeniably clear. Her brass knuckles knife through the air like a piston in a well-oiled machine.

But the element of surprise is gone now. And the creature reacts to the blow before she can connect. It lunges to the side. The hook rips out of its shoulder with a wet, jagged *slurp*. Then the monster's heavy arm slams into her throat, knocking her off her feet.

Pain explodes in her neck, and she's treated to a brief, disorienting glimpse of the night sky—dirty clouds, blurry stars, a moon that looks like a glob of curdled milk—then the street slams into her back, crushing the breath out of her.

She coughs and rolls to her knees just in time to see the beast turn away and hurl itself down the street, its catlike tail whipping behind it like a snake, its body shedding strips of clothing, tufts of hair, and tiny flecks of blood. It bounds to the end of the block, throws itself around the corner in a flurry of dark limbs, and vanishes from sight, leaving behind only tiny remnants of itself and a stretch of cobbles that suddenly feels too quiet to be natural. Too empty to be real.

Brielle staggers to her feet and stuffs the blood-slicked chain back into her satchel, avoiding the hook's sharp prongs. Then she takes a slow, staggering breath—just enough to make her throat and lungs ache.

How could she be so stupid? How could she let the thing mess with her head?

Her mind flickers and she's treated to another glimpse of that horrible pantry door, its hinges slowly creaking, the darkness behind it looming like a nightmarish void. When her chest tightens and her eyes start to burn, she lowers her head and runs after the monster, throwing herself away from that death-filled closet. Away from those cowardly tears. In the ragged space between her breaths, she makes a promise to herself. To *Mom*.

She won't just kill this beast. No . . . she's going to make it *suffer*.

# 49

Kemple hurls himself down the street like a dark-furred nightmare, his claws stabbing into the gritty gaps between the cobbles. The cool air bites at his snout and stings his shoulder, but he keeps moving, stumbling, bounding in a panicked fury, as if his body has become a mass of fire and oiled springs. It's horrible and wonderful and dizzying all at once, and the more he tries to make sense of it, the more his mind echoes with a voice that isn't his—a voice that keeps shoving his own thoughts down under its thick, terrible weight.

Seek. Hunt. DEVOUR.

The words feel . . . right. Pure. Absolute. A simplified philosophy for life that even Josephyn would appreciate.

Really, why can't everything be so easy?

He lunges around a corner, skids to a stop beside a darkened storefront, and sucks greedily at the wind. The night air is teeming with scents. Rosy hints of decay. Bitter whiffs of smoke. A sour, briny odor that could only come from a trillion gallons of festering bay water.

The aromas are pleasant, but overwhelming, like too much perfume in a windowless room, and he finds himself snuffing and swiping at his maw, as if he can somehow bat the torrent of scents away. Then a new sensation slaps at his nostrils: a salty, leathery, pocket-sized whiff of sweat and rust and something terribly familiar, something that smells like . . . meat. Like *blood*.

Like a metal-handed, skin-and-bones girl, just waiting to be torn open.

The voice in his head turns from a growl to a roar, stuffing every inch of his skull.

SEEK. HUNT. DEVOUR!

If he could grin with this new jaw of his, he would. Instead he pivots toward the girl's scent, twisting the pads of his feet over the worn cobbles. He crouches down, flattens his ears against his skull, and squeezes his body as low as he can until the crank on his chest scrapes against the street. The contact shoots a dull jolt of pain into his heart, and he snarls, then cranes his neck around the edge of the building to look for the girl.

Something moves at the edge of his vision, and he freezes in place.

It isn't the wind, or the savage girl with the metal hand. No—what he sees is a pair of glowering eyes and a mouthful of snakelike fangs. He sees matted fur stretched taut over a muscular, catlike body, its limbs draped in the remains of a thin, chalk-white shirt.

A shirt that, once upon a time, was gray like a dreary sky.

A shirt that used to be his.

It takes a moment to piece it all together. When he finally does, he lurches backward with a hiss. He's looking at his *reflection*.

But that's . . . impossible. How could it be *his* reflection? The image is of something horrible. Something monstrous. Something huge and terrifying in the darkened storefront window that moves whenever he moves, mimicking his posture, mirroring his gait, copying every tilt of his head and flex of his muscles, parodying every gulp of his throat.

He snaps his jaws and the thing in the window does the same. He bares his teeth and the creature in the glass snarls, too. Finally he can't take it anymore, and he lashes out with his claws, slashing furiously at the windowpane.

The blow shatters the glass, sending a flurry of shards into the empty store, and he lets out a triumphant roar.

He isn't a monster. This is all an illusion. A terrible trick of the brain. That girl with the chains and that metal glove—this must be *her* doing. What mind-altering chemicals did she put on that hook?

What kind of drugs are coursing through his veins?

The beast in his head rasps again, uttering that same three-word command— *Seek. Hunt. DEVOUR!*—but the voice doesn't feel *right* this time. It feels ragged and splotchy, like a bandage stuck carelessly over a secret wound, or a monstrous hand clamped tight over his eyes.

It feels . . . like a lie hiding the truth.

He glances down at the cobbles and braves a hard look at one of the shards of glass.

His reflection stares back at him like a nightmare: those yellowed, slitted eyes; the huge, fang-lined jaws; that dark, glistening fur wrapped around every inch of his inhuman face.

This time, there's no uncertainty about it. No drug-induced twist of the mind. This is real. This is *him*. This is . . . what he's become.

A creature. A monster. A *beast*.

He waits for the horror to flood his veins, for his mind to scream out, for his insides to clench in that hot, awful way—the same way they always did whenever

Abner wrapped that belt around his grimy hands. But the feeling doesn't come. Because some part of him has always known it would come to this. How could it not? Gideon's device couldn't hold forever. Viola's elixir would eventually turn to mist. The beast inside *had* to come out, one way or another; it was simply a matter of time.

Now, that time has run out.

*Seek*, the monster growls, its voice thundering through his mind.

But he shakes his head and twists his animal body away from the road.

*Hunt*, the creature bellows.

But he merely digs his claws into the street's worn cracks and hurls himself toward the harbor.

*DEVOUR*, the beast screams, but Kemple isn't listening anymore. Because he's already made up his mind.

He uses those monstrous limbs to lope toward the bay, steadily closing the distance between the darkened city and that tattered boat that he calls home. The closer he gets, the thicker and wetter the air becomes. The storefronts dwindle away. Warehouses rise in their place. The cobbles turn to water-slicked asphalt, then to weather-worn wood. Finally the *Nameless* rises into view, her hull gently sloshing in the ink-black waters, her fractured mast wobbling in the salty wind.

The monster in his head twists and lurches, like it finally realizes what he's trying to do, and the muscles in his limbs suddenly clamp tight, stiffening at the joints. *NO*, the beast roars, but Kemple has momentum on his side. He lunges toward the *Nameless's* peeling hull, fighting against the terrible tension in his bones, and all his animal weight comes crashing down onto the pier.

The wood is slick from years of oil, grime, and rot, and his furred body goes sliding across the planks. The beast tries to slash out at the dock, tries to dig its claws into the gaps between the boards, tries to stop its slide in any way it can, but its limbs belong to Kemple, too, and he fights to keep his arms tight against his ribs and his legs curled against his torso. The animal pries his mouth open and lets out a furious roar, then the pier slips out from under him. For the briefest of moments, there's nothing beneath him but air and the murky waters of the bay. Then his furred limbs smash down onto the *Nameless's* splintered hull.

The beast fights to get back to its feet. It thrashes to get back onto the dock. It gnashes and bellows and lunges for dry land, but Kemple wrestles the monster toward the boat's tether instead and slashes the rope apart with his claws.

The *Nameless* floats in place for a moment, as if she's not quite sure what he wants her to do. Then the tide begins to pull her out into the murk of the bay. Her mast clatters against a neighboring yacht. Her hull scrapes against the pier.

Kemple holds the beast through all of it, digging his claws into the deck, pinning the animal in place. It snarls and roars, and even manages to slash at his face once, tearing open a burning gash along the side of his snout. But he doesn't release his grip.

Soon the *Nameless* will slip past the mouth of the harbor, out into the deeper waters. Soon the sounds and lights of the city will shrink into muffled points in the distance. Soon he'll be where he should've been all along: alone and adrift on a broken boat, lost to the whims of the sea.

Maybe, after the *Nameless* sinks and the beast succumbs to the pummeling waves, after his monstrous body washes back to shore, lifeless and bloated beyond all recognition, maybe *then* Viola will finally forgive him. For everything.

The creature lets out a desperate scream in his head, a primal blast of noise that almost sounds like a *plea*, but his mind curls away and wraps itself around an image of Josephyn, her slender body sitting cross-legged on some starry rooftop, her face buried in the fold of a book.

What would she feel right now, if she were reading his story?

Would she think he's being cowardly . . . or brave?

# 50

Brielle follows the monster's trail with her lenses zoomed out, the cobbled streets bending around her like waves. The creature's blood glints in the dim light from the streetlamps, every droplet glimmering like a coin. It's a winding path that's easy to track, for now. But it won't last long. Soon the blood will dry, pulling all the shine out of it, and no amount of goggle-twisting will make the splatters visible again.

So she picks up the pace, lunging down the gritty sidewalks and around the brick-lined corners. At one point her boots crunch on a heap of shattered glass, and she skids to a stop, twisting her lenses back to a normal view. She squints down at the shards, glances up at the broken storefront window beside her, and lets out a thoughtful hum.

The beast is careless. Inexperienced. It hasn't yet learned how to hide. Which is all the better for her.

Come to think of it, it's been a while since she had a good chase, hasn't it? Shaw has always been more excited about the *thinking* part of the hunt—the finding of clues, the careful guesswork, the slow and meticulous act of luring the beast into a well-crafted trap. But not her. Forget the lab work—give her dirty air in her lungs and sweat-streaked goggles on her face any day of the week. Give her gritty cobbles and crunching shingles under her worn boots. Give her the thrill of plunging toward literal life or death—that rare opportunity to slay another vile creature before it attacks someone else's loved one.

Give her the chance to do the very thing that she couldn't do for Mom.

She blinks at the shards one last time, then turns and continues following the blood flecks. Eventually the creature's destination becomes obvious: it's heading straight for the docks. But what would a monster want near the bay? Every Aílouros she's tussled with so far has stayed as far from the harbor as possible. Shaw even came up with a theory to explain the behavior: maybe the beasts *fear* the water on some deep, visceral level. Perhaps they can sense the larger, gilled predators lurking beneath the waves.

Or maybe they just don't know how to swim.

Whatever the reason, the theory makes sense. The creatures do seem to stick to dry land. Always lurking in the shadows. Always seeking cramped spaces in dark alleyways, the grimiest nooks and crannies to pounce from.

Except this beast.

The inconsistency is enough to drag her boots to a stop, mere inches before she steps onto the rotted wood of the docks.

Could this be a trick, perhaps? The creature's attempt to fool her? A clever form of misdirection, just to catch her off guard?

She frowns and pivots in a slow circle, scanning the pier and the tethered boats sloshing against it. There aren't many hiding spaces out here—not for a creature that's considerably bigger than a man. Really, the only plausible way for an Aílouros to vanish in this harbor would be if it climbed *beneath* the pier, like a spider fleeing the light. But the tide is high tonight, the dark waves sloshing against the planks. The sound is relentless. And the idea of a monster clinging to the underside of the dock—and holding its breath against such a tide, no less—is so absurd that it's not even worth considering.

But the blood trail . . .

She scowls at the last few droplets on the damp wood. Their shine has begun to dull and fade, but the path the creature took is still visible, still leading *toward* the bay, the blood ending in a thick, blurry smudge at the edge of the pier. She gives her goggles a sharp twist until she can see the individual grains in the wood—and the fresh, glistening claw marks scraped into it.

She frowns and swivels her lenses back to their normal position. If she didn't know better, she'd think that the beast simply lost its footing and slid right into the sea. But she *does* know better. Or at least she knows enough to scoff at the idea of an agile, catlike monster tumbling to its demise from a sudden bout of *clumsiness*. Especially when all she did was stab the thing uselessly in the shoulder.

So, no. It didn't simply *fall* into the water. No way would she ever believe it. That leaves only one possible scenario: the beast, for some reason, must've pounced onto one of the boats. And judging from where the blood trail ends, there's only one vessel she can see that the monster could've leapt onto: a small, pitiful sailboat with a broken mast, its battered hull rocking aimlessly in the waves, its stern bobbing pitifully away from the pier like it's making a slow-motion escape.

She glances back at the dock and eyes a short strand of rope that's been left to dangle over the edge. The rope's frayed end grazes the water, the exposed strands dark and glistening, and though the thing could've simply unraveled from soaking so long in the sea, from all the days being stretched and slackened, from all those nights being heated and chilled, somehow she knows that none of those things caused this rope to finally break.

No, the line was clearly *slashed*.

All in all, it's enough circumstantial evidence to convince Shaw, even on his most stubborn of days.

Without another thought, she lunges off the dock. Her body sails over the dark-watered gap before reaching the nearest yacht, and for an instant, the night air seems to pause, as if the planet is holding its breath. Then her boots hit the weathered deck and the world starts up again. She slides to a violent stop against the yacht's starboard rail, and for the next few wobbly seconds, her mind staggers, her balance teetering off-center.

Clearly, leaping onto a rocking boat is nothing like jumping onto a stable rooftop.

But she adjusts, tilting her body with the rhythm of the water, and soon she's leaping from handrail to handrail, from one yacht to the next. By the time she stumbles onto the last yacht in the line, the battered sailboat has drifted nearly out of reach. She frowns, steps quickly onto the yacht's handrail, and crouches on the rusted metal like a gargoyle preparing to take flight. She doesn't have time to scan the ragged-looking boat for threats, even though she probably should. No—scratch that; she *definitely* should. She doesn't have time to come up with a plan, either, other than the most obvious one: leap into the air as hard as she can and try to land on something that isn't wet. Beyond that? Well . . . she'll keep her clockwork hand crimped into a fist, just in case she needs it.

She takes a deep breath and jams her elbow against her satchel, pinning the bag against her side. Then she jumps with everything she's got. Only when she's fully airborne, with the salt-thick wind pulling at her hair and shoving against her skin, does she finally realize how utterly *reckless* she's being. Throwing herself onto a tiny boat that almost certainly has a monster onboard?

Has she lost her mind?

She doesn't get much time to ponder the question; the sailboat's jagged stern rushes toward her, its chipped edge sloshing just above the surface of the bay. She lands on it awkwardly, sprawling out like a starfish, just to stop herself from slipping off and into the dark water. The last time she swam anywhere, she was a kid. And she didn't have a clunky metal glove weighing her down. If she fell in now, who knows if she could even tread water, let alone *swim*? Maybe her clockwork hand would yank her straight down to the depths, like her own horrible anchor.

That makes this little sailboat jaunt of hers a double threat: a cramped boat with a ravenous creature inside, and the deep waters of the bay sloshing on all sides, preventing any hope of escape.

She *really* should've thought this out better.

But at least she's on the boat now. One step closer to finishing off the beast, which . . . should be around here somewhere. She clambers to her feet, grips the boat's flimsy rail with her good hand, and waves her brass-plated knuckles in front of her like she's brandishing a torch. Like she's trying to beat the darkness away with just a rusty, leather-strapped glove.

Then she hears it: the sound of the creature chuffing below deck, shuffling and clattering across the floorboards. The movements sound pained and disoriented, like nails digging frantically into wood. Like furniture being knocked over and shelves coming loose. Like an animal that doesn't quite know what to do with itself in such a small, confined space.

Like a predator in a room without prey.

She doesn't need to think at this point—she's danced this waltz so many times by now, she can practically do this next part with her eyes closed. She plunges her good hand into her satchel, scoops out one of the injection vials, and carefully thumbs the rubber plunger off the needled tip.

She won't need a compression gun in such close quarters. A metal-handed punch to the beast's horrible face—followed by a quick, venomous jab to its furry neck—and whatever fight the monster has left will drain away quickly, like water spilling through the crack in a glass. The part *after* that is certainly the most squeamish step in the process. All the ripping and tearing. All the crunching and gore. But until someone thinks up a cleaner way to rip out an Aílouros's heart, it's the only method she's got. And she's perfectly fine with that, to be honest. If nothing else, at least it makes her clockwork hand feel useful, like a tool that she *needs* to get the job done, rather than a deformity that she'd do anything to live without.

Really, the act of crunching those leather-wrapped, metal-bound, ghostly fingers of hers right through a monstrous chest? It's . . . therapeutic, in a grim sort of way. A sudden, violent release of all that soul-straining tension in her life. The one thing, these days, that keeps her sane.

Aside from Shaw, there probably isn't a person on earth who'd understand that.

Something below deck shatters, the sound resonating through the boat's dirty floorboards, and the noise startles her, spurring her into action. She grips the syringe between the knuckles of her good hand and points the poisoned tip outward, like a knife blade. Then she leaps down the boat's darkened steps in a rush to the cabin below. The door is jammed shut, the wood splintered around the handle, and she smashes the whole thing inward with a stomping kick.

She doesn't waste the element of surprise—she knows firsthand how dangerous it can be to let such an advantage slip away. Instead, she lunges into the shadowy space with her gloved hand in front of her, her geared fingers curled like claws, until she collides with another figure in the darkness.

The beast staggers backward, clearly startled and confused, and its body crashes through a small wooden table. In an instant she's upon it, her knees jamming onto the thing's heaving torso, her clockwork hand wrenching tight around its pitiful throat. She thrusts her good arm upward and is halfway toward stabbing the animal's vile neck when a voice wheezes out in the darkness—a voice that's not monstrous, but *human*.

A voice that belongs to a *boy*.

"*Josephyn?*"

Brielle freezes. Suddenly she's aware of the strangeness of the figure beneath her: the startling warmth of it, the glaring lack of fur, the pure and utter *nudity* of this gasping body on the darkened floorboards—this entirely *non*-monstrous boy that she has pinned under her knees.

She drops the syringe with a gasp, not just because of the awkward position she's in, but because what just happened is *impossible*. Monsters never come back from the brink.

Beasts don't turn back into *boys*.

# 51

To say that Kemple is confused would be the understatement of a lifetime. No, it's so far beyond that. He feels . . . *unhinged*. Like he's one wrong thought away from losing his grip on reality altogether. Like he's *this close* to losing his mind.

To make matters worse, there's a girl kneeling painfully on his stomach. It takes him a moment to place her. Those huge, goggled eyes; the leathery, metallic glove around her wrist that looks so much like one of Viola's own terrible hands.

This is the girl that leapt out of the carriage to yell at him, isn't it? The same one that stabbed a hook into his shoulder. The one he could *smell*, even from a distance, when he was still . . . when he was a . . .

His eyes widen and he grabs frantically at his face, jamming his fingers against his cheeks. He braces for the terrible coarseness of all that animal hair . . . but he finds only soft, sweat-dappled skin. He gropes at his nose and mouth, too, ready to feel the horror of those monstrous jaws; those terrible fangs; that nightmarish, steam-pluming snout . . . but his fingertips only graze against a normal nose and a pair of lips that are simply chapped.

He's human again. Not a monster. Not a beast. Just . . . himself.

The relief is so overwhelming that when he lets out a sigh, it almost sounds like a moan.

The girl scrunches her face around her goggles, then quickly clambers off him. The sudden loss of her weight on his stomach makes his head spin, and he jams his palms over his eyes, just to stop the cabin from twirling.

"How'd you do it?" the girl snaps. Her gritty voice clatters against the cabin walls, filling the cramped space. Before he even has a chance to breathe, she barks out, "How'd you change back? *How?*"

How, indeed? He racks his mind for an answer, but right now his brain feels like a bucket of smelt. The only thing he can remember with absolute clarity is a surge of gut-wrenching *pain*. That, and a growling voice in his head that kept telling him to . . . to do *something* . . .

He winces and slaps his head with the heel of his hand, but all that does is make his forehead sting. "I don't know," he admits. "Everything is . . . foggy right now." He tries to squint up at the girl, but the cabin is so dark that all he can see are the barest of details—her hair: straight and choppy, as dark as the shadows around her; her face (the parts of it that he can see, anyway): slender and pointed, with a ruthless clench to her jawline; her clothes: thin and boyish, with a clear emphasis on function over fashion. Lastly, her body: narrow and angular, like she's nothing but shoulders and elbows, hips and knees.

Of course, there's also the most obvious thing about her: that metal glove ticking on the end of her arm like some horrible, five-fingered clock. He scowls at the thing and says, "Who're you, anyway? And what're you doing on my boat?"

The girl pinches her lips into a line and tilts her head, like she's looking him up and down. Then she quickly turns toward the nearest wall and says in a wobbly, almost embarrassed voice, "Maybe you can . . . find some new clothes to put on before we continue this discussion."

He scrunches his face so hard that his cheeks hurt. New clothes? *That's* her big concern here? He's tempted to point out that *her* clothes aren't exactly the pinnacle of fashion, either. But then he looks down and sees what she means: aside from a few mercifully placed strips of fabric, he's completely and utterly *naked*. His face blazes and he scrambles to his feet, but the sudden movement only seems to draw her attention more.

"Get back!" she says, curling her mechanical hand into a fist. She squats quickly, scoops something small and pointy off the darkened floorboards, then stands in a hard, fluid motion. The swiftness of it all makes a word leap into his head: *dancer*.

Maybe she's a stage performer of some kind.

But then she gives the pointed object an aggressive thrust toward him, and he finds himself shaking his head. Definitely not a dancer. He clamps his hands over the part of himself that she's probably already seen, then repeats himself more forcefully. "Who *are* you? And what're you *doing here?*"

The girl lifts her chin to an awkward angle, like she's making a conscious effort not to look down at his hands. "I should be asking you the same thing," she says. Then, with a sudden grittiness to her voice, she adds, *"Aílouros."*

Again, he finds himself shaking his head. This is all becoming too weird. Too *much*. "I what?" he says. "No, you know what? Never mind. Just get the hell off my boat, thanks."

The girl flinches and cocks her head. "Your boat," she mutters softly.

"That's right. My boat." He jabs his thumb against his chest and says, "Me. Mine. All of it."

The girl huffs and looks up at the roof of the cabin. "Can you put that hand back down, please? Or better yet, can you just get some clothes on already?"

He puts his hand back down, but otherwise doesn't move. Why should he? He's not the one in the wrong here. "This is *my boat*!" he shouts, as if this explains everything.

The girl looks back at him and visibly tightens her grip on the sharp object, it's glinting edge pointing at him like a blade. "So what if it is? This is *my city*."

This time he doesn't even bother to shake his head—he just scoffs and glares at her. He was wrong to peg her as a performer. No, it's so much simpler than that: she's obviously flat-out *crazy*. "Your city," he says. "Do you even know how ridiculous you sound?"

The muscles along her jaw twitch and bulge. If the bay wasn't steadily sloshing against the boat, he'd probably hear her teeth grinding right now. Instead what he hears is the whir of a dozen or so tiny gears as she contorts that clockwork glove of hers, turning it from a fist to an accusing gesture. That metallic index finger jabs menacingly in his direction. "Do you even know how ridiculous you *look*?" she says.

He has a brief, fleeting urge to throw the insult right back at her—her and those weird, bug-eyed lenses; her and that oversized metal hand. But there's something about the way her chest keeps heaving—like she's one nudge away from mentally tumbling off a cliff. Like she's *daring* him to go ahead and say it.

Like she *wants* him to give her an excuse.

So he bites his tongue and waits until the urge passes. Then he says quietly, "Can you just leave me alone? I don't know you, and I'm already dealing with . . ." He's not quite sure how to end that sentence, so he simply lets his voice trail off.

The girl jerks her head, making her dark bangs whisk against her goggles. "You're a *monster*," she says. "You may not look like one right now, but I've seen what you are." Her voice tightens in an almost emotional way. "I know what you're capable of doing."

"Capable?" he mutters. Heck, he doesn't need her to tell him what he's *capable* of. He tries not to think of Gideon, but his mind dredges up an image of the old man, anyway—his face slackened, his eyes closed, his throat and chest covered in so much blood . . .

When his eyes start to burn, he shakes his head and tells the girl, "You don't know a thing about me."

"It doesn't matter. I know what you are. And I've killed enough of your kind to know that whatever you're thinking of trying, it's not going to work."

Kemple furrows his brow. *Your kind?* Is she saying there are . . . others like him?

"So save us both the trouble," she says, "and tell me how you did it." She jabs at the air with the sharp object again, and this time he finally sees what it is: some kind of liquid-filled syringe.

Now he understands the threat: *answer me, or get pumped full of . . .* whatever that fluid is.

"How the hell did you turn *back?*" she demands.

The question makes his mind teeter and sway. Maybe he really *did* become a monster, after all. Maybe it wasn't just some horrible dream. He jams the heels of his hands against his eyes, as if he can press all this confusion away. As if he can take all the awfulness in his life and somehow shove it back into his head. The girl curses and tells him to *cover it back up,* but how can he worry about being *naked* right now? How can he think about *anything* when there's a creature writhing in his veins—a horrible darkness that's twisting him from the inside out?

How can he hope to defeat such a beast when the only defense he's got is a failing tangle of tubes and gears in his chest, and a crank that's so rusted it barely even—

He gasps and lets his hands fall away from his face. "My crank," he says.

"Your *what?*"

"My *crank*," he says again, straining the word. He blinks down at the handle on his chest and waits for a memory to surface, because *surely* that rust-tinged contraption is the reason he came back, isn't it? What else could've pulled that monster back into his skin?

"If this is your way of stalling," the girl says, "it's not going to—"

He shushes her by chopping at the air with his hand, not because he's tired of hearing her threats, but because he can feel a memory coming—like a ship slowly breaching the fog. When it finally arrives, it comes in short, illuminating bursts, like lightning strikes on the horizon.

*The cedar-stink of the cabin around him, smothering his snout.*

*The starchy crunch of wood and old fabric shredding between his claws.*

*That mindless, insatiable* hunger *and* rage, *draping over everything.*

*And then, like a spark deep in the shadows of his mind, his own voice screaming out from the void: "The crank! Try it! Before it's too late!"*

*Then the struggle, the fight, his limbs wrestling with the monster's, his muscles straining against those inhuman bones, that last heaving effort to shove the beast's paw toward his chest, and the guttural roar that the animal lets out when he finally forces it to wrench the handle.*

*Then the pain, like a wildfire scorching his heart. Like the universe plunging into his chest, wedging his soul apart. Like . . . dying.*

The memory sucks away, plunging him back into the darkened cabin, and he staggers into the nearest wall. Pain lances through the wound on his shoulder, and he grits his teeth until the worst of it passes.

"If this is you turning again . . ." the girl growls, raising the syringe above her head.

"I remember," he mutters, more to himself than to her. "I remember being that . . . thing. I remember twisting the crank." He looks up at the girl's goggled face and, despite the horror of all of this, he finds himself chuckling. "Thought I was done for," he says, "but damn it if Viola isn't every bit the genius Gideon claimed." His laugh fades. In its place, he's left with a warbling numbness. He blinks at his hands and marvels at how normal his fingers look. There isn't even a *hint* of the claws that came out of them. "All this time," he mumbles, "and her potion still works." He looks back at the girl and cracks a smile. "Can you believe it? It still wor—"

The girl lunges at him, cutting him off, and before he can even raise his arms to defend himself, she stabs the syringe into the side of his neck. He yells out and shoves her away, but it's already too late. He can feel the fluid gushing from the needle, like ice water snaking through his veins. He tries to rip the syringe out, but his arms suddenly feel like they're made of lead. He tries to stagger away, but the sensation drains into his legs, too. Suddenly he's stumbling, gasping, garbling his words. *What've you done?* he tries to say, but all that comes out is a groan.

He hits the cabin floor hard, his face smacking against the splintered wood, and the next thing he knows, the girl is wrapping something cool and metallic around his ankles and wrists.

Chains.

The girl is *shackling him*. Like a *prisoner*.

He tries to struggle. Tries to shout. Tries to do something, *anything*, but his body doesn't belong to him anymore. Every inch of him feels disconnected, like his flesh has been scattered a thousand miles in every direction. When he tries to curse at the girl, his mouth only manages to shove out a pitiful bubble of spit.

"I don't know what you're going on about," the girl says, her voice uncomfortably close to his ear. She wrenches at the chains with that mechanical hand of hers, knotting the links together. "But I know someone who might." Then her voice drops to a whisper, her lips grazing his cheek. "And if any of your story doesn't add up," she hisses, "I'll rip your heart from your chest without so much as a blink."

Kemple wheezes back at her, because it's the only thing he can do. Then something cold and heavy pulls at his mind—an unnatural, chemical version of falling asleep. When his eyelids finally drag themselves shut, his last thought before spiraling down into the darkness is of Viola and her bitter, gear-wrapped eyes.

She and this metal-handed girl would probably be the best of friends.

# 52

It takes Brielle at least twenty minutes to get the attention of a passing boat, and another twenty minutes or so after that for the boat's crew to tow the battered sailboat back to the docks. By then most of the clouds have flitted away, leaving the night sky glittering with stars. Any other evening, she'd find it beautiful. Right now, she just finds it *frustrating*.

All it would take is one curious sailor to glance down at the sailboat's cabin steps. Then they'd see her boot print on the shattered door, plain as day. Good luck to her after that; no way would she be able to explain the unconscious, naked, chained-up boy on the cabin floor.

So she stands awkwardly on the steps, using her body to block most of the view of the doorway, and she keeps her lips pressed into an unreadable line while a gruff-looking man from the other boat tethers the sailboat to the pier. Only after he hops back onto his own vessel, and the thing churns noisily back out into the harbor, does she allow herself to let out a slow, shuddering breath.

The sailboat, at least, has a telegraph onboard, nestled into a crook beneath the ship's wheel. The machine is nothing like the one Shaw gave her—this one has buttons instead of levers, and switches instead of keys, and its gears are crusted with so much rust that it's almost to the point of being useless—but after a few flailing attempts to switch it on, and a handful of colorful curses, she finally manages to tap out a message out to Shaw.

*At the docks. On a boat. Caught a—*

She hesitates, her fingers hovering over three faded switches: *b-o-y*. For an achingly long minute, she doesn't move. Can he really be called a *boy* when he's also a monster? Is there even a word for a demon in human skin?

Another teeth-clenching minute passes, then she finally types the word—not because it's the best way to describe the young man, but because she just plain doesn't want to say anything more. Not over a stupid telegraph, anyway.

She can explain the crazier details to Shaw in person, when he gets here.

She smacks the button at the base of the telegraph and waits while the thing whines, clatters, then finally goes still. In the silence that follows, she sits on the warped deck, hugs her knees to her chest, and peers out at the sludgy waters of the bay until the gentle sway of the boat makes her eyelids droop.

There's a *monster* in the cabin below her, shackled and asleep.

There's a *person* in the cabin below her, shackled and asleep.

There's a *boy* in the cabin below her, shackled and asleep—a boy with eyes like seawater and hair the color of dark earth. A boy that somehow turned into a beast and then back again. A boy who seems to have found a way to *beat* the disease ... or at least a way to wriggle around it.

The whole situation has her reeling, her mind stretched thin, her insides a quivering mess of coal smoke and jagged ice. Is she supposed to hate him? Pity him? To feel something horribly in between?

What will Shaw suggest they do? ... What would *Mom* have wanted?

What, what, *what*?

She grimaces and clenches her misty hand inside her glove, jamming those iron fingers into her leg until her calf begins to ache. Then she squeezes even tighter, pinching her muscle until her leg radiates with pain. She stays like this with her eyes winced shut, her teeth clamped together, because at least *this* is simple.

At least *this* she can understand.

# 53

Kemple doesn't fall down, but *in*—into an abyss so dark and endless that he finds himself wondering: was the girl's syringe full of poison, perhaps? Is this what it's like to be . . . dead?

The void doesn't answer him. It offers no clue, no insight. It simply keeps *going* and *going* in every possible direction, stretching and unfurling like a bottomless well filled with the thickest, bleakest ink.

Like a universe where every star has collapsed, leaving nothing but an infinite stretch of gaping black holes.

Like—

"Tell me everything," says a low, gruff voice, the words echoing all around him.

Kemple twists toward the sound. His body twirls weightlessly in the dark. "Is someone here?" he calls out.

His voice bubbles from his lips, then fades to nothing.

Then a new voice fills the shadows. "He was . . . one of those things," the voice says, the words thin and gritty. "And then he just . . . *wasn't*. I don't even know what to think anymore."

The voice is familiar in a grating way, and it takes him a moment to place it. When he finally does, his face flushes with an angry sort of heat. It's the girl with the metal hand. And she's talking about *him*.

But to who? And why?

. . . And where the heck is he?

"He told you this is his boat?" says the first voice. A man's voice.

There's a pause, then the girl replies flatly, "Yes, but he could've been lying."

*Lying?* Kemple grits his teeth and writhes in the blackened space. Of all the things he could've done to the girl, *lying* would've been the last on his list.

The conversation continues, warbling around him, the voices stretched and muffled. It's as if he's trapped in giant fishbowl while two strangers speak on the other side of the glass.

Or . . . it's as if he's still lying on the cabin floor of the *Nameless*, naked and shackled, while some terrible drug courses through his veins, shoving his consciousness down into this bleak, unnatural abyss.

Which would mean that the two speakers aren't strangers—they're his *captors*.

He thrashes and claws at the void, but he might as well be slashing at outer space.

"He could've lied, sure," the man says. "Or not. We won't know until he wakes. In the meantime . . . " The man trails off, and Kemple finds himself straining to hear better.

What's the next maddening assumption that these two fools will come up with?

Finally the girl lets out a sigh. "You want me to search the boat."

Kemple scowls and yells out into the shadows. This is his boat! What gives them the right?

The pair falls silent for a moment, and Kemple tenses in the darkness. Are they looking at his body, right now?

Did he make some kind of noise?

If he screams loud enough in this strange limbo, will his voice somehow reach the other side?

"Someone needs to keep an eye on him," the man finally says, and the casualness in his voice tells Kemple all he needs to know: his body didn't stir. He didn't make a sound.

No, he's too far down in the depths to send out even the smallest of ripples.

He sighs and lets himself drift. Directionless. Aimless. Like a rudderless boat in a sea of muddy ink.

"Besides," the man continues, "I can see the emotion in you right now. Don't want you doing anything rash. Lord knows you've got a knack for that."

The girl scoffs and starts to say something, but the man talks over her. "So, yes," he says, "I'll watch the boy. You search the boat. Use those lenses of yours. Find the clues that're no doubt hiding in plain sight." He clears his throat and says, "We'll solve this riddle, one way or another."

Kemple sags in the darkness. He should be livid about this. The thought of two strangers rummaging through his belongings—which, admittedly, are pretty sparse—*should* be enough to make him scream. Especially while he lies on the floor, drugged and exposed. And knotted in *chains*, no less.

He *should* be screaming at the top of his lungs. But right now he just . . . doesn't want to feel anything at all. He's so tired of all of it—the heart-pinching loss of Josephyn; the gut-clenching guilt over Gideon; the mind-gripping worry over Viola, and now the mystery of this iron-gloved girl; the way his life has just been one tiresome struggle after another, a hopeless spiral that only seems to get worse, no matter how he tries to fix it. A plummet with no apparent end.

Not until he finally gives up and gives in, anyway.

Not until he's dead in some grave.

And of course there's the monster inside him, too—the horrifying presence that he can feel even *here*, down in these dark, chemical depths. That beastly pressure thrumming against his insides, like a ghastly balloon between his organs—one that feels like it's, once again, starting to inflate.

As if on cue, that terrible growl rumbles through the void, the weight of it shuddering his bones. *Seek.*

*Hunt.*

*DEVOUR.*

This time, he *does* feel something: a heat in his stomach. A weight in his veins. A steaming, fiery pressure that comes not from the creature, but from some deeper, warbling part of himself.

To hell with the beast. To hell with the strangers trampling his things. To hell with *everything.*

It's time for him to wake up.

He grabs at the darkness with his fingers curled like claws. He kicks at the void like he's climbing a mountain. Somewhere in the abyss below him, he can feel the creature doing the same: lurching and rising, snarling and thrashing, its monstrous body struggling to connect with his own, its ravenous mind straining to be *free.* But he's closer to the surface, closer to the voices in his cabin, closer to that frayed, dusty cot where he's spent so many nights blinking up at the glass-streaked stars, nights where the tears burning his eyes felt like the only proof he had that his soul was still *there*, somewhere lost inside him, still clinging on. Still worth fighting for.

The beast lets out a horrible roar and suddenly a furred arm slashes up from the depths. Jagged claws sink into the flesh of his legs and the pain is like an explosion in his thighs, the heat of it scorching his nerves. The monster twists and yanks, tugging him back toward the shadows. But he doesn't stop climbing. Doesn't stop pulling. Doesn't stop *fighting*, because suddenly it all makes sense: *this* is what his life has taught him. *This* is the lesson he was meant to learn all along: it's *all* a struggle, and it always will be. And he can lie down like a worm and let the world roll over him—or he can grab that darkness by its throat and shove it the hell out of his way.

So he kicks at the beast until its claws tear free. He wrenches at the darkness until it crumples away. Suddenly the world fills with sound: the rush of air and water, the creak of old wood and damp rope. The clattering of rusted metal.

He coughs, gasps, and forces his eyelids apart.

A dust-cluttered beam of sunlight lances through his cabin window. The splintered floorboards dig into his back. He tries to sit up, but his wrists and ankles are still bound, his skin still pinched by those cold, immovable chains. Then the stairs to the cabin thunder with a flurry of footsteps, and suddenly there's grizzled-looking man looming above him—and the man is aiming a pistol at Kemple's face.

"You're going to answer every one of my questions with complete and unyielding honesty," the man barks, "or I'll blast your brains out the back of your skull."

Kemple tries to speak, but his throat feels like it's been hollowed out with sandpaper. His mind feels even worse. In the end, he barely manages a nod.

"Good," the man says, uncocking the gun. He narrows his eyes, leans threateningly close, and says, "Let's start at the beginning."

The beginning? Kemple frowns. Honestly, where does he even start? He glances away from the man, just to find something less intimidating to look at, and this is when he spots her: the metal-handed girl, sitting tensely on the stairs. His eyes connect with her gray-lensed goggles, and her lips twist into a frown. Then she sighs and turns away.

He's not sure what to make of that look. Maybe she's not even sure, herself. "I guess," he rasps, speaking more to her than to the man, "it all started with Abner." He gulps slowly, just to give his throat some relief.

Then he winces his eyes shut and tells them . . . everything.

# 54

Brielle hates to admit it, but the boy's story really is quite . . . compelling. And, if she's being completely honest with herself—it's a little bit sad, too. Which only adds to her anger. *And* her fatigue. Last night was exhausting—of course the *boy* was allowed to snore away in the cabin below, while she and the detective were forced to alternate shifts. She quickly learned that it's impossible to sleep on a battered sailboat—especially when there's a slumbering monster onboard. Not even the steady slosh of the bay could put her mind at ease.

Now she's sitting on the boat's dingy stairwell with her brain feeling like curdled mush, while the boy calmly explains everything. By the time he's done, her head is practically spinning.

A cat scratch? He says he caught the disease from a *cat scratch*, of all things? And then there's the whole absurdity of this scientist who connected a *device* to the boy's heart. To top it all off, the man even had a bizarre *clockwork daughter*?

Is anything even real anymore?

By the time Shaw grips her elbow and leads her back up to the boat's sun-bleached deck, she's practically seething. "Just let me kill him already," she mutters, keeping her voice low. She yanks her arm free from the detective's grasp and glares at him through her dark lenses. "You heard all the nonsense he was spilling," she whispers. "He's just trying to confuse us to buy time."

Shaw doesn't respond. He merely turns toward the handrail and gazes quietly at the early morning sky, his eyes creased into slits.

She looks, too, just to see what the heck he's peering at.

The sun has crested somewhere behind the clouds, staining everything a dazzling pink and orange. Even the bay looks like it's been filled with peach-colored ink. The view is elegant, and soothing, and so horribly pristine that Brielle has a sudden urge to light the whole harbor on fire, just to stain the sky with putrid black smoke. Just to smear something *ugly* onto all that prettiness. "Did you hear what I said?" she hisses.

Shaw finally acknowledges her with a nod, his gaze still pinned to the sea. "I did hear you," he says. The sailboat tilts and sloshes against the tide, and the detective calmly leans with the motion.

Brielle's teeth grind so hard, her jaw starts to ache. *"And?"*

"And," the detective says, turning to look at her lenses, "how did you sleep?"

Brielle can only blink. "I didn't," she finally says. "Or if I did, I don't remember it."

Shaw nods and says, "Same here."

"Good. Great. Wonderful," she says, her voice dripping with sarcasm. "Now that we've got that out of the way, can we get back to the topic at hand?"

Shaw yawns openly and stretches like a scruffy, unwashed cat. Then he sighs and tells her, "I think killing the boy would be a terrible mistake."

If she were an animal right now, her fur would be bristling. "Keeping him *alive* would be a terrible mistake," she snaps. "He's an Aílouros. And everything he said is so out of line with what we know."

"I noticed that," Shaw says, thumbing his lip.

"And *you're* the one who told me that if something doesn't line up, just look for the most obvious conclusion."

The detective's mouth curls into a lopsided grin, as if he finds this whole conversation amusing, and she's struck by another wild impulse: to smack the grin right off his face.

"And what, in your opinion," he finally says, "is the most obvious conclusion here?"

Brielle just gapes at him. Does she even need to say it aloud? "That he's *lying*, of course! That he just . . . made everything up!"

Shaw frowns and shakes his head. Below them, the cabin echoes with the rustle of chains. They both pause to listen. When the boy doesn't make any more sounds, Shaw clears his throat and says, "He didn't make up the part where he turned into a beast and then turned back again." He points at her chest with a grubby finger. "And that part *does* line up. His clothes look like they were torn apart from the inside out. There's blood and hair on your grappling hook—hair that looks a lot more animal than human. And you even told me that you saw the boy change, then change back." The detective pauses and mumbles something under his breath. Then he glances at her goggles and says, "Really, the only obvious conclusion here is that the boy must be telling the truth. Maybe not the whole truth—but enough of it to be taken seriously." Before she has a chance to protest, he raises a finger and adds, "Enough, at least, to warrant further investigation."

The whole speech lasts barely half a minute, but it practically knocks the breath right out of her. *Further investigation?* Is he out of his mind? How would they even *start* to verify any of the boy's wild claims? She squeezes her eyes shut, shoves her goggles up onto her forehead, and pinches the bridge of her nose, as if this might somehow relieve the throbbing pressure in her skull. It doesn't. "I thought you'd have answers," she mutters. "I thought you'd make this whole mess go away. Now it sounds like you want to . . . to . . ." She shakes her head and jams her goggles back into place. "Heck, I don't even *know* what you want to do. But I can tell I'm not going to like it."

Shaw looks back out at the churning bay, and Brielle does the same. The day has ripened a little more, giving everything a scorched look. Even the air feels warmer. Stickier. Inside her glove, her wispy hand feels like a miniature storm cloud. She frowns, and fidgets, and the silence stretches out until she can't bear it anymore, until her voice is tumbling out of her mouth before she even has a chance to think. "What do you want me to do?" she grumbles.

The detective finally looks her way, his haggard face creasing in the sunlight. "I'll need to talk to some higher-ups. But I should be able to wriggle things our way."

The storm cloud in her glove curls and twitches, making her iron fingers clatter and bend. "What *things?*"

Shaw clicks his tongue against the roof of his mouth and musses her hair. "Stay with me, here. Of everything the boy said, what's the part that we'd want to look into the most?"

Brielle frowns, steps out of his reach, and smooths the mess of her hair back into place. Frankly, she doesn't *care* what Shaw wants to look into. But he's obviously made up his mind. "I don't know," she admits. "And I'm tired of thinking about any of it, to be completely honest."

Shaw exhales slowly, then says, "The mechanical girl. *Viola.* The one that makes the potions." He pauses, as if he's waiting for her to respond. When she doesn't, he says, "The *potions* that, according to our young captive, allowed him to transform back into a human being."

Brielle lets the boy's story warble through her head once more. The details are still blurry, but she remembers one thing the boy said—the only thing that really stuck with her: "He said," she mumbles, "that the clockwork girl wants to kill him."

"That he did," Shaw replies. "Which is why *you* are going with him. To meet her."

The suggestion is so outrageous that her mind literally goes blank. "What?" is all she's able to say. "*What?*"

"I'd do it myself," he says, "but let's face it: I'm no spring chicken anymore. You've got youth on your side. Plus, you're fully capable of taking care of yourself. And to be blunt: you're the only person, besides myself, that I would trust with a task like this."

The pressure in her head has become so horribly muddled that she doesn't even know what to think. Or how to *feel*, for that matter. If she had to guess, she'd pick *anger*. Or rage. No—right now, it's something stronger than either of those. Something closer to . . . fury. "And what if I tell you to screw the hell off with your so-called *task*?"

Shaw blinks at her lenses, then frowns and looks out at the bay. "Then I suppose I'll just have to accompany the boy myself." He pauses in a deliberate way, as if he wants his words to sink in.

As if he *wants* her to picture him in her place—the tired, middle-aged detective, escorting a monstrous young man to meet a violent clockwork girl.

He doesn't have to say a word to imply the obvious: he wouldn't survive the trip home. Not even with his trusty revolver.

Her voice comes out in a wobble. "Why even bother taking such a risk?"

Shaw replies quickly, as if he's been waiting for her to ask this question all along. "Because of what it could *mean*, Gabrielle. Think about it: this *Viola* girl made a potion that suppressed the beast in that boy's veins. She didn't have to hunt him down. She didn't need to rip out his heart. She only needed tubes and gears and chemicals—and the know-how, which she clearly possesses." He takes a slow, steadying breath, then says quietly, "This could change everything. Not just for Iron Bay, but for *you*, Gabrielle. You've been on a quest to avenge your mother for so long now—a tireless mission to somehow right that horrible wrong. Wouldn't it be nice to finally consider that mission *accomplished?*"

Brielle lifts her good hand and, before she even realizes what she's doing, she slaps him across the face. Not roughly. Not cruelly. But just hard enough to let him know that he's crossed some invisible line. "I'll never feel *accomplished* when it comes to Mom," she says, her throat already tightening, her eyes already starting to burn. "I'm grateful for everything you've done for me," she whispers, looking away from the detective, "but right now, I hate you for even saying such a thing."

Shaw doesn't say anything for the longest time. When he finally does speak, his voice is soft and creaky. "Guess I should consider myself lucky you didn't use your other hand." When she doesn't respond, he sighs and says, "You're right. I shouldn't have said that."

"It's fine," she mutters. "I shouldn't have hit you."

Another stretch of quiet falls between them, filled only by the distant screech of gulls, the creaking of wood, and the endless slosh of the bay. Brielle tries not to think of the boy, but her mind drifts toward him anyway. She pictures him below deck, still struggling against his restraints, his attention fixed on the cabin roof.

Would the monster in his blood enhance his hearing?

Has he been listening to their conversation this whole time?

. . . have those strips of fabric shifted at all, revealing more of his naked skin . . . ?

This last thought makes her cheeks flush, and she scowls and shakes her head until her brain feels thoroughly scrambled.

Shaw finally breaks the silence with a cough. "I'll do it myself," he says. "It was wrong of me to suggest you do it, anyway."

Part of her wants to say, *Yes. Yes it* was *wrong of you.* But she finds herself uttering something else entirely, something that even she can't believe she's saying: "No," she whispers. "I'll do it. Just tell me when and where."

Shaw doesn't argue, or question, or explain anything further. He simply pats her shoulder with a heavy hand, then climbs slowly off the boat. Only when he's standing on the dock does he finally say, "I'll get the wheels into motion." He nods in her direction without fully looking her way. "You just keep an ear out for our new friend down there."

"*Our new friend,*" she parrots with a scoff. Then she says nothing else, because what else *is* there to say? How do you respond to madness without going insane yourself?

How do you even begin to try?

She watches Shaw trudge off the pier with her lips clamped shut, her breath thick and fiery in her chest. She doesn't move. She doesn't even breathe.

Only when the detective turns a corner, his hunched figure slipping out of sight, does she finally let out a bitter, lung-emptying scream.

# 55

Kemple's morning is a jumbled blur. He can't tell if his confusion is from the girl's syringe, or if the monster in his blood is simply messing with his head. Probably a combination of both.

What he *does* know is that he spends a lot of time stumbling and groaning, and even drooling, while somebody stuffs his arms and legs into a starchy set of clothes. He knows that his mouth is held open, and mushy food is jammed between his teeth. He knows that two pairs of hands take turns scrubbing his skin with cold, soapy water, while that unnatural fog wraps around his brain.

And then, at some point, the mist around his thoughts finally clears, and he finds himself sitting on a fractured wooden bench, in a weed-strewn field, beneath a gray mid-morning sky—with that goggle-eyed, metal-handed girl sitting quietly beside him, her face twisted into a scowl.

"Okay," he says, turning to look at the girl, "what is this?" He can tell the dirt-brown shirt he has on has never been worn, because the collar is so stiff that it keeps itching his neck. When he tries to scratch at it, though, his wrists snag on something hard, and he lets out a tired sigh.

Apparently, he's still wearing that lovely set of chains.

"Nice touch," he says, shaking his arms. The shackles clatter and clink. "Threading the restraints *under* my clothes. That must've been quite a challenge." He imagines the girl and that sour-looking man working together, struggling to pull an outfit over his limp body, weaving those chains under his sleeves, and the absurdity of it all makes him laugh.

The girl twists on the bench to look at him, her face tight and unreadable behind those dark lenses. "You were naked," she says. She clenches that metal hand of hers around one of the bench's slats, and the wood crackles in her grip. "And judging by the look of things, you must've been *cold*, too." She stares at him, unflinchingly, like she's waiting for him to grasp the insult. Like she *wants* him to feel embarrassed.

Like she . . . cares what he thinks.

But why would it matter to her if she made him feel bad? Come to think of it: what is it that she even *wants*? "Good one," he says, rolling his eyes. He tries his best to look casual, careless, but the tightness of the chains only allow him to look *cramped*, at best. So he sighs and asks the girl directly: "Why are we here? And what do you want from me?"

The girl doesn't respond. Not immediately. For a while she just sits there, staring at him with those coal-colored goggles, her eyes a frustrating mystery. Then she frowns and jerks her head toward the dead grass in front of them. "You've got two normal eyes," she says, with just a hint of jealousy. "Use them."

So he does, peering out at the dry, weather-worn field. Only then does he see it: a thin, barely visible line of rusted metal and dark wood, snaking all the way to the horizon. "Train tracks," he mutters.

"Good-looking *and* smart," the girl blurts out. "What a winning combination." She winces and mutters to herself, and he looks at her sideways.

"Was that supposed to be a compliment," he says, "or an insult?"

The girl shakes her head and turns away. "I don't know what that was supposed to be," she admits. She sits there for a moment, staring off into the distance. Then she turns back around and jams one of those metal fingers into the meat of his shoulder. "Look, I don't want to be here any more than you do, okay? If I had things my way, you'd be dead already. Lucky for you, Shaw thought otherwise. And once he's got his mind set on something . . ." She waves her non-gloved hand vaguely through the air. "Well, that's why we're here now."

"Shaw," he says, repeating the name. He waits for some kind of bodily response, like a bitterness in his throat or a tightness in his chest, but the man's name doesn't make him react at all. The girl beside him, on the other hand, has his body reacting in so many different ways that he's not even sure where to begin. Does he find her compelling, or revolting? Something else altogether?

Heck, maybe it's a mixture of both?

He frowns and, just to put his mind on something simpler, he asks, "So if he's the one who pointed a gun at me, then who are *you*?"

The girl sighs and shifts on the bench, moving a little farther away. "I'm nobody," she says. "End of discussion. Now let's just shut up and wait for the train, okay?"

But it's not okay. How could it be? He's still in *chains*, after all. "Then where are we headed?" he asks, even though the question feels . . . dangerous. Come to think of it, he's not even sure he *wants* to know the answer.

This time when the girl twists on the bench, she turns her whole body toward him, like she's one twitch away from flat-out punching him in the jaw. "What part of *shut up and wait for the train* do you not understand?"

"You put me in *shackles*," he counters, shaking the chains. "And before that, you stabbed me in the neck with a syringe." The girl opens her mouth to say something, but he cuts her off before she can get a word out. "And before *that*," he says louder, "you kicked your way onto *my boat*."

"And before *that*," the girl shouts, lunging into his personal space, "*you* turned into a *monster!*" She glares at him with her lenses nearly touching his face, her breath coming out of her in short, angry huffs. Then she flinches and moves away from him again, clutching that leather bag of hers closer to her side. "Or have you conveniently forgotten that part, too?" she says.

"I can never forget that part," he admits, quietly. "It'll haunt me every day of my life."

This time when the girl looks at him, he can almost feel the thoughts swirling in her head. The confusion. The frustration. That same desperate search for an answer that'll never come, no matter how long or how hard you look. "I never knew my mother," he says, the words tumbling out of him.

The girl twists her face, bunching her cheeks against her goggles. "What?"

"I don't know," he says. And he really, truly doesn't. But the words keep coming, anyway, shoving their way past his lips. Clawing their way into the open air. "It's just, you were looking at me like . . . like someone jammed a puzzle into the center of your life, one that you can't seem to solve, no matter which way you look at it. And I know that feeling too well. That's how I've always felt about my mother."

The girl's face slackens. Then she sniffs and looks away. "If you're waiting for me to talk about *my* mom, you can forget it."

"I wasn't—"

"Because so what if you didn't know yours? Why should I care?"

"I never said you—"

"And you know what's a million times worse than not knowing your mom?" she snaps. She moves into his space again, so close that he has to lean away, just to stop her lenses from crashing into his chin. "Try *knowing* your mom," she says, "and *loving* your mom, and then try watching her get *ripped* out of your life in front of your eyes, by the very same kind of monster that *you are*." She shoves him with her mechanical hand, nearly pushing him over. Then she turns away and says, in a voice that's suddenly small and distant, "So don't even talk to me about not knowing, because I'd rather not know. I'd give *anything* to not know."

Kemple glances down at the chains around his ankles, because he doesn't quite know where else to look. It's not exactly clear what happened to this girl, either— something about her mother, obviously, and a creature like *him*—but there's no denying the emotion beneath her words. Not just anger, but *pain*. A sadness that sounds like it's been tied into a hopeless knot around her heart.

Kind of like the chemical-filled tubes that Gideon knotted around his own.

He touches the bulge in his shirt, pinching that crank through the fabric, and when that familiar barb of pain stabs at his heart, he winces and says, "I'm sorry."

The girl bunches her face, but doesn't say anything.

"I don't know what that's like," he continues, "but I can imagine how much it hurts."

The girl smacks the bench with her metal glove. "Will you just stop talking already?" She glances at the empty tracks and shakes her head. "And where the heck is this stupid train? I just want to get on, get this over with, and be done with all of this. I don't want to talk. I don't want to *bond*. And I sure as hell don't want to trade sob stories, least of all with *you*. So can you just sit there with your mouth shut until it's time to board? Think you can manage that?"

The girl sounds so much like Viola right now that he almost blurts out an insult about her inhuman looks, just from habit alone. But he catches himself just in time. Thankfully. He's pretty sure a punch from that mechanical glove would hurt just as much as one of Viola's clockwork slaps. "Look," he says, "how am I supposed to know how you want me to act if you won't even tell me what we're doing?"

"Waiting for a train."

The words come out of her with such a sense of finality that it almost feels wrong to ask a follow-up question. "For . . . what purpose?"

The girl clenches her teeth, making the muscles of her jaw bulge under her skin, and he finds himself bracing for another angry lecture. Instead, she merely looks at him and says flatly, "Shaw thinks your story is worth looking into. Especially the part about that man's clockwork daughter."

"Viola?" he says. Her name leaves a sour taste in his mouth, and an even worse feeling in his gut.

The girl turns to look at the horizon, twisting the edges of her goggles with her gloveless hand. Then she lets out a sigh. "There it is. It's about time."

He follows her gaze and spots a thin tendril of smoke in the distance. The plume looks . . . ominous. Like a giant minute hand, lurching just a little bit closer. Like a monster crawling from the depths. Like . . . he's running out of time.

"Wait," he says, straining against his shackles, "what about her?"

The girl glances at him, then shoves off the bench, her boots gritting against the dirt. The noise is so familiar—so much like the sound of Viola's feet grinding against Gideon's warehouse floor—that he instinctively flinches. "It doesn't matter," she says. "Get on the train. Do what I say. That's all you need to know."

Like hell it is. "What. About. Viola," he says, shoving the words through his teeth.

The girl stares hard at him with those ash-colored goggles, the cloudy sky reflecting off her lenses. Behind her, the train has finally trudged over the horizon. From where he's sitting, it looks like a huge, diseased worm. When the girl finally speaks again, she sounds tired. Of everything. "You told us that thing in your chest only works because of the girl's potions. You also said that the scientist died because *she* fell into him."

The memory of that night threatens to surface all over again, like an air bubble ready to burst, and it takes everything he has to shove it back down. "I don't follow," he says. But then something clicks, and his eyes go wide. "You want to . . . to *blackmail* her?"

"*I* don't want to do any of this," the girl says. "But Shaw gave me no other option." She turns to look at the approaching train, then says quietly, "And no. Not blackmail. Not exactly. We're going to offer her a choice. She can show us how she made the elixir that brought you back, or . . . she'll be held accountable for that man's death."

The train has become audible now, the air filling with its steady chuff and groan, and for a moment they both just . . . listen. Then his voice flies out of him like a bullet. "That's the worst possible plan in existence. You *do* realize that she wants to kill me, right? How do you think she'll feel when I turn up with you at my side, throwing a *threat* her way? And here I am, bound by *chains*, of all things." He yanks and kicks at the shackles, as if she needs the reminder. "You might as well tie a bow around my neck and sing *Happy Birthday* to her." When the girl doesn't respond, he puts it as simply as he can: "She's going to end me. And you won't be able to stop her."

The girl's face tightens. Then she looks away. "Sorry to tell you, but that's not exactly a bad outcome in my eyes."

His shoulders sag. His arms slacken. For an instant his mind goes so thoroughly blank that all he can sense is that dull thrum at the base of his spine, like the relentless ticking of a monstrous clock.

Like the pulse of some terrible beast, slumbering in the dark.

"And what if I turn first . . . ?" he says flatly. "What if my crank doesn't work again? What if I can't stop—"

"Then I kill you myself," the girl says quickly. The answer is so swift, so devoid of hesitation, that he doesn't bother asking anything more.

Only when the train puffs and creaks to a stop in front of them, its dark bulk ticking and steaming, does he finally say, "If you're sending me to my death, the least you can do is tell me your name."

The girl wraps her metal fingers around the chain between his wrists, yanks him to his feet, and says, "Brielle." Then she adds quickly, "And no, I don't want to know yours."

"Brielle," he repeats, rolling it over his tongue. It's a nice name. Kind of pretty, actually. Now that he's heard it, he can't imagine her being called anything else. "It suits you," he says.

She pulls him toward the locomotive with a frown—not an angry one, but one that just makes her look ... sad. Then she whispers a word so quietly that he almost doesn't hear it. "Thanks."

Despite everything, he finds himself smiling. At least now, if he really is heading to his doom, it won't be beside a *total* stranger.

At the very least, when Viola finally gets her metal hands on him, it won't feel like he's dying alone.

# 56

Shaw never prepared her for this.

Of all the thoughts swirling through Brielle's head right now, *this* is the one that she keeps snagging on. The one that keeps making her pause. Shaw never prepared her for this.

Not for a boy who's a monster. Not for a monster who's a boy. Not for all these conflicting feelings surging inside her, like a storm inside a glove.

Sure, the detective taught her to hunt and kill, but he never *once* suggested that she might, one day, come across an Aílouros that expresses sorrow and regret, a monster that *sympathizes* and *compliments*, a beast of a boy with eyes so startlingly blue that when he peers at her lenses she simply *has* to look away, otherwise it feels like she might just . . . fall right in.

She grips her hair with her good hand and slumps back against the leather seat.

"Are you okay?" the boy asks.

His voice is annoyingly smooth—too calm and steady to be anything but practiced—and she finds herself grimacing. How can he ask her such a thing right now? Why would *he* be worried about *her*? "I'm not the one chained up," she reminds him. When he merely blinks at her, she lets go of her hair and twists around on her seat to look at . . . anything but him.

The rest of the train appears to be empty. Diamond-patterned carpets. Beige leather seats. Windows lined with smooth brass trim, and an endless line of clear gas lanterns. The locomotive is pretty, and expensive, and utterly . . . abandoned. Aside from whoever is conducting the train, they might as well be the only people on earth.

She grits her teeth and whirls back around to glare at the boy. "Where the heck are the passengers?" she grumbles, more to herself than to him.

The boy squints up and down the aisle, then frowns. "I'm guessing your *Shaw* arranged for this to be a private trip."

"It's just *Shaw*," she says. "Not *my* Shaw." She unfastens her satchel and starts rummaging through it. Then she stops to scowl at the bag. What the heck is she even looking for? "And damn him," she says, "if you're right."

The boy cracks a lopsided smile and rests his hands on the polished table between them. His chains clatter against the wood, and the sound makes her heart flutter a little, not from excitement, but from *panic*—did she secure the links firmly enough? Did she remember to take out the slack?

If he snaps his restraints right now and lunges over the table, will she be able to defend herself in time?

"I'm not feeling any violent urges," the boy says, as if reading her mind. "So you don't have to worry. To be honest, I can't even sense the monster at all, which . . . worries me a little."

She tries to look uninterested, but she can't stop herself from asking: "Do you normally feel it?"

The boy swallows and looks away. "Almost always," he says gently.

Again, she tries to act bored, but another question slips out. "What does it . . . feel like?"

The boy furrows his brow and looks down at the table, where he's dug his fingernails into the varnish. "Mostly it's a pressure," he says. "Like something is weighing me down from the inside. Like gravity has been flipped around, and it's pulling on whatever's inside me, trying to get it out."

She waits for his answer to do something to her—to ease some of the tightness in her chest, or to soften some of that maddening curiosity that's plagued her since the day she met Shaw.

. . . Since the day she lost Mom.

But all she gets is *angry*. Not at the boy, but at herself. She's supposed to be *delivering* him, like a package. Which means she should view him as an object. A thing. Something to be thrown away.

Nothing more than a means to an end.

But the more she hears him talk—heck, the more she *looks* at him—the more of a person he seems to be. And not just a person, but a thoughtful one. An *emotional* one.

One that's not exactly hard on the eyes, either.

"You okay?" the boy asks. Again.

She blinks and shakes her head, hoping the movement might clear her mind. It doesn't. "Of course I'm okay," she says, maybe a little too harshly. "Why wouldn't I be?"

The boy shrugs and looks away. "No reason, I guess." He tilts his head until the bones in his neck crack, and the motion makes a lock of his hair swing down over his eyes.

She has a sudden, irrational urge to reach across the table so she can brush his hair back into place. With her good hand.

. . . What the heck is wrong with her?

She scowls and stands from the booth. "I'm going to look around," she says. "If you try anything—"

"I know," the boy says wearily. "Another poisoned dart to the neck, I'm sure."

The flat, almost *bored* tone of his voice makes her teeth grind. "If you want more variety," she says, patting her glove against her satchel, "I can always pull out my hatchet."

When he doesn't say anything to that, she smirks and pivots away—far enough to get a better view of the rest of the train, but not far enough to let him out of her sight. She may be restless, but she isn't *dumb*. And she certainly knows well enough to—

Her eyes catch on something, and she stops. A slip of parchment has been taped onto one of the cabin windows. In the center of the page is a block of handwritten text.

She wastes no time lunging for it and yanking it off the glass.

*The train is all yours*, the note starts out. Immediately, she recognizes Shaw's terrible cursive.

*Just stay on it. I've labeled your trip as a "prisoner transport." Even described the crank on the boy's chest. Blasted the notice through the telegraph, all over Iron Bay. If that clockwork girl is as determined as the boy claims, she'll find you both soon enough. See you at the end of the line. —Shaw*

*P.S. Use your head, Gabrielle.*

She squeezes the parchment between her iron fingers, but she can't crumple the note fast enough. *See you at the end of the line?* When Shaw cooked up this whole train idea, he never said anything about riding it *all day long*. She lets the wadded message fall to the carpeted floor and looks back at the boy with a grimace.

The boy studies her face for a moment. Then his eyes track down to the crumpled note by her boots. "Bad news, I'm guessing."

"Great detective work there," she says bitterly. "What gave it away? The look on my face? The scrunched piece of paper?" She crosses her arms over her chest, just because she doesn't know where else to put her hands. "Apparently, I'm stuck with you until this train finally stops. Or at least until your metal girlfriend decides to show up."

"She's not my girlfriend," he says, shaking his head. "Not even close. If anything she's more like . . ." He waves his hands around, making his shackles clatter against the table. "Like an evil, metallic sister." His eyes flick up toward her lenses, then he quickly looks away. "To tell you the truth, I've never actually had a girlfriend. I don't even know what that's like." He lets out a soft chuckle, then sighs. "How pathetic is that?"

She wants to say, *It's not pathetic.* Because if it were, then that would mean *she's* pathetic, too. And she's not quite sure she can handle that right now. So she keeps her mouth shut and twists her goggles until his face is all she can see—and what she sees is a boy who looks too pretty, too kind, too *heartbroken* to be a monster. A boy who, in another life, would have no problem finding a girl to love him. She takes her time winding her goggles back into place. When she finally speaks again, her voice comes out thin and wobbly. "At least you don't need these just to see," she says, flicking her iron thumb against the frame of her goggles. "And good luck finding a boy to *look* at you, let alone date you, when you've got this on the end of your arm." She clenches and unclenches her steamy hand inside the glove, and those clockwork fingers respond dutifully, curling and uncurling like metal-plated worms.

"I think they're both kind of neat, actually," the boy says, and he sounds so honest, so *sincere*, that she can't stop herself from blushing. Luckily, he doesn't seem to notice. "I mean, you're a little cruel to me sometimes," he adds with a smirk, "but otherwise, you seem alright."

She starts to laugh, then catches herself and forces her frown back into place. Why is he being so nice to her?

What is he planning to do?

"I don't know what you're up to," she says, "but you're not going to catch me with my guard down. So just forget it, okay?"

The boy slumps back in his seat, making the leather squeak and wheeze. "You're probably the last person I'm going to see before . . ." He swallows. "Before Viola gets here. So I figure we might as well *try* to get along in the meantime."

This time when her laugh slips out, she doesn't fight it at all. Her and an Aílouros, chumming around like the best of friends? That's possibly the most ridiculous thing she's ever heard. When she finally stops laughing and looks at the boy, however, his face is stern, his eyes wide and eager.

"I'm Kemple," he says. "Now we aren't strangers anymore."

She stares at him then, with her eyes stinging and her chest flooding with an uncomfortable sort of heat, until the engine car lets out a shrill whistle, and the whole train starts to move. Then she slips into the seat across from him, making sure not to look his way. She fixes her gaze on the window, instead, as if the slow-moving hills on the other side of the glass can somehow settle the chaos in her head.

*The boy is a monster, but . . .*

*The monster is a boy, and yet . . .*
*A package to deliver, that's all he . . .*
*Kemple, his name is . . .*
*How has he never had a girlfriend when he looks so . . . when he acts so . . . ?*

Soon the train reaches full speed, smearing everything outside into a meaningless blur. Everything *inside* Brielle gets even worse. Eventually she twists her lenses until the cabin shrinks to a distant point, pulling her thoughts down with it, funneling all the madness of the world into a single, horrible truth: she's not traveling with a beast. She's just . . . leading a poor boy to his death.

# 57

As soon as the train picked up speed, all the worries in Kemple's head just . . . slid away. Now his skull feels like it's been hollowed out, leaving nothing behind but pure, empty space. It's the same feeling he used to have during those quiet hours whenever Abner was asleep. That muscle-easing sense of safety. Of relief. Of knowing that, at least for the time being, there was nothing else in the world that could hurt him.

Of course, he wasn't in shackles then. And he wasn't riding on a train, against his will, toward a clockwork girl who wanted to end him.

And he *definitely* didn't have a demon lurking in his veins.

So why does everything feel . . . *fine*?

Perhaps it's the chains. As crazy as it seems, there really *is* something freeing about being so helplessly bound, like a fly caught in a web. No control over what happens next. No pressure to make any decisions. No point in forming a plan. Maybe—in some weird, twisted way—getting shackled is the best thing that's happened to him in years.

Let someone *else* worry about his life, for a change.

But he finds himself shaking his head. Because that just . . . isn't it. So, what *is*? What's made all the tension drain out of his limbs?

Why doesn't he give a damn?

He sneaks a glance at the metal-handed girl. At *Brielle*. Maybe the answer lies with her.

She frowns, squirms on her seat, and lifts her chin like she's ready to spar. "What?" she asks.

*What*, indeed. How do you tell the girl who wants you dead that you suddenly don't . . . care? "Never mind," he mutters.

"Just spit it out," she says. "You've been staring at me since we left, and it's really starting to get on my nerves." She drums her metal fingers against the table, tapping out a steady rhythm. "If we're going to . . . what was it you said again?"

When he just blinks at her, she huffs impatiently. "Something about me being the last person you'll see . . ."

"Ah." He nods. *That.* "I said we should try to get along in the meantime."

She stops thrumming her gloved fingers. "Right. If we're going to do *that*, then I'd prefer you stop gawking at me like I'm some kind of a freak. Otherwise, forget it."

He frowns and looks out the window. "I can do that," he says, aiming his words at a blurry line of trees. Then he glances back at her, not to steal another glimpse, but to look right into the center of those coal-colored lenses. "And for the record, I've never once thought of you as a freak."

She scoffs and shifts on her seat, turning her body away. The movement is subtle. Obvious. Like she doesn't believe him one bit. "Whatever. Just . . . quit looking at me, alright?"

So he doesn't argue. He doesn't say a word. He just glances back out the window and watches the blur of trees flatten into a smudge of hills. For the longest time, neither of them make a sound, until the quiet becomes horribly awkward. When he finally can't take it anymore, he blurts out a question without even thinking: "What if there's another way?" As soon as the words leave his lips, it feels like everything slots into place. Like it all suddenly makes sense. The softness of his muscles. His unnatural lack of concern. Because *of course* there's another way. There's *always* another way.

They just need to find it.

"Another way?" Brielle repeats. She leans back in the booth, moving as far away from him as she can without actually leaving her seat. "You're joking, right?" When he merely raises an eyebrow at her, she frowns and shakes her head so hard that her bangs slap against her lenses. "No," she says. "This is the plan. It's not up for discussion."

"Why not?" he counters. "Nobody knows Viola as well as I do. Shouldn't that fact alone give me some say in the matter? Doesn't that make me worth listening to?"

"I already listened to you on that crummy boat of yours," she fires back. Her metal hand grips the edge of the table, and the nozzle by her thumb lets out a startling puff of steam. He glances at the leather bag on her hip and waits for her to pull a set of tools out of it. Wrenches, perhaps. Pliers. Maybe some kind of ratchet.

He can only imagine how much maintenance a glove like that would need.

But the steam evaporates as quickly as it appeared, and Brielle doesn't even seem to notice. Or rather: she doesn't seem to care. She just keeps those gloomy lenses of hers fixed intimidatingly on him. "I listened to you blabber on about fish guts and sleeping bags," she continues. "I listened to you talk in circles about your book-thief friend and the open-heart surgery that you *kind of remember but kind of don't.* And I definitely remember every word you said about *Viola*—mostly because she sounded so absurd, I was convinced you'd made her up." She pauses here, as if she's waiting for him to say something. As if she's *hoping* he'll admit that Gideon's clockwork daughter is just a figment of his imagination.

If only.

"She's real," he assures her.

She frowns and says, "Fine. Doesn't matter. My point is that I listened. Way more than I wanted to. And you even said yourself that you left *nothing* out. So that means you either have nothing new to tell me, or you weren't being truthful when you said that you mentioned *everything*. In either case, I'm better off with the information I already have. Anything you add to your story now will only sound like a lie."

He tries to come up with a response, something logical and coherent, something *convincing*, but all he manages to say is, "You remind me so much of her right now." The words come out before he even realizes who he's talking about: Josephyn.

She reminds him of *Josephyn*.

Come to think of it, they even *look* similar: straight, dark hair; short, slender bodies; delicate faces that have the uncanny ability to turn as hard as stone.

Brielle scowls, unfurls her mechanical fingers from the edge of the table, and tucks her gloved hand onto her lap, out of sight. "Remind you in what way?" she asks bitterly. "Because of my metal hand? My clunky goggles?" Her voice becomes strangely thin and small, like the voice of a hurt little girl. "*Clockwork Brielle*, is that it?"

It takes him a moment to catch on. When he does, he lets out a laugh. "No, I'm not talking about *Viola*. You're . . . nothing like her at all."

This seems to relax her a bit. The angles in her shoulders soften. Her scowl turns back into a frown. "You mean the book thief, then."

He nods. "Josephyn." Just saying her name makes something pinch in his chest. "She always seemed to talk circles around me." His mouth twitches, and he can't decide if he should smile or frown here. So he goes with something in between. "A lot like what you just did," he continues. "And I never quite knew what to say back."

Brielle sighs and looks out the window. Her bangs drape over her lenses, but she doesn't bother to brush them away.

"It's a compliment," he adds. "Really."

She lets out another sigh. When she finally speaks again, she sounds . . . tired. Stretched thin. "What do you mean, *another way*?"

"I don't know," he admits. "Another scientist, perhaps? I mean, if Viola put those chemicals *into* me, there must be someone in the world who can pull them back out." His mind flickers, and for a split second, he finds himself back in that darkened warehouse, staring at Gideon's pained face. The memory is quick, like a knife-jab to the heart. Then it's gone just as fast. "I refuse to believe," he says, his voice tightening, "that Viola is the only way."

Brielle twists her lenses, then rests her forehead against the window, letting the edge of her goggles clink against the glass. She stays like this for a while, slumped over and silent, until a cold tinge of worry begins to creep up his spine.

Is this how she concentrates? Or did she just . . . pass out, mid-conversation?

Should he give her arm a shake, just to be sure?

. . . Should he try to get away?

"I'm not asleep," she mumbles, "if that's what you're wondering. I'm just . . ."

She goes quiet again and stays that way, even while the train plunges through a darkened tunnel, then rattles back out into the gray sunlight.

Finally he clears his throat and says, "You're just . . .?"

"Thinking," she says, without skipping a beat.

"About?"

This time when she answers him, her voice is so soft that he almost doesn't hear it. "You," she whispers. "I'm . . . thinking about you."

This is . . . not the answer he expected at all. His insides flutter and flip, and the sensation is so strange and alien, so *different* from the beast's violent pressure, that he can't even tell if he's flattered or afraid. Maybe a mixture of both. "What about me?" he whispers back.

Brielle finally looks up at him, her lenses fogging around the edges. "That's just it," she says. "*What about you?* You're a beast, but you're not. I'm supposed to kill you—heck, I've been *trained* to kill you—but every time you open your mouth, you say something *kind* or *thoughtful* or *whatever*, and it makes me wonder if I'm even doing the right thing anymore." She sighs and tilts her head, as if she's trying to see him from a new angle. Then she clenches her jaw and mutters, "And of course you have to look like *that*, on top of it all. Do you have to be handsome, too? Can't you just be ugly? Can't you at least *look* like a monster?" She groans, tangles her mechanical fingers in her hair, and mumbles, "It would make all of this so much easier."

Did . . . did she just call him handsome? "I . . . don't really know what to say to that."

"Of course you don't," she mumbles. "Because everything has to be difficult. That's how the universe works, don't you know?"

Kemple furrows his brow. It's obvious from the strain in her voice that she's talking about so much more than just their current situation. So much more than *him*. And suddenly it dawns on him: this is an opportunity. An opening. A chance to escape. She's emotional right now. Conflicted. Vulnerable. Heck, she even said that she finds him *attractive*. Really, there are so many ways he could play this.

But then his gaze catches on her jaw, and he spots the slightest tremble—like she's on the verge of breaking down completely. And he realizes, for the first time since she kicked her way onto the *Nameless*, that she and him are . . . one and the same. They're both outcasts. They've both suffered their own terrible losses.

And they're both trapped in some never-ending struggle with their own personal demons.

When he finally speaks, he does it gently. He doesn't tease her. He doesn't try to convince. He doesn't *do* anything, really, other than sympathize and connect, because to do anything else just seems . . . wrong. "It doesn't have to be difficult," he says. When she doesn't say anything, he adds, "You could say that I attacked you. You could say that I gave you no choice but to defend yourself."

Finally she responds. "What are you saying?"

He takes a deep breath, then pushes his words out before he has a chance to swallow them back down. "I'm saying you could kill me, like you've wanted from the beginning. Then you won't have to deal with Viola. You won't have to deal with *me*." When she just gapes at him, he adds, "It's win-win, really. It's only a matter of time before the monster in me wants out again. And between you and me, I'd rather die as a person than a *thing*."

For the longest time, she doesn't move. She just stares at him, her face taut and unreadable behind those goggles, her mechanical hand still clutching her hair. Then she climbs out of the booth, grabs him by his shirt collar, and starts yanking him violently down the aisle. He stumbles after her the best he can, his ankles straining against the chains, and when they finally come to a stop near the back of the train car, he takes a deep breath and closes his eyes.

How will she do it? Another syringe to the neck? A sudden blow to the head?

Will she plunge her metal fist right through his chest, like she threatened when they first met?

"I'm ready," he whispers, even though he's really not. How can a person *ever* be ready for the end?

When she doesn't say anything back, he finds himself straining to hear . . . everything. The relentless thunder of the train over the tracks. The random gushes of fluids inside the walls. The floorboards creaking under the carpet and the heat ticking above the ceiling panels and the steady *huff, huff, huff* that could only come from a pair of lungs, from a person standing too closely, from a girl who is about to do something awful to him. Something merciful. Something *right*.

Suddenly there's a pressure on his chest—a hard, forceful weight that could only come from a shove with a metal hand—and the next thing he knows he's falling backward, and the floor is tilting away. He clenches his eyes shut even tighter, so tight that the darkness behind his eyelids turns glittery white, and he braces for that final, life-ending impact, an impact that'll—

His legs collide with something soft and padded. Then his hips and back do the same. His head hits last, his skull bouncing off some sort of fabric cushion, and when he opens his eyes, he finds Brielle looking down at him from a narrow doorway with her arms crossed over her chest.

"You're in a sleeper car," she says, answering his question before he's even thought to ask it. Then she adds, in a softer voice, "I'm not killing you today, Kemple. But I *am* locking you in here. For your sake. And for my sanity." She starts to close the wooden door, ready to seal him in, but then stops halfway, as if she's forgotten something. She gives him a hard look, and he has a sudden urge to leap up, to lunge across the room, to rip off her goggles just so he can see the emotion in her eyes. Just so he can see *her.*

"And just so you know?" she says. "Charming a girl, and then asking her to kill you right after? That's a really awful thing to do. Even for a beast."

The door slams shut before he has a chance to reply. The lock clicks loudly into place. And his head becomes such a swirl of heat and confusion—such a tangle of emotions and questions, all knotting around the mystery of *Brielle*—that he doesn't notice the strange pressure sliding up his spine. Doesn't feel the terrible weight shuddering his bones. Doesn't sense the monster crawling up from the depths, its maw gnashing hungrily toward the light.

# 58

B rielle jams the key to the sleeper car into her pocket.

She groans and yanks the key back out.

She scowls and tucks it away once more.

This jittery dance continues for nearly a minute, until there's no denying it: she's absolutely *lost her mind*.

What the heck is she supposed to do here? She can't just *hand Kemple over* to that clockwork girl. Not now. Not since she's gotten to know him.

Not since she's realized that he's so much more than just a monster.

He's clever, and he's funny, and he actually seems to care about her, even though she's done nothing to deserve it. And that face, those lips, those *eyes* . . .

But what if it's all just an act?

What if he's merely saying what she wants to hear?

What if he's just . . . playing her for a fool?

She grabs a fistful of her hair with her good hand and storms up and down the aisle, as if her footsteps might somehow jostle an answer loose from one of the overhead compartments.

As if Shaw hid another note somewhere, one where he describes, in perfect detail, what she should do in this exact situation.

But no answer comes. No scribbled-on slip of parchment tumbles off the paneled walls. The train keeps jostling along the tracks, and the door to the sleeper car stays agonizingly shut, and all the while she just keeps marching back and forth like a glass-eyed, metal-handed *maniac*.

Like a girl who's finally tumbled off the deep end.

She smacks the heel of her glove against her head so hard, it fills her vision with sparks. "Think!" she growls.

What would Shaw do?

But that question just makes her scrunch her face. She already knows what Shaw would do; he'd toss the boy at Viola's feet without a second thought.

She can't do that. She *won't*.

But what other option is there? Shaw already started a chain reaction. Anyone in the city with enough curiosity, and a working telegraph, would know who's on this train right now.

Which means that Viola is almost certainly on her way.

Which *further* means Kemple's time is running out.

She smacks her head again, sending a streak of pain through her temple. "*Think!*"

... What would *Mom* do?

She frowns and shakes her head until the question tumbles away. Mom wouldn't do anything because Mom is *dead*—and she's dead because of someone *just like Kemple*.

Her steamy hand swirls inside her glove, making her iron fingers clatter and twitch. Her insides feel even worse—all fire and lightning, all ice and smoke—and before she even realizes what she's doing, she clenches her glove into a creaking fist and she slams her brass knuckles into the nearest wall panel, punching and swinging and swiping and jabbing until her bicep feels like it's going to shred down the middle, until her shoulder feels like it's going to pop out of its joint, until the wall is nothing but a splintered hole and there's nothing left for her to punch anymore. Only then does she slump down into the nearest bench seat, panting and slick with sweat.

Only then does her mind begin to clear.

She'll ... have to stop the train. *Before* Viola shows up. She'll have to give Kemple a chance. Heck, Shaw will probably have a stroke when he finds out, but this is the only way she'll be able to live with herself. And who knows? Maybe Kemple is right—maybe there *is* someone else who can help. Maybe Viola isn't the only one in Iron Bay who knows how to chemically smother a beast.

Maybe ... monsters really can turn back into boys.

# 59

Kemple's body has become a battleground. His mind has turned into a raging sea. The beast has clawed its way into every part of him, and now it's slashing to get out. To be *free*. It tears at his muscles and shoves at his skin and strains against his bones, and the weight of it all is so monstrous, so inhuman, so utterly and completely overwhelming that no matter how hard he fights, it just keeps driving him *down*; down into that thick, inky void; down into those cold, empty depths; down to that horrible nothingness, that infinite bottom of everything.

But Kemple has found a lifeline, a trembling rope in the void, a frayed little thread of light to cling to in that realm of endless dark: *Brielle is still on the train.*

*Brielle is still . . .*

*Brielle . . .*

Of all the thought-shards spraying through his mind, *this* is the one keeping him human. Not his determination to survive. Not a fear of losing control. No, the one thing that's stopping him from fully becoming a beast is his ridiculous concern for *Brielle*—for the goggle-eyed, gear-handed girl who's wanted to kill him all along.

And maybe the feeling is misplaced. Maybe his worries are absurd. Maybe she's crouched somewhere at this very moment, sharpening her hatchet, ready to carve her name into his blackened heart.

Maybe he completely deserves it.

Either way, he can't turn now. Not while she's still onboard. He'd never forgive himself if he became the thing to finally end her. His role in Gideon's death was already more than enough. He will not take a *second* soul off this earth.

So he curls against the mattress while the monster claws at the sheets. He tucks his limbs together while the beast thrashes against the chains. And he clings, desperately, to the one flailing thought that, for some insane reason, seems to be keeping him from tumbling away forever: her eyes.

He's never even seen *her eyes*.

# 60

Brielle stumbles through the train like a madwoman. Somewhere between the flat plains and the parched hills, the locomotive picked up a considerable amount of speed. Now everything is jostling and swaying so intensely, if she wasn't already feeling out of her mind, she'd probably be sick.

But she keeps her focus, keeps her goggled eyes pointed forward, keeps pulling herself along with her geared fingers tearing holes into the headrests of each padded seat.

There's a pull-chain somewhere on this stupid train. There *has* to be. She just needs to find it. To rip it free from the wall. To yank it until all that ghostly pressure comes screaming out of the engine's metal veins, and then . . . then . . .

Well, then she and Kemple can sit down and figure out the rest. Maybe they'll go on the run, together. Maybe Shaw will have a better idea. Maybe—

Something glints on the wall in front of her, two seats down and to the right, and her breath catches in her throat. She doesn't need to twist her goggles to make out the silver chain with its thick, red-painted handle. Below it, five words have been stenciled onto the wall in bold, dark ink:

*TO STOP TRAIN, PULL CHAIN*

It sounds so . . . devastatingly simple. One hard tug with her gloved hand, and everything will change. It almost seems *too* easy. Suspiciously so. Like there's something missing. Something crucial that she's forgotten. And as she pulls herself along those final two rows of seats and reaches her iron fingers toward the handle, this is when it she spots it: the horrible *something* that she's forgotten.

She frowns and twists her lenses to see it better, and her gaze moves *past* the chain, zooming through the bug-splattered window beside it and even farther still, until she's peering at a patch of thick-branched trees far in the distance, their limbs draped over the tracks.

It's not the trees that catch her eyes, but the *figure* perched on one of the branches—a silhouette that's so small and slender, it's almost childlike; with a dark coat so billowy and tattered that it practically looks like a cape; and hair that's fluttering so madly in the wind, the locks don't even seem to be real.

"Viola," she whispers. The name makes her shudder, and she wrenches her goggles back into place with a shaky hand. Then she mutters a curse. She waited too long. Even if she pulls the chain now, the train won't be able to stop in time. No—all she can do is watch as the cluster of trees rushes closer. All she can do is hold her breath as the branches scrape against the windows. Then something heavy and metallic clatters onto the roof—something that sounds like a body made of gears and coiled springs, like a mechanical girl with a score to settle, like Kemple's own bizarre angel of *death*—and Brielle doesn't waste another second: she pivots on her heels, scoops the key from her pocket, and makes a wild dash for the sleeper car.

*Chains.* A murderous clockwork being just leapt onto the train, and here she left that poor boy in *chains*.

# 61

How long has Kemple been dangling in the dark? How many lifetimes has he spent in this void?

Is there even a reason for him to hang on any longer?

He tugs at that flickering rope, pulling with everything he has, but no matter how far he climbs, nothing seems to change. That horrible cold keeps drilling into his bones. That terrible pressure keeps straining against his veins.

If he doesn't find a way out of this ink-colored hell soon, well . . . that will be it. The darkness will consume him. The monster will be free. And then . . . then . . .

Then . . . what?

He pulls at that pitiful thread, clutching it to his chest, clinging to some sort of hope, hanging on to some kind of *meaning*, but the tighter he grips it, the more it frays and unravels between his fingers, and the more he keeps slipping. Down. In. Away from the light, away from the warmth, away from everything but that monstrous growl, that horrible voice that keeps rumbling closer and closer.

He needs to hang on for *her*. For . . . for *who*?

*SEEK.*

She has a hand like . . . like a . . . like a *what*?

*HUNT.*

But her eyes! Her eyes are . . . he never got to . . . they don't . . .

*DEVOUR!*

The thread strains against his weight and cuts into his palms and he stares at that trembling lifeline with wild eyes, because what else can he do *but* look? What else can he possibly *do*?

The line shreds in his grip, from three strands into two.

And those two strands unravel into one.

Finally he turns away and glares into the void, because if this truly is his last moment, he'd rather not watch it happen. He'd rather see nothing at all.

# 62

Brielle twists the key so hard that it bends in the lock, and she lets out a shuddering curse. "Kemple!" she hisses through the door. "I'm coming in! We need to get—"

Somewhere on the train a window smashes, letting in the roar of the wind, and Brielle's heart clenches like a fist.

Viola is inside the train now. Viola is coming for them.

There's no time to fix the key. No time for anything, really, other than brute strength. So Brielle wraps her glove around the doorknob and swirls her misty fingers inside the gears until the knob squeals and crumples and finally rips off the door in a *crack* of loose screws and wood shards. Then she kicks the door inward, lunges inside, and finds the boy limp on the crumpled mattress with his eyes tightly closed, his clothes sticking to him, his skin dappled with sweat.

"Kemple!" she hisses, still keeping her voice down. "We need to go! Viola is here! On the *train!*"

He doesn't move.

She curses, straddles him on the mattress, and shakes him violently. "Wake the hell up!"

Still, the boy with earth-colored hair—hair that's sopping and plastered to his forehead—he doesn't move. He barely even *breathes*.

Brielle raises her clockwork hand and, in one swift motion, slaps her metal palm against his glistening face so hard that it leaves a dark red mark.

And still, the boy who's a monster—the monster who's a boy—he doesn't move. He doesn't even flinch.

Something worse than panic beings to swirl in Brielle's chest, something that feels like darkness and glimmering eyes, like half-open pantry doors—something that feels like *dying*—and in a moment of desperation, she rips open his shirt, grabs at the shackles around his body, and begins wrenching the links apart with her clockwork hand. "Get up!" She tugs, and the chain above his crank snaps loose.

"Move!" She yanks, and the chain over his stomach crackles apart. "Come *on!*" she begs, but the bare-chested boy under her doesn't open those startling blue eyes. He doesn't sit up, confused, and call her *Josephyn* by accident. He doesn't frown in a mournful way and ask her to kill him.

He doesn't do *any* of the things that she's come to expect from him. All he does is lie there. Sweating. Breathing. Like he's trapped inside his own skin.

Like he's waging a war in his mind.

Like he's fighting against the monster inside.

Somewhere in the train, somewhere closer this time, there's a sound of wood splintering apart. Then the sound comes again, closer still.

Brielle balls her good hand into a fist and looks wildly over her shoulder at the doorframe. *Doors.* Viola is moving through the train now, kicking doors off their frames.

How long until they're found?

How long until that man's clockwork daughter finally gets her revenge?

. . . How long until Kemple is dead?

Brielle's throat clenches. Her vision swims with tears. Suddenly this all feels so ridiculous, so utterly *insane.* She's crying over a *beast,* for crap's sake. She's mourning for a *monster!* What would Shaw think if he saw her now?

What would *Mom* say, if she were still . . . alive?

But then she looks down at the boy between her knees and something else takes hold of her. Something new and different, something strange and horrifying, something delicate and wonderful and utterly bizarre and . . . and is *this* what it feels like to want something more than just a life with two normal eyes, and two normal hands, and a Mom who's still around? Is this what it feels like to want something beyond her own imperfect existence?

Is this what it feels like to want . . . *another?*

Then it happens so fast that it feels slow, so sudden that it seems like it's been happening all along: she cradles Kemple's head in the scoop of her metal hand, closes her eyes behind her dark lenses, and she mashes her lips against his.

The kiss is awkward and clumsy, sticky and hot, and the frames of her goggles jam hard against her cheeks, and his lips are so soft that it's making her dizzy, and it's crazy, she knows it, it's all so horribly wrong, but her body won't listen, won't pause, won't stop pressing her closer to the handle on the boy's chest, and her breath, *his* breath, keeps fogging her lenses—and if there was a time before this moment, a time before *Kemple,* she can't remember it now, doesn't *want* to remember it. And suddenly there's movement between her knees. Suddenly there are hands in her hair. Suddenly Kemple's lips are parting, and his eyes are opening, and she leans back, dazzled by the sudden loss of heat on her skin, disoriented by the sudden abundance of *space* around her, *bewildered* by the sudden alertness of the boy who she just . . . shared her first kiss with.

He blinks up at her slowly, his eyelashes glittering with sweat. "Brielle?"

She nods, because right now talking feels too heavy. Speaking feels *too much*. Then something shifts in her awareness, some twinge of a memory from a time before their lips met, and a wave of panic floods through her. "Viola," she gasps, her eyes going wide. "Kemple, Viola is on the—"

The rest of her sentence gets muffled against the palm of a cold, metal hand. The hand tightens around her face, squeezing her jaw shut, shifting her goggles loose. Another hand grips the back of her shirt, cinching her collar around her neck, and she's given just enough time to gasp, just enough time to look into the eyes of the bare-chested boy on the mattress, before she's flung backward through the doorway.

Something hard splinters against her back. Something even harder clangs against her skull. Shadows bleed in from the edges of her vision, a darkness so thick and absolute, and the last thing she sees is the carpeted floor rushing up to meet her.

Then the darkness swallows her whole.

# 63

Kemple's mind is a hurricane right now. One moment he was in the darkness, dangling from a thread. The next, he was kissing Brielle. And not just kissing her, but really, truly *kissing* her in a way that felt like falling—not down, but *up*. Toward the light and everything beyond it. A kiss that somehow pulled him back from the brink.

A kiss that made him whole.

Then Viola *literally* ripped her from his arms.

"No!" he shouts. He scrambles up from the mattress. His clothes are loose. The shackles tumble off him and clatter to the floor. He looks over Viola's shoulder to the hallway behind her, and what he sees makes his heart ache in a way that's so far beyond the pain of that crank. So much worse than what the monster could ever do.

Brielle is slumped against the wall and the floor, with a head-shaped dent in the pipe above her. A thin trail of blood trickles down her bangs and beads against her lenses.

He lets out a sound that's halfway between a sob and a shout. Then he whirls on the metal-faced girl standing in the doorway. "If she . . . if you . . . if . . ." He can't even find the words.

"If she what?" Viola says. "If she dies?" She twists her corded neck around, pivoting her body in that inhuman way until she's looking at Brielle's unconscious body. Then she turns back around with a near-human sigh. "Judging by what you two were just doing, if she *dies*, then it will be a fitting punishment for you." The gears around her eyes click and grind, narrowing her gaze into slits. Then she adds softly, with all the spite and sourness that he's come to know so well from her: "Monster."

And he doesn't think. He doesn't pause. He merely throws himself at her—at the clockwork girl who caught him in that alleyway all those years ago; at the spiteful, gear-faced sister who he never wanted to have; at the daughter of the man who took him in, the man whose death he would do anything to reverse.

The struggle doesn't last long. He wraps his hands around her cabled throat. She snarls and rips his hands free. He shoulders her iron body into the doorframe. She twists her torso with the motion, knocking him to the floor. He grabs at her leg and tries to pull her down, too, but Viola doesn't budge, because Gideon made her out of stronger stuff than flesh and bone, stronger stuff than Kemple could ever imagine, and somehow he's always known it would end like this. Somehow he's always known.

Gideon's clockwork daughter looks down at him with her eyes glinting, her gaze darkened by ink-black tears. She doesn't say a word. She doesn't even pretend to breathe. She merely reaches down, grips the crank on his chest between her clockwork fingers, and in one ruthless yank of her childlike body, she rips Gideon's device right out of him.

The pain is instant and everywhere at once, as if the entire universe just exploded out of his heart. He tries to scream, but all he manages is a gurgle. He tries to move, but his body doesn't respond.

The sleeper car fades and darkens, and he's dimly aware of a small, childlike figure turning slowly, then walking away. His head slumps to the side, and his gaze settles on the motionless body of a girl with a metal hand, and two gray lenses where her eyes should be.

The wound around his heart wrenches in a mournful way, and there's a vague sense of familiarity about the sleeping girl. Does he know her? Does she know him?

Did they know each other in some strange, twisted way? Had they once been friends?

The air around him turns dark as tar, and he feels himself tumbling into it. His last thought before falling away completely is:

Were they ever something *more*?

# 64

Brielle swims back to consciousness like she's crawling through mud. The ache in her head is the worst she's ever felt. The pain in her body isn't far behind. When she opens her eyes, the light around her is so harsh and white that she lets out a groan.

Something moves beside her—a body wrapped in fabric, the fabric wrapped in smoke—and a familiar voice rasps, "Thought I'd lost you there for a while." Calloused hands graze her face. The light behind her eyelids dims. Then the man who helped raise her gently lifts her head and buckles a strap behind her ears. "Figured you'd want these as soon as you woke," Shaw says.

Brielle sighs under the weight of her goggles. "Thanks."

"Sure thing," Shaw says back.

She tries to open her eyes, but even with her lenses on, everything keeps spinning. She groans and winces her eyes shut again. "Where am I?"

For a moment, the detective doesn't say anything at all. Then he finally whispers, "Home."

And Brielle doesn't have the energy to ask which *home* he means. The one she calls her own? The one where he took her in? Or the one she grew up in . . . the one she shared with Mom?

Maybe it doesn't really matter in the end.

"Home," she whispers.

"That's right." The detective clears his throat and fiddles with something papery. "*So*," he says, dragging the word out, "there are a lot of questions that need answering. Are you ready to tell me what happened on that train?"

Brielle's mind fills with the face of a boy with night-blue eyes. Her jaw aches from the ghostly grip of a metal hand. Her misty fingers clench inside her glove, and her insides swirl in a delirious sort of way, and soon it all collapses into a blazing point—a name that forces its way past her lips as if gravity itself were pulling it out of her. "Kemple," she blurts out. "Where's Kemple?"

Shaw clears his throat and says, "The boy? I was hoping you could tell me. There was a lot of blood left behind. And clear signs of a struggle. But our . . . friend is nowhere to be found."

The detective's words feel like claws digging into her skin. Like a pantry door creaking open all over again. Her throat tightens and her voice comes out in a whisper. "How much blood?"

"Enough to expect that he couldn't have gotten far."

Brielle tries not to picture Kemple bleeding out somewhere, his eyes squeezed shut, his body going limp, but the image slithers into her mind anyway, and a whimper escapes her lips. "We have to find him," she mutters, forcing her eyes open. She blinks up at Shaw's hazy silhouette and says, "He was more than just a monster. And Viola must've known it. We have to find him before . . . before it's too late."

Shaw lets out a weary sigh and paws at his messy hair. For a moment it looks like he's about to give her an annoying lecture on loss and grief. Or worse: about love. But then he stuffs his notepad into his coat and gives her a slow nod. "Okay," he says firmly. "Then that's exactly what we'll do."

Brielle lets out a slow, shaky breath—just enough to take the edge off the storm raging inside her. Then she sits up with a jolt.

"Easy there," Shaw says, resting a hand on her shoulder. "You still got some healing to do."

But Brielle isn't listening anymore. She's already shoving his hand aside. Already getting to her feet.

She has a score to settle with a certain clockwork girl . . . and a monstrous boy to save.

# 65

Kemple always thought that dying would feel like . . . nothing at all. Like spiraling down into that monstrous void, never to come up again. But right now, his world is . . . anything but empty.

The air smells of grease and motor oil. Everything is warm and sticky. And the wind is stuffed with noise: metal clanking, fabric rustling, and the gruff sound of a pair of . . . men singing?

He tries to open his eyes, but his eyelids merely flutter, like he's too weak to use them. Like his body is still struggling to repair itself from . . . from what?

From *something*. He knows he went through *something*.

Then he hears it: a noise so faint that it almost sounds like breathing. Like a cat's tail swishing gently across the floor. Like . . . a pair of feet that have spent a lifetime sneaking around.

And though her name sounds so out of place, so unlikely, so *distant*, he finds himself croaking it out anyway. ". . . *Josephyn?*"

For a moment, all he hears is the sound of gentle breathing, and the thrum of propellers in the distance. Then a voice echoes in the dusty space around him—a voice that's straight from the past. "Hey there, Belt Boy. Long time no see."

# Acknowledgments

To my mom, for taking me to the "book house" when I was a tadpole, and for putting up with all my nonsense; and to Tricia, for always demanding more, more, *more* from my writing, only to vanish, mid-edits, so she could play tennis; and to Sarah, for reading the first version of this story, though I'm still eagerly waiting to hear what she thought; and to Kai and Lucy, for being such adorable little monsters, and for repeatedly smacking my keyboard while I tried to write; and especially to Michelle, for her soul-hugging love and support . . . and for wanting to punch my novel in the face.

# About the Author

Kyle Richardson lives in the suburban wilds of Canada with his adorable wife, their rambunctious son, and their adventurous daughter. He writes about shape-shifters, superheroes, and the occasional clockwork beast, moonlights as an editor at Meerkat Press, and has a terrible habit of saying the wrong thing at the most inopportune moments. His short fiction has appeared in places such as *Love Hurts: A Speculative Fiction Anthology* and *Daily Science Fiction*. He can be found at: www.kylerichardson.ca

## Did you enjoy this book?

If so, word-of-mouth recommendations and online reviews are critical to the success of any book, so we hope you'll tell your friends about it and consider leaving a review at your favorite bookseller's or library's website.

Visit us at www.meerkatpress.com for our full catalog.

Meerkat Press
Atlanta